Exordia

Sarah E. Ott

Uncommon Universes Press

Uncommon Universes Press LLC

621 N. Mulberry St.

Berwick, PA 18603

www.uncommonuniverses.com

This is a work of fiction. Names, characters, businesses, places, events, and incidents are either the products of the author's imagination or used in a fictitious manner. Any resemblance to actual persons, living or dead, or actual events is purely coincidental.

Content editing by Janeen Ippolito – www.janeenippolito.com

Line editing by Sarah McConahy

Proofreading by Sarah Delena White – www.sarahdelenawhite.com

Cover Design by Julia Busko – www.juliabusko.com

ISBN-10: 1-948896-00-1

ISBN-13: 978-1-948896-00-9

Dedication

To Aaron.
Thank you for drop-kicking me into success, over and over
and over again.

Part One

Chapter One

The first time Brant met Lena, he tried to punch her in the jaw.

He propped himself against the glass counter of a bar in Second City. It was stupid to come here. Second City's nightlife clientèle came from all over Exordia, but he should have known that his unobtrusive gray clothing would draw attention in a crowd of black factory-leather jackets and metal-studded shoes. Like most of Second City, nearly everyone in the bar sported neon hair, headbands, jewelry, or—he took a second glance at the bartender's vivid lipstick—even makeup.

I just want a drink, he thought. *One drink, then I'll leave.*

His right leg twinged painfully, and he leaned heavily on the counter. He raised a hand to catch the bartender's attention—there was no way she would be able to hear him over the loud buzz of laughter and music.

She glanced at him and sneered. "You want something?"

Brant leaned forward and pointed to one of the two beverage dispensers that didn't glow. "That one," he shouted.

The bartender filled a mug and set it down with a *tap*, her bright orange lips pressed tightly together, waiting.

Brant pulled a small coin pouch from his back pocket. It was depressingly light. He shoved a few coins across the bar and accepted the mug. "Can I get a couple of the sliders, too?"

The bartender rolled her eyes and turned away, her shoulders heaving with a heavy sigh that was lost in the noise of the bar.

"Thanks," Brant muttered under his breath. He shoved the pouch into his back pocket and picked up the mug. The wound on the back of his hand throbbed. It had been phaeting difficult to cut out his ID chip, but he had managed it. The last thing he wanted was for his old bosses to find him by tracking his purchase of cheap alcohol and sandwiches.

He took a cautious sip of his drink and grimaced at the sour taste. Putting the mug down in disappointment, he glanced at the couple beside him. They were dressed a little too brightly to belong in this sector—probably wealthy students from Seventh City, here to squander their parents' money on Second City's mostly-illegal commodities.

Brant took another gulp of his drink. Terrible as it was, he'd paid for it, and he didn't have money to waste right now. The electric dissonance of the dance music grated his nerves with every beat, and the bartender showed no sign of bringing him his food. He brought the drink up again. If he reached the bottom of the mug before his sandwiches appeared, he would find something to eat in a more welcoming establishment.

The bar was crowded enough that a few people elbowed him in their efforts to find places at the counter. He ignored the pushing as best he could, clenching his jaw when someone demanded he move over. Getting thrown out of a bar in Second City took special talent, and Brant had no intention of drawing attention to himself.

Someone shoved his shoulder from behind. His drink, halfway to his mouth, sloshed down the front of his shirt. Brant grit his teeth and mopped up the alcohol with his jacket sleeve before taking another sip. He had nearly finished his drink when he felt his coin pouch slide out of his back pocket. He turned around and grabbed the slim wrist of a boy, maybe thirteen orbits old. Brant shook his head, the buzz of alcohol fading in a rush of adrenaline.

"Kid, pickpocketing is not a good idea in Second City."

In response, the boy pulled out a laser-edged knife and swung it at Brant's chest. Brant dropped his mug and caught the boy's knife-wielding arm with his other hand, tightening his grip until the boy cursed loudly and dropped the humming laser. It hit the ground and gouged a shallow divot in the floor just shy of Brant's boots before shutting off. The smell of singed plastic filled the air.

The bar went silent, except for the heavy music still pumping through the speakers.

Revelator, Brant swore. *That's not good.*

The guy at the bar next to Brant slugged him in the jaw. Spots clouded his vision as the boy kicked him in the shin of his bad leg. Pain wracked his body from his old injury, and Brant released his hold on the boy. He reached into his jacket pocket for his own knife, but before he could get a good grip on it, someone else hit him in the stomach. He dropped the knife, wind knocked out of him,

Great. There are two of them. He lashed out at the
second face and felt the crunch of bone beneath his fist.
The first guy grabbed his arm and held it. Brant tried to twist
away but his leg wouldn't hold his weight, and the alcohol,
cheap as it had been, left him uncoordinated. The second
assailant, with a freshly-broken nose, kicked him viciously
in the knee. Brant cried out and slumped, gasping in pain.
Someone grabbed his other arm, and he was dragged toward
the side of the bar and out into the alley. His boots scraped
the ground as he tried to regain his balance. One final shove
against the wall and he was released.

His arm wrapped around his aching stomach, Brant
braced himself against the wall, blinking away involuntary
tears of pain. He raised his head and looked at the man with
the bleeding nose. He had the same brown eyes as knife-boy.
Brant glanced at the man to his left. Both faces looked like
older versions of the pickpocket's. *Great. They're phaeting
relatives.* He leaned over, trying to catch his breath. *I've lived
through a war, for Revelator's sake. I won't let some Second
City punks knife me in a side alley*

Out of the darkness came a flash of electric blue light.
The man to his left crumpled to the ground, and Brant lunged
forward. *Never waste an opportunity to act.* Enforcement's
motto flashed through his mind as he slugged the other man
in the jaw with all the strength he could muster. The thug hit
the pavement hard, whimpered, and went still.

Brant wavered, his knee buckling beneath him. Someone
grabbed his elbow. He swung around, fists ready, but the

glint of neon light off a black stun gun stopped him.

A woman held the stunner. She was pretty, her dark hair cropped short around her face. She stood nearly as tall as he would, if he hadn't been standing crooked. Her jacket and pants matched her hair, and her knee-high boots accentuated her long legs. *Definitely my type of woman,* he thought as he tried to regain his footing. His stomach turned, but he ignored it and opened his mouth to speak. Instead, he fell to his knees and threw up the sour alcohol barely a span away from her boots.

To her credit, the woman didn't flinch or wrinkle her nose at the smell. She did, however, take a step back, away from the splatter. She reached into the bag over her shoulder and drew out a small bottle of water, holding it down toward him as he finished vomiting. After his stomach had been emptied, Brant raised his eyes to the dark-haired woman and took the proffered bottle. She silently waited as he rinsed his mouth and spit before she held out her hand.

Brant ignored it and pushed himself to his feet, giving the woman a more careful once-over. Even in the dim light of the alley Brant could see the expensive clothing she wore. Whoever she was, she didn't belong to Second City—and he doubted she wanted to speak with someone who couldn't stand on his own.

"I didn't need help." He gestured to the two unconscious men on the ground. "I had it handled."

The woman crossed her arms and leaned into the busy street in front of the bar. She glanced pointedly at a third man lying on the ground. Patrons of Second City's nightlife stepped around the body, too drunk, in too much of a rush, or too illegal to care about calling for help. There were always bodies in the street when the sun rose over Second City. No one wanted to add to the count by asking questions. Brant grimaced. *I'm losing my touch. I didn't even see that guy.*

"Okay," he conceded. "Maybe I needed a *little* help."

The woman laughed. "So do I." She tucked the stunner into the back of her waistband beneath her jacket and held out a hand. "I'm Lena Ward."

Brant took her hand this time. "Brant Hale."

"I know." Lena's hand was small in his, but her grip was firm. She released the handshake and wound one arm around him, supporting his bad side. She stepped out of the alley, pulling him with her.

The crowd of pedestrians didn't part for them, but Lena shoved her way into the street. Brant stumbled on the uneven pavement, but Lena steadied him easily. He leaned heavily against her as they walked, jostled on all sides.

It had been the middle of the night when Brant caught a gravbus to Second City, but by now Luna One had set. Luna Two gave the sky above them a warm, yellow glow. Starlight was obscured by flashing signs advertising food, drink, or company. Most of the people crowding the street at this hour were Second City born, wearing garishly bright orange and pink splashed against their dark clothing. Still, a few outsiders lingered around the entrances of bars or crowded around outdoor food stands, their comparatively somber clothing making them easy to spot. It was enough variety to keep Brant and the mystery woman invisible.

He hoped.

Halfway down the street, Brant realized they had a shadow.

"Who's the redhead?" he asked. "Gloves, glasses, frown—is she your muscle?"

Lena chuckled. "Ah, no. Dani is...technical support."

They walked by a bar blaring discordant music, and Brant had to lean closer to hear Lena's next words. "Actually, I hoped you'd be the muscle."

Brant remembered the ruthless, close-range stunner shot Lena had fired at his assailant. The guy would be lucky if he had any feeling in his face for the next moon cycle.

"Lady, you don't need any more muscle than you've already got."

She shook her head. "I do for this job. And please, call me Lena."

The fight and subsequent walk through Second City left Brant more winded than he'd been since he joined Enforcement. He tried to keep his breathing steady and not let his exhaustion show in front of Lena. His limp was obvious and getting worse, the pain from his old injury forcing him to lean heavily on her. If Lena was looking for help on a job, why would she choose him?

Brant shook his head. "Why me?"

"I read your file."

Brant inhaled sharply. "My *Enforcement* file?" Those were encrypted nearly as well as Council files. "How did you—"

"My tech support is *very* good," Lena interrupted, steering them around a pothole in the pavement. "This job is too important. I can't just hire the first alley scrapper I come across. I need someone with experience."

Brant didn't answer. The first stage of the Hazing had removed almost every memory he had of working for Enforcement. His stomach tightened at the thought that a stranger might know more about his service than he did.

Lena must have sensed his unease, because she squeezed his arm. "Enforcement has most of your records stored somewhere other than the CityGrid, so I haven't seen them. But I know you didn't go through with the Hazing. You still retain the combat skills you were trained in, and I need those. Like I said, muscle."

Brant let Lena pull him farther down the street. His thoughts jumbled together in a fog of adrenaline and confusion. She'd hacked Enforcement. She'd tracked him down in Second City, not an easy thing to do with his ID chip cut out. She was carrying an illegal stunner, and she clearly knew how to use it.

Well, I might not be interested, but I'm definitely curious. He jostled Lena's arm to get her attention. "What's the target?"

"Pallagen."

Brant stopped short. Lena, still walking, jerked back a step as he froze. Pedestrians parted around them, ignoring them in typical Second City style—pedestrians who knew nothing about the battles fought to preserve their neon-lit life of crime. They knew Pallagen as a name only, nothing more than a white-shrouded building fenced in by secrets. They didn't know its true, dark nature, whispered in the ranks of Brant's fellow Enforcement officers as an awful machine, turning out weapons that won wars.

Pallagen had offered to give Brant his leg back, but the price they had demanded—Brant shuddered at the recollection. He hadn't slept through the night sober since that conversation. He wished they'd Hazed that memory when they took away his memory of serving Enforcement. But no, they had left it there. An open offer.

Or a terrible warning.

"You don't want me," he said, voice hoarse, drowning in memories. "I didn't run from Enforcement because I didn't like what they were doing. I ran because I couldn't handle the Hazing. I never even finished the first stage."

"I want you," Lena said. From the certainty in her voice, Brant could tell she saw through the lie—that she knew what he had done, and exactly why he'd run. "I came to Second City just to find you."

Brant shook his head in disbelief. *Revelator.* What was in his Enforcement file that made Lena so sure about him? "Pallagen has more security than the Council tower! Half of Exordia is on their payroll. No one messes with them. What are you planning?"

Lena smiled and released his arm, then stepped away. Unbalanced without her support, Brant faltered and nearly fell. When he looked up again, Lena had disappeared into the crowd.

Rich, well-informed, and sneaky. Brant's curiosity rose again.

Brant felt someone tap his shoulder. He turned and saw the redhead that had been following them. Her face was rounder and softer than Lena's, and she had the bored shoulder-slouch of a teenager. *Pretty young to be in a place like Second City on her own.*

She held out an actual paper card and pushed her dark glasses—goggles, really—up on her forehead. Brant almost laughed at the way loose hairs stuck out over the top of the goggles but remembered Lena's stunner just in time.

"This apartment, first thing in the morning." The redhead held the card up. "Lena pretends being late doesn't bother her, but it does." She flipped the card over, and Brant saw it was covered in cramped writing. "Hangover cure." She pushed the card into his hand, pulled her goggles over her eyes, and walked away.

The printed address on the front of the card was for a suite in Seventh City. Brant turned the card over and squinted at the cramped, handwritten instructions to *eat light and stay hydrated*. He rolled his eyes.

He didn't move, not quite sure where to go now that Lena had disappeared. He stared down at the card, turning it over and over in his fingers. A few Second City natives gave him odd glances, a solitary, still figure in the middle of a busy street, but Second City was, above all things, used to ignoring outsiders.

Brant took a deep breath and considered what he was doing for the first time since he'd run from Enforcement. He found himself in the heart of Second City, surrounded by blinking neon lights, breathing damp air. Half the people jostling against him were drunk while the other half were ready to take advantage of anyone dull-witted enough to let them. *Like me.* Brant shuddered. He'd almost died in an alley tonight, almost let the city he'd sworn to protect swallow him up.

The hopelessness weighing him down fell away. This job—illegal, dangerous, probably impossible—was the most enticing thing he'd encountered since he left Enforcement.

I need to think this through. I shouldn't agree to anything until I know more about her and that redheaded kid. He shoved the card deep into his coat pocket and started to limp slowly down the street toward the gravbus station.

The small terminal shelter held only a few waiting passengers. The blinking screen on the back wall advertised an incoming gravbus bound for Ninth City. Brant settled himself carefully onto a plastic bench and waited.

He thought of Lena's stunner. A new model, hard to come by. Goggles girl, probably an Enhanced human. The paper card, expensive and impractical.

If nothing else, this job could be interesting.

Brant let the Ninth City gravbus roar past and waited for one to Seventh City.

Chapter Two

Lena's Seventh City apartment was spacious and placed high enough in the complex to see the smooth metal of the Council tower gleaming in the dawn. It was her own place. She'd moved here after her last fight with her parents, so it was under her new name. It was safe. For now.

Dani had made herself at home. She was sprawled across the couch, shoes propped up on the lush, cream fabric, shadowed goggles covering half her face. Her hands were tucked behind her head, but her fingers twitched once in a while as she communicated with the apartment complex's AI.

"Do you need your hands to work?" Lena asked curiously. She'd hired the teenager a couple of moon cycles past, and while she knew the extent of what Dani was capable of, she knew little about how she interfaced with the CityGrid.

Dani didn't answer. Lena sighed and poured milk into her bowl of cereal. She grabbed a bowl of strawberries—fresh-grown, expensive, definitely something she'd miss—from the fridge and carried her breakfast to the kitchen table. She sat down and shook her head. *Guess I'm not getting an answer to that one.* Lena scooped a spoonful of cereal into her mouth. At this point, she was used to Dani being unresponsive.

Dani sat up suddenly and faced Lena, pushing her goggles up on her forehead. "Not really," she said, blinking rapidly as her eyes adjusted to the light of the apartment. "But sometimes it helps me keep track of what I'm doing."

Lena nodded. She pushed the bowl of fruit toward an empty chair and tapped the tabletop with her fingers. "Breakfast. There's more cereal, or toast if you want."

"I'm not really hungry."

"Breakfast isn't optional," Lena said, hoping she sounded more like a bossy friend than a nag. She scooped another bite of cereal and chewed slowly, staring pointedly at the technopath. Dani ignored her for a few minutes, then plopped into the chair next to Lena and picked up a piece of fruit.

Lena eyed her partner. Dani's normally braided hair hung loose around her face, and her eyes were squinted and tight. Lena tapped her mobile and commanded it to tint the windows, keeping out the bright sunlight of early dawn. "Headache?"

Dani popped the fruit into her mouth and picked up a second piece. She shrugged. "Nothing unusual."

Lena rolled her eyes but didn't say anything. The first time she'd offered Dani standard painkillers for a headache, the technopath had turned her nose up at them. Lena knew better now.

She pushed back from the table and took her bowl to the sink. She rinsed it out and pushed it through the cleaning unit to the side of the sink. It emerged from the other side, warm from the hot air that dried it and the UV light that sterilized it. Exordia's water reclamation system had never failed, but living on a desert planet left everyone careful of their water consumption.

Lena opened the cabinet, put away the bowl, and pulled out a mug. She turned on the drink dispenser set into the wall and keyed in the code for black coffee. She glanced around her apartment as she waited for the coffee to brew.

Before Dani had moved in with her, it had been spotless, the white plastic counters and table gleaming, the soft carpet well-cared-for, the furniture carefully kept clean of any crumbs or drink stains. Now, several tablets were left haphazardly wherever Dani lost track of them, and pieces of miscellaneous tech—disassembled cameras, deactivated plastiscreens, and hacked ID chips—were scattered on Lena's sofas and tabletop.

Lena drummed her fingers on the counter. The clutter clashed with her meticulousness, but when she thought of how scrawny and haunted Dani had looked when Lena first offered her a job, she couldn't regret also offering her a place to stay.

She sighed. She'd had this apartment for a few orbits, and the thought of leaving it made her...not sad, exactly. Melancholy. Thoughtful.

Once she left this apartment, she was crossing a line she couldn't uncross.

Dani carried the now-empty fruit bowl to the kitchen and set it down. "Do you think he'll come?"

"He'll be here," Lena said. She pushed the bowl through

the sanitizer and put it away.

"Why'd you pick him, anyway?" Dani flopped back down in her chair. She leaned back and pulled her goggles over her eyes. "He got in a bar fight. That's not exactly a stellar resume."

"I don't know. He did all right for someone with only one properly functioning leg." Lena smiled as she remembered the way Brant Hale had fought. He'd been about to lose that fight—badly—but he hadn't given up, and he'd jumped right back in as soon as Lena had given him an opening. Since he'd skipped the last part of his Hazing, she hoped he still retained as much of his knowledge of martial arts and weaponry as he did his fighting spirit.

Only one of the reasons Lena needed to recruit him for her team.

Lena's coffee finished brewing. She picked up the mug, but before she could take a sip, the door chimed.

Dani pushed her goggles up again and looked at Lena.

"I told you so." Lena smiled and carried her mug to the table. She took a deep breath and faced the door. "Open."

The door slid to the side, and Brant poked his head in, not quite entering the room. He was wearing the same worn jacket from the night before, and he looked as if he hadn't slept at all. "Lena?" he asked, leaning farther into the apartment.

Lena stepped closer to the door and waved Brant in.

"Please," she said. "Come in. Make yourself at home." She glanced at the mug in her hands. "I can get you some coffee if you want. You look like you need it."

Brant stepped in, and the door slid shut behind him.

"Thanks, but I'm good." His face was mottled with bruises from the fight, and his blond hair was tangled, though it looked as if he'd run his fingers through it in an attempt at style. All in all, he was a dark and dirty splash against Lena's light and airy home.

Dani frowned and stared mutely at the ex-soldier. *Let her.* Dani had been on her team before Brant, and if he couldn't put up with her silence, he wasn't staying.

"This is a weird place to recruit criminals." Brant shifted to one side, keeping weight off his injured leg, but he didn't ask to sit.

Lena wondered if he did that out of pride or the need to stay alert. Either way, it looked painful. She sat down on the couch and picked up one of Dani's discarded tablets, motioning to the cushion next to her. "Have a seat."

Brant hesitated, then nodded. He limped across the room and sat at the other end of the couch.

"Dani, the lights." Lena said. The brightness in the apartment dimmed even further as Dani increased the window tint and lowered the lights.

Brant narrowed his eyes, looking from the redhead back to Lena. "Technical support, huh?"

"Dani is a technopath." Lena refused to say more. *I want you on my team, but you don't get all our secrets yet.* Making a face at the lines of alphanumeric code scrolling across the tablet screen, she swiped it away. *I hope Dani wasn't working on anything important.* Lena pulled up the personnel file on Brant Hale that Dani had stolen off the CityGrid. "You ran halfway through your Hazing. Why?"

Brant met her eyes. "I didn't like people messing around with my brain. And...some of the things they wanted me to forget, I needed to remember."

"Such as...?"

"Pallagen, for one." Brant licked his lips. "They offered to give me a new leg." He motioned to his right leg, stretched out stiffly in front of him. "They offered to fit me with some kind of exoskeleton brace, but they wanted too much in return." Brant glanced at Dani, and his eyes narrowed again. Lena suspected he knew what had happened to Dani. Enhanced humans weren't unheard of in Exordia, but they were few and far between, and always artificially created.

"They wanted me on their security team," Brant continued, refocusing on Lena. "I was pretty dangerous before my gravship crashed. They said they'd fix my leg if I helped them keep people quiet."

Something you never would have agreed to. She'd read the psych profile Pallagen had on Brant Hale. What had they expected? There was nothing about Brant's character that would suggest anything other than a deeply imbedded sense of honor. He'd volunteered to join Enforcement on his own, not because of any legal trouble. Perhaps Pallagen simply made the same offer to every soldier leaving Enforcement.

"Is that why you recruited me?" Brant demanded. He shifted his leg and leaned closer to Lena. "Did you hear about me from someone? Expect me to work for you since I can't work for anyone else?"

Lena arched an eyebrow at his challenging tone, but Dani was smirking at her. She shot the technopath a glare.

"I worked for Pallagen." She grimaced, trying to decide what to tell Brant without giving too much away yet. "I did research in a very specific field, and Pallagen was the only organization that paid me to do it."

Brant raised an eyebrow in return.

"I know. I was naïve. I didn't grow up in circles exposed to the worst side of Pallagen's actions."

Brant tipped his head, examining her face and glancing around the well-kept apartment. "Ah-ha. Council kid?"

"Yes." Lena tapped the tablet and brought up three psych profiles—hers, Dani's, and Brant's. "I researched personalities. I analyzed how people connect, why they connect, why relationships succeed or fail, studies like that. I wanted to use my research to help people succeed in business and personal relationships, but Pallagen wanted to use it to further their own good." She glanced at Brant. "That's when I started digging deeper into what Pallagen was doing. I didn't have to look far before I found the truth. They used my research to test individuals' compatibility with their...projects." She looked at Dani, who had her goggles off and was watching them closely. The technopath nodded slowly, and Lena continued. "Dani is one of the many people my research was used against, without my knowledge or consent. I know some of the projects my colleagues were working on are potentially more dangerous than mine— everything from advanced weapons research to human technology integration. If Pallagen twisted any of it the way they twisted mine, all of Exordia could be in danger. We need to know what they're doing." She swiped the profile information to the side and tapped another file. She turned the screen so Brant could see it. "Before I left, I downloaded as many project files as I could without getting caught. I want to know every secret Pallagen is hiding."

"So quitting on moral grounds wasn't enough for you?" Brant asked, humor in his voice. "You decided to poke your nose where it didn't belong instead of just walking away?"

Lena raised her chin. "Walking away wouldn't have solved anything. I want to stop Pallagen from doing any more harm."

Brant stared at her.

Lena put the tablet down and crossed her legs. She folded her hands over her knees and waited him out.

"Okay." Brant blinked a few times and took a deep breath. "So you're not just, I don't know, robbing them?"

Lena frowned. "What did you think I was doing?"

Brant ran a hand through his hair in agitation. "Theft, maybe. Exposing inside information. You know, typical disgruntled ex-employee stuff. But *stopping* Pallagen? That's crazy!" He looked over at Dani, expecting more of an explanation, but the technopath only stared back at him.

"Of course it's crazy," Lena said flatly. "But it needs to be done." Her stomach twisted at his hesitance. She had the names of a few other ex-soldiers she could hire if Brant refused, but now that she'd spoken to him, she was convinced that he was the ideal person for her team. She sighed. "It's an open offer. I have a plan, I have the knowledge I need, and I have an ex-criminal technopath."

"All those charges were dropped," Dani snapped.

"Whatever," Lena muttered. "Like I said, I intend to find

everything Pallagen is hiding. Dani can access the information Pallagen has stored on the CityGrid, but we'll need to break into their secure facilities sooner or later. For that, I need a defense specialist. You can take the offer or leave it."

"And if I leave it?"

"You can walk away."

"That seems kind of careless." Brant crossed his arms. "What if I run back to Pallagen? Take that new leg they offered in exchange for telling them all about you?"

"I have your psych profile, remember?" Lena nodded toward the tablet. "I have a pretty good idea of what you will and won't do."

Dani tipped her chair back on two legs and crossed her arms behind her head. "Besides, no one would ever believe you. Two people can't take on an organization like Pallagen."

Brant snorted in agreement. "And what do you plan to do with the files you find?"

"I suppose that depends on what they contain," Lena said quietly. "I would like to dump the information onto the CityGrid for everyone to see, but that might be too dangerous." She stood and walked over to the floor-length windows and looked out at the city, her hands clasped behind her back. "Exordia is divided enough as it is. You can tell what sector a person is from by the way they dress or talk, and it's becoming increasingly rare to see someone in your sector who doesn't live or work there—except, perhaps, in Second City. If, for instance, we let it slip that Pallagen has been letting Seventh City medtechs experiment on Fourth City street kids..." She turned around and met Brant's eyes.

"Exordia is well-established, but it's easy to forget we're just a colony. We're completely cut off from Old Earth. All the sectors have to work together, or we face disaster. We can't afford to cause more conflict between cities. I don't know what we'll find, but we may have to handle it ourselves instead of pulling the rest of Exordia into it."

"And that's why you need a defense specialist," Brant said slowly.

Lena watched him and thought of what his psych profile said: *driven, strong conscience, needs a sense of purpose.* She hoped she was the first person to offer him a purpose since he ran from Enforcement.

He pushed himself up off the couch. If he didn't limp so badly, Lena thought he'd start pacing. Instead, he ran a hand through his already-chaotic hair. "I won't let you use me like Pallagen." He faced Lena. "I can fight, and I want to help you, but I won't be your hitman."

"No." Lena stepped away from the window. "You're here to keep Dani and me alive—no more, no less."

"Okay," Brant said. He took a deep breath. "Okay, I'm in."

Chapter Three

Alex woke up and didn't know who she was.

She was in a white room with a window. There were white sheets on the bed. White ceiling. White tile. White lights. She looked to her right and saw a bush full of white roses outside a white-framed window.

She lifted her arm and blinked at the plastic ID band wrapped around her wrist. *Alex Kleric.* Her name. Right. That was her name. She was wearing a soft, light gown with short sleeves. She was...in a hospital? No, that wasn't it. Was it? Her brow furrowed as she tried to make sense of the tangled threads in her mind.

"Well!" A cheerful voice echoed off bare, white walls. "Staying awake this time, are we?"

I know that voice. She looked up at the nurse. "You told me my name."

The nurse smiled. Her uniform was a soft blue, and Alex was glad for the contrast in color. "At least you remembered me this time. I've told you your name every morning for the past several days."

Alex frowned. Several days? "How long have I been here?"

"Ah. No memory recall yet." The nurse fiddled with the IV drip, eyes on her work. "Accident, your file says. A bad one. Severe head trauma. No one thought you'd wake up."

Alex flexed her fingers and took inventory of every part of her body. The back of her left hand was stiff where the needle was taped down. There were sharp aches in one of her knees as well as in her chest, and it was difficult to breathe deeply. Her head was foggy. Very foggy. *Drugs. Well, I'm in a hospital.*

"Which hospital?" No, no, not a hospital. Why couldn't she remember?

"You're not in a hospital," the nurse said, pinching the toes of Alex's injured leg. "Feel that?"

Alex curled her toes away and grimaced at the pain that re-ignited in her knee. "Yes." She pushed herself up on her elbows. She felt weak, but her arms didn't give out. "Where am I?"

"You're in a long-term rehabilitation center in Sixth City. Like I said, your injuries were so extensive, no one thought you'd wake up." The nurse—Tabba, her clear plastic badge read—gently pushed her back onto the pillows. "There, now. Maybe this is the last time we'll have to go over this."

"Hope so." Alex stared at the ceiling and lost herself in the new information for a few seconds. Tabba patted her shoulder. Alex turned her head and watched the nurse leave the room. The door clicked shut behind her.

No handle on the inside of the door, Alex thought drowsily before falling asleep.

Alex blinked at the ceiling, trying not to let the last vestiges of her dream fade. She closed her eyes and scrunched her nose, but she couldn't remember. It hadn't been pleasant, she knew. There had been pain and fire. Alex sighed. *At least I remember my name this time. And Tabba. And where I am.*

She rolled over on her side, wincing as she repositioned her knee. She reached out and grabbed the tablet she saw sitting on her bedside table and activated the screen.

7:30. Still early morning. Good. Maybe she had recovered enough to sleep and wake up like a normal, uninjured person. She tapped the screen thoughtfully. If she could access the CityGrid, she would be able to look up her chart and perhaps fill in some of the gaps in her memory. Alex fiddled with the displays on the screen, but none of the icons led to her chart or any other useful information. Just the date and time, a weather report, and a breakfast menu full of options that made Alex's stomach churn. *I don't remember what any of these taste like.* Disturbed, she placed the tablet back on the table and rolled over onto her back. She crossed her arms carefully, wrapping her fingers around her sore ribs.

Her head felt clearer than it had before, enough to sort through the wisps of memory still clinging to her mind. Most of the memories fluttered away as soon as she tried to grasp them, but a few stuck. She closed her eyes and remembered tile beneath her knees. A bedroom. Heavy weight bearing down on her shoulders. Everything overlaid in a red haze— grief, anger, blood.

Alex didn't know. She couldn't remember.

"Awake and sitting up! Definite improvement."

Tabba's voice startled Alex from her reverie. She straightened too quickly. The ache in her chest flared and her breathing hitched.

Tabba hurried to the bed and helped her lean back against her pillows. "Sorry about that. I've been told I can be a little *too* awake this early in the morning."

Alex forced herself to smile. Her ribs hurt too much to breathe deeply, and it was hard to catch her breath enough to speak. "I don't know if I'm a morning person or not."

Tabba laughed and wrapped her fingers around Alex's wrist to check her pulse. "Joking about your condition is a sign of good spirit—I think. I'm a nurse, not a shrink." She winked at Alex and handed her the tablet. "Now, would you like fruit, grains, or liquid for breakfast?"

Alex hesitated, searching her memory for a preference. "I'm not sure. I..."

"How about all three?" Tabba's voice was gentle. "Try a little of everything. See what you like."

"I'd like that." Alex relaxed. "Please." She handed the tablet back to Tabba.

Tabba smiled again and placed the tablet on the side table. "It will get easier. Be patient, Alex. You've only been awake for a few days."

"Right." Alex sighed. Even that made her side twinge. She closed her eyes again. She wished she could remember a time when she knew what she liked for breakfast.

Alex stayed awake for the few minutes it took Tabba to bring her breakfast. She sniffed at the steam rising from a bowl of hot cereal. Her stomach growled. "I'm pretty sure I like that."

Tabba placed the tray of food on the table and grinned, handing her the bowl. "Eat up, then! You've been well cared for, but you've lost quite a bit of weight. If you can keep it down, you can have as much as you like."

The cereal was creamy and sweet. Alex chewed the first few bites slowly, letting the buttery grains melt in her mouth. She scraped every last bit from the bowl, then poked at the fruit. She tried the juice and screwed up her face. It tasted sour, a sharp contrast to the cereal, and she pushed the glass away.

While Alex ate, Tabba tidied the small room. The nurse scrubbed away dust and smudges Alex had never noticed. She pulled back the white curtains and threw open the window. A warm breeze filtered in, carrying with it the smell of roses. With the window open, Alex could hear the low hum of a force field. She wouldn't be able to escape through the window.

Alex frowned at the strange thought, her spoon halfway to her mouth. She was here to recover. Why would she want to leave by the window?

"There," Tabba exclaimed, hands on blue-skirted hips. She looked satisfied—with her cleaning job or the amount Alex had eaten, Alex couldn't tell. Tabba cleared the tray and balanced it against one hip, then reached into a deep pocket. "You'll get bored now that you're awake. You likely won't feel like moving around much, but this should keep you busy." She held out a data chip. "News from the last few months, in case you want to catch up. Your file is on there, too—the accident report, list of personal belongings, even the weather report from the day you were admitted to the rehab center. If you're curious about yourself, this is a good place to start."

Alex nodded, knuckles white as her fingers tightened around the chip. "Thanks." She rubbed the chip between her fingers, tracing the engraved logo. It felt familiar. She looked up at Tabba. "Which rehab center is this, again?"

Tabba raised an eyebrow. "Sixth City Rehab. Pallagen owns it. Why?"

Alex shrugged. "Just wanted to see if I recognized it."

"Do you?"

"No," Alex said. She tried to sound unconcerned, but guessed by the look on Tabba's face that she hadn't succeeded.

Tabba reached out and squeezed her hand. "Don't be afraid, Alex. You're awake now. It will get easier from here." She released her hand and left the room, smiling at Alex as she closed the door.

Alex set the chip on the table next to the tablet. She needed more sleep before she tackled the outside world. Breakfast had exhausted her.

She curled up on her side, facing the warm breeze from the window. Careful of her sore ribs, she wriggled beneath the thin, soft blanket until she was comfortable. The back of her hand itched. She rubbed her fingers over the puckered tissue and felt the outline of her ID chip beneath it. She frowned. Chip implants didn't leave a scar. She should hardly have noticed it was there. One more mystery to add to the list of questions that needed answers. The solution was probably on the data chip. Curiosity chased away some of her drowsiness, but she was too comfortable to roll over and pick up the chip.

Later, she promised herself, and fell asleep.

Chapter Four

Lena had been to Second City only twice before: once to recruit Brant, and once when she'd needed a fake ID chip to gain access to Pallagen's secured records.

Now she was moving in.

In contrast to its vibrant, bustling nightlife, Second City was nearly empty during the day. The inbound gravtrains were unoccupied, but the outbound transports were filled with Second City residents who worked outside the sector. Most of the city's restaurants and bars were closed during the day. A few cafés catered to the early-morning crowd that lingered until their jobs called them to other parts of Exordia. Around dusk, visitors would begin to filter in, and Second City would come alive.

It was the perfect place to live if you wanted to come and go unnoticed after dark.

Dani stopped in front of a dilapidated building "The apartment's in here." She pulled an access card from her jacket pocket and keyed the door open.

Lena stared. "I'm not sure breaking in is the best way to make an impression as a possible tenant."

"What possibility?" Brant reached into his back pocket and pulled out two other access cards. "I already rented the place."

"You *what*?" Lena turned to glare at Brant. "You didn't think to ask me first?"

Brant looked back at her curiously. "You gave me the coin and told me to find a place to set up. You didn't say anything about picking out paint colors first."

True enough. "I'd at least like to see it before moving in," she grumbled.

"You want to fit in here, right?" Brant shrugged. "If you're renting an apartment in Second City, it's not because you care about the view."

The lift inside the building was broken. From the look of it, Lena didn't think it had ever worked. She didn't mention Brant's uneven steps or heavy breathing as they plodded up the steps to the apartment, but she resolved to ask Dani to take a shot at fixing the lift. Three flights of stairs was difficult enough with two good legs.

The technopath easily beat Lena and Brant to the third level. By the time they caught up, she was standing outside a battered plastic door, tapping her foot impatiently. Lena smiled at her annoyance. "Go ahead, show us what we're stuck with for the next few cycles."

Dani waved her access card in front of the door panel, and it slid open with a groan. Lena stepped inside with Brant and Dani close behind.

The room was small and felt crowded with all three of them in it, even though it was nearly devoid of furniture. There was a couch slumped in the middle, and a table and chairs next to a small kitchen area. The floor was covered with a thin rug that might have been black once, but was now a sickly slate color.

Lena closed her eyes and sighed. "This is a terrible idea."

"It's better than an army barracks."

"Or the street," Dani added.

Brant stepped closer to Lena. "I know it's not what you're used to, but there's not much empty real estate in Second City. It's small, but it's all that's available."

"And it won't break the bank, either." Dani pulled out a kitchen chair and sat backward in it, arms folded across the back. "I can only scam so many coin claims before getting noticed, which is the last thing we need right now."

Brant gasped in mock horror. "You mean you're not omnipotent?"

Dani scowled at him and jerked her goggles down over her eyes.

Lena dropped her backpack on the beat-up plastic table. "Leave her alone, Brant."

Brant ignored her. "You can see most of the sector from up here," he said, walking over to the balcony door. "And it's in the middle of the city. No one is going to turn us in to Enforcement or Pallagen. There are too many ways that could backfire. No one in Second City has clean hands."

Lena tipped her head, conceding the point. Second City was a little like Pallagen: full of things the wealthy were willing to pay for and largely free of consequences from the rest of the colony. As long as what happened in Second City *stayed* there, no one bothered them. Only when violence spilled over the boundaries did Enforcement take serious notice.

"I get the bedroom," Dani said, interrupting Lena's thoughts. She hopped up from the chair and disappeared through a doorway.

Lena watched her leave in dismay. "*The* bedroom?"

Brant shrugged and flopped onto the couch, giving her a grin as he stretched out his legs.

Lena rubbed her forehead. She'd hoped that Brant, being a few orbits older than her, would understand the weight of this job, but he seemed to be treating their mission as casually as Dani. *So much for mature company for the next few cycles.*

"So where am I supposed to sleep?" Lena threw her hands up in frustration. "This is *my* apartment."

Brant tipped his head back against the couch and closed his eyes. "You're resourceful. You'll figure it out."

Lena pinched the bridge of her nose. She knew her background was vastly different from that of her teammates. With her mother serving on the Council, her family had never lacked funds—or well-kept living space. She'd thought she was prepared to accept the consequences of her choices. She was willing to live on the fringes of society outside of Enforcement law. She was prepared to face the dangers of breaking into Pallagen's labs. She'd never considered that she might have to share decrepit living quarters with two other people.

"Hey!" Dani shouted, poking her head back into the living room. "I can hear something dripping in here!"

Lena closed her eyes and groaned.

Brant disappeared to get his gear from...wherever he was keeping it. Lena didn't ask. She had only a small locker of personal belongings and one backpack of equipment. They'd need more, but Lena had sold most of her possessions for hard coin. She was dragging her locker toward the bedroom, determined to share the space civilly with Dani, when the technopath appeared in the doorway and threw a bundle of black cloth at her.

Lena looked up just in time to catch it with her face. Sputtering, she dropped the locker and glared at Dani.

"It's part of your image," Dani said, shoving her hands into her pockets and leaning against the doorframe.

Lena blinked. "My what?"

"You know, your image." Dani reached out and pulled the cloth away from Lena's shoulders, where it had come to a rest in a tangle. She shook it out and handed it to her.

It was a coat—long, black, and hooded. It fastened up the front with a line of small metal buttons. The cut looked vaguely military, like a knockoff Enforcement uniform jacket. Lena held it carefully by the shoulders. The fabric beneath her fingers was thin enough to be worn during Exordia's mild winter days.

"It's...it's a very nice coat, Dani," she said slowly. "But it's the middle of spring."

"We'll be out at night, mostly. It's cooler then. And you need something that looks intimidating." She reached out and straightened the bunched-up collar. "Between this and those boots you wear all the time, you'll look a few inches taller than you actually are."

"Which is important for my image."

Dani raised her chin and smiled. "Right."

Lena held the coat out in front of her, trying to see the potential Dani had picked up on. "What image is that, exactly?"

Dani sighed and took the coat back. "You're going to war against Pallagen, right? You need a uniform." She pointed a finger at Lena and twirled it. "Turn around."

Shaking her head, Lena turned and let the technopath help her slip the coat on. It fit comfortably across her shoulders, and the sleeves settled just at her wrists. She fastened the buttons down the front and shoved her hands into the deep pockets. Looking down at herself, Lena had to admit the coat made her look a little less like she was taking on the most powerful corporation in Exordia with three people and a couple of tablets.

The doubt she hid when Dani and Brant were around slithered into her thoughts. She tugged at the collar of the coat, trying to give herself room to think. She'd been furious when she left Pallagen, and her anger had fueled her determination to find Dani and Brant. Now, cycles later, she felt the first twinges of uncertainty. Could she and her team truly hope to stand up to Pallagen in a way that made a difference to Exordia?

She shook her head, pushing the thought away. It was too late for that now. She'd already crossed too many lines to be able to give up and go home.

"Nice choice." She forced a smile and turned to face Dani. "When did you become the fashion expert?"

Dani smirked. "After I spent hours marathoning holodramas." She pulled her goggles down and wandered to the living area.

Lena frowned and reassessed the coat, hoping she looked intimidating and not like a holodrama's villainess.

She dragged the locker the rest of the way into the bedroom and pushed it against the wall. She'd have to find a couple of pallets for them to sleep on. The room wasn't big enough for a bed frame. She opened the locker and dug through the few things she'd held on to from her old apartment—a couple of data chips full of music and technical journals, some clothes, a small holo tablet loaded with pictures of her parents that she hadn't turned on in orbits. She reached into the pocket of an old jacket and pulled out the data stick that held what little information she'd been able to steal from Pallagen.

"You wanted to know if we could do this," she murmured to herself, holding up the data stick. "There's only one way to find out."

Chapter Five

Alex settled easily into the routine at Sixth City Rehab. It would have been difficult not to. Her meals arrived at precise times, always brought by Tabba, and the nurse checked on her once or twice between meals. Sometimes she simply poked her head in to say hello; other times she helped Alex select food from the menu.

"If you're bored," Tabba constantly reminded her, "there's an entire data chip full of information waiting for you."

Alex didn't load the chip, though. There were a hundred questions she wanted answers to, and most of them were probably on that chip. What kind of person had she been? Did she have friends? A boyfriend? What was her family like? She hadn't asked about visitors, but Tabba hadn't mentioned anyone trying to contact her. Was she alone, or was there a happy reunion waiting for her?

As long as she didn't know the answers, she could imagine whatever past she wanted for herself.

She waited, and slept, and ate. She sometimes held the chip in her hand, the small piece of plastic heavy with the weight of the knowledge it held. She watched the roses outside her window bend and sway in the wind.

Days later, while shoveling savory pasta into her mouth, she noticed a few of the blooms had died. Alex blinked. She felt more awake than she had since...well, since she could remember. She swallowed. Suddenly, ignorance didn't feel safe anymore. It felt empty.

"All right," she said to the empty room. Her voice sounded loud in the quiet, but in a way it was comforting. It was one thing she recognized as part of herself. "Let's do this."

She pushed her dinner tray to the side of the bed and switched on the tablet. She slipped the data chip into the port. Her finger hovered over the tablet: news or personal file? *I'm still panicking over what to eat for lunch. I'm not ready for the personal file.* She selected the news file. There were several articles saved. One about an upcoming Council election, listing the views of each candidate. A few opinion pieces from both sides. A few heartwarming stories of good deeds done by citizens, someone complaining about a new building and the unsafe work practices of the contractors, a video interview of a man in a white, starched shirt explaining why housing costs in Fourth City rose while living conditions remained atrocious.

There was a light knock on the door, and it cracked open. Tabba poked her head in. Since she'd startled Alex that first time, she'd always made some kind of noise before entering. She walked across the small room to the bed and leaned close to Alex, peering at the tablet's screen.

"Find anything interesting?"

The story about the cat stuck in the puddle was interesting was what she meant to say, but what came out was, "I think I came from Seventh City."

Tabba nodded. "That's possible. Your ID chip listed only age, physical description, and current address."

Alex looked up, surprised. "Current address? I have a home somewhere?"

Sighing, Tabba shook her head and settled on the bed next to Alex. "I'm sorry, Alex. I doubt it. Any lease you may have had would have ended long ago. And vacancy laws would have taken effect by now, even if you'd owned a home."

Vacancy laws. Wait… Her hands shook, and she lowered the tablet into her lap to hide it.

"How long have I been here?" Alex asked quietly, afraid of the answer.

"Almost two orbits." Tabba pulled the tablet from Alex's fingers and pulled up her personal file. She opened the rehab center's admission form. "There, see the date?"

Alex's heart pounded against her aching ribs. Her vision tunneled and she clenched her fists, trying to control her rapid breathing. "I don't understand."

"Take a minute," Tabba said. She placed her hands on Alex's shoulders, and Alex leaned against them. "It's okay. You're okay. Breathe deeply."

Closing her eyes, Alex sorted through the questions that raced in her mind, trying to keep the panic at bay. "Two orbits—that's a really long time. No facility would have taken me on. Who's paying for this? Do I have family left?"

Tabba sighed, and her hands moved from Alex's shoulders

to her arms, squeezing lightly. "I'm sorry, Alex. No family. You're a ward of Exordia. The colony is paying for your stay."

"But—"

"Read your personal file," Tabba said firmly. "I understand your confusion, but you're going to get secondhand information from me. Start with what's in the file, and if I can answer any questions for you, I will."

Alex nodded, rubbing her forehead. For the first time since she woke up, she could think clearly without the haze of drugs. Unfortunately.

"Do you want to be alone?"

No. "Yes, please."

She felt Tabba nod and pull away. The nurse's shoes squeaked against the tile floor as she walked toward the door and pulled it shut behind her. It closed with the same click Alex had heard dozens of times. Same lock on the outside. Same force field on the window.

Revelator, Alex thought. *Who am I, and what happened to me?* She took a deep breath and scrolled through the file.

It didn't contain much. Date of birth, physical description—brown hair, dark eyes, average height—home address, gravbike registration. She took a moment to admire the bike's sleek design and dark chrome. At least she had good taste in vehicles. She swiped quickly past the picture of the bike broken and twisted in the aftermath of her accident.

She couldn't say much for her old hairstyle, though, cut short and ragged. Alex fingered the ends of hair that hung over her shoulders and wondered how it looked now. There was no mirror in her room. She'd have to ask Tabba about that.

The face that stared out from the ID file looked young, much younger than Alex felt now. Younger than the two orbits Tabba said it had been since she took a bad spill on her gravbike and lost everything about herself.

The initial shock of lost time was wearing off, and Alex felt her curiosity returning. She swiped over to a file labeled "Personal History."

According to the report, she hadn't listed her parents on her emergency contact information. Were they dead? Perhaps she and her parents had been estranged. No siblings either. Friends? Revelator, the questions were endless. Surely she'd had a job, coworkers to wonder about her disappearance. Was she a people person? Maybe she was a drifter, someone who formed no attachments and left no one to miss her.

No. That's not right. There was...someone. Someone that left an ache in her chest deeper than the physical ache that was fading daily.

The accident report was long on words and short on detail. She'd been traveling—along a regular commute?—between Fourth and Seventh City. The skyroads of Exordia were apparently very crowded, and a reckless driver had crossed into Alex's lane.

Alex felt a little better knowing she hadn't done anything stupid to get herself or anyone else injured. The amnesia was bad enough. She didn't need the burden of guilt as well.

The accident report ended, and she swiped over to her admission forms and charts from an Eighth City hospital. Several days in intensive care, several surgeries on her knee and chest, and she had been installed in the rehab center.

Indefinitely. Due to the severity of her head injury, none of the doctors gave much hope for a full recovery. Alex felt grateful to be awake.

What was disconcerting was Exordia sponsoring Alex's recovery. Her memory might be gone, but the private room, the soft blankets that spoke to both care and comfort, and the hot meals made exactly the way she liked couldn't be something the rehab center provided to every patient. Her stay couldn't be cheap. Anyone willing to keep her alive in a place like this must owe her a great deal. Or want a great deal from her.

There was a knock on the door, and Alex looked up from the tablet. Tabba poked her head in. "Get some sleep, Alex. The files will still be there tomorrow. Stop reading and rest."

Alex checked the time on the tablet and was startled to see that she had been reading for hours. Now that she had started, she wanted to finish, to keep reading to see if she could resolve her questions. But the look Tabba was giving her told her not to argue. She tossed the tablet onto the bedside table.

"What, do you live here?" she grumbled.

Tabba grinned. "Yes. Several of the nurses do. Now, go to sleep. I'll be here in the morning, don't worry."

Alex relaxed into the pillows and folded her arms over the blanket. It was easier to close her eyes knowing Tabba would be around to wake her up with quiet chatter and point out the tastiest breakfast options. She realized that Tabba was, currently, her only friend in the world.

Alex slept, and for the first time, she dreamed about waking up instead of dying.

Chapter Six

The outdoor café was one of Lena's favorites. It served some kind of Old Earth food, full of sweet and spicy flavor. She pushed the fried noodles and vegetables around her plate, sopping up the thick sauce, but didn't take a bite. It had been Brant's idea to monitor their first target from a restaurant, and now, with nerves knotting her stomach, she didn't think she'd keep down anything she ate. She looked across the table at Brant and wondered if her new teammate was just as nervous.

His plate was clean.

"Are you going to finish that?" he asked, fork poised.

Lena rolled her eyes and pushed her plate of food toward him. Apparently not. She tapped her earpiece, unsure if she would be able to hear her teammates over the noise of Tenth City dinner hour. "Comm check." She spoke quietly, hoping none of the business men and women around them caught enough of their conversation to get curious.

"*Clear,*" Dani said. Lena glanced across the street toward the roof of the Pallagen lab they were about to break into.

She imagined Dani hunched over a dim tablet, fingers poking out of her black gloves as she manipulated the infrastructure of Pallagen's security system.

"*Loud and clear, boss,*" Brant answered, much louder and in surround sound.

Lena glared at him. "You're sitting on the other side of the table."

"I was making sure Dani could hear me." He shrugged and shoved another forkful of food into his mouth.

"*I wish I couldn't,*" Dani retorted. "*I can hear you chewing. It's disgusting. Lena, make him stop.*"

Lena sighed. "Let's just focus on breaking into the building."

"*I already have control of the cameras,*" Dani said. "*There are a few people working late. A couple of receptionists at the desk. Four of the administrative offices are still occupied, and there are three scientists in one of the labs. I've seen at least five different security guards so far.*"

"The scientists will leave soon." Lena tapped the menu icon on the screen set into their table and ordered dessert to give them some extra time to loiter without attracting attention.

"Order me that orange cake thing, will you?" Brant pushed back Lena's now-empty plate. "You're sure the scientists won't work late?"

"I'm sure." Lena submitted the order before leaning back in her chair and crossing her arms. "We've been over this, Brant," she said, exasperated. "Several times now."

Brant shrugged. "This is a big target to start with. I want to make sure you know what we're getting into here."

Lena looked across the street to the lab. It sat back from the main gravtrack behind a small sage-green lawn peppered with benches that offered a false sense of welcome. Exordia's sun sank slowly toward the horizon behind it, giving the glass-fronted building an ominous cast. It was only five floors tall and looked short compared to the towering skyscrapers in this part of Tenth City. Lena knew the lab well. Most Pallagen employees started their careers here. It was a lab scrubbed clean of most of Pallagen's unsavory experiments, serving as a front for business investors, prospective scientists, or the curious public. But it was also a data bank, full of employee records, laboratory locations, and project files. It was the perfect target for Lena and her team.

A waitress brought out their dessert: an alarmingly orange slice of cake for Brant and a bowl of pink frozen yogurt for Lena. She picked up her spoon and scooped out a bite.

"I still don't like how many people are inside," Brant said around a mouthful of cake.

"Trust me, it will be empty of anyone but guards by the time we break in." Lena poked at her frozen yogurt with her spoon. It was strawberry, one of her favorite flavors, but not even the dessert was tempting her appetite. "It's mostly administrative staff and a few low-clearance scientists. I worked here for several weeks before Pallagen moved me to their main lab. I know the routine."

Brant put another bite of cake into his mouth. "Look, you're the boss, but isn't breaking into your old office a bad idea? They'll match your face with your employee record soon enough, and then they'll know exactly who you are."

"Good. I want them to know I'm not afraid of them." Lena frowned at her dessert. "I don't suppose you like frozen yogurt?"

Brant wrinkled his nose. "Not the strawberry kind."

Lena sighed and put her spoon down. "Look, I know this is a risk, but I want to hit this lab for a few reasons. First, there will be project files there—high-clearance files that may or may not be stored at the main laboratory. Dani pulled what she could off the CityGrid, and none of it was helpful."

"*It's not my fault Pallagen doesn't keep all of its files on a hackable system like the rest of the colony,*" Dani put in.

"Second," Lena went on, "it's not enough to simply get Pallagen's attention. We have to keep it. If we disable, even temporarily, one of their public fronts, they won't be able to cover it up easily."

Brant shrugged again. "Like I said, you're the boss."

Lena frowned, not sure if he was agreeing with her or simply conceding. She opened her mouth to ask, but Dani interrupted her.

"*Can I do street recon next time?*" Dani asked. "*I can smell that restaurant from here, and my sandwich sucks.*"

"It wouldn't suck if you had let me make it." Brant scraped the last of his cake crumbs off the table and grinned cockily in the direction of Dani's rooftop perch.

"*Whatever. Next time, someone else gets the roof.*"

Lena kicked Brant under the table. He winced and rubbed his shin, giving her a wounded look. Lena ignored him and tipped her head in the direction of the lab. There were people in dark suits and sharp business skirts exiting the building. Some of them wore lab coats.

"See?" Lena said. "Told you. How many are left, Dani?"

"*One scientist and two of the admins. They're wrapping up, though. Give them ten minutes and they'll be gone.*"

Brant stared sadly at his empty plate. "We can't keep sitting here, though." He looked up hopefully. "Unless we order more cake?"

Lena shook her head and tapped the screen set into their table. "We'll walk around for a bit. We don't want to be seen anytime near the break-in. Pallagen's going to figure out who we are sooner rather than later, but I don't want any civilian witnesses remembering us." She pulled a small plastic card out of her pocket. There was a fake ID chip embedded in it, programed by Dani with just enough credit to purchase their dinner. Paying with coin in Tenth City was out of the question. It would draw too much attention. She swiped the chip over the screen and then shoved it into the recycling slot next to it so the chip couldn't be traced back to them.

Lena and Brant stepped out of the café and joined the stream of pedestrians headed home for the evening. Tenth City was primarily a business district, full of towering glass-sided skyscrapers and carefully-maintained green spaces. The few pedestrians wore dark business suits and walked quickly toward their destinations. An occasional gravtrain or private vehicle skimmed through the narrow alleys between buildings, but soon everything would be silent save for Enforcement patrols and an hourly gravtrain. The ordered quiet felt far more familiar to Lena than the crowded chaos of Second City.

Streetlights began to turn on as they made their way down the street, providing the illusion of security for Tenth

City's business establishments.

Brant glanced nervously at the lights. "Shouldn't we be worried about the streetcams?"

"Dani will keep them from seeing us."

Brant frowned. "Can she control the tech inside the building, too?"

"She could, but she won't." Lena slipped her hands inside the pockets of the coat Dani had given her. "I can't believe you talked me into wearing this," she muttered.

"*Helps though, doesn't it?*"

Lena shook her head and looked up at one of the streetcams with a wry smile, letting her expression speak for her. Dani's laugh, short and sharp, filtered over the comm.

Brant ran a hand through his hair. He looked agitated. "Okay, explain to me why we're not going to hide from the lab cams? If we can, we definitely should."

"Pallagen is going to figure out who we are eventually— or who I am, at least. I worked there for a few orbits. Someone will recognize me or match my description with my personnel file." She nodded at Brant. "I'm all right with them knowing my identity. But outside any Pallagen facility, Dani keeps us off every camera, we don't use traceable tech, and we keep a low profile."

"*If they can't trace our movements, they can't figure out where we're based or what we'll do next,*" Dani put in. "*We'll just show up, hit their lab, and disappear again.*"

"Hmm." Brant limped silently for a few steps. "That could work, I guess," he said indifferently.

Lena could tell Brant didn't agree with her, but at least

he was willing to trust her. She glanced at him out of the corner of her eye. He looked as comfortable walking down the upscale Tenth City street as he did lounging in their shabby apartment. She wondered what kind of man he'd been before he joined Enforcement, before the Hazing. His Enforcement file was full of character-based psychological information but held almost nothing personal.

"Do you remember your family at all?" Lena asked.

Brant didn't answer right away, and Lena winced. She shouldn't have asked. She wanted to know more about Brant than what was listed in his file, but she wasn't sure what conversation was off limits. "I'm sorry, I..."

"No, not really," Brant said quietly. The scuff of his boots against the gravel was uneven, his limp noticeable this late in the day. "I remember they existed," Brant went on, his head tipped back slightly, his voice thoughtful. "I know I had a couple of siblings. I know my parents weren't happy with my choice of Enforcement as a career."

Lena snorted. There might have been a time in Exordia's history when Enforcement served to protect the people, but now they worked for any organization or individual wealthy enough to bribe them. There were still a few men and women like Brant who enlisted for altruistic reasons, but they didn't usually last long. They learned to play the ruthless games of their employers, or they ended up dead. Lena thought Brant was lucky to have been injured and discharged.

"I had a girlfriend, I think," Brant said softly. "Yeah...I remember her."

Lena's heart sank. That certainly hadn't been in his file. She hadn't spoken to her own parents since going to work for Pallagen, but that had been her choice. The idea that Brant might have left behind someone he loved shouldn't be surprising to her, but it was. Had he planned to find her after running from Enforcement, or had Lena taken that chance from him? She turned to Brant.

"You could go back to her, you know." She meant it. Dani could work some of her identity magic, and any involvement Brant had with Lena would be erased off the CityGrid forever. "The civilian re-entry program would still take you. You could claim you had a breakdown, finish the Hazing, and go back to your life."

Brant shook his head and grinned wryly. "Nah. They wouldn't take me, not after I ran from the Hazing. Besides, I'm pretty sure I had a fight with her before I left. I don't remember what it was about, but I'm pretty sure she wouldn't be happy to see me."

Lena sighed. Knowing a little about Brant's attitude, that was probably true.

"So how does re-entry work, exactly?" She watched Brant carefully to gauge his reaction. This was the most serious conversation they'd had since she hired him. "If you remember your family, do you remember anything about when...when you were serving?"

Brant gave her a sideways glance. Obviously, he wasn't believing her feeble attempts at detachment. He laughed. "I'm not as fragile as Dani, Lena. You can ask me whatever you want."

"*Hey*," Dani said. Her mouth was full, probably of dry, stale sandwich. "*I heard that*."

Lena grinned, feeling relieved that Brant was willing to talk about his past. "Okay, then. I know Pallagen developed the Hazing process as a memory-wipe program, but I don't know how it works. My parents knew a few high-ranking Enforcement officers, and they remembered everything about their lives before Enforcement."

Brant walked a few steps before answering. "An Enforcement contract lasts five orbits. At the end of your contract, you get the chance to sign on again, or go through re-entry."

Lena nodded. That made sense. "So the memory wipe happens when you're ready for re-entry?"

"Yeah. They can't pick and choose what memories to take, so they just Haze everything. The first stage is base memories—your family and friends, your past, your history with Enforcement. It allows Enforcement to erase any knowledge of cover-ups you might have been a part of, or of any undercover identities," Brant said bitterly.

Lena resisted the urge to reach out and touch his arm, unsure if the gesture would be welcome. "You couldn't have done anything too terrible. You're helping two people fight Pallagen. I doubt Enforcement could force you to do something wrong against your will."

Brant grinned at her, but the smile didn't reach his eyes. "They were probably glad to get rid of me."

Lena silently agreed, but she didn't think saying it out loud would help. "What's the second stage?" she prompted.

"Physical skills. Martial arts, weapons training...I ran

before that stage." Brant glanced at Lena. "You already know that, since that's why you hired me."

"It was one of the reasons," Lena said smoothly. It had been her first reason, but the more she got to know Brant, the more she knew she'd made the right choice. "Your character had quite a bit to do with it as well. Which brings me to another question: why sign on in the first place? Enforcement's reputation isn't exactly a secret."

Brant shrugged. "I wanted to make a difference. And Enforcement does that sometimes. They've stopped almost as many terrible people as they've helped."

Lena did reach out then, lightly touching his arm before pulling away. "You get the chance to do that now."

Brant's expression lightened, and some of his cheerfulness returned. "True enough."

They stopped walking in front of a small park full of white plastic tables and benches. Gray and black metal sculptures dotted the landscape. A few plants bloomed in carefully-arranged beds, adding a dash of color against the gravel. Brant dropped onto one of the empty benches. "Hazing only works on a person's memories. Anything rooted deeper than that—personality, emotional connections—is left untouched. After the Hazing, they put you through memory therapy to re-introduce you to the details of your former civilian life. Family, friends, prior occupation, that kind of thing. They also do some pretty extensive questioning to make sure you don't retain any memories you shouldn't." He grinned up at her. "Like how to break into buildings with armed security personnel."

Lena smiled back before turning to look toward the

Pallagen lab, far behind them now. "Dani, how does it look?"

"*Empty. The guards changed. There are five of them now.*"

Lena looked at Brant. He shook his head dismissively.

"Not a problem," Lena said, offering Brant a hand up. "We're headed back your way."

"*Street is empty, too. I'll have the front door unlocked by the time you get there. Just walk in.*"

Lena didn't ask any more questions, and Brant didn't volunteer any more information as they headed back toward the lab. She was too nervous to talk, palms sweating inside her pockets. More than once, Lena found herself taking long, quick strides, leaving Brant a step behind. She took a deep breath and forced herself to slow down. *Stay calm. You've been planning this for weeks. You can do this.*

The glass-fronted entrance had a row of automatic doors. They didn't open when Lena and Brant approached as they would have during business hours, but Lena pulled the handle of one and it swung open easily.

She paused, door held open. There were answers inside this lab, but also risk. She didn't know what Pallagen was hiding or what she would do when she found out, but once she walked through this door, she couldn't walk away. Pallagen would see her intrusion as a declaration of war, and she would have no choice but to fight them or die trying.

She looked up at the building, twilight glinting off the glass, to where Dani—wounded, angry—was perched. She glanced at Brant, who'd had a girlfriend before Pallagen stole that from him. She wasn't just facing down Pallagen because of what they'd done with her research. This was about what they'd taken from the people around her. Some of her nerves faded. She licked her lips and turned to Brant.

"Are you ready?"

Brant unzipped his jacket, revealing the armored vest he was wearing beneath it. He pulled a dark scarf over the lower half of his face and nodded. Lena pulled the door open wider and walked through the entrance.

There were three guards wearing Pallagen gray in the reception area: one behind the desk monitoring cameras, and two lounging on comfortable-looking chairs, facing away from the windows. They snapped to attention at Lena's entrance, completely surprised at their approach, thanks to Dani's control of the cameras.

"Good evening, gentlemen," Lena said, smiling, hands in the pockets of her overdramatic coat. Brant stood behind her, slightly to her right. He had his blaster out, both hands wrapped around the grip and aimed at the guards. Set to stun, Lena hoped. They were only here for information.

Before the guards had time to draw their weapons, Brant stunned the two by the chairs, the blue light of the stunner bright in the dim office. He was quick and accurate. Lena nodded in approval.

Behind the desk, the third guard, young and wide-eyed, raised his hands. "Revelator! Who are you?"

"Should we tell him?" Brant's voice was muffled by the scarf. "Or should we take the wise path of criminals everywhere and remain anonymous?"

Lena resisted the urge to roll her eyes. "Stun him. We have a job to do."

The guard's face twisted in panic before Brant stunned him. Blue light washed over him, and his eyes rolled back into his head as he slumped in his chair.

Brant pulled the scarf down and smiled. "See? This isn't so hard."

Lena huffed. "Don't get too cocky. This is the reception area. There will be other guards back in the labs." Still, she felt some of the tension across her shoulders release at their successful entry. "Besides, we had the element of surprise on our side. Pallagen wasn't expecting us. They'll be ready next time."

"If there is a next time." He glanced at the ceiling. "Where are we headed, Dani?"

"You want the first floor lab. Take the hallway past the administrative offices and make a right."

Brant strode across the tiled reception area to the adjacent hallway. Gun up, he swept the hallway, then motioned Lena in with one hand. "It's clear."

"I could have told you that." Dani's voice was so dry, Lena could practically hear the accompanying eye-roll.

She followed close behind Brant down the dark hallway. "*If* there's a next time? What's that supposed to mean?"

"You're after project files, right? If we find them here, you can dump them onto the CityGrid, let public outcry do the rest of your job for you, and —"

"Shut up! There's a guard right around the corner from—"

Brant turned the corner and came face-to-face with the guard.

"Hi." He stunned the guard in the face.

"*Okay, never mind.*"

"A little more warning next time, Dani-girl," Brant said.

"*Well if you hadn't been* talking *so much—*"

"Where's the next guard, Dani?" Lena interrupted, stepping over the body sprawled on the floor.

"*Other side of the building, second floor. You're good for now.*"

Brant led her down the long hallway, past dark, empty offices. Dani turned on the low hallway lights as they walked, and soon they reached the double doors of the lab entrance.

"Doors, Dani," Lena murmured.

"*Yeah, hold on. The lab has a higher clearance requirement, just...there.*"

The doors slid aside, revealing a small lab. A long table against one wall held a row of clear glass computer screens with wireless keyboards set in front of each one. Another table was covered with disassembled tablets. There was a second metal door on the back wall of the lab.

"Okay," Lena said, "light it up."

The monitors flickered to life.

"*Your turn,*" Dani said.

Lena pulled a data stick from her pocket and placed it on the keyboard data dock to allow Dani to download information.

"*Okay, I see the files. Give me a minute.*"

There would be time to go through the files later, but Lena was impatient to learn what they contained. Would they find out the extent of what Pallagen was doing with their research? Or would they simply find the locations of other labs? Lena wasn't sure which option she wanted. One would give her a task to focus on—finding and breaking into Pallagen labs across Exordia. The other option left her with choices that carried colony-wide impact.

"Does this bring back memories?" Brant poked a screen with one hand while keeping an eye on the door.

"Quit fidgeting with the tech, Brant. You're a whole floor away from anyone else in the building. At least, anyone who's conscious."

Lena activated one of the screens and pulled up the security camera feeds. It was a shallow distraction, since Dani was watching every sensor in the building, but Lena hoped it would make Brant drop his question.

"So? How long did you work here?"

No such luck. She swiped her hand across the screen, hiding the security feed. "Did it ever occur to you that the last thing I want to talk about while stealing from Pallagen is my history with them?" she asked, voice taut.

"Hey, I told you about my past in Enforcement."

"What little you remember," Lena said dryly. She sighed and drummed her fingertips against the table. "I was only here for a few weeks. Pallagen starts all of its scientists here. It's lower risk than letting someone into the main lab right after being hired."

"Hmm." Brant looked at her, eyes narrowed. "So why go to Pallagen?"

"My research was highly theoretical. Where else was I supposed to go?"

Brant tipped his head to the side, accepting the

explanation, then went back to checking the lab doors. "Are we almost finished here, Dani?"

"Just a few more seconds...and we're done."

Lena grabbed the data stick and put it back in her pocket. "Okay, that's it. Let's go."

"One small problem. The guard on the second floor tried to check in with his buddies."

Brant snorted. "Bet they didn't answer."

"Nope."

Brant made a show of checking his stunner. "So why is he a problem?"

"He's armored. He was the only real threat in this building to begin with, and now he's headed your way."

Lena tensed, and her hand reached for the stunner tucked into her waistband. It wouldn't do her any good. The guard's armor would disrupt the stunner's signal. Her weapon was made using Pallagen technology, and any weapon Pallagen invented, they built another to counteract it.

"Wish you'd said something about that before we walked in, Dani-girl," Brant said, shoving his stunner into its holster. "Lucky for you, I came prepared."

He reached beneath his jacket and pulled out another gun, an Old Earth model that used bullets for ammunition.

Lena's eyes widened. "That still won't do you much good against his armor."

"It'll do better than the stunner." He stood against the wall next to the lab doors and motioned with one hand for Lena to stand on the other side. He pointed the old gun toward the ground and waited for the guard to step through.

The doors slid open. The guard stood in the doorway assessing the lab, the stock of his energy rifle against his shoulder. Lena held her breath and stood completely still until he moved into the room.

Brant stepped forward and raised the gun. "Stop right there."

The guard spun around and froze at the sight of Brant's gun pointed at his face.

"That plate's pretty thick," Brant said quietly, nodding toward the guard's clear visor, "but I bet it would hurt if it shattered in your eyes. Raise the visor."

The guard tapped a button on the side of his helmet, and the visor slid to the side. The guard's face was grim. "I don't know who you are," he said, his voice low and gravelly, "but breaking into a place like Pallagen is a terrible mistake. If you surrender yourselves now, I can—"

Lena stepped forward and shook her head. "Don't. Just give me the rifle and take off your helmet." She held out a hand and waited. A beat of silence, two, and the guard, his gaze flicking from Lena to Brant's gun and back again, lowered the rifle and passed it to Lena.

Lena held it by the grip, barrel pointing down. It was heavier than she had expected. She reached out her other hand for his helmet, and he handed it over.

Leaning forward, she looked at the guard's badge. It read *Severn, Jacob* and held a 2nd-level access code. "So, Severn, Jacob." Lena tipped her head in the direction of the metal door at the end of the lab. "What will we find behind door number two? What's Pallagen using this lab for?"

The guard's mouth tightened.

"Power in the next room is higher. It's insulated. Refrigeration, maybe?"

Lena raised an eyebrow. "It's a blood bank, isn't it?"

The guard's face remained impassive, but his shoulders slumped just a little.

Lena smiled. Dropping the helmet, she brought the rifle up to point at the guard. "Brant?"

Brant put the Old Earth gun away and pulled out his stunner. "What do you think, boss? Should we tell him why we're here? He did try to warn us."

Lena stared at the guard for a moment, considering. "Tell Pallagen…" She trailed off, took a deep breath, and squared her shoulders. She met the guard's eyes. "Tell Pallagen we're coming for them. This is only the beginning. Their days of hiding the truth from Exordia are over."

The guard sneered. "Just who do you think you are, lady? Pallagen is everywhere. Even Enforcement works for us now. Just because you managed to break into a beginner's lab with a washed-out soldier—"

Brant fired the stunner, and the guard convulsed and fell to the ground.

Lena's hands tightened around the rifle, eyes fixed on the guard. She shouldn't be bothered by his words. They were only meant to unsettle her, but they'd worked.

There might have been a little truth to them, as well.

"Ignore him." Brant's words interrupted her thoughts. He reached down and grabbed the helmet. "We need to move." His finger hovered over the helmet's kill switch. "We don't want them listening in on us, but Pallagen will be notified the moment his helmet goes offline. We'll only have a few minutes until someone shows up."

"Go ahead and shut it down. Dani, get us into that cold storage room." Lena said, shifting the unwieldy rifle in her arms.

"I'll take that." Brant holstered his stunner and dropped the helmet. He took the rifle, settling it across his chest with the practice of someone familiar with it.

The door at the end of the lab slid open under Dani's control. A blast of frigid air billowed out, and Lena shut her eyes until it passed. When she opened them, she saw dozens of shelves stacked with blood samples. Lena shivered, but it had nothing to do with the cold air. She wondered how many different people the vials represented, and how Pallagen was using them.

"Revelator," Brant said, breath fogging in the cold, "what are they using all of this for?"

Lena stepped closer to the shelves and glanced toward the security camera. "How do you think they knew Dani was compatible with the technopath project?" She tapped the barcode wrapped around a vial. "They'll screen all of this to see if anyone can handle one of their experiments."

Brant swallowed, and his face paled.

"*We can't leave it here.*" Dani's anger was clear over the comm link.

Lena understood. "I know, but how do we get rid of it?" Lena turned to examine the room. There was a drain in the middle of the floor, and she nodded toward it. "We could dump it, I guess."

Brant's face twisted. "You know all of that gets filtered

into water reclamation, right?"

"Do you have a better idea?" Lena's voice held a note of panic. "Pallagen will be here in a few minutes!"

"Four and a half minutes. Streetcams show an unidentified grav vehicle heading our direction from Third City."

"Great." Lena reached up and grabbed a handful of test tubes, but when she turned around, Brant was grinning. He held up the guard's rifle.

"Actually, I do have a better idea."

He aimed the rifle at one of the shelves and fired.

Lena jumped at the shrill whine of the shot. "Revelator, Brant. What the phaeting—" She stopped. The shelf was gone, melted by the energy blast. The blood had either evaporated or melted against the wall, along with the glass containers it had been stored in.

"Okay then." Lena dumped the test tubes back onto the shelf. "That's definitely a better idea."

Brant destroyed the rest of the shelves with precise aim. Lena made a mental note to ask him for shooting lessons before their next mission.

"You know we're keeping this, right?" He vaporized the last shelf and shouldered the rifle.

"It did come in handy." Lena stepped out of the cold storage room, and Brant followed. The door closed behind them at Dani's direction. "If you can figure out how to get it back to Second City without getting caught, you can have it."

"Two minutes. Hurry up, guys."

Lena jogged through the hallway toward the front doors with Brant only a step behind her, despite his limp. She pushed open the wide glass doors of the lobby.

"We're out."

They walked across the lawn, not wanting to be spotted running from a building. When they reached the street, Lena paused to look back at the lab. She tried to steady her breathing, but her heart was pounding and her palms were slick with sweat. Her body pulsed with adrenaline and the thrill of success.

She took a deep breath. "Hit it, Dani."

The lab blinked into silence as the hum of air circulation, lights, and computers shut off. A couple of the streetlights near Lena sputtered out, caught in the small electromagnetic pulse Dani had sent from the rooftop.

"See you at the apartment," Lena nodded to Brant. He pulled the scarf off his face and disappeared into the dark. Lena walked the other direction. She heard Dani scrambling off the roof over the comm link.

One lab down, only a hundred or so to go.

Chapter Seven

No matter how busy her shift was, Tabba always found time to putter around Alex's room. Sometimes she cleaned and tidied, and sometimes she helped Alex through exercises to strengthen her healing knee. Today she was digging through a cabinet set against the far wall, hunting for a sweater in Alex's size.

She was quieter today, Alex noticed. It might have nothing to do with her. The nurse could be tired or worried, or not feeling well. But Alex had been awake for a week now, and she'd only seen the inside of her tiny room and talked to one other person. She couldn't help but feel like Tabba's mood had something to do with her. Alex squirmed where she sat on the edge of her bed, the tile floor cold beneath her bare feet.

"Am I dangerous?" she asked, letting her words shatter the silence of the room.

Tabba stopped pulling clothes out of the cabinet and turned to face Alex. "Well, I should hope not! They let me in here alone with you." She bit her lip and smiled, but it didn't quite reach her eyes.

Alex's shapeless white shift bunched uncomfortably as she crossed her arms. "The door locks from the outside." She felt like a child demanding answers from an authority she didn't know or understand. "There's a force field on the window. You're in here alone, but I know there's someone in the hall. I can hear their steps when you come in. And you're not the one that unlocks the door."

Frowning, Tabba propped her hands on her hips. "Well, that's terribly observant of you."

Irritated, maybe, but not angry. Good. Perhaps Tabba would tell her the truth after all.

"Will I ever be able to leave?"

Tabba's face softened. She rummaged in the cabinet until she found a comfortable looking sweater. She handed it to Alex, then sat next to her on the bed. "You're not a prisoner here. When you're cleared medically and psychologically, you'll be released. This is a long-term rehabilitation facility. There are many patients here with various medical or psychological conditions. The locked doors, the force fields... they're for your safety as well as everyone else's."

Alex took a minute to process that, weighing Tabba's words against her tone, her face, and Alex's own observations. *Truth*, Alex decided. *At least, truth as she believes it.*

"So how does this work, then? The mind thing. Why can I remember what a force field is and how to read and how the tablet works but not my own name? Where I lived, my family, the accident?"

"The mind is a complicated thing," Tabba said slowly, as if choosing her words carefully. "Not even Pallagen fully understands how it works. I haven't seen all of your scans, but I'm guessing that the injury you sustained only affected the part of your brain that forms certain kinds of memory— you still have automatic skill sets like reading or driving, but you can't remember learning those skills."

Alex pulled the sweater over her head. She wondered how many "automatic skills" were hiding, waiting to be discovered. Noticing the door locked from the outside was just the start of it. Every time Tabba brought in a tray of food, Alex found herself analyzing the utensils for their effectiveness in disrupting the window's force field. She'd categorized the shift changes of the guards outside her door by the sound of their footsteps. She felt restless in the small room, comfortable though it was. Even weak and aching, she wanted to be away from the white walls and antiseptic smell. She never remembered what happened in her nightmares, only the fear they left her with, but she knew this room was making them worse.

She knew better than to tell Tabba any of that. Alex shook her head, as if the motion would somehow allow her thoughts to fall perfectly into place. "No offense meant, but why haven't I seen a doctor? It seems like I would need extra help with such a traumatic injury."

Tabba did smile then, a real smile that lit her eyes. "You're past needing that much help, physically. A little therapy and you'll be able to leave. There will be a psychiatrist here in the next few days. Exordia is providing one of the best. Claire Tverdik is a good woman. You'll like her. She's highly respected in her field."

Tverdik. Alex let the name roll around in her brain, curious to see if she recognized it. Nothing. Her past life must not have had anything to do with the medical profession.

Tabba patted her hand and stood to leave.

"Thank you," Alex said just before Tabba closed the door. This time, the nurse left it open a little longer, allowing Alex a glimpse of the white hallway and an orderly in a dark blue uniform. Tabba flicked her hand to the side—*think nothing of it, no big deal*, Alex could almost hear her say—before letting the door slide softly shut.

Alex shifted uncomfortably on the bed, pulling the sweater tighter around her. There was something about the white of the room that was unsettling, something that touched a fear deep inside of her. Something she had to hide from Tabba.

The nurse was unfailingly kind. Whatever terrible thing had happened to Alex, she was sure Tabba was only there to help.

Alex hoped she would be allowed to roam the rehab center, see some of the other patients, and maybe get a better feel for the place. See if it was truly as innocent and calming as it pretended to be.

Then again, Alex didn't feel nearly as innocent or calm as *she* pretended to be.

Chapter Eight

"Hey, listen to this!" Brant exclaimed through a mouthful of toast, spraying crumbs across the table.

"No." Lena took a gulp of scalding coffee and wished she could zone out like Dani. The technopath sat with them at the tiny kitchen table, goggles pulled down, chin resting in her hands. Lena frowned. Dani had been sitting like that for over an hour. She'd have to wake her soon to make sure she didn't get lost inside the jumbled mess of her mind and the building's AI.

But there were no distracting AIs for Lena to lose herself in. She was stuck listening to Brant read the latest Exordian gossip while he consumed his breakfast, and most of Dani's.

She sighed. "I asked you to summarize whatever news pertains to us, not read off celebrity gossip."

"Oh, come on, don't you want to know what your old Council-sponsored university buddies are up to?"

If Lena's eyes were lasers, her glare would have burned through the tablet in Brant's hands.

Brant ignored her look but began scrolling through the less salacious section of the news. "They're accrediting the break-in at the lab last night to an unknown black market group. Someone looking to sell plasma to the underworld."

Lena chuckled at that. "It's a pretty poor cover up, but Exordia is used to Enforcement covering up incidents." She turned her attention to Dani and poked her in the shoulder. "Hey, you in there?"

Dani *hmmed*, and Lena figured that was the best response she'd get for a while. "Can you put up some conflicting reports of what happened at the clinic? Make it look like there's more than one story going around?"

"Sure." Dani pushed her goggles up, her unfocused eyes blinking in the morning light. "Want me to throw your name out there yet?"

"No, not yet. It won't take long for Pallagen to match my face with my employee records, and they're the only ones that need to know who we are right now."

Dani nodded and pulled her goggles back down, her attention already back on the CityGrid.

Brant frowned at the tablet. "The description in the first guard's official report says Lena is taller than she is."

"Told you the coat would work." Dani's voice was distant, like it always was when she was interfacing with an AI, but she sounded distinctly pleased with herself.

"That first guard described us as 'armed to the teeth' and a good foot taller than our actual height." Brant glanced up at Lena. "I think we scared him."

Lena smiled and took another sip of coffee.

"The armored guard was more realistic, but he played us up a little, probably to save face."

"I doubt it worked," Lena said.

All five of the guards probably found themselves demoted. They would be lucky if that was all that happened. Pallagen was known to make people disappear to preserve their secrets.

"Either way, you've made your first move." Brant put down the tablet and folded his arms across his chest. "What's next, Robin Hood?"

Lena's brow furrowed. "Who is that?"

"You know, Robin Hood? Bow and arrow? Outlaw? Old Earth story?"

Lena shook her head. "I don't know that one."

"He robbed from the rich to give to the poor," Dani broke in. "Which is not at all like what we're doing."

Brant rolled his eyes. "Whatever, freak show. How do you even know about Robin Hood?"

"I have access to almost every database in the city," Dani retorted loftily.

"That's just not fair."

Lena sensed another squabble forming between Brant and Dani. She'd learned that these arguments could go on indefinitely. She also knew that joining them or choosing a side wasn't helpful. The only way to get the two to stop bickering was to derail the conversation. She put her coffee cup down on the table with a solid *thunk*. "Have you found anything useful in the information we pulled from the databank?"

Dani didn't look at Lena, but she pushed her tablet across the table. "Nothing helpful, yet. A lot of subject information. They're doing drug tests as well as physical endurance tests, interestingly enough."

Brant leaned forward. "Could they be trying to create a superhuman?"

"Probably not." Dani said, pulling off her goggles. "Old Earth tried that, just before they started colonization. They wanted to see if they could give humans an edge when facing the unknowns of space. Nothing worked. Not well enough, anyway."

Brant's face fell and he sat back, crestfallen.

"There's a bunch of location intel, but it's encrypted. Once I get to it, I can tell you where the other labs are and what they're being used for." Dani met Lena's eyes. "I'm sorry. I know you wanted something more impressive than a list of buildings to break into, but..."

Lena forced a smile. "It's hardly your fault." She didn't refute the disappointment, though. She knew the chances of finding damaging evidence at a small clinic were slim. Still, part of her had hoped to find more.

"At least we know your suspicions weren't misplaced." Brant tapped his tablet. "That blood bank proves what happened to Dani isn't an isolated incident. They're planning to do something like that again, if they haven't already."

Lena nodded in agreement. It felt good to know she was right about Pallagen, but more than that, it felt good to be able to *act* on her suspicions. Even if the results weren't what she'd hoped for.

She wrapped her hands around her coffee mug. "Pick a location," she told Dani. "High profile this time. I want Pallagen to know we're not afraid of them, and we're not going away anytime soon."

Dani picked up her tablet. "You want flair?"

"Lots of flair." Lena went to take another sip of coffee and discovered her mug was empty. She pushed back from the table and walked over to the kitchen, moving a mess of tech and dirty dishes aside to get to the drink dispenser. While she waited for coffee, she surveyed the rest of the apartment.

The two rooms were already a disaster. Brant had dragged a mattress into the living room the day after they'd moved in. He'd claimed it was so he could sleep better, but Lena had noticed his limp was worse after only one night on the couch. She wasn't about to call him out on the lie. His shirts and socks were strewn across the room. Dani had a tangle of electronics on the table. There were two-day-old dishes on the counter. Lena refused to become Team Mom and clean up after everyone, but she had a feeling she'd give in to her need for tidy space long before she won the battle of teaching everyone to take care of their own dishes.

"We wouldn't have such a scary reputation if people saw our apartment," she said, her voice carrying a note of mocking disapproval. "What is this, university housing?"

Brant laughed.

Dani looked at the mess, eyes wide. "Wow." She poked at the dirty mugs in front of her. "You guys really are slobs."

Lena's eyebrows shot up, and Brant laughed even harder. She folded her arms and glared at him until he calmed down.

"If you get the dishes," he said between chuckles, "I'll go find a box for Dani to keep her tech in."

"Deal."

Dani spread her hands protectively over the tangle of wires and screens. "Don't touch my stuff!"

"I'm not going to." Brant pushed away from the table and tapped Dani's shoulder. "But *you're* going to store it somewhere out of the way where we don't, y'know, eat."

Dani mumbled something derogatory about food, but Lena ignored her and started running dishes through the sanitizer. She tuned out Brant and Dani's bickering. It was easier now than it had been a few days ago, and sometimes she found it amusing instead of annoying.

I'm getting used to them. She glanced back into the living area. Brant was shoving Dani out the door, tablet clutched to her chest and a deep scowl on her face. He slung his jacket over one shoulder and gave Lena a wave and a grin before following Dani. The door slid shut, and the apartment fell silent. Once, Lena would have found that comforting. Now, it felt empty.

She shook her head and shoved dishes into a cabinet. She didn't know what would happen to the three of them if they succeeded in taking down Pallagen, but she didn't think they would stick together without a common cause to unite them.

Pallagen wasn't going anywhere for quite a while yet. Lena might be stuck with this job longer than she'd planned, but for now, she didn't mind.

Chapter Nine

Alex talked Tabba into getting her a pair of sweatpants to go with her bulky sweater. They were gray and shapeless, but now she could curl up comfortably in a chair by the window without wrapping herself in a blanket. The morning of her appointment with Dr. Tverdik, she managed to put on her clothes without Tabba's assistance. The effort left her knee aching, so she stretched it out on the bed and tipped her head back against the pillows, breathing deeply. She had her finger on the call button to ring for Tabba when the nurse opened the door.

"Well!" Tabba exclaimed. "Up and dressed without my help. You'll be ready to leave sooner than I thought."

Alex smiled tightly and pushed herself up.

"Ready for the big day?" Tabba placed her breakfast tray on the bedside table and handed Alex a full glass of water. Reaching into her pocket, she brought out two white pills and handed them to Alex.

Alex accepted the medication, but paused before swallowing the pills. "These aren't going to knock me out, right?" She was nervous enough about talking to someone other than Tabba for the first time. The last thing she needed was a hazy mind.

Tabba laughed. "You're past needing anything that strong, except maybe to help you sleep." She gently tapped Alex's injured knee. "Something you should ask for. I know how restless you are at night."

Alex flushed and took a large gulp of water, downing the pills. "It's not my knee that keeps me awake."

"Nightmares, then." Tabba rolled the little table over to the window. "You should speak with Dr. Tverdik about them. Perhaps she can help."

"Maybe," Alex mumbled. She swung her feet to the floor and closed her eyes, bracing herself to walk across the room. She jumped when Tabba wrapped a hand around her arm.

"Slowly," the nurse said softly. "We're in no hurry." She placed one hand against Alex's back, keeping her steady as she walked the short distance to the window.

Alex sank into the chair with a sigh. "Thank you, Tabba."

"Of course." Tabba pulled the table closer and tapped the tray. "I want to see most of it disappear."

Alex wrinkled her nose. "I know."

"You may not be hungry now, but you need to eat something with the medication you took." Tabba squeezed Alex's shoulder. "Don't finish it all now. Wait until after you've spoken to Dr. Tverdik. You'll feel better."

Alex nodded and gently rubbed her knee. Tabba patted her shoulder and left her alone.

She drained the glass of water and managed to swallow

a few bites of cereal. It felt sticky in her mouth, and she soon pushed the bowl away.

There was a soft knock at her door, and Alex straightened, running a hand through her hair. "Come in," she called before quickly pushing the table to the side. She didn't want someone analyzing both her breakfast habits and her psyche.

Dr. Claire Tverdik stood in the doorway. She wore a soft beige skirt suit and platform heels, and in her hand was a real spiral-bound notebook instead of a tablet.

"Tablets get hacked, or stolen, or lost, or dropped," she said, noticing Alex's raised eyebrows. Either that, or she was used to giving an explanation for the notebook. She sat down in a soft gray chair Tabba had brought to the room last night and waved a hand at Alex's breakfast. "I hope I'm not interrupting."

Alex tried not to scowl. Claire's cool tone was nothing like Tabba's bedside manner, coaxing and kind. Instead, Alex felt like a scolded child. "Notebooks get stolen, too," she argued. "And they're not passcode locked."

Claire chuckled. "True. But if anyone can decipher my terrible handwriting, they deserve my secrets!"

Alex felt a little sorry for not laughing at Claire's attempt at a joke, but Claire didn't seem bothered. She simply settled into her chair and opened her notebook.

"I'm Dr. Claire Tverdik. You can call me Claire."

"I know. I looked you up on the CityGrid." Alex didn't want to speak anymore. She knew Claire had all of her information tucked away in a file somewhere and didn't need an introduction, but it didn't take long for the silence to become awkward. In the hallway, someone dropped a tray, the crash sounding muffled through the door. Alex's knee was still aching, and she had to stretch it out again. She shifted forward and held out a hand. "I'm Alex Kleric."

"It's lovely to meet you, Alex." Claire's voice was warm and her handshake firm. So far, she was everything the CityGrid proclaimed her to be. Starched stiff, flawless smile, perfect posture.

Alex wasn't buying it. She leaned back in her chair and folded her arms, unimpressed.

Claire seemed undeterred by Alex's animosity. She opened her notebook and held her pen poised and ready to write. "Can you tell me how you ended up at Sixth City Rehab?"

Is she serious? "You've read my file, right?"

"Of course I've read your file," Claire said evenly. "I want to know what *you* know."

Alex rubbed her knee. "An accident, they told me. Another vehicle skidded into my lane. They were drunk, the file said. They walked away, and I slept for the next two orbits."

Claire wrote for a moment in her notebook. Alex tried to read what she wrote, but the notebook was tilted at an angle, and she couldn't see without obviously straining.

Claire looked at Alex again. "Does that make you angry?"

"Angry because it wasn't my fault and I'm the one who's stuck here?"

Claire didn't respond to her harsh words, just tapped her pen against the notebook.

"Maybe? I don't know. There's so much I'm trying to figure out. I haven't thought a lot about whose fault it was."

"Fair enough," Claire said. She wrote something else. "To be honest, Alex, I can't say I've ever had a patient who's lost two orbits of their life. Would you help me understand what that's like?"

It wasn't quite a lie, Alex could tell. Claire probably hadn't dealt with an amnesiac with a two-orbit gap in her memory. But Alex was quite sure Claire knew the answers she wanted and was feeling Alex out for the best way to get them.

"It's confusing," Alex said finally. There. That was a safe answer. "I'm sure everything's different, but I can't remember what things were like two orbits ago. Everyone's moved on, and I stopped. I know I'm off, but I don't know how."

Claire nodded. She didn't write anything this time, and Alex didn't know if it meant she'd given a right answer or a wrong one. "Can you tell me anything you do remember?"

Uniforms. Shouting. Something burning. That red, red haze over everything.

"No," Alex kept her voice and expression even. Huh. That had been disturbingly easy.

Claire made another note. "Have you spoken to anyone since you woke up?"

"Just Tabba. She's nice."

Claire smiled. "It's good to make connections. You'll need those in your recovery."

Claire had kept control of the conversation, putting Alex deliberately on her guard, but she was too curious to let the comment pass. Verbal trap or not, she had to ask. "Yeah, about that. Tabba said Exordia was paying for my rehabilitation. Why?"

Claire frowned. "Are you opposed to the colony's intervention?"

"Not opposed, exactly. In my experience, people don't hand out favors unless they want something in return." *And I'm pretty sure "Ward of Exordia" means "We want something from you."*

"In your experience?" Claire latched on to the phrase. "I thought you didn't remember anything."

Scowling, Alex shook her head. "I don't. But I'm not an idiot. Exordia doesn't give something for nothing. No one does."

Claire tilted her head to the side, her eyes meeting Alex's. "It's true. Exordia does want something from you. But if your file is correct, you won't mind giving it to us." Claire pulled a data chip from her jacket pocket and leaned forward. "This is your file from Sixth City's official records. It's got more than what the rehab center was able to give you."

Alex grabbed her tablet off the bed and immediately loaded the chip, eager to get to the bottom of one solvable mystery. She flicked through information as Claire continued to talk.

"The reason for the lack of personal information is because you were working for Sixth City. You were a lieutenant with Enforcement." Claire leaned forward and tapped on the ID file. Alex stared at the image that filled the screen. It was a picture of herself in the blue uniform of Enforcement, looking older and less vacant than she had on the vehicle registration in Tabba's file. There was a determined set to her jaw. She looked like she was facing a mission—one she was proud of.

Alex knew Claire was watching her for any reaction. She just shrugged. None of it sounded familiar, and Claire's explanation lacked the conviction of truth Alex was searching for.

"You were working undercover," Claire continued when Alex didn't say anything. "Your father abandoned your mother before you were born, and your mother died before you finished your education. Enforcement recruited you, and you aced your way through the Academy. You had no connections, few acquaintances, and even fewer friends. Enforcement sent you deep undercover in Fourth City with one of the gangs there. They were working with the Dallusin, and Enforcement asked you to feed them information. You were one of their most valuable assets until your accident."

Alex raised an eyebrow. "Wow. I'm impressed with myself."

Claire smiled. "You should be. Exordia owes you a great deal. Sponsoring your rehabilitation was the least we could do."

"Wait." Alex pointed at the ID picture. "Is Alex my name or my cover?"

"You were born Alexandra Kleric," Claire said. "Your cover was destroyed, and you were reported killed in action so no one would come after you if you recovered."

Nodding, Alex flipped through the various files on herself. Though still sparse, the information was more detailed than what Tabba had been able to provide, full of personal details that filled in some blanks in her mind. There were a few images of her with other uniformed officers and a couple of kids at a social function. "Is there anyone left that I know?" Alex asked, stuck on a picture of her laughing with a light-haired man.

Claire sighed. "I'm sorry, Alex. For your safety, you were

reported killed in action to all of your colleagues so no compromise of your identity could be made."

Alex's mouth tightened. Yep. There was the Exordia that felt more like an efficient machine than a doting parent.

Her thoughts must have shown on her face, because Claire began to explain. "You have to understand, you weren't on a short-term mission. You'd been undercover for nearly an orbit, and Enforcement had no intention of pulling you out. The Dallusin have tried to undermine Exordia for decades. Your position with them was precarious. If any of them found that you were still alive..."

Claire let the implication hang. There was a thread of steel in her voice that Alex knew better than to argue with, whether or not she agreed.

"I guess I'll have to try not to recognize anyone on the street," she said, forcing humor into her voice. She could tell Claire didn't believe her, but the psychiatrist relaxed a bit. And made another note.

Alex was really starting to hate that.

She looked back down at the tablet, slowly scrolling through her service record. She paused over specific case details, picking out names and locations. She'd chased down a ring of counterfeiters manufacturing ID chips, caught the leader of a street gang, fed information to Enforcement about the Dallusin spies infiltrating Fourth City. She'd received a commendation after stopping an armed robbery, and another when she was injured getting her partner to safety. If her record was accurate, Alex had been quite a daring Enforcement officer.

She didn't feel anything close to daring or brave now, though. She swallowed, trying not to let her despair show. "I don't remember any of this. I don't know who the Dallusin are anymore."

"You may or may not regain your memory of what happened before the accident," Claire said, leaning forward and folding her hands.

"Isn't that what you're here for?"

"I'm here to help you process what has happened to you, not resurrect your past life. If you have memories you'd like to discuss, we can do so, but if you want assistance recalling life before your accident, you'll need to seek out a memory therapist."

Alex was silent. She wasn't sure she was ready to restore her past life. Her nightmare last night, full of white walls and hands streaked with blood, didn't seem like something she'd want to remember. She shuddered at the thought of making that dream her new reality.

"Do you have any more questions for me?"

Revelator, did she have questions. How did her mother die? Who had she worked with? Who had she left behind? Did anyone still visit her empty grave? Alex badly wanted to ask, but there was no way she trusted Claire to tell her the truth. Instead of giving voice to the thoughts in her mind, Alex shook her head. "Can I keep the data chip?"

"Please." Claire closed her notebook. "Passcode the tablet, though. Even though the information on it is two orbits old, it would be best if no one found it."

Alex nodded, for the first time feeling the delicacy of her

situation. Her waking moments had been consumed with sorting out who she was. Now that she had some answers, she had to acknowledge the possibility of enemies. How was she supposed to protect herself if she didn't know who she was looking for? Revelator, Tabba could be plotting to slip something fatal into her lunch at any moment.

Great. Alex's fingers tightened around the tablet. That was going to do wonders for her sleep tonight.

"I hope I've been able to fill in some of the gaps for you," Claire said, frowning at the tension on Alex's face.

"Yes." Alex pointed to the tablet. "This will help. Although I admit, it's made me want to start sleeping with one eye open."

"Don't worry," Claire's face cleared, and she patted Alex's knee gently before leaning back in her chair. "Pallagen and Enforcement have always worked closely with each other. Several of your fellow patients are former Enforcement officers, injured in the line of duty. This is the safest place you could possibly be right now."

Alex smiled, but her stomach was twisting. She didn't *feel* safe.

Claire stood. Alex rose stiffly, more from pain than attitude, and shook her hand. "It was lovely to meet you, Alex. Pallagen has asked me to speak to you again in two days to evaluate how soon you'll be ready for release. In the meantime, Tabba told me she plans to let you explore the rest of Sixth City Rehab. I hope you enjoy yourself."

Exploration sounded nice. She must have done okay with this first test if they were allowing her out of her room.

She waited until the psychiatrist had left before she

crawled back into her bed. Her chest felt heavy, and her knee ached. She hoped Tabba didn't expect her to do much walking.

Alex disconnected the data chip from her tablet and held it in her hand. It seemed light for carrying the weight of her former life. The information was detailed, certainly, and there was no reason to disbelieve it, yet Alex didn't quite believe everything Claire had told her. Maybe it was because she'd just met Claire, and wasn't ready to trust her yet. But that didn't seem right either. Alex trusted Tabba easily enough.

It could be Claire herself. Tabba fully believed Alex's story, but Claire lacked clear conviction.

Mostly, Alex thought, it was because nothing in her file explained her nightmares.

Still, the room felt emptier after Claire left. To her surprise, Alex found herself looking forward to the next visit. The woman might be lying to her face, but there was something about her that drew Alex in.

Or maybe it was just because Claire could help her get out of Sixth City Rehab.

Alex shook her head and reloaded the data chip, determined to scour every part of the report until she found something—or someone—familiar.

Chapter Ten

When Lena quit Pallagen, her entire world had turned upside down. She'd questioned her work, her character, her superiors, her morals. She'd lost her home and her routine, things that had always given her a sense of balance. There was little in her life that could be called steady at the moment, almost no certain ground to stand on.

But one thing she knew—Brant and Dani would only get along on opposite sides of the city.

They stood in the middle of the apartment a few inches from each other, shoes off. Brant's mattress was pushed against the wall out of the way, and Lena sat on the sagging couch, her feet pulled up out of stomping reach.

"Keep your chin down," Brant said. "And *pay attention*."

"I *am* paying attention." Dani tucked her chin and glared at Brant. "This is boring."

"It won't be boring if a Pallagen security team finds you on their roof with illegal tech. You need to know how to get away from them." Brant reached out and wrapped his fingers around Dani's wrist. "Now, your best bet is to run, but if they catch you..." He pulled her closer and frowned as Dani rolled her eyes. "Listen, freak show, this is important."

Dani's mouth tightened into a thin line and she jerked back the wrist Brant was holding, pulling him off balance and straight onto her bony knee. She jabbed him in the stomach with her elbow and he grunted, the wind knocked out of him. He let go of the technopath and leaned forward to catch his breath, hands on his knees.

"Don't call me freak show," Dani hissed. She stalked into the bedroom, grabbing her goggles off the table on her way.

Lena sighed and switched off her tablet. "Are you all right, Brant?"

He straightened and shifted his weight to his good leg, putting one hand on his stomach. "Kid's stronger than she looks."

"She's managed to hide from Pallagen for quite a while now. I doubt she needs our help to look after herself."

Brant ran a hand through his hair and shook his head sharply. "No, Lena, she's managed to keep off their radar. That's all. And it's not difficult to do if you've learned how to manipulate every circuit on the CityGrid." He limped to the couch and dropped heavily next to Lena. "We're putting her in the center of each target. If they find her, she's going to need more than a few disappearing-off-camera tricks."

Lena frowned. "You're right. I'm glad you're teaching her, even if it is a challenge. She needs more people looking out for her." She watched him rub his stomach muscles where Dani had kneed him. "But you might try making friends with her before you tease her. She doesn't always catch the subtleties of human conversation."

"I noticed." Brant grimaced. "Where'd you find her, anyway?"

"Robbing banks." Lena grinned. "She was good at it, too."

"So she's a criminal."

Lena's eyes narrowed at the flat tone of Brant's voice. "I wouldn't say you're a paragon of virtue yourself. I found you picking a fight in a bar."

Brant smirked. "True." He looked at her sideways. "I mean...you picked me out of a crowd. Was Dani the same, or did you hire her because she had a useful skill set?"

Lena didn't answer right away. She heard his unspoken question—had she hired *him* for his skill set alone? Had she picked Brant just because he could fight, or had there been a deeper motive?

She wasn't sure what she should tell him. She'd had a stack of files on soldiers or criminals, and Brant's had been on top. If he'd said no, other options had been available. Lena believed in careful planning, not fate. She'd expected Brant to agree to work for her because she knew he needed something—or someone—to live for beyond himself. Brant needed purpose for the same reason Lena needed to stop Pallagen: to give his existence meaning.

She couldn't tell Brant that.

"Dani needed help," she finally said. "And I need her technopathy for this operation to be successful." Lena gave a short laugh. "Revelator, I probably need her more than she needs me right now. But she was going to get herself killed robbing banks."

"And you felt responsible."

"Some." A lot, if she was being honest with herself. It had been her personality-based algorithm that matched Dani as compatible with Pallagen's technopath project. Saving Dani from a life of crime would stem the guilt Lena felt about getting the technopath involved with Pallagen in the first place.

Brant nodded. "How long do you think we'll be sneaking in and out of Pallagen labs?"

"I don't know. Before that first raid, I thought ..." She trailed off and waved a hand. "It doesn't matter now. We can keep this up for an orbit or so. Maybe a little longer than that. I don't want to do this for the rest of my life, and we don't have the resources to fight Pallagen long-term. They'll catch on to us eventually." She paused and turned to look at him. "Why do you ask? Is there somewhere you need to be?"

Brant pushed himself off the couch and straightened, his face tightening for a moment as he put weight on his bad leg. "No plans." He grinned down at Lena. "I just want to know how long I'm gonna be stuck with you two." He limped toward the bedroom—hopefully to make up with Dani for calling her names.

Lena switched on the tablet and began flicking through schematics, but her thoughts were elsewhere. She'd left her family when she decided to work at Pallagen to further her research, and she'd lost what few acquaintances she'd made when she went underground. It was a little disconcerting to think that, as soon as this job was done, she'd lose her only two friends in the world.

She shook her head and pushed the thought from her mind. She'd decide what to do with her life *after* they survived the wrath of Pallagen.

For now, she had a raid to plan.

They waited until after Luna Two had risen to raid the second lab.

"Late at night? I thought you wanted flair." Brant dumped a box of tangled gear on the table and started sorting it.

Lena picked up a small, suspiciously sword-shaped laser from the pile. "Where exactly does all this come from?" Brant opened his mouth, but Lena held up a hand. "Never mind. I don't want to know. And yes, there will be flair. But in the smaller project labs, scientists keep irregular hours, and I don't want civilian casualties."

Brant pulled on a pair of dark goggles—night vision, it looked like—and tilted his head. "I thought anyone who worked for Pallagen was the bad guy."

Lena tucked her stunner into the holster clipped to her waistband. "Pallagen employs almost 18 percent of Exordia's population, from cleaning staff to researchers, security, even landscaping. Not everyone is aware of what Pallagen does off the books." She held her coat at arm's length and frowned. The style hadn't grown on her, but it was easy to hide weapons underneath it. She glanced at Dani, who nodded approvingly, and Lena reluctantly pulled the coat over her shoulders.

"Maybe they've gotten really good at looking the other way." Brant said as he stuffed a tablet into his shoulder bag and headed for the door.

Lena refused to admit it, but he was right. More than a

few suspicious projects had passed across her desk before one stuck out and made her look deeper. She slipped her comm into her ear and followed Brant out of the apartment. Dani trailed behind her and punched a few numbers into the keypad by the door, locking it.

"Nevertheless," Lena insisted, "we're giving Pallagen's employees the benefit of the doubt until proven otherwise."

Brant turned to face Lena, and she straightened her shoulders. She never liked having to justify her actions to anyone, much less Brant, but he needed to remember who they were fighting

"Pallagen is the real enemy, not necessarily the people who work for them. We'll deal with security when we have to and take down ringleaders, but for now, we're after their information, not their people."

She expected an argument, but Brant just shrugged. "Your job, your rules." He turned and walked down the cluttered hallway toward the stairs.

Lena slumped against the wall in frustration. "I don't get it. He challenges everything I say, then turns around and does everything I ask of him."

Dani twisted a piece of her hair between her fingers. "Is that a problem? Don't you want him to do everything you tell him to?"

"Of course." Lena frowned. Did she? Not really, now that she thought about it. "I want him to trust me," she said slowly.

"Just because someone questions you doesn't mean they don't trust you. Besides, someone has to poke holes in your ridiculous plans."

Lena bristled. "My plans aren't ridiculous."

Dani pulled her goggles down and gave Lena a disbelieving look over the top of them. "The only reason we're in this mess is because no one was around to tell you that you'd need more than three people to take out Pallagen." She let her goggles snap back into place. "Trust me. Your plans are ridiculous."

Lena followed her teammates down the stairs, grumbling. She let herself sulk until they reached the gravtrain out of Second City. It was easier to brood about imagined injustices than focus on the nerves that accompanied their second foray into Pallagen territory.

Lena and Dani boarded the waiting gravtrain. Brant would take a later one out of Second City. Dani interfaced with the security cameras and chip readers on both trains to allow them to pass any electronic security unseen. Lena perched on the edge of her seat, tense and alert, a direct contrast to the technopath, who slouched nearby with the practice of a teenager and the confidence of someone who knew exactly how invisible she was.

Lena took a deep breath and let it out slowly. *Think about the mission.* Think about the steps they'd taken to prepare. The research they'd done, the schematics they'd memorized, the likely rosters of security guards. Nothing in this job was certain, but Lena did her best to control the outcome of every confrontation. Still, she was aware that anything could go wrong—a scientist working late, a guard walking the wrong hallway at the wrong time, being recognized by an old colleague.

Thinking about the mission was definitely a bad idea.

Lena sighed.

The gravtrain slid to a stop, and most of the passengers left the train. This late at night, almost no one boarded. Lena relaxed and leaned closer to Dani.

"Hey," she said, pausing until the technopath shoved back her goggles and looked at her. "I can tell Brant to stop."

Dani frowned. "Stop what?"

"I..." Lena trailed off, shrugging. "He's kind of hard on you."

"I probably need it." Dani sighed, pulling her goggles off her head. She turned them over in her hands for a moment. "Do you know why I didn't stay with my family?"

Lena shook her head.

"Everyone I knew treated me like glass—like I was going to break any second. So I decided I was better off on my own. Sometimes part of being unbreakable is believing that yourself, y'know?"

Lena remembered the first morning she'd gone to work after discovering how Pallagen had used her research. She remembered how she'd smiled at her coworkers, read reports, and compiled data, all while pretending her world hadn't collapsed beneath her. She nodded.

"You don't exactly treat me like that, but I can tell sometimes, when you look at me, you're not really seeing *me*." Dani met Lena's eyes briefly.

Lena shifted uncomfortably on the hard plastic seat. "Dani, I—"

"No. It's fine." Twisting the strap of her goggles in her fingers, Dani shrugged. "Brant acts like nothing's wrong with me—like Pallagen never did anything to me. It's annoying, but it helps me feel normal."

Lena didn't answer. Dani gave her a nervous sideways glance and put her goggles back on. The technopath hadn't offered any personal information until now. The first time she had showed up at Lena's Seventh City apartment after accepting her offer of employment, she'd simply handed Lena a data stick with every file the CityGrid had on her.

Lena shook her head, realizing she didn't know much about her teammates outside of what was recorded in some impersonal files. She had read the interpretations of others rather than the people themselves. That was something that needed to change. If she was going to develop an effective, corporation-breaking team, they needed to trust each other. A grin slowly spread across her face. Dani, not as self-absorbed as she was pretending to be, leaned forward at the change in Lena's expression.

"What are you planning now?" she said, wariness marking her words.

"How do you feel about ion tag?"

Dani's grin answered her question.

Chapter Eleven

"No ion tag." Brant drained the last of his coffee and slammed the mug on the table with enough force to make Lena jump in her seat.

"Come on," Dani said in a voice that was closer to whining than Lena had ever heard from her. "Don't you want the opportunity to beat us?"

Brant's face looked like he very much enjoyed that idea, but he shook his head. "It's too close to what we do for our day job." He looked out at the city sky, barely lit behind the tall towers of Second City, and frowned. "Night job. Whatever. The point is, we just finished a raid. Ion tag loses its appeal when you've been shooting at people—and getting shot at—for real."

Lena sighed. Brant had a point. Their raid on the small clinic last night had nearly ended in disaster. They'd been caught by the guards. She'd missed her first stunner shot and would have gotten stunned herself if not for Brant's quick action with his rifle. The smell of burned flesh from the guard's injury still lingered in her memory.

"I'm sure there are other things we could do to break the ice," Brant went on.

Lena tilted her head in confusion. "Break the ice?"

"Old Earth saying."

Of course. "All right then, what do you suggest?"

Brant opened his mouth, then closed it. Lena felt smug, but realized she had no other suggestions either.

"What do normal people do to...*team build*?" Dani spoke as if she were tasting the strange phrase and finding it disgusting.

Lena thought about the social hoops she'd had to jump through as part of Pallagen's orientation process. "Depends. Sometimes it's just dinner, sometimes going to a holodrama, sometimes playing a game."

"Like ion tag."

"You'd cheat, Dani-girl. You know it." Brant poked her shoulder.

Dani huffed but didn't deny it. She pushed food around on her plate.

Eat your dinner, Lena wanted to say, but Dani was—almost—an adult, and Lena didn't want to throw that kind of weight around. She sighed. "Maybe this wasn't such a good idea."

Brant shook his head. "It's a good idea, but what can we do? Our faces are probably being broadcast on every screen outside of Second City."

There was silence for a few moments as everyone stared at their plates contemplating the things they couldn't do, or wouldn't agree to do, or would get arrested for doing.

"We could sort out the rest of the location information I got from the first lab," Dani finally said.

"Sure, why don't we do that?" Brant asked before Lena could protest. He shoved his plate to the side and scooted closer to Dani.

The technopath eyed him suspiciously. "You don't know anything about hacking."

Brant shook his head. "True, but I know Exordia inside and out. You hack the information, I'll log the locations."

Dani didn't answer, but she slid a tablet across the table to him and pulled her goggles down.

Lena picked up her plate and tossed the remains of her sandwich into the recycling hatch beneath the sanitizer before cleaning it. That idea had failed miserably. So much for building trust.

Then she watched Brant and Dani bend over tablets together, trading civil information instead of insults.

Maybe it hadn't been a complete failure.

Within hours, Brant and Dani had compiled a list of Pallagen labs and their locations, and within weeks they began to take them down, one by one. The third lab they hit was an easy job. The building was nearly empty, and they were in and out in under two hours. Raids on the fourth and fifth labs were spaced out more after Brant ran into a well-meaning Enforcement officer and had to stun him. Raid six was a bust. The lab had been abandoned days before Lena and her team found it. Raid seven gave them the location of at least ten other research facilities, and ended with Dani on the run after a Pallagen security team spotted and chased her. Raid eight

left Brant with a burned side from an energy rifle blast, and
Lena with a black eye and sore ribs.

Team building, indeed, Lena thought ruefully as Dani
carefully wrapped a cold pack around her ribs. The three
armored guards at the lab had almost been too much for
them. Brant had shot one, but in the few seconds it took to
charge the rifle, the second guard had flattened Lena. The
third had fired at Brant while he got rid of Lena's assailant,
searing Brant's side. But Brant was a crack shot. The third
guard had never stood a chance.

"We really need another rifle," Lena muttered. She
glanced toward the bedroom door. Brant was already asleep
on his mattress in the next room. His burn was painful but
not dangerous. Dani had slathered it with cream and shoved
a bottle of pain tablets into his hands before retreating into
the bedroom to help Lena.

Lena glanced at Dani. The technopath's hands were
shaking, and she refused to meet Lena's gaze.

"Dani," she said softly.

"Where was Brant?"

Lena blinked in surprise. "What?"

"When the guard hit you. Where was Brant?"

There was a tension in Dani's voice Lena hadn't heard
before. "It wasn't his fault, Dani."

"He's there to protect you!"

"He's there to get us both out safely, which he did." How
he had done it, Lena wasn't sure. Brant had been white to
the lips, face lined with pain, but he hadn't said a word or
changed the way he moved until they were safely aboard a

gravtrain. Lena tugged her shirt down over the cold pack, feeling instant relief from the pain of her bruises. "It wasn't his fault," she repeated, trying to catch Dani's eyes. She did, just for a moment, and saw raw fear hiding under Dani's anger.

Sometimes Lena forgot that Dani was still young. Her skills made her seem older than she was, but the fear that she saw in her eyes reminded her that she was the closest thing to family that Dani had. Lena wanted to wrap her in a hug and tell her she was sorry for scaring her like that, but she knew Dani would only push her away. Lena couldn't promise it would never happen again. She could only promise the opposite.

"I'm sorry," she said softly.

Dani ran a hand over her face. "It's fine. It's the job, right?" She smiled, but there was no humor in her eyes.

Lena sighed slowly and carefully, hands bracing her ribs. Yeah, that was the job.

Revelator, she didn't want to lose these people.

Chapter Twelve

"Have you been dreaming?"

Alex certainly had, but she wasn't going to tell Dr. Tverdik that. She shrugged.

Claire sighed. "Alex, I understand that you must be very confused right now. Not knowing what happened to you, not knowing who to trust…"

Alex didn't answer. She simply sat, arms crossed over her chest. Part of her knew she was being petty. She had no real reason for refusing to answer Claire's questions, but the rest of her didn't care.

"Look." Claire closed her notebook and leaned forward. "If you don't like me, I can arrange for another psychiatrist to be assigned to your case. If it's simply a distrust of your current situation, there isn't much I can do about that. I can tell you that opening up to someone will be the first step in your recovery."

"What recovery?" Alex asked, letting her bitterness spill out. "You said yourself that I'll probably never get my memory back. I have no idea who I was, and I never will." Alex swallowed hard and gestured to the room around her, torn between anger and fear. "I'll be stuck here forever."

Claire tossed her notebook onto the empty bed and pulled her chair closer to Alex. "Listen, Alex. You're not stuck here forever. Physically, you could be released at any time. Psychologically, there's nothing besides your memory loss to keep you here, and that's hardly debilitating. It certainly won't keep you from functioning on your own."

Alex's throat tightened and she clenched her fists, her fingernails biting into her palms. "I don't know who I am. How am I supposed to have a life if I don't know who I am? I don't know what foods I like, or colors, or clothes, or music, or—"

"Alex." Claire sighed. She placed a hand on Alex's knee and met her eyes. Alex didn't say anything or flinch away, so Claire left her hand there. She took a deep breath. "All right. So you don't know who you are. That's not the end of the world."

"It's the end of *my* world." Alex folded her arms more tightly and sank back into the chair.

"No. You might not know who you were, but you get to decide who you're going to be." Claire removed her hand and leaned back in her chair. "We are always changing as people. Our personalities, our temperaments, and our mannerisms shift with age, life experiences, and the people we spend time with. Just because you're starting with a blank slate doesn't mean you have nothing to work with."

Alex blinked back the tears she refused to let fall in front of Claire.

Claire stood. "I think that's enough for today. Remember Alex, whoever you were before, you get to decide who you are now."

"I don't even know where to start," she whispered hoarsely, refusing to look at Claire.

"You like Tabba, right?"

Alex nodded.

"Then start there. Ask her what she notices about you. You're in there, Alex. You just have to find yourself again."

Claire patted Alex on the shoulder before she left the room. Alex stayed curled up in her chair by the window and angrily scrubbed tears off her cheeks. If she had to decide who she was, she knew she didn't want to be someone who cried in a corner over something she couldn't fix. She stood up and limped over to the tablet next to the bed to call Tabba.

"Fruit, sweet and sour. Dessert, sweet and salty. We're not going to try vegetables because honestly who wants to eat a dozen different vegetables just to find out which ones they don't like?"

Alex laughed. As soon as she'd suggested trial-by-error to discover what foods she liked, Tabba had jumped on the idea. Alex was fairly sure she was doing this off her shift. Tabba still wore the starched blue nurses uniform, but she wore a fuzzy sweater over her scrub top, and she had a mug of steaming coffee in her hands.

"Can I try the coffee first?" Alex asked, nodding toward the mug. The smell coming from it was tantalizing.

Tabba curled her fingers around it. "Sorry. No caffeine until you've been discharged, and even then, you shouldn't have any for a while."

Alex pouted and poked at a yellowish fruit.

"Peaches?" she hazarded.

Her memory of commonplace things was slowly returning. Though some of her word-fumbles were hilarious in retrospect, Alex knew that if she was ever going to fit back into society, she needed to remember as much as she could.

"Peaches. The finest Third City has to offer." Tabba took another sip of coffee. "As good of a place to start as any."

Alex speared a slice with a plastic fork and stuck the peach into her mouth. The fruit was firm, the juice sweet, the peel fuzzy on her tongue. Alex closed her eyes in contentment as she slowly chewed it.

"I definitely like peaches," she said, opening her eyes.

"Of course. Everyone likes peaches. Try the strawberries next."

The strawberries were plump and bright red, and a memory arose in her mind, bringing with it a twinge of pain. Alex paused, fork halfway to her mouth.

"Aren't they usually freeze-dried?" she asked, staring at the fresh fruit.

"Usually." Tabba reached for the plate and took a strawberry for herself. "Sixth City Rehab gets priority food shipments. Unless Third City goes offline, the freshest food is always available to us."

Third City. The image of a hydroponic greenhouse flashed in Alex's mind. She winced.

"Are you all right?" Tabba asked around the strawberry in her mouth.

"I'm fine." Alex shook her head to clear it and picked up

the next fruit. "Apples. I definitely remember apples."

Tabba settled into a chair. "Does it hurt every time you remember something?"

The question was asked so innocently that Alex answered before she could think. "Yes. No. That wasn't fair."

"If you're not going to talk to Dr. Tverdik, then you'll have to talk to me. Unless you want to chat up the guard."

Alex rolled her eyes. "No, thank you." She took a bite of apple. "Sometimes it hurts. I only get vague images. Sometimes a voice. Then usually a headache."

Tabba nodded. "The headache I can fix. The weird memories, not so much." She finished her coffee and curled her legs beneath her in the chair.

"They're not weird." Alex stuck her chin out and pushed hair out of her face. "They're just...detached. I don't have any context. I have no idea why one minute I see a hydroponic garden, and the next a tablet screen full of data."

"That sounds pretty weird to me."

Alex scowled. "Aren't nurses supposed to be understanding and sympathetic?"

"That's Dr. Tverdik's job. You want a gentle touch, talk to her instead of me."

Alex sighed. "I walked right into that one."

Tabba smiled. "She's a good person, Alex. You can trust her."

Alex poked at the rest of the fruit with her fork. "I don't think she's telling me the truth." She kept her eyes on her plate to avoid seeing Tabba's reaction.

"You have a point." Tabba stood and rubbed strawberry

juice off her fingers. "She works for Exordia. She might be a good person, but she's definitely not an honest one." Tabba pointed to the tray of food. "Please help yourself. I have to go back to work, but I'll come pick it up later, and you can tell me what you liked." She pulled a data stick out of the pocket of her scrubs. "And in case you get tired of the quiet, I loaded some of my favorite music on this. See if there's anything you like there, too."

Alex nodded, still thinking about Tabba's description of Claire. Not honest, but good. For some reason that sounded appealing—and familiar. Alex shoved another slice of peach in her mouth.

Maybe next time she'd tell Claire a little more about her nightmares.

Chapter Thirteen

Lena sat reading in a corner booth of a low-end diner in Second City, paying more attention to her tablet than her food. With all that she and her team had been doing recently, she hadn't had time to keep up with her colleagues' research, so she was taking the chance to eat a meal by herself and read something other than security system schematics. Second City was no place to be relaxed to the point of distraction, but Brant was up front playing a holo game and would warn her if anyone from Enforcement showed up.

Not that they would dare. Second City's residents would resist any intrusion from Enforcement. If there was one thing Second City hated, it was outside interference, and Lena and her team had been around for several cycles now—long enough to be considered part of the sector. Second City was, in a strange twist of fate, the only place in Exordia that Lena felt safe anymore.

A stranger slid into the booth across from her, and she started, nearly dropping her tablet.

The woman was middle-aged, dressed in casual

clothing. Her haircut alone marked her as a resident of another city, and Lena wondered a little that she'd braved the inevitable stares and jeers to get this deep into Second City in the middle of the day.

"Can I help you?" Lena asked.

The woman's eyes darted around nervously.

Lena could sympathize. When she had first moved to Second City, she'd stuck out like a sore thumb until she learned to dress and act a little more like she didn't care what others thought of her. With a sigh, she shut down the tablet and forced a smile. "What's your name?"

"I'm—" The woman stopped and shook her head. "Call me Janaye."

Lena almost rolled her eyes. There had been four Janayes in her graduating class alone. The woman might as well have introduced herself as Mrs. Smith. "What are you doing here, Janaye?"

Janaye leaned forward. "I heard you could help me." She spoke so quietly that Lena had to strain to hear her over the sounds of the lunch crowd.

Lena raised an eyebrow. That was new. "Help you with what?"

Janaye hesitated. "You're Lena Ward, right?"

Lena leaned back in the booth and crossed her arms. Enforcement wouldn't be stupid enough to send a middle-class civilian in as a trap, would they? Get her to admit who she was or what she'd done? Either way, Lena was taking no chances. She waited for the woman to keep speaking. If she had something important to say, she'd overcome her nervousness and say it.

Janaye's mouth tightened. "My daughter has disappeared. I need you to help me find her."

Lena stared at the woman for a few seconds, waiting for more of an explanation. When none came, she finally spoke. "Look, ma'am. I'm not sure what you've heard I can do, but if you think I can help you find your daughter—"

"I know what it is you do," Janaye interrupted impatiently, anger tingeing her voice. "But I need you to do something else right now."

Lena slipped her hand into her pocket and touched the screen of her mobile, activating her earpiece. Wherever this conversation went, she wanted Brant and Dani to hear it, too.

Janaye sighed, propped her elbows on the scarred, sticky table, and buried her face in her hands. She rubbed her fingers across her forehead before looking at Lena again.

"I know a little about Pallagen," she said, her voice low. "My husband is a medtech in one of their clinics. He never tells me anything, but I see in his face that he doesn't like what he's doing."

Lena bent forward. "Go on."

"My daughter moved out two orbits ago," Janaye continued. "We don't really get along. Her father was gone a lot, and she was kind of a wild thing stuck with just me, you know?" Lena did, a little, and she nodded. "She doesn't talk to us, really, but I call the university every once in a while to make sure she's all right. The last time I called they said she hadn't checked into any classes for almost three weeks."

Lena frowned. "You said she's kind of wild. Maybe she

wanted to get away? Or maybe she dropped out?"

Janaye shook her head. "I don't think so. Her boyfriend got my contact information from the school and came to talk to us. He hasn't heard from her either."

It was undoubtedly a suspicious disappearance, but people went missing all the time.

"Look around you," Lena said, motioning with one hand. "Second City is full of people who disappeared for one reason or another. I'm sorry for your loss, but you're not the only person to have a child go missing. If you want help, you need to speak to Enforcement."

Lena pushed her plate away and threw some coin on the table. She grabbed her tablet and was halfway out of her seat when Janaye spoke again.

"I think Pallagen took her."

Lena sat back down. "Pallagen doesn't operate that way," she said flatly. "They occasionally take people off the streets, but only those that won't be missed, and only for high profile projects. They certainly don't kidnap students."

"They do now," Janaye hissed, "and it's all your fault. You showed everyone that Pallagen wasn't invincible, that if you fight back there's a chance they'll leave you alone. I don't know how you keep Pallagen or Enforcement from finding you, or how you are still alive with the entire colony hunting you, but whatever it was you meant to do, you showed people that resistance can be successful. You know why they abducted my daughter? Because the street kids they used to take decided to watch out for each other. They took my daughter because the underworld isn't a safe place for them to kidnap subjects anymore. They took my daughter because of you."

Lena's hands clenched into tight fists. Her heart pounded. She didn't know if it was in anger or fear.

Brant slid into the bench next to Janaye. "Hi," he said, holding out a hand, "I'm Brant. Look, lady, I'm sorry about your daughter, but unless you have proof that Pallagen took her, we're not going to help you."

And maybe not even then, was the unspoken end of the sentence.

Thankfully, the woman didn't seem angry at Brant's callous words. She did refuse to shake his hand, though. Brant shrugged and dropped his hand into his lap, glancing across the table at Lena.

The woman pushed a data stick toward Lena. She took it but didn't activate it. She'd let Dani look at it first.

"That's information on a new drug test," the woman said. "My husband came across it by accident. The medical information on the test subject is identical to my daughter's, and the drug trial started a day after she disappeared."

Lena still didn't answer. It was all circumstantial evidence. She felt Brant watching her, waiting for her answer, and she met his eyes. He looked tired. Lena admitted to herself that she was too. For every lab they raided, Pallagen built two more. They could destroy equipment and steal records for another ten orbits and still not make any headway. Maybe helping even one person would feel more like a victory than anything they'd done so far. She took a deep breath.

"Okay," she said slowly. The woman sat up straighter, her eyes wide. "No promises that we'll find her, or if we do, that we'll be able to do anything about it. But we will look, if we can, without compromising our cover."

The woman's face crumpled, and Lena bit her lip. *Don't start crying, please don't start crying...*

Brant stood up and offered Janaye a hand. "Come on. I'll walk you out of the City. This is no place for you to be alone."

This time she took his hand. She slid out of the booth and paused, looking at Lena, her eyes dark and solemn.

"Her name is Arya," she said softly, then turned and left. She pulled her hand out of Brant's, but she didn't move away when he hovered close to her side. Knowing the ex-soldier, Lena was sure he wouldn't leave Janaye alone until she was safely on a gravtrain back to her home.

Lena sighed heavily and dropped her head into her hands. "Revelator," she groaned, "what did I get us into?"

"*Excuse me,*" came Dani's voice, and Lena jumped. She'd forgotten that she turned on her earpiece. "*Did you just agree to play detective?*"

"Shut up," Lena muttered. She tapped the data stick on the table. "Meet me here, okay? We'll see if this file has anything we can use."

"*I'm in the middle of something,*" Dani complained.

"Come on, Dani. If this girl has been missing for three weeks already..." Lena let the implication hang. Dani hadn't been missing for more than a week before Pallagen turned her into a technopath.

"*I'll be there in ten minutes.*"

"And find out how she knew where we were. Reputation or not, I don't like that she was able to walk into Second City and find us on a lunch break."

"*On it.*"

Lena stared down at the data stick. A warning pulsed in the back of her mind. *Don't get involved.*

Revelator. This was a bad idea.

Chapter Fourteen

Sixth City Rehab was the same outside Alex's room as it was inside: white, spotless, and mostly void of people. Tabba kept a hand on Alex's elbow as they walked down the hallway, and Alex leaned on it for support more than she wanted to admit. She felt old and slow. Her fists tightened. She wouldn't be able to protect herself like this.

"This is exhausting," she muttered.

"Give it time." Tabba helped her down a few steps. Alex was grateful her knees hadn't collapsed by the time they reached the bottom of the stairs. "Sixth City Rehab has the best equipment in Exordia, even for coma patients. You'll be fine in a few weeks with plenty of good food and slow walking."

Alex stopped, and Tabba pulled out a monitoring tablet to check her vitals.

"I'm fine." Alex waved the screen away. She took short breaths, trying not to pant from the effort of walking. She hoped Tabba wouldn't notice. "I was thinking of something a little more intensive than walking."

Tabba frowned. "You're not up for much of anything.

Three stairs were enough to set your heart racing."

Alex grimaced. So much for fooling Tabba. "Martial arts, maybe?"

Tabba crossed her arms and stared curiously at her. Alex wavered without her support. She locked her knees to regain her balance. "What?"

"Combat knowledge is illegal for civilians on Exordia," Tabba said, her eyes narrow.

Whoops.

"Sorry." Alex shrugged. "I don't remember anything like that. It was just something Dr. Tverdik said." There. Let Claire take the fall for her slip-up. She was the one who'd scared Alex in the first place.

Taking her elbow again, Tabba sighed and pulled her along the corridor. "The world must be very confusing for you right now."

"It's not exactly simple," Alex said, glancing at Tabba. The nurse's mouth was tight and her shoulders stiff. There was a tension about her that Alex had never felt before. Was it what she had said? Alex sighed. There was so much to learn. "Maybe running, then. Instead of...anything illegal."

Tabba smiled, but it didn't reach her eyes. "Maybe you should start with walking to the dining hall first."

They shuffled slowly down the hall until they reached a large glass room with high ceilings and open windows. The doors were thrown open, leading to a tangle of trees and slate-colored pathways. There were a few patients and nurses near the tables and chairs, and Alex saw flickers of movement in the foliage of the garden.

"Well?" Tabba asked.

Alex had stopped in the doorway, frozen at the sight of the world that existed beyond her window. It was the middle of the afternoon, and the dining area was close to empty, but the noise was deafening. She could hear plastic utensils tapping against plastic plates. Someone was running water. Three patients were grouped around a table playing a holo game, and the sound effects were unbearably loud. She looked sideways at Tabba, her eyes wide.

The nurse sighed. "Maybe it's too soon for this."

"No." Alex's voice was hoarse. She licked her lips. "No, I want to do this. I just..."

"Why don't we skip lunch? Come outside where it's quieter."

Alex let Tabba lead her through the open glass doors to a bench in the garden. She dropped onto it, one hand braced against her knee, the other pushing against the ache in her chest.

"Slow down, Alex. You're all right. Take a deep breath."

Alex let Tabba coach her through the next few breaths before she looked up.

Tabba's forehead was wrinkled with worry, and her fingers were tight on Alex's shoulder. "Too much for your brain or your body?"

"Body, I think." Alex took another deep breath. "I'm all right. It was just a lot."

Tabba didn't look convinced, but she didn't pull out her tablet either, so Alex took that as a point in her favor. She patted the empty spot on the bench next to her, inviting Tabba to sit. After staring at her for a moment, Tabba sat down. For once she didn't say anything. Maybe she sensed that Alex needed quiet. Alex closed her eyes and listened to the sounds around her, sorting through them in her mind. She could hear someone talking, though not clearly enough to distinguish the words. Footsteps shuffled along a garden path. A muffled laugh came from somewhere behind her.

"I can't hear any birds," Alex said quietly, unwilling to disturb the peace of the garden.

"There aren't any." Alex heard the smile in Tabba's voice. "Look up."

Alex raised her eyes skyward. She'd been focused on her feet since she left the dining room and hadn't paid attention to anything but the garden path. As she looked up, she could see they were beneath a large glass dome that let in the bright sunlight. Gravbikes and trains shot past the dome, but none of the traffic noise reached the garden. Alex let the quiet wash over her.

"You're being released the day after tomorrow," Tabba said abruptly, interrupting Alex's reverie.

Alex was surprised, both at the news of her release and the anger in Tabba's voice. "Isn't that a good thing?"

"Yes and no." Tabba frowned. "Dr. Tverdik arranged it. Like I told you, she's one of the best psychiatrists in Exordia. But, Alex, I won't lie to you. As a nurse, I am concerned. It's too soon for someone with your history."

"I thought you said I'd fully healed. Surely two orbits was long enough for me to recover."

Tabba shook her head. "Your body is physically weak

but otherwise healthy. It's your mind I'm talking about. You nearly passed out walking into a dining room with half a dozen people in it. Do you really think you're ready for the City?"

Alex didn't answer her. She knew Tabba was right. She wasn't ready to leave, but her need for escape was overriding her trepidation at facing a world she didn't remember. Sixth City Rehab had a deep sense of *wrongness* about it. The guard at the door, the force field on the window, even Tabba's constant presence, made it feel too much like a prison. Not for the first time, Alex let the steady beat of *I don't want to be here* pulse through her mind.

"I can handle it."

Tabba snorted.

"No, really. There's a lot you don't know about me, but I can tell you this won't be the scariest thing I've ever done."

Tabba's mobile buzzed. She looked at the screen and sighed. "Will you be all right out here? I'm being called to another patient."

Alex nodded.

"You know the way back to your room, right? If you're tired, you can go lay down."

"I'm good." Alex held up her hands. "I promise, Tabba, I'll be fine."

Tabba squeezed her shoulder and left, answering her mobile.

Alex leaned back on her hands. She knew she should be nervous about leaving Sixth City Rehab. She didn't remember anything about the rest of the colony—what it looked like, how to navigate it, the people it held. But she felt claustrophobic here, and she wasn't sure why. Maybe it was the way her skin crawled at the thought of being locked in, or maybe it bothered her to rely so heavily on Tabba for everything, even to leave her room. Either way, Alex felt sure her mental and physical recovery would be easier when she had some space.

She looked up at the sky and watched the people of Sixth City fly by. They were traveling well above the dome, far enough away that all Alex could see was a blur of movement. *Must be a no-fly zone,* Alex thought, frowning. Why in the worlds would a place like Sixth City Rehab be a no-fly zone?

Just another reason she wanted to get out.

She had almost decided to return to her room when someone flopped onto the bench next to her. Alex flinched at the sudden movement. The only people she had been near were Dr. Tverdik and Tabba, and their movements were always calm and controlled. The abrupt motion startled her, sending her heart racing as she looked to see who had caused such a disturbance. A man wearing the same shapeless clothes as Alex smiled at her, his dark hair unkempt, face lined, eyes vague and empty.

"Are you here for long?" he asked pleasantly.

Alex's fingers tightened on the edge of the bench. "Isn't everyone? I mean, it's long-term care, right?" She wished she was back in her room, behind the force field and the door that locked from the outside. She bit her lip and glanced down the path where Tabba had disappeared.

The man smiled. "True." He held out a hand. "I'm Carter. Definitely here for a while."

Alex didn't answer right away. She studied the exoskeleton brace that wrapped around his wrist and stretched across his fingers. After a moment, she carefully shook it. The metal was hard and cold in her grip.

"Alex," she said. "Leaving tomorrow, in fact."

Carter looked up at the sky as Alex had done. "Lucky you." He glanced sideways at her. "Did Dr. Tverdik swing that for you?"

Alex froze. First Tabba's comment about Dr. Tverdik's influence, now Carter. How much authority did Dr. Tverdik have here?

Carter laughed. "It's not a secret. Dr. Tverdik is one of Exordia's most trusted psychics. She controls who gets in and out of Sixth City Rehab."

"You're wrong. She's a psychiatrist," Alex pointed out. "Psychics are an Old Earth story. They don't exist on Exordia." How she knew that, she wasn't sure.

"Don't they?" Carter chuckled. "Good to know. I'll remember that the next time she tries to dig around in my mind."

Alex's palms began to sweat. *He's a mental patient,* she reminded herself. *He could be completely crazy.* She wiped her hands on her pants. The soft, gray fabric reminded her that she too was a patient here. She could be just as crazy as he was.

Suddenly overwhelmed by her racing thoughts, she stood clumsily. "It was nice to meet you," she said stiffly. She turned and walked down the path, leaving Carter alone on the bench in the garden.

She remembered the way back to her room easily enough, but she was exhausted when she arrived. The guard was still stationed by the wall, standing at attention. He opened the door for her but didn't help her inside. Alex wouldn't have let him anyway. She stopped to catch her breath just inside the door, and it slid shut with a *click* behind her.

Alex collapsed into the chair next to the window. She rubbed her fingers against her forehead. Carter could be right about Claire being a psychic, but Alex had no way of knowing if it was true. One thing was for sure: she wasn't going to ask Tabba if the words of a fellow patient were true. She wanted to leave too badly to be detained for further psychological evaluation.

She'd known Claire was lying to her, but now Alex found herself wondering if she had done anything to her mind while she tried to get Alex to talk. Alex squeezed her eyes shut. She hadn't exactly trusted Claire, but the thought that the psychiatrist might have manipulated her already-vulnerable mind stung.

I don't want anyone else in my mind. The words—not in her voice, but in someone else's—flashed through her memory. Alex gasped and hunched over in pain, but the memory didn't stay. She rubbed her temples against the developing headache and opened her eyes.

The red haze was back. She blinked a few times and it went away, leaving her in the stark white of her room. Alex took a few more deep breaths, and her heartbeat settled.

She was fine.

And she'd be even better once she was out of Sixth City Rehab.

Chapter Fifteen

They found Arya by accident when they raided a lab Pallagen had listed under "weapons research."

They expected the lab to be heavily guarded. On previous raids, Lena had worn a concealed vest. She couldn't move as well in heavier armor, even with the self-defense training Brant had been putting her through. Besides, part of her wanted to show Exordia that you didn't have to be armed to the teeth to fight Pallagen. An idealistic thought, but no more ridiculous than Dani's refusal to wear any protective gear.

This time Lena wore black and gray, like her partners. An armored vest was strapped under an impact-absorbing jacket. She had on heavy boots, and the inside lenses of her glasses displayed whatever information Dani chose to send her. She still refused a combat helmet, but she did pull a stocking cap over her hair.

Brant's rifle was slung across his shoulders, and he had a stunner strapped to each thigh. Lena was sure he had more than a few knives hidden somewhere, too. The stunners were non-lethal, but the rifle was deadly. Lena didn't know if he thought it was poetic justice to use it against Pallagen or if he simply thought it was a cool gun, but she didn't make him get rid of it. They needed all the firepower they could get against Pallagen's security teams. The scientists and lab techs they encountered were a different story. Some of them were cold and calculating, but most were like Lena had once been—looking for a job. Lena didn't want to harm anyone unnecessarily, so she only carried a stunner. She didn't tell Brant or Dani that she'd tampered with the electric circuits, amping them high enough to kill someone if she needed to.

She was an idealist, not an idiot.

Lena and Brant stopped on either side of an alleyway entrance to a noisy bar in Fourth City.

"*It looks clear,*" Dani said. An image of the inside hallway popped up on Lena's glasses. There was one tall, muscled bouncer standing on the inside of the door. On the wall opposite him was a keypad. "*I've already hacked the keypad, but you'll have to take care of the guard.*"

Brant hefted his rifle. "No problem."

Lena scowled at him and held up her stunner. "I'll take the guard. You watch the hallway." She was sure of her aim this close to the guard, but if anyone started shooting at them from either end of the hall, she wanted Brant taking care of them. She flicked the safety off. "Dani, open the door."

The door slid open with a quiet hiss. The guard turned to face them, but Lena stunned him before he could raise his rifle. Brant stepped inside and looked quickly from one end of the hallway to the other.

"Clear," he announced quietly.

Lena pushed the guard's limp arm out of the way of the door sensor. "Shut the door. We're in."

The hallway led to another set of steps, but instead of leading them up, the steps led down into the ground. Brant and Lena looked at each other uneasily before creeping slowly down, their rubber-soled boots squeaking against the slick plastic floor.

"Is Pallagen excavating labs now?" Brant muttered.

"Maybe it was already here." Despite her words, Lena's stomach twisted. It wasn't easy to dig a basement out of the loose desert soil of Exordia. What was so terrible that Pallagen had to hide it underground?

There were no guards at the bottom of the stairs, though there was another door with a keypad.

"That's weird. I wanted to shoot more people."

Lena shook her head, reading his underlying concern—there should be more guards. "Maybe they think no one knows about this lab yet. Or maybe they're inside that door."

Brant grinned at her and unslung his rifle.

Lena rolled her eyes. "Open it up, Dani."

"*Hold on,*" Dani said.

A few tense seconds passed before the door slid open.

The lab was dark and empty. Lena relaxed. She wanted to make a statement, not leave a trail of bodies. Still, something about the room felt off.

"Can you bring the lights up?" Lena asked quietly as she and Brant moved into the room. The lights flashed on. The room was small, painted a stark shade of white. There were a couple of metal tables, a few chairs scattered haphazardly around the room, but nothing else. No tablets strewn across the tables, no half-empty coffee cups, no equipment, none of the junk that accumulated in the workspace of focused genius.

"Why abandon a functional lab?" Brant stepped farther into the lab. His boot crunched on a glass beaker and it shattered, breaking the still reverence of the abandoned basement.

"Maybe we've made them nervous." Lena hoped her words sounded more confident than she felt.

"But if it's abandoned, why are they still guarding it?" Dani asked, her apprehension clear over the comm.

"They'll guard it until they're done cleaning up." That, at least, Lena had an answer to.

Brant looked up. "What?"

"If they abandoned it, that means their project is over. They'll send a cleanup crew to erase anything that's left."

Brant's face tightened. "A finished project like Dani?"

"Why do you think I have her stationed on the roof?"

"I can hear you, you know."

"Whatever," Brant said, kicking the glass shards under a table.

There was another door at the end of the room, and Lena nodded toward it. "Let's check in there before we leave. Even if Pallagen isn't using this lab anymore, we should make sure they didn't leave anything behind."

It was an old-fashioned door that swung on hinges instead of sliding into the wall. Brant tugged it open, revealing a wall of doors on the other side. Doors with tiny, clear windows in them.

Lena's apprehension increased. Her heart pounded as

Brant stepped toward the first door. "Brant, no, wait..."

Brant stepped up to the viewing window on the first door. Lena reached out and grabbed his sleeve to stop him, but he didn't pay attention. He pressed his face to the window and jolted back as a hand slapped the glass.

"*Revelator!*" he swore, swinging the rifle up.

"Calm down. Just...calm down." Lena's shaking voice belied her reassuring words.

"*What?*" Dani asked. "*What happened?*"

"Is this what you meant by 'cleanup?'" Brant turned to look at Lena, face flushed, eyes narrowed and hard. Her fingers still clutched his sleeve, and he jerked his arm away. "There are still people here!"

"I know." Lena swallowed. "They...they probably abandoned the lab anyway."

Brant stared at her.

Lena bristled, her own shock wearing off. "I didn't think they'd just *leave* people somewhere to—to die." She stumbled over the words.

Brant looked away. His face paled, losing some of the anger and none of the horror.

Lena took a deep breath to steady herself. "Dani, did you find any specifics on this lab?"

"*Yeah.*" Dani's voice was distracted. For once, Lena was glad for Dani's experience at the hands of Pallagen. She wouldn't be as blindsided by what they saw. "*Looks like standard drug testing. Don't let anyone out. They'll still be coming off whatever high Pallagen put them on. If you open the doors, you may end up having to shoot them.*" Her last

words came out sharper than usual, and Brant pulled his
hand away from one of the door keypads.

"What do we do with them?" Brant asked, holding tight to
his rifle. He looked unnerved. Lena wished she had words to
help dispel the horror on his face, but in a way she was glad.
During previous lab raids, Pallagen had been a faceless enemy
for Brant, a corporate entity with no real personal connections.
Lena felt a little less alone, knowing that both Brant and Dani
felt the same horror she did at Pallagen's atrocities.

"How many cells?" Lena asked.

"*Eight,*" Dani said. A weighty silence followed her answer.
Brant and Lena looked at each other, Brant's face hard and
frowning, Lena's eyes and shoulders heavy with the guilt of
knowledge.

Finally, Dani broke the silence. "*Lena, we can't—*"

"I know," Lena said, cutting her off. She wasn't sure how
Dani was going to finish that sentence. The technopath was
remarkably pragmatic sometimes, and Lena didn't want
to mediate another argument between her teammates. "I
know, we can't leave them here, but we don't have a place to
take them, either."

"Can we drop them off at an emergency med center?"
Brant asked, voice tight.

"And then what?" Lena spread her arms. "They come
around after a few hours and begin raving about underground
laboratories and human experimentation? We'd be condemning
them to a mental institution. That won't get them the help they
need."

"*Pallagen would locate them, anyway. They'd find a way*

to get rid of them, and it would be easy enough if they were considered mental patients."

Brant slung his rifle over his shoulder and crossed his arms. "A safe house, then."

"We have no medical knowledge," Lena said. "And we can't involve anyone else—at least not yet."

"But I—"

Lena held her hand up, stopping Brant's protest. She knew he had connections, and she was willing to use the information he was able to gather, but she wasn't ready to drag anyone else into her war on Pallagen. "Just...let me think a minute."

Brant didn't give her a chance. "I joined you to protect people."

Lena sighed. "We've been over this, Brant. If we want to stop Pallagen, we have to —"

"I don't want to stop Pallagen!" Brant shouted. His voice echoed through Lena's earpiece and bounced off the walls of the lab. "I wanted to help people. I thought stopping Pallagen was the best way to do that, but clearly you think otherwise. Do you care at all about these people?"

"Of course I do!" Lena's tone echoed Brant's frustration and anger. She clenched her fists and took a breath to calm herself. "Of course I care," she said softly. "Why do you think we're here in the first place? I know what happened to them. I used to *help* the people who hurt them. But we're not a rescue network, Brant. We don't have the resources, or the people, or the time—"

"Then *make it work*," Brant said menacingly.

Lena's jaw clenched and she glared at him, measuring the resolution she saw in his eyes. Brant had always questioned her plans, second-guessed her gut instincts, but he had never challenged her directly. His face hardened as he stepped toward her. Lena forced herself to remain rooted to the floor, meeting his harsh gaze with one of her own.

"We can't leave them." He jerked a thumb over his shoulder at the cell doors. "Just because we don't have the resources to help them doesn't mean we shouldn't try."

"We could harm them more," Lena said quietly. "If we turn them out on the streets, Pallagen will recapture and eliminate them."

"What if it were Dani? What if Pallagen caught her again? What would you do if we found her locked in a cell with no hope of escape?"

"That's different!"

"No, it's not!" Brant lowered his voice. "What are you trying to do here, Lena? Are you really interested in stopping Pallagen, or are you just angry at them for what they turned you into?"

Lena stepped back as if she'd been slapped. *Of course that's not why*, she wanted to snap, but she couldn't. She wasn't sure if it was true.

"We're getting them out," Brant said after a moment.

"We can't."

Brant started toward the cell doors, then paused and looked back. "You can help me, or leave. I don't care."

Lena hesitated, then reached out and grabbed Brant's arm. "Fine. We'll get them out. But we do it my way."

Brant met her eyes, and Lena didn't look away. *I want him to trust me,* she'd told Dani, and now was her chance to show that she was worthy of his trust. Finally, Brant nodded. Lena squeezed his arm once—*thank you*—and pulled her hand back.

"Dani, get down here."

Lena tapped a lifeless screen by the first cell door and brought up patient data. She sighed in frustration. There was little information, besides vitals taken at regular intervals and a few sedative administrations.

"Fine." She switched the screen off and turned back to the door. "We'll have to play it by ear."

"Oh, great." Brant rubbed the back of his neck. "That sounds like a fantastic idea."

"*You* were the one who wanted to stay and help. Quit complaining."

Dani stepped into the lab, goggles up and eyes wide.

Lena reached out and tapped her elbow. "Are you okay with this?"

Dani's jaw tightened, and she nodded.

"Brant, be ready to stun." Lena reached for the first door. "Dani, start scanning them as soon as the door opens."

Her team nodded, ready and tensed. The person on the other side could have been through almost anything: drug testing, sensory testing...who knew? Pallagen hadn't attempted biological weapons yet—at least they hadn't when Lena worked with them—so she felt fairly confident they wouldn't be facing a viral threat. But there was no guarantee. Lena rubbed her sweaty palm against her pant leg and pulled an access card out of her back pocket.

"All right," she said, and took a deep breath. She swiped the access card across the panel, and the door slid open.

Inside was a girl in a shapeless white shirt and pants, stained with sweat. She was huddled in a back corner of the room, knees pulled to her chest and her face hidden by an unkempt mop of dark hair. Lena glanced back at Dani, who shook her head.

"High stress levels, malnutrition, dehydration," Dani read off the medical scanner. "Whatever they had her on, it's worn off by now." Dani stared at the girl. "Elevated temperature as well."

Which, combined with everything else, probably meant altered perception. Lena swallowed and pushed her hair out of her face. She stepped into the cell, hoping her all-black attire would help distinguish her from the Pallagen scientists the girl was presumably used to seeing.

"Miss," she said, slowly stepping forward, keeping her voice low and calm. It was the same tone she used when Dani was lost in thought. "Miss, can you hear me? We won't hurt you." Lena was close enough to put a hand on the girl's shoulder, and she hesitated for a moment before gently resting her fingers on the white shirt.

The girl flinched tighter into the corner. Lena frowned and knelt next to her. Out of the corner of her eye she saw Brant step into the cell, one hand gripping a stunner, the other holding out a water bottle.

Lena took it and rested the weight of her hand firmly on the girl's shoulder. "We won't hurt you," she repeated, injecting more force into her voice. "I promise. We don't want to hurt you."

The girl slowly raised her head. Her face looked even younger than Dani's. She couldn't be more than sixteen or seventeen orbits. She was pale and malnourished, and her eyes were bright with fever and fear. There was a weary acceptance about her, as if with the knowledge that whatever happened next would be received without protest.

She looked like the woman in the diner.

Lena held out the water. The teenager eyed the bottle with suspicion, so Lena twisted off the cap and took a mouthful of water. As soon as she offered the water again, the bottle was snatched out of her hand, and the teenager tipped her head back, gulping down its contents.

"Slow down." Lena pulled the bottle away. The girl resisted but was too weak to do much more than pull ineffectually at Lena's grip.

"Brant." Lena motioned him closer.

He nodded and stepped forward, holstering his stunner. They each took an arm and helped the teenager stand. She was unsteady on her feet, but with their help she managed to walk to the main lab. They lowered her into a chair, and Dani draped her jacket gently over her shoulders.

"We need to go back for the others," Lena told the girl. She looked small and vulnerable under the glaring lab lights. Lena wanted to stay and help her, but there were seven more prisoners, their conditions unknown, waiting to be released. There was no way to know when Pallagen would send their cleanup team, and they needed to get out of the lab as soon as possible.

Dani passed the med scanner to Brant and sat down next to the girl, talking softly to her. Lena paused and watched Dani, surprised to see this side of the technopath. She often forgot that Dani was a young girl herself underneath the attitude, and that she, too, felt deeply for others affected by Pallagen.

One by one, Brant and Lena opened the isolation cells and released the occupants. There were four men and four women, all about the same age and size. Lena guessed they were a control group for whatever drug tests Pallagen had conducted. They were hollow-eyed and vague, and though a couple reacted with more hostility than the first girl, they were so weak that Brant was able to hold them long enough to convince them that the team was there to help.

Finally, the group of worn, ragged people huddled around one of the metal tables in the main lab. Dani ran the medical scanner over each person while Brant recorded their identities so they could create similar ID profiles under different names.

After she had finished, Dani pulled Lena to the side. "We need to take them somewhere safe. We can't just let them leave. They'd collapse before they walked a block."

Lena pinched the bridge of her nose. "Where, exactly, do you have in mind? We're not hauling them all back to our apartment."

Dani shifted uneasily from one foot to the other. "I have a safe house we can use."

Lena glared at the technopath, but she didn't have the energy to scold her for keeping secrets. She folded her arms. "How do we get them there?"

"Same way we got here. We'll use the gravtrain."

"Dani, that's public transit. We can't just—"

"Yes, we can. I can clear a whole car for just one commute. I'm already blocking us from all streetcams, and it won't be hard to hack everyone's chip to pay their fare."

Another risk—a big one. But some of the more coherent victims were watching Lena, waiting for her answer. "Okay. If you think you can handle it, let's do it."

Dani's eyes lit up before she pulled her goggles down and got to work.

Lena didn't like the cold feeling that settled in her gut at each concession she made, but a blossom of warmth helped drown out the dread she felt. This was the right thing to do. She knew it, despite her fears about what might happen next. Brant had been right about her. For so long, she'd wanted to stop Pallagen because she felt responsible for helping them. She'd told herself she could atone for her past actions by destroying their reputation. Now, for the first time, she was angry on behalf of someone other than herself or her team, and it felt good.

"We'll have to make a few trips. The gravtrain isn't close, and no one here is able to walk on their own. Luckily, we're in the middle of one of the worst parts of Fourth City. I doubt anyone will stop us to ask what we're doing. If they do," she raised her voice and met the eyes of everyone listening, "let us do the talking. Dani, you're with me. Brant, stay here with the others."

Brant nodded and unslung his rifle. He threw out a casual salute. "Yes, ma'am."

Many of the victims were still in shock, but a few were coming around. The first girl they'd rescued looked much more alert, and she gripped Lena's hand tightly. She waved away Dani's offer of help and leaned heavily on Lena.

"You're Arya, right?" Lena whispered as they picked their way across the lab. The girl flinched as if she'd been struck, but Lena steadied her and continued. "Your mother asked us for help."

Arya nodded. "Who are you people?" she asked in a hoarse voice.

Lena took her next steps silently, thinking about her answer. Interacting with people had not been on her agenda. Revelator, who could she be to these people? Who did she *need* to be?

She stepped into the alley. Cold air hit her face, and she took a deep breath.

"I'm Lena Ward, and we're here to help."

Chapter Sixteen

Whoever had picked out Alex's apartment had good taste. She wondered if it had been Claire. It was a few stories up, past the crowded streets of Exordia. The apartment was small, but it had open spaces and large windows that overlooked a balcony with a fantastic view of the Seventh City skyline. There was a plush gray couch against one wall and a shining chrome and white kitchen across from it. From the slate-colored walls to the soft, thick carpet, it stood in complete contrast to her room at Sixth City Rehab.

It felt like coming home.

She didn't realize she'd stopped in the doorway until Tabba gently pushed her into the room. Alex stumbled forward, and Tabba and Claire followed her in.

"Oh, how lovely!" Tabba exclaimed. "It's perfect. Alex, you'll love it here."

Tabba immediately started opening kitchen cabinets and inspecting the dishes and food stored inside. Claire seemed more sensitive to Alex's sudden quiet and stood silently beside her, waiting for her to make the first move.

"Where did the boxes come from?" Alex asked, stepping over to the gray storage crates stacked in the middle of the apartment. She cautiously lifted the lid of one as if it held a desert snake.

"Sixth City had some of your things." Claire patted the top of another box. "Your partner boxed up what was left in your old apartment, and we pulled it out of storage when you woke up. Maybe some of it will help jog your memory."

Alex hurriedly closed the box. She didn't want Tabba or Claire around if she suddenly regained any memories, afraid they would overreact to the migraine that always accompanied them.

Claire smiled at her, clearly not fooled. "We'll leave you alone to get settled. You're out of the rehab center's care, but we're still here if you need help. I'll be by every few days to check on you. I've had the apartment stocked with basics to last you a few days, but please, let us know if you need anything." Claire held out a mobile.

Alex accepted the device. She activated the screen and saw Tabba's and Claire's numbers pre-programmed into its memory. "Thank you," she said gratefully. She wouldn't have thought to ask, but having a way to reach Claire or Tabba made her feel less like she'd been cut adrift.

Claire smiled, and Tabba hugged Alex gently. Then they were gone. Alex took a deep breath. It was the first time she'd been left completely alone since she woke up, and it felt good. She tucked the mobile into her back pocket and explored her new home.

All the crates had labels with her initials and a number—

ID number or badge number, maybe?—but Alex didn't open them right away. Instead, she walked into the kitchen and pulled out a plastic cup. The faucet switched on when she held the cup beneath it. She took a sip and almost spit the water back out. Obviously the taste of unfiltered city water was something else she'd forgotten. She wandered over to the floor-to-ceiling windows in front of the balcony and folded her arms, enjoying the view and trying to match it to something—anything—in her mind. The tower where the Council met seemed familiar, but that could have been from any news vids she'd seen.

She turned back to the boxes, trying to decide which one to tackle first, when the doorbell chimed. Rolling her eyes, she walked to the door. "For the last time, Tabba, I'm fine," she called, fumbling with the lock code. It disengaged after a moment and the door slid open. "It's not like I've never lived alone before..."

The person in the hall wasn't Tabba. A tall man stood in the entryway with a confused expression on his deep brown face. In his hands he held a container.

"Hi." Alex frowned up at him, resisting the urge to step backward. Revelator, he was tall. Thin, too. He had the lanky appearance of someone who had more arms and legs than he knew what to do with. "I...thought you were someone else."

"Obviously," the man said with a grin, and held out one hand. "I'm Liam. I've got the apartment next door."

"Right." Alex shook his hand. Her fingers disappeared in his grip. Neighbors were a thing. Everyone had neighbors.

Who were my neighbors before? Alex shook her head. That wasn't helping. She realized she was staring at their clasped hands silently. "Right! Sorry. Umm, I'm Alex. Alex Kleric." Her verbal fumbling hadn't seemed like a big deal when talking to Tabba or Claire, but they knew who she was and why she sounded that way. To a complete stranger, she must seem like an idiot. She covered her awkward stuttering with a smile. "Sorry," she said, trying again. "I was distracted. Moving and...stuff." She waved a hand vaguely at the crates.

"Yeah, moving will do that to you." Liam's smile widened. "Need any help?"

Alex met Liam's eyes and stared at him for a moment. She listened to her instincts, measuring the man's gaze against the feeling that had never steered her wrong—as far as she could remember. He seemed sincere enough. She needed to stop being so suspicious. Not everyone was out to kill her.

Also, Liam had a *very* nice smile.

"Sure. But not today. I'm tired and... how about tomorrow morning?"

Liam nodded. "Sure thing. I'll be around all weekend. Just knock when you're awake." He held out the container. "Here. In case you don't have anything on hand, it's always nice to have a hot meal the first night in your new home."

"Wow," Alex said, taking the container. The contents sloshed. "Thanks. Do you always keep soup on hand for emergencies?"

She winced a little at the sarcasm in her voice, but Liam chuckled. It was a warm, friendly sound that made Alex want to laugh, too.

"I saw the boxes being carried in, and I fired up the stove. Let me know what you think. The entire building loves my cooking!"

He waved and walked away.

Alex stepped back and let the door slide shut. She stood there staring at the door, the container warming her hands. Was that how normal neighbors acted? Sharing food, introducing themselves, offering to help? She wished for a moment she'd listened to Tabba. She wasn't sure she was ready for life outside the rehab center after all.

But there was no turning back now. Alex sucked air through clenched teeth and shifted her fingers around the container, cracking the lid. The soup did smell good. She rummaged through a few kitchen drawers before finding a spoon and plunging it into the soup before she could change her mind. Considering her history, should she really be eating food from a stranger? Her other alternatives were cold cereal or a frozen dinner. In the end, hunger—and the knowledge that Claire wouldn't have given her the apartment without running background checks on the other tenants—won out, and Alex ate the soup.

The next morning, she poked her head out of her apartment door and glanced down the hallway. She wanted to take Liam's container back, but after the constant supervision of Sixth City Rehab, it felt strange to simply open her door and leave at will. The hallway outside was quiet

with no other tenants in sight. Taking a deep breath, she
stepped out and walked to Liam's apartment.

She tapped the control panel next to Liam's door, empty
container in hand. "You're right," she said as soon as Liam
opened the door. She handed him the container. "It was
good. If you feed all the new neighbors like this, I bet no one
ever leaves."

Liam laughed. "I should make the landlord give me a
discount for securing tenants. Or maybe open a restaurant."
He took the container. "You still up for unpacking?"

"Are you still free?"

Liam smiled and stepped into the hall, letting the door
slide shut behind him.

Alex couldn't help returning his smile as they walked to her
apartment, Liam taking one long stride for every two of Alex's.
She keyed her door open and stepped aside to let him enter.

"So, Liam, what do you do?" Alex asked, curious to talk
to someone who wouldn't hedge their answers or be careful
of her mental state.

"I work for the city. You?"

Alex grinned. "I'm...in between jobs right now. I used to
work for Exordia, too, though."

"You don't strike me as a receptionist."

"No. I was...information, I suppose."

"Can't tell me, huh?" Liam's tone was teasing, but it set
Alex on edge.

"Well, what do *you* do for the city?" she asked, miffed,
and not sure how to cover with an alibi. She realized she'd
need one if she was going to interact with anyone other than

Tabba or Claire.

"Filing, believe it or not." Liam stopped in front of her stack of boxes, hands on hips. "Is this all you have?"

"I travel light." Alex wasn't too nervous about the contents of the boxes. If her personal file hadn't helped her remember anything, she doubted a box of clothes would jog her memory. Still, she didn't want to face the tangible evidence of her forgotten past alone. Tabba would have helped in a heartbeat, but she was too cheerful for a job like this. Alex would have been smothered with encouragement and overzealous assistance. Liam's presence, with his warm laugh and steady smile, was a much more appealing prospect. After the isolation of Sixth City Rehab, Alex was willing to risk a memory-triggered migraine if it meant she could have company.

She tugged a box closer. "So what does filing look like these days?"

Liam gave her a strange look. "Well, it usually consists of sitting at a desk and making sure the right people get the right documents sent to them."

Alex mentally slapped herself, realizing she'd asked a question that was strange to anyone that didn't know she'd lost a couple of orbits. She hid her frustration by opening a box and burying her attention in the contents. Maybe this wasn't such a good idea after all.

The box Alex opened held neatly folded clothes and a dark jacket made of sturdy material. A few pairs of slim-cut pants, several plain-colored shirts, and a couple of dressier blouses. At least she had sensible taste in fashion. She pushed the box behind her toward the small bedroom. "Any clothes you find can go in there. All of the…everything else… can stay out here. There's no other place to put it."

Liam nodded and opened another box. His eyebrows rose. "Are you some kind of foot messenger, maybe?"

Looking in the box, Alex flushed. "Wow. That's a lot of shoes."

A very specific type of shoe, too. No fancy heels or sandals, just comfortable sneakers or boots that looked like they'd run through the rain and mud more than once. It made sense for someone who had spent their life chasing criminals.

Liam laughed. "What, you just now realized?" He carried the box into the bedroom. "Don't worry. Noticing you have a problem is the first step to recovery!"

Shaking her head, Alex rolled her eyes and opened another box. She froze. Sitting on top, carefully folded and starched, was a dark blue uniform jacket. Hers, she guessed. She couldn't remember wearing it. She carefully reached out and straightened the collar, then ran her fingers over the embroidery of her name.

"Enforcement, huh?"

Liam's voice startled her, and she quickly closed the box. She looked up, her shoulders tense and mouth tight, but Liam's face was soft, his eyes full of compassion.

"Retired," Alex said after a long pause. Her palms were sweaty, and she rubbed them fretfully against her pant legs.

"Kinda young for that, aren't you?"

Alex sighed. "I was injured in the line of duty. I lost some time. So if I'm a little bit off, that's why."

Liam nodded. "I figured it had to be something like that when I saw Dr. Tverdik here yesterday."

Alex groaned. "Great. Does the whole building know I'm a psych case?"

Liam took the box from Alex. "Filing, remember? I know lots of things the average person doesn't!" He carried the box away. "Seriously. I'm an encyclopedia of random facts."

"I believe it," Alex said, shoving another box at him. "Here, see if you can discover any more secrets of my past."

There were no more secrets, though. Some more clothes, a tablet, and some data chips that Alex boxed up and put on the couch to look at later. A couple of drama vids, a small set of mismatched dishes, a pillow, a half-used makeup set. All of it felt very impersonal to Alex. There were no pictures or knickknacks, no childhood leftovers or anything that appeared to be a gift. Nothing kept for sentimentality's sake.

Not that she would recognize something like that. She could hold some of her most prized possessions, and she would have no idea what they meant to her.

Liam helped her put away the dish set and opened her freezer. He gaped at the pre-packaged food. "We're going shopping tomorrow. You'll waste away on all of that junk." He looked at her with narrowed eyes. "Who did your shopping?"

Alex huffed. "Dr. Tverdik, not that it's any of your business. Why? Are you offering to help me cook?" She'd agreed to let Liam help her unpack because she wanted company, but she didn't know if it was normal for someone to offer help as casually as he did.

He gestured to the frozen meals. "Only because you

obviously need it."

Alex bit her lip. Had she ever been able to cook? More importantly, did she want to take the chance that Liam would figure out how damaged her memory was?

Liam didn't seem bothered by her hesitation. He grinned at her, eyes glinting with amusement.

Alex sighed. It would be smart to keep her distance until she had a better handle on what her new life looked like.

But, Revelator, Liam was cute.

"Fine," she said, matching Liam's smile with one of her own. "But only if you teach me to make that soup first."

Chapter Seventeen

Lena found Brant on the balcony of the apartment, hands braced against the rail. It was too dark to see his face, but Lena could read tension in the tight line of his shoulders. She stepped beside him and leaned her hip against the rail, waiting. The sights and sounds of the city surrounded them. They listened to the neighbors arguing. A group of unruly teenagers splashed the side of a building with neon paint. The distant sounds of gravtrack traffic reached the balcony, resonant with life and motion.

"The Hazing didn't work," Brant said softly.

Lena looked at Brant. "I know. You ran—"

"No." Brant ran a hand through his tangled hair. "I mean, it didn't take. They Hazed me, but it didn't work. I kept getting flashes of memory, so they kept trying. That's when I ran."

Lena's stomach twisted. She imagined Brant under the constant influence of mind-altering drugs, undergoing session after session of therapy intended to erase his past life. She could only imagine the agony he must have felt when his memories returned, knowing that he would have

to repeat the process again until his mind was blank. The
incredible mental and emotional strength he must have to
be willing to walk into Pallagen labs again and again after
multiple Hazings … her fingers tightened around the railing,
until they ached almost as much as her heart.

Brant turned and faced Lena. "I don't remember much
about my time with Enforcement. Some faces, a few names.
Bits and pieces of a job here and there. Whatever makes me
resistant to the Hazings kept Enforcement from completely
wiping my memory, but no one can go through that process
multiple times without some consequences." Brant's mouth
twisted bitterly. "But I do remember how I got my limp."

Lena swallowed, mouth dry. "Yeah?"

"I was in some kind of wreck. I remember the transport
ship, a little. I remember it was on fire, and I couldn't
breathe. My leg was stuck, but someone came back for me."
He shrugged. "I don't remember who dragged me out."

"I'm sorry." She hadn't given any thought to what
Enforcement friends Brant might have lost in his Hazing.
Stories he would never be able to tell about his adventures
serving Enforcement.

"Whoever it was, they're probably still alive, if they
were well enough to get me out. I feel like I owe them some
kind of debt, whether or not I remember them." He turned
around to look at the city. "I can't do much to repay that
debt, but what I can do is help the kids Pallagen has taken."

"They're hardly children. And if they're anything like
Dani, they probably aren't helpless."

Brant ignored her. "That's not the only live-testing lab

Pallagen has, is it?"

Lena didn't answer. She didn't need to.

"We go after them, Lena. We have to."

Lena pinched the bridge of her nose with her fingers. A thousand thoughts ran through her mind. They would need safe houses and new identities for each victim. They'd need better transportation, better information. They'd need more than three people to stage a rescue of this magnitude. Lena closed her eyes. Releasing Pallagen's victims put more people than herself and her team at risk. Their chances of being caught would multiply with every victim they freed. The fallout if they were caught grew exponentially. If they shifted their focus like this, they could lose any advantage over Pallagen they'd gained so far.

But if she said no and turned her back on the people only she could help, how did that make her any different from Pallagen?

"If we do this," Lena said, "it changes everything. We're not going after Pallagen anymore. We don't get to be dramatic. We'll have to be faster and quieter."

Brant shifted, his face hopeful. "You were the one that wanted flair."

The door from the apartment slid open before Lena had a chance to answer, and Dani stepped out onto the balcony. She wasn't wearing her goggles at all, not around her neck or pushed up on her forehead. It was the first time Lena had seen the technopath without them. She looked vulnerable, somehow. But when Dani met her eyes, Lena understood. Dani cared too much about what Pallagen was doing to hide any longer.

"You didn't turn your comm off." Dani tapped her earpiece. "I'm with Brant. If we can help these people, we should."

Lena stepped closer to her, trying not to let her concern show on her face. "Can you handle that? We'd need you on the mission, not staying up on the roof."

Dani nodded. She looked more present than Lena had ever seen her, mind fully disengaged from the building AI and the CityGrid. "I can do it."

Lena nodded once. "If Dani can handle it, then I think the rest of us can." She looked over at Brant. "All right. You win. We hit the live labs."

Part Two

Chapter Eighteen

Liam was a collector of holodramas, and so, it proved, was Alex.

"I can't believe you have all nine episodes." Liam held the data chip reverently as if it were glass.

Alex laughed at the look of boyish excitement on his face. "Well, I don't have anywhere to go tonight. And I don't remember if I've ever seen it, so..." She spread her hands.

Liam's face lit up. "I have a bigger screen in my apartment. Are you feeling up to a walk down the hall?"

It was easier to think about leaving her apartment than it had been a few days ago, and in those few days, she'd become more comfortable around Liam. She wasn't sure why. Maybe it was the food he kept bringing over. Maybe it was because he treated her like a person rather than a patient.

Or maybe he just had a really nice face. Alex shrugged and smiled. "I guess it's your turn to host."

Liam bounced up off her couch. "Great! Hey, if you let me borrow the chip for a couple days, I'll throw in dinner, too."

Alex's stomach growled at the thought. "Sure, why not?"

Liam's apartment was identical to Alex's with its open living area and kitchen, floor-to-ceiling windows, and small back rooms. It was cozier, though, the colors all light browns and creams and rich blues. There were overstuffed pillows and a soft blanket thrown across the couch. Data chips and tablets lay strewn across the table, a jacket was draped over a chair, and a few stray pillows littered the floor. There was a pile of laundry in the doorway of one of the back rooms. It felt like a home that was lived in rather than a place to sleep.

Liam's home smelled as delicious as the food he'd cooked for Alex. She took a moment to breathe deeply the aroma of pungent, earthy spices—curry, Liam had called it.

"Water?" Liam called from the kitchen. "Coffee?"

Coffee sounded good, and Tabba had never let her have it at Sixth City Rehab. "Coffee, please."

"Sugar?" Liam pulled two mugs out of a cupboard and watched Alex, waiting for an answer.

She hesitated.

Liam frowned. "Is something wrong?"

Alex sighed. If this friendship was going to get anywhere, she was going to have to open up about her past. "You know how I said I lost some time?"

Liam turned his water to hot and filled the mugs. "Yeah?"

"I lost more than time. I lost..." Alex gestured to herself, and swallowed. "I lost *me*."

"Ah." Liam nodded and opened a jar of instant coffee. The rich, nutty aroma filled the apartment, overpowering the lingering scents of curry. Alex took a deep breath and waited, but Liam only poured a couple of spoonfuls of coffee into each mug and stirred.

"So, that doesn't bother you?"

Liam shrugged and took a sip out of his mug. "Should it?"

Alex opened her mouth to speak, then closed it. Up until now, her memory loss had loomed large in her life. It affected everything—how she thought, how she acted, how Tabba and Claire treated her, how she made breakfast in the morning.

But maybe it didn't have to be that way.

"Huh," she said aloud. Liam looked at her quizzically, and she shook her head. "No. It shouldn't bother you. And sugar in the coffee, please."

Liam grinned, stirred sugar into her mug, and handed over her coffee. He tried not to laugh when she took a large gulp and choked. The coffee was hot and far too sweet in her mouth, and she spluttered, trying not to spew liquid all over him.

"No sugar?"

Alex handed the mug back, one hand on her chest. Revelator, that had hurt. She shook her head and grimaced. "No sugar, please."

Liam made her a fresh mug of black coffee, and Alex settled on the couch with all the pillows. Liam loaded the data chip onto his screen.

"Do you sleep out here?" Alex tried to arrange the pillows so she wasn't sinking into them. No luck. She quit fidgeting and settled in.

"Nah. I have a friend that stays over sometimes." Liam flopped onto the pillows next to Alex. "He's such a slob." He looked dolefully at the living area.

Alex laughed. "This can't all be your friend's clutter."

"No." Liam threw an arm across the back of the couch behind Alex, his fingers brushing her shoulder. She didn't move away, and his hand settled more firmly on her shoulder. "But he's not here to point that out, is he?"

Liam's hand felt warm and heavy on her shoulder, a grounding feeling, not uncomfortable or claustrophobic. Alex wrapped her hands around the coffee mug and stole a glance at Liam. He was focused on the screen across the room, his eyes wide and his leg bouncing a bit as he waited for the holodrama to load. She wondered if it was normal to feel this comfortable and safe around someone so quickly, wondered if it had anything to do with the dearth of people in her life right now.

She relaxed into the pillows, leaning just a bit closer to Liam, and decided she didn't care.

The coffee was perfection. Alex spent the first half of the holodrama episode with her eyes closed, breathing in the scent and taking tiny sips. Then the caffeine hit her system, and she was forced to remain awake until after Luna Two had risen, watching the most horrible holodrama she had ever seen in her life.

"I can't believe I own this," she said when the last episode ended.

"I can't either!" Liam looked vaguely spaced out, still staring at the empty screen. "It's the first holodrama made after we declared independence from Old Earth."

Alex shook her head. "That explains it. It was *terrible*."

Liam turned toward her, mouth open in surprise. He

sighed. "Unbelievable. You have absolutely no taste in holodramas."

Alex arched an eyebrow and scrambled to her feet, scattering pillows as she stood. "It was badly acted, the sets were poorly constructed, and I'm not even sure there was a plot."

"It's a classic, Alex. You have to make allowances."

Alex rolled her eyes and gestured toward the door. "Fine. You make all the allowances you want. I am headed to bed."

Liam pushed himself off the couch and held out a hand for Alex's long-empty mug. "Thanks for letting me borrow the chip."

"Keep it. *Please*," Alex insisted, holding up a hand. "Really. I do not want it back."

Liam smiled. "I forgot about dinner. Maybe tomorrow?" He looked out the window at Luna Two, and grimaced. "I mean, tonight?"

"Sure." Alex let Liam walk her to the door. "Thank you. For the coffee and..." She didn't finish, unsure how to tell Liam what spending a normal evening with someone meant to her. What it had done to center her. How she felt more at home now in her own skin. For the first time since she'd woke up, she felt connected to the world outside Sixth City Rehab.

Liam shrugged, and his smile softened. From the empathetic look in his eyes, Alex had a feeling she didn't have to explain. "I get it, Alex. You're welcome any time."

She carried the words with her the few steps to her apartment door. She wondered if Liam knew what *welcome any time* meant to someone with no home and no idea how to make a new one.

Finally rid of the caffeine in her system, she drifted off to sleep with a warm feeling in her chest instead of aching loneliness.

Alex suspected Claire was far too busy to spend her time helping one patient baby-step her way into a new life, but she dropped by every few days and called on the days she didn't see Alex.

"Liam seems nice," she observed, making a note in her book. Since she began visiting Alex in her home, she'd dropped her painfully professional facade. Now she was curled up on one end of Alex's couch, shoes kicked off and her light hair loose instead of pulled back into a bun. Her jacket lay draped over the back of the couch, revealing her slim, tanned shoulders. She glanced disapprovingly at the coffee mug cupped in Alex's hands. "I wouldn't overdo it on that, though. You still need plenty of sleep."

Alex shrugged and took another sip. "I feel fine."

She did, too. After that first sleepless night, her body had seemed to adjust and metabolize the caffeine quickly. "I must've drunk pots of it—before."

Claire's mouth tightened a little. "Well, don't tell Tabba. Or if you do, tell her I warned you. How are you sleeping, by the way?"

Alex shifted in her seat. "Well enough." It was almost true. She gave Claire her most open-eyed and innocent face.

Claire didn't seem impressed. "I thought we were over this, Alex. You know you can trust me. Why not tell me what's going on so I can help you?"

"I know you want to help," Alex admitted. That wasn't enough, though. Alex wasn't sure *why* she wanted to help. Until she figured out why Claire was sticking around, even after she'd left the Rehab Center, she wasn't ready to trust her with the nightmares.

Claire tapped her pen against the notebook. "All right then. What do you feel comfortable sharing?"

Alex's mind raced, her need for answers warring with her caution. She had to give Claire something, or the psychiatrist would never leave. "I haven't left the apartment building yet."

There. That was safe enough. And it was something she needed help with. She couldn't bounce between her apartment and Liam's forever.

"Are you frightened of leaving?"

"No, not exactly. It's just...comfortable here."

Claire nodded. "It's easy to do only what you are comfortable with when the rest of your world has fallen apart. But you'll have to confront the outside world sometime."

Alex silently disagreed, remembering her panic attack in the dining room of Sixth City Rehab.

Claire leaned forward. "You're ready for more, Alex. More than you think you are, I believe. It seems you've made a friend in Liam. Why not take him with you for a walk?"

That didn't sound terrible. Alex tipped her head in concession. "Maybe I will."

Claire closed her book. "Make plans. The weather will be cooler soon, so take advantage of the sunshine while you can." She stood up and grabbed her jacket, then paused. "Oh.

I forgot." Slipping a hand into a jacket pocket, she pulled out a data stick and held it out to Alex.

What is it?" Alex asked hesitantly as Claire started pulling her shoes back on.

Claire stood a few inches taller in her platform heels, and Alex stood up so she didn't have to crane her neck.

"Exordia is offering you a job."

"What kind of job?" She held the data stick carefully as if it might bite her.

Claire laughed. "Nothing dangerous. They want information from you—they'll send you case files and you can cross-reference them with your old files or anything you remember, and maybe help them with some of their current work. You have a unique perspective. Enforcement hopes you'll be able to make connections no one else can."

Alex turned the stick over in her fingers. "I can do that from here?"

Claire nodded. "You'd never have to leave the apartment. Although I strongly suggest you do so," she added. She pulled on her jacket and untucked the hair caught between her coat and dress. "What do you think?"

Alex was silent. While she liked the idea of being fed more information and having access to files that could help her remember her past, something about the idea didn't sit well with her.

It was Enforcement, Alex realized with a start. It was the thought of working with Enforcement that unnerved her. It made her uneasy in a way she couldn't explain, just like the white walls of Sixth City Rehab.

She'd been staring at the data stick for too long. She started when Claire put a hand on her arm.

"Are you all right?" Claire asked softly.

Alex stepped back, pulling her arm away from Claire. "I'm fine." She tossed the data stick in the air and caught it. "What do you think I should do?"

"That's not my decision to make."

"No, but I want to know your opinion."

"Well." Claire crossed her arms and frowned. "Speaking as your psychiatrist, it would be good for you to have something to occupy your time, something to think about other than what happened to you."

Claire stopped talking. Alex waited a few seconds, then tipped her head. "And as my friend?"

Claire stepped closer, her brow furrowed. "You're right to be hesitant. This information mining doesn't seem dangerous, but anything Enforcement is involved in is rarely what it seems." Claire's voice was low and more serious than it had ever been. "Whatever you decide, be careful, Alex."

Claire patted her on the arm and left.

Alex walked over to her kitchen, snagging her empty coffee mug on the way. She filled it with cold water and drank it slowly, still turning the data stick over in the fingers of her other hand.

Enforcement Lieutenant Alex Kleric had been a risk-taker. She'd worked underground with some of Exordia's worst gangs and had come out on top. She would have been smart, fast, and dangerous. But what was she now? Afraid to leave her apartment, incapable of cooking herself a meal that didn't come out of a freezer, unwilling to open up to a friend.

Alex finished the water and closed her hand around the data stick. When she put it like that, she didn't have much choice, did she?

She grabbed her tablet and loaded the data stick. She might not remember who Lieutenant Alex Kleric had been, but it couldn't hurt to pretend for a while.

Chapter Nineteen

There were moments when Lena wondered what her
old Pallagen colleagues must think of her. Did they hold her
in contempt, or were some of them secretly awed by her
audacity? Did she have underground support within the
ranks of Pallagen scientists? Did Pallagen's leaders see her as
a threat, or were they simply biding their time, waiting for
the right opportunity to crush her?

Whatever they thought, Lena was certain they didn't imagine
her plotting their demise hunched over a table with uneven legs
that was covered in dirty dishes and sandwich remains.

"Pallagen's main laboratory." Lena poked the large tablet
in the middle of the table and pulled up an image of the
facility. A sprawling, squat building, surrounded by fences,
armed security, and carefully-manicured grounds. "It's mostly
a front, somewhere to bring officials for inspections or to
demonstrate their research to prospective buyers. A few
of the more valuable experiments are housed there once
they're past the initial testing phase." She swiped the image
left and brought up the list of labs and their locations. "They

have almost a hundred smaller labs scattered across the city in abandoned houses or buildings."

"Like the ones we've been hitting." Brant was sprawled back in his chair, arms crossed.

Lena gave him a pointed look, but he only raised an eyebrow and refused to straighten up. She shook her head. "These temporary labs are the first places victims are taken. According to what Dani's found, they're conducting research on everything from drug compatibility to aptitude testing. Every abducted subject travels through one of these facilities before making it to the main laboratory."

Brant leaned forward. "We know all of this already, Lena."

"Of course you do. I'm just making sure we're all on the same page." Lena crossed her arms. She met Brant's gaze for a moment, then looked to Dani—who was working with her goggles off. She'd been doing that more often lately. "Look, I told you before: this isn't simply breaking and entering anymore."

"I wouldn't exactly call what we were doing before safe."

"No, but the stakes are higher now. It's not just us on the line." She waited, letting it sink in for a moment. For once, neither Brant nor Dani had anything to say. "If we get caught, they're going to want to know what we did with everyone we've rescued. We're not only putting ourselves at risk, but every single person we've helped."

Brant shifted in his seat. "It's still the right thing to do."

"No one's arguing that." After seeing the condition of Arya and the others in the lab, she knew they couldn't have made any other choice. "But that doesn't make it any less dangerous. And I'm not convinced it is the best way to fight Pallagen."

"I don't know about that." Dani picked up the tablet and pulled up the locations they'd determined were likely to be live testing labs. "These labs and their human contents are Pallagen's lifeblood. There is no way Enforcement knows everything they're doing. They need a place to get through the...the mess..." She paused and swallowed. "They need somewhere to test a product before they sell it to Enforcement."

Brant's eyes gleamed with anticipation. "So, which little lab do we hit first?"

Dani rolled her eyes. "Can we please not call them little labs?"

Brant drummed his fingers against the table. "*Micro* labs?"

"Revelator, no."

Lena rapped her knuckles against the tabletop to regain the attention of her bickering teammates. "Here's what we do: we start by letting people know we can help them. We keep an eye on missing person reports and try to catch the people that slip through the cracks." She gave a sidelong glance at Dani, hoping the technopath caught the weight of the unspoken apology. "If we know when people have disappeared, maybe we can stop some of Pallagen's testing before it advances too far."

Dani scrunched her nose. "How do we know if people have legitimate cases, or if it's a trap?"

Lena shrugged. "We'll make a judgment call. Correlate it with any other data we have on Pallagen."

"Hold on. You didn't want to rescue these people in the first place, and now you're going to take a stranger's word that they need help?" Brant asked, folding his arms and raising his eyebrows.

"I trust my instinct." Lena held Brant's gaze until he looked away. "But right now, our biggest problem is what to do with those we rescue."

The seconds ticked by silently.

"Safe houses?" Dani ventured.

Brant shook his head. "For a couple of weeks, maybe, but they'll need new identities, new homes, new jobs..."

Lena shoved her hands in her pockets. "Okay. That's a place to start. Dani, you're in charge of forging new identities. Start with Arya and the others we found the other day. Brant, see if you can find us some empty buildings to use as safe houses."

Her team nodded and rose from the table. Brant grabbed his jacket from the back of the couch and left the apartment, while Dani took a tablet from the kitchen counter and furiously began tapping the screen as she walked to the bedroom. Lena rested her elbows on the table and buried her face in her hands, letting the doubt she hid from Dani and Brant rise to the surface. Her gut may be telling her this was the right decision, but her brain disagreed. Would they be able to handle the pressure of seeing Pallagen's victims, day after day? Would they be able to walk away when they needed to? Was changing their strategy going to make any difference?

This was too big for her.

She had meant to expose Pallagen, or at the very least, embarrass them. Wipe some files. Let them know that they couldn't use people without their consent, couldn't get away with using research like hers to hurt innocent civilians. Now it was turning into a struggle that stretched across the Cities. It was something they couldn't handle alone. She was beginning to think that Brant was right. Maybe it was time to ask for help.

Lena closed her eyes. No. No one but herself, Brant, and Dani. They had enough to lose. It was better not to drag anyone else down with them.

If she kept telling herself that, she'd convince herself her reluctance to bring anyone else on the team had nothing to do with the vague fear she felt when Brant and Dani were out of her sight.

Chapter Twenty

"I have money, right?" Alex asked Claire when she walked into the apartment.

Claire's eyes widened. "What, ready for a shopping spree already?" she asked, amused.

Alex shook her head. "I'm still not sure I'm ready to leave my apartment yet," she said, motioning out the window. "But I'm going to need food and transportation at some point. Is Exordia paying me for information mining, or do they expect me to get a second job?"

Claire smiled. "So you took the job. That's a good sign."

She sat down on the couch and patted the cushion next to her, pulling out her ever-present notebook. Alex sighed. Apparently they were going to be finishing their consultation before addressing any of her personal concerns.

"Have you met any more of your neighbors?"

"The lady next door is pretty snippy." Alex shuddered. "And her cat sits in the hall and stares at me every time I walk by."

Claire laughed. She looked appraisingly around the apartment. It was still sparse, but it no longer looked as if someone had just moved in. "I'm sure Tabba would approve of your organization, but not your lack of housekeeping skills." She eyed the stack of dirty dishes next to the sanitizer.

"I don't think I was very good at housework." Alex frowned. "It doesn't feel natural to me."

"Are there other things you've discovered that do feel natural?"

Alex wanted to kick herself. She'd been trying to get Claire's mind off track, but as usual, she'd laid a verbal trap for herself.

"Talking to people," she said. *Lying* to people, actually. And being able to tell when someone was lying to her. She'd like to see Claire puzzle that one out. "It was easy to talk to Liam. And I don't like spending evenings alone. I think I was a people person."

Nodding, Claire wrote something down. "That makes sense. The file the city has on you isn't extensive regarding your personal life, but I know you were well-liked."

Alex looked past Claire to the window behind her and kept her voice casual. "By all my friends at Enforcement?"

Claire looked up, eyebrow raised. *Whoops.* Not casual enough, then.

Claire slowly tucked her pen into the notebook and tossed it onto the couch next to her. "Is this about the job?" She spoke cautiously—nothing like her usual confident tone. "If you're uncomfortable with it, no one is going to force you to keep it."

Alex swallowed. There was no turning back now. "I looked at the case files on the chip you gave me. The CityGrid says they're all closed, or cold cases, and they're all public records. Whatever you gave me, you didn't get it from Enforcement."

Claire didn't say anything. The silence unnerved Alex, and she twisted her fingers together to keep them from shaking. She hesitated, unsure of how to question Claire, then plunged ahead. "You weren't telling me the truth at the rehab center, either."

"What makes you think I was lying?" Claire said, her voice frosty. "I only told you what was on the data chip I gave you."

Alex shook her head. "I don't know about the data chip. I don't know how to tell if it's been tampered with. But I can tell that you're lying to me."

"How?"

"I just know." She tossed her hands up in the air. "I can tell. I can always tell."

Claire was silent for a long time. Alex knew she'd made the psychologist angry, but she didn't care. Not much, anyway. Claire wasn't her only link to the outside world anymore. Alex was making her own life now, or trying to. She had the right to know. It was her memory, and she needed to know if someone was tampering with it.

Finally, Claire sighed. "I'm not lying to you, Alex. Someone else is." She stood and stared down at Alex, her expression a mix of worry and resignation. "I arranged your early discharge from Sixth City Rehab because Pallagen wanted to keep you there. I don't know why, but I can't imagine their reasons were good. I gave you your official personnel file so you'd keep a low profile, not because I believed anything in it."

"You got me out," Alex said. She felt numb. "Why?"

"I told you: Pallagen wanted you. That was reason enough." Claire straightened her skirt. "I needed to find out why Pallagen was interested in you."

Alex's heart pounded, and she had to concentrate to keep her breathing steady. "Is any of this real?" she asked, waving her hand around the room. "The boxes of my stuff, what you've told me about myself...is any of it actually *me*?"

Claire didn't answer.

Alex closed her eyes and turned away. Her mind was a swirling maelstrom of confusion and fear. Her head throbbed, and she rubbed her forehead, trying to ease the headache. "I'm living the life they created for me, right?"

Claire nodded.

Alex dropped her hand and lifted her chin. "Then I don't want to know why. As long as I stay here and act the way they expect me to, they'll leave me alone, right?"

"Alex..."

"No." Alex stood. "I don't know what happened to me. I don't know why Pallagen wanted to watch me. But if I try to find out, they'll come for me, and I..." Alex squeezed her eyes shut. She breathed deeply, remembering the scent of chemicals and blood. "I can't do that again."

"Again?" Claire stepped forward and gently touched her arm. "Alex, did you remember something?"

Alex pushed Claire's hand away. "Yes. No. I don't know, and I don't care."

Their eyes stayed locked for several moments. Finally, Claire nodded and backed away. "We should talk about this another day."

Alex's hands clenched at her sides. "Fine."

Claire picked up her notebook and walked to the door. She stopped, hand on the frame. Her mouth opened, but she didn't say anything. After a moment, she shook her head and left.

Alex dropped back onto the couch and covered her face with her hands. *I was lying too,* she wanted to say. *I do care. I do want to know.* She couldn't ask Claire, though. Claire worked for Exordia, and the only thing Alex had left was her distrust of the colony.

Her door chimed. She tapped her mobile and keyed open the door without getting up, and Liam walked into the living area. She pulled her hand away from her face, trying to hide her distress behind a smile. Liam had accepted her for who she was. She didn't want to mess that up by falling apart in front of him.

"Ready to leave?" He stopped, hands in his jacket pockets, and frowned at Alex. "Are you all right? You look pale."

Alex took a deep breath and shook her head. "I'm fine." She stood up, ignoring Liam's raised eyebrows. She could tell he didn't believe her, but she didn't want to explain that nothing in her life, past or present, was what it seemed. As she locked the door behind her, a thought struck her. "Hey… you work in filing, right?"

"Yeah." He shrugged. "I send documents to everyone in Sixth City. I see every bit of news, both official and off-the-record, that passes through the city." His shoulders squared and he lifted his chin, pride in his voice. "It's not an easy job."

"I'm sure." Alex grinned. What harm could it be to ask? "You want to look up a name for me?"

Chapter Twenty-One

Brant plopped a tablet on the table in front of Lena as soon as she sat down to eat breakfast-for-dinner. "We need a gravcar."

Lena closed her eyes. She'd just woken up, and her body hadn't adjusted to sleeping during the day and waking up at night. Revelator, she hadn't even finished her coffee yet. "It's too early for grand larceny."

"The moons aren't even up yet!"

"I don't care. We're not stealing a gravcar." She gestured around the apartment. "Where would we put it?"

Brant rolled his eyes. "Well, not in here, obviously."

"We need a way to transport people," Dani said. She slathered some green jelly Lena didn't recognize over her slice of toast. "We can't take the gravtrain again. It was bad enough last time—we've never been that close to getting caught."

"We're still not stealing one."

"Who said anything about stealing?" Brant asked, affronted. "I know a couple of guys that could get us a cheap one."

Lena tapped her foot against the plastic flooring,

considering the idea. Dani had a point. Moving people to a safe house would be much less dangerous if they had private transportation.

"If we get one, it needs to be functional and inconspicuous, not some flashy statement vehicle," she warned.

Brant grinned. "Of course."

"But also zippy," Dani put in, her eyes sparkling with enthusiasm. She was far too eager about the prospect of a vehicle. Lena made a mental note to check Dani's file for any driving experience. "We need something with speed so we can get away from Enforcement if they spot us."

"I thought the reason for getting a gravcar was so they *wouldn't* spot us," Lena pointed out dryly.

Brant and Dani glanced sideways at each other and shrugged. "We should prepare for every possibility," Brant said solemnly.

Lena caught the glint in his eye and looked from one teammate to the other, exasperated. And cornered. She sighed. "How many seats, and how much coin?"

Brant activated the tablet, and the screen displayed the merits of a middle-grade private gravcar, the kind that could transport either people or goods. Lena nodded in approval. It was dark gray, good for traveling at night. It was boxier than some of the newer models, but older gravcars were harder to track. "Is it...*zippy*?"

Dani grinned. "If it's not, I can fix that."

Lena handed the tablet back to Brant. "Fine. Where will we keep it?"

Brant waved off the question. "Let me worry about that."

"Oh, I will." Lena crossed her arms. "You can also worry about the registration and insurance, since it needs to look official in case we're ever stopped."

The ex-soldier gave her a dirty look. Dani abandoned her toast and stood, winding her arms around one of Brant's and bouncing up and down on the tips of her toes.

Lena couldn't help but smile at the technopath's eagerness. "You know what? I think I'll come with you. This, I want to see for myself."

The gravcar looked as good in person as it did on the tablet. Lena shook her head as Dani ran her hands over the gray plating. The technopath crawled inside and started lifting the covers off the control panels, making crooning noises under her breath. Lena peeked inside the gravcar. There were four seats covered in dark nylon and plenty of cargo space in the back—no windows except the front windshield. *Good. Much easier to hide people that way.* Lena didn't waste a glance at the controls. Dani would let her know if there were any problems. She pulled her shoulders out of the hatch and came face-to-face with Brant and his contact.

"Revelator," Brant breathed, his eyes wide and fixed on Dani. "I've created a monster."

Lena jabbed him in the ribs with her elbow. "I told you this was a bad idea."

"It's an excellent idea!" Brant's contact boomed. He was taller than Brant and nearly as wide, and his jovial face was wrinkled with laugh lines. He was wearing plain black, an anomaly for anyone living in Second City, but he did have a swath of bright yellow material wrapped around his head. He spread his arms wide. "A finer gravcar you won't see inside Second City."

"What about outside of Second City?" Lena asked dryly.

"Ah, but no one outside of Second City will take your coin, will they?" The contact winked.

Brant pointed at the man. "Lena, this is Reigel. Reigel, my boss, Lena."

"A pleasure, I'm sure," Reigel said. He folded his hands behind his back and bowed at the waist like a Sixth City official. "Always happy to help out my old friend Brant!" He clapped his "old friend" on the shoulder hard enough to send him stumbling. Lena grabbed his elbow to steady him.

"Yeah, your 'old friend' and his money." Brant smirked. He nodded toward the gravcar. "Is she clean?"

"As clean as a whistle."

Lena frowned. "Clean as a what?"

"Old Earth thing," Reigel and Brant chorused.

Lena sighed. "Should've known. How come everyone but me understands these references?" She glanced back at the gravcar and cringed. Dani had the control panel wiring pulled out and was examining each wire carefully. "We should probably settle the deal before Dani marries it."

Brant laughed. "You still offering the same terms?"

Reigel nodded. "Anything for you." He tipped his head toward Lena, his face more serious than before. "And anything for you especially, lass."

Lena stared. Was he hitting on her? No, he looked

grateful, not enamored. Lena shifted uncomfortably. "We appreciate your help."

"We appreciate yours," Reigel said quietly. He leaned closer. "Second City may have a funny way of showing it, but you'll always be safe here."

Lena swallowed. "Look, I'm not sure what you've heard, but—"

Reigel shook his head and took a step back, waving his hands emphatically. "Not a thing, lass, not a thing." He winked again. "Just thought you should know." He turned and walked back to the gravcar. "You! Dani! She's not yours yet, so get your mitts off of that panel."

Lena stepped closer to Brant. "Word travels fast," she muttered. "I know I said to spread the word about us, but did you have to tell everyone in Second City?"

Brant laughed. "Lena, nearly everyone in Second City already knew what we were doing." He turned to look her in the eyes. "I know you think we're alone in this, but we're not as isolated as you think we are."

He limped over to the gravcar where Dani and Reigel were heatedly arguing over something—lights, it sounded like. Lena stayed back, shoving her hands in her pockets and mulling over Brant's words.

She still didn't trust Second City, but it felt good to know that she wasn't the only one looking out for her team—even if the other person was a Second City gravcar salesman.

She smiled. *Maybe we do have a chance after all.*

Chapter Twenty-Two

Seventh City was primarily residential, its streets well-kept and clean. Alex tried not to stare at the buildings towering above her. They shone dull white against the deep blue sky. The glass of hundreds of floor-to-ceiling windows, like those in her own apartment, reflected light that nearly blinded her. Here and there, a balcony sported a splash of color, where some enterprising tenant was attempting to grow flowers or herbs. The street she and Liam walked down was pedestrian, with only a single gravtrain track running through the middle. Far above them, gravcars sped past on invisible paths, following CityGrid traffic lanes.

Eyes wide on the sky above her, she tripped over Liam's heels. He reached out and caught her arm, steadying her.

"You all right?"

"Fine." Alex tried not to snap at Liam. She wanted to pull her arm out of his grip and run back to the safety of her apartment, but she met his eyes and saw only amused concern, none of the careful pity Tabba always showed her. She smiled. "I'm fine. I just haven't had much of a chance to look around yet."

It was true. Tabba had hustled her inside the building when they first arrived because Alex had been hyperventilating at the sheer press of people and space.

Now, Liam was a solid presence at her side. He let go of her arm but stayed close, his elbows brushing her upper arms as they strolled. It gave Alex a warm feeling in the pit of her stomach. She didn't feel like holding hands, but she felt safe with Liam, even on the crowded street. Alex flinched closer to him as a gravtrain passed, momentarily silencing the crowd as they waited for the rush of wind to stop.

"Hungry for anything in particular?" Liam asked. He pointed toward a café sign. "I'm guessing coffee is a must."

Alex smiled. "Please."

Liam laid a hand on her elbow and guided her into one of the shops that inhabited the lower lobby of every apartment building in the city. Alex glanced around curiously. There were tables and chairs scattered across the open space, and the low hum of conversation filled the room. There were several people in there, some talking with friends and others studying tablets. She followed Liam to the low counter where he ordered coffee for both of them.

"Is there anything beneath our building?" she asked. They'd taken a back elevator out of their apartment complex, one that led directly into the street.

"Vegetables, mostly. The colony can't expand into the desert, so most of the buildings in Seventh City house something useful." Liam held out his hand and let the attendant scan his chip. A moment later, two steaming coffees were placed on the counter. He scooped them up and held one out to Alex. "On me."

Alex smiled and accepted the cup. The coffee was hot, black, and smooth. Alex couldn't remember anything tasting quite as good. She closed her eyes and swished the coffee around in her mouth for a few seconds before swallowing.

Liam laughed. "Come on. Let's go find real food that will put meat back on your skinny bones."

Liam led Alex through the groceries, bakeries, and delis until their arms were full of fresh bread, bundled vegetables, and a basket full of strawberries and peaches.

"Well, you'll be healthy, if nothing else." Liam eyed the fresh food with a little despair. "You're still missing so much. We need to find spices, and there's a place nearby that makes noodles. You need some canned foods too..."

Alex laughed. "Let's start with this." She patted the wrapped loaf of bread. "Honestly, I don't remember a thing about cooking. It's probably not a good idea to throw me into the deep end." Besides, her knee was aching, but she'd been trying to hide that.

Liam tilted his head in defeat. "True." He took one of the bundles from Alex. "One more stop, then we can get you back and off your feet. You keep limping."

Alex flushed. *Not hiding it very well, I guess. Or Liam's paying close attention.* Her face heated at the thought, and she looked down at the bags she was carrying to hide her embarrassment. "Fine. I'm hungry, anyway. What are we making with all this stuff?"

"Sandwiches," Liam said decisively.

Alex looked up. "Seriously? You're not concocting some Old Earth secret recipe?"

Liam shrugged and grinned. "I can't come up with amazing ideas *all* the time. Besides, what else are you supposed to make with fresh-baked bread?"

They slowly wound their way through the crowd of people wandering the streets of Seventh City. Alex sidestepped to avoid a woman with a toddler in one arm and a bag of groceries in the other. "It's a weekend, right? There are a lot of people out here."

"Mm-hm. Speaking of which, are you looking for a job? That apartment you're in isn't exactly cheap."

"No, I have a job. For the city." Alex frowned, a flash of memory tugging at the back of her mind. "Doesn't everyone in Seventh City work for Exordia?"

Liam chuckled. "Just about. That, or the hydroponic gardens. Those are the two callings for anyone looking for a steady income."

That, or Pallagen. Alex gasped as white-hot pain flared in her head, just behind her eyes. She dropped the bread, but she didn't hear it hit the ground. Stumbling back, she opened her eyes. Her fingers tangled in her hair, trying to push back the pain. Liam was standing close with the bread on top of his other bundles.

"Are you all right?" he asked, his voice soft. His brow was furrowed, and his eyes held a mixed look of confusion and concern.

Alex forced a smile. "I'm fine." She shook her head. "It's just a headache. It happens every time I remember something."

Liam frowned. "Some headache." He handed over the bread. "Was it something I said?"

Their fingers brushed as Alex took back the bread, and she had the wild urge to grab his hand and hold tightly until the pain of memory faded. Instead, she stepped away. "No, no." Alex resumed walking, and Liam followed. "Claire—Dr. Tverdik—said it's probably a side effect of my head injury."

"Hmm." Liam didn't look convinced, but he dropped the subject. Alex sighed and felt relieved. The pain was fading, but, Revelator...She rubbed her forehead again. It hurt so much she never wanted to remember anything ever again.

Maybe that's why it hurts, her mind whispered, in a voice that sounded suspiciously like Claire. *If Pallagen doesn't want you to remember anything, maybe this is their way of making sure you don't.*

Alex clenched her jaw and firmly pushed the thought from her mind.

"Here," Liam murmured, stopping suddenly and pushing her through a small doorway overgrown with vines into a tiny shop overflowing with green. The store was made of glass windows and filled with shelf after shelf of plants and pots. Gardening tools were scattered haphazardly across the bare sandy ground. There were larger plants dispersed around the room with narrow paths between them. Exordia was on a dry, desert planet, but in this little greenhouse, the air was damp and humid, weighing heavily in Alex's lungs.

She took a deep breath. The shop smelled of damp soil and flowers and clean air. She turned to Liam, eyes wide and headache forgotten.

Liam shifted from one foot to the other. "In some parts of Old Earth, it was tradition to bring a gift to someone who'd just moved into a new home. I wanted to get you something, but I wasn't sure what you would like ..." He trailed off and began to examine a small pink flower in a tiny pot, avoiding Alex's curious gaze.

Alex grinned at his embarrassment. She had no idea if she'd liked plants before, but here, in this tiny corner of Seventh City, surrounded by a profusion of living green, she felt more at peace than she had since she woke up. She stepped closer to Liam and wrapped her fingers around his arm. "This is perfect."

Liam smiled, and suddenly the shop seemed even warmer. His hands were full, so he tipped his head in the direction of a little spiked plant. Alex reached out and gingerly lifted it from the crowded shelf.

"Aloe vera," Liam said. "It can cure everything from sunburn to heartburn. It's the perfect plant for a place like Exordia."

Alex carefully poked at the spikes.

"Also, it's very hard to kill. Like someone I know."

Alex looked up sharply, but Liam's eyes were bright with amusement. She shook her head. "That's classified information," she said. It sounded like a lame excuse.

Liam's eyebrows rose. "Well, I could've suggested you choose a forget-me-not."

Alex snorted, surprised by his joke, and started laughing. The effort made her chest ache, but she couldn't stop. She didn't want to stop. It felt good to joke with someone about her condition, to be lighthearted about something that weighed on her day and night. To be reminded that she was more than just a shadow of an unremembered past. She leaned her forehead against Liam's arm, gasping for air as her laughter subsided.

Liam rubbed his arm against her forehead and she looked up, blinking back tears. He grinned down at her, and nodded his head toward the back of the shop. The attendant had appeared, alerted to their presence by her resounding laughter. He was as tiny as his shop and as round as the loaf of bread Alex was starting to crave. There was dirt under his fingernails and a smudge of mud across his cheek, and he did nothing but smile broadly as he scanned Liam's chip and carefully checked the aloe plant for any imperfection.

They trudged back to Alex's apartment and dumped the food on the table. Liam sliced bread and Alex chopped vegetables, and before long they were eating the best sandwiches Alex could remember. The *only* sandwiches she could remember.

"I'll leave you to organize your stuff," Liam told her when they'd finished, stacking his dishes next to the sanitizer. "I've meddled in your kitchen enough."

Alex chuckled. "I needed someone to meddle." But she was worn out by their shopping trip—something she wouldn't admit to Liam, though she suspected he knew. She'd seen more people today than ever before, and she needed some time to herself.

After Liam left, she picked up the aloe plant. "You're all right," she said thoughtfully. "You don't look like you'd be too helpful, but I suppose looks can be deceiving."

Alex put it on the ledge between the kitchen and living room where it would get the most sunlight. She pulled out her tablet and looked up how to care for her new plant. She chuckled as she read.

"Thrives in unstable environments." She patted the spines on the aloe plant gingerly. "You and me both, buddy. You and me both."

Chapter Twenty-Three

Relax, Lena. It'll be fine, Lena. What could go wrong, Lena?
Lena sighed and pushed back from the table. She limped across the room to the kitchen, her worried thoughts racing. She needed more coffee.

The team had to move faster now. Pallagen changed the location of its live testing labs every few days, trying to stay ahead of Lena. It wasn't quite working. Dani's ability to interface with the CityGrid kept them informed of the location changes, but if they didn't hit a lab as soon as they found it, they lost the lead. They didn't have time for delays, and they certainly didn't have time for Lena to clumsily scale a fence and wrench her ankle when she landed. Their next mission had already been planned. Lena knew that Brant and Dani were capable of handling the rescue on their own, so Lena let them go and waited to indulge her frustration until they had left the apartment.

She had always been a stress-cleaner, but there was only so much she could do in the tiny apartment. She rearranged her clothes in the bedroom and straightened the blankets on the bed. She wiped down the kitchen and table, ran the dirty dishes through the sanitizer, and took inventory of their food. They needed to stock up. The fridge held some sandwich ingredients and a few frozen meals, but Lena wasn't going anywhere for a while. Her ankle was already achy and swollen from the few fretful steps she'd taken around the apartment.

Sighing, Lena stretched out on the couch and propped up her ankle. She turned on a tablet and pulled up the news stories Brant had flagged as pertinent to them. The first was a vid clip that started in the middle of a special press release.

"...and although the number of missing persons has not increased drastically, the Enforcement officers investigating the disappearances say they're keeping a close watch on any reports in case there are any connections. Anonymous sources have stated that they believe the research corporation Pallagen to be responsible for some of these abductions."

Lena bit her lip. They'd told the people they rescued to keep a low profile. She hoped they weren't drawing Pallagen's attention by spreading stories. Restless, she stood again, realizing she'd never made coffee. Dropping the still-playing tablet onto the counter, she pulled a mug and the jar of instant coffee out of a cupboard.

"Pallagen declined to comment on the recent accusations that they are conducting non-consensual drug testing. They claim full cooperation with Enforcement in finding the source of these recent rumors as well as in any investigation the colony of Exordia wishes to make."

The newscaster paused in his report as a video of Pallagen's public relations manager began to play. Lena knew the man personally, having spoken to him when Pallagen first hired her. More importantly, he knew who she was, and he knew what she was doing. Lena wondered if he knew she'd be watching, wondered how many of his words would be aimed specifically at her.

Lena shook off the thought and dumped sweetener in her coffee. Normally she drank it black, but Brant and Dani were on a mission without her for the first time, so she deserved a little indulgence. She leaned her elbows against the counter, mug in her hands, and refocused on the tablet.

"There are always enemies of progress," Pallagen's public face said, his voice smooth and cultured. His dark hair was slicked back perfectly, and his face was calm. He didn't look at all disturbed by the accusations against Pallagen. He tugged at the hem of his over-starched gray tunic and smoothed the orange badge on his chest. *"Pallagen has led progress in Exordia since Old Earth first landed here. As we have done in the last two centuries, we will continue to forge ahead, in spite of all opposition."* He looked straight into the camera—straight at Lena, it felt like. She stiffened. *"Pallagen exists to serve Exordia. Any who argue otherwise may consider themselves enemies of the peace and stability we work to preserve."*

Lena thought about finding Arya, frightened and alone, left to die in an unforgiving cell. Dani, experimented on and turned into something inhuman. Brant, still running from nightmares of unsuccessful attempts at Hazing. She shut off the tablet viciously, hard enough to make the casing creak in protest. She'd accepted Pallagen's propaganda once. She'd thought she was doing the right thing. How could she have been so blind?

And how could she be sure she was doing the right thing now?

The door slid open behind her, but she didn't turn around. Dani had made sure it would open for no one but the three of them. She heard Brant's uneven gait and waited for him to lean up against the counter next to her.

"How are we any different?" Lena asked. She gestured toward the tablet. "Pallagen fights for peace and stability. So do we. What makes us any different?"

"We don't have people confined in underground laboratories against their will," Brant said, flat and hard.

Lena turned to face him. "We've killed people." Brant opened his mouth to protest, but Lena held up a hand to stop him. "And not just the guards who attacked us. No one responsible for the security of those labs escaped Pallagen's retaliation."

Brant sighed. "This is a war, Lena."

"It isn't even close to—"

"No, it is—whether you meant it to be one or not. People are going to get caught in the crossfire."

Lena raised an eyebrow. "You sound like Pallagen."

"Their motivation might be just as solid as ours. Bad guys never see themselves as the bad guys, Lena." Brant ran a hand through his hair. "Most people want the same things— to enjoy life, to protect the people they care about, to leave the world a little better than it was before. Some people go about it the wrong way."

"And that gives us the right to stop them? To tell them our way is better?"

"I don't know." Brant met her eyes. "But I know what they did to Dani, to Arya. And, regardless of any motivation, that needs to stop."

Lena swallowed. *How far am I willing to go to stop them?* "I don't want to become the same kind of person, Brant."

"Then don't."

Lena rolled her eyes. Typical Brant, brushing aside the nuances of a situation to cut through to the heart of it. "It's not that easy."

"Yeah, Lena, it is." Brant reached out and lightly touched her elbow. "Come on. You shouldn't be standing on that ankle."

Lena let Brant guide her back to the table and settle her into a chair. She frowned. "Where's Dani?"

Brant sighed. "About that."

Lena's eyes narrowed, and cold fear settled in her gut. "What happened?"

"Nothing. The mission went fine. But something's wrong with the family we found."

"They took an entire family?" Lena shook her head. "That's pretty bold."

Brant shrugged. "Dani's still with them. You need to come talk to them."

"Brant, why don't you just tell me what—"

"Please." There was an edge to Brant's voice. "Just come and talk to them, ok?"

Lena sighed. She recognized the look on Brant's face— the same resolve he'd showed when he insisted on rescuing Arya. She wouldn't be able to argue him out of this.

"All right," she said. "But the coffee's coming with me."
She had a feeling she was going to need it.

Chapter Twenty-Four

Alex cooked for Liam with equal parts eagerness and trepidation. She owed him at least a dozen meals at this point, so when he suggested dinner a few days after their walk, she insisted on preparing the meal herself. She found an Old Earth recipe on the CityGrid that looked like something Liam would eat and required ingredients she already had in her apartment. She followed each step meticulously and set her table according to the most formal standard she could follow with her basic utensils.

"Clean kitchen, check," she muttered. "Main course, check. Dessert, check." She glanced at the thriving aloe plant on the ledge in her kitchen. "What about appetizers? Should I have made an appetizer?" She groaned and buried her face in her hands. "Get a grip, Alex. Quit talking to plants." She hit the apartment intercom and invited Liam over before she completely lost her nerve.

Liam smiled at the sight of the set table, but he sat down without a word. His smile was strained and his shoulders were tight. Alex bit her lip as he picked up his fork and poked at the food, taking one bite and chewing it for a long moment.

Alex waited expectantly, sweaty palms clutching her fork tightly, watching his face. His forehead was wrinkled, and he stared at his plate. Nervousness curled in her gut. Tapping her foot against the ground, she waited for him to take another bite. Same slow chewing, same staring. *Revelator. That's enough of that.* She smacked her fork down onto the table, relishing Liam's guilty jolt at the sound.

"What? Are the beans too salty? Is the texture of the breading off? Did I violate some unspoken culinary rule?"

She'd meant it to be a joke to break the tension, but Liam didn't laugh. Instead, he sighed and put his fork down. "Your cooking is fine."

Alex raised her eyebrows. "Fine? That's it? I think I'm offended. Coming from you, I suppose 'fine' is a compliment—"

"Alex." He picked up his glass and took a big gulp of water. "Okay, look. Just...answer my questions, and let me talk this out, all right?"

Alex's stomach turned to ice, and her hands clenched in her lap, aching to hold something—anything—to release the turmoil she felt at Liam's words. She wasn't sure she wanted to hear whatever it was he had to say, but after all he had done for her, she knew she at least owed him her attention.

"Okay," she said, mouth dry.

"I know you said you were injured, that you lost time." Liam paused, and Alex nodded. "How much time did you lose?"

"Um." Alex blinked. This wasn't the direction she'd thought the conversation was going. She'd thought Liam was going to tell her he was moving out of the building, or that he regretted agreeing to help her, or...something. She didn't think he was going to ask about her past. She didn't have a good reason to lie to him, though. "A couple of orbits, actually."

Liam leaned back in his chair. "Wow. I guess that makes sense."

"Makes sense with what?" Alex demanded.

Liam took a deep breath and folded his hands on the table. "I looked up your name and file, like you asked." He shifted in his chair and wouldn't meet her eyes. "I don't know who you are, but I don't think you're Alex Kleric."

Alex blinked a few times, staring at Liam. After a moment, she gave a sharp, humorless laugh. "That's ridiculous. Who else would I be?"

Liam leaned over the table, rubbing his forehead. "There were only a couple of files attached to your name. And maybe I should have given them to you before I read them, I don't know, but I was curious. There was one public ID file with basic information—probably a cover document." Liam paused, waiting for her reaction.

Alex shrugged. "I knew about the cover-up. Claire told me it was to protect my undercover work for Enforcement."

"Right." Liam took another gulp of water and pushed his plate away. He pulled out his mobile and tapped the screen. "I found a press release about your death, an obituary in a news archive, and one Enforcement file with your service record, but that was it. Just one file on the CityGrid."

Alex's breath caught, and time slowed to a crawl. "What?"

"I stole the file." Liam swiped a file across the screen to Alex's mobile. "Everything I found is there."

Alex opened the file. She scanned the lines of the document, but she didn't need to read any of it. It was identical to the service record Claire had given her—she'd memorized every name, sifted through each piece of her history, trying to make connections.

"*Just* this file? Where did you find it?" Alex asked, fingers trembling as she scrolled through the file.

"I hacked Enforcement's personnel archive. It's missing pieces, though. Personnel files are attached to archives all across the CityGrid. Birth and death certificates, medical records, family records, residential or gravbike permits... yours has nothing."

"Revelator," Alex whispered. "This is it? This is all the CityGrid has on me?" Her voice pitched higher with each word, and she bit back frantic questions. "Maybe you missed something."

"Alex." Liam reached across the table, hand outstretched, but Alex pulled back. Liam's face tightened. "I hacked Enforcement, Alex. Do you know how hard that is?" He shook his head. "If there's any other information about you, it's not on the CityGrid."

Alex met Liam's eyes. "What does that mean?"

"It means according to the CityGrid, you don't exist." Liam watched her carefully. Was he worried about her, or trying to gauge her reaction? "It takes a lot of work to wipe someone from the system like this. If I were to guess..." Liam trailed off.

"Well?" Alex demanded.

Liam took a deep breath. "The files attached to Alex

Kleric are probably fake. It's easier to plant something like that than to erase someone completely. As for who you actually are..." Liam shrugged helplessly. "I have no idea. Your real identity isn't anywhere on the CityGrid."

Alex felt numb. She slumped in her chair, staring at the table full of nearly untouched food. *Erased. Just like my mind.*

Liam finally broke the silence. "You didn't know?"

Alex's chin came up, her face flushed with anger. Her fingers tightened around her mobile until her knuckles turned white. "You think I'd live a lie on purpose?"

Liam held out his hands in defense. "I don't know! I only met you a few days ago. For all I know, you got yourself erased from the system on purpose."

"Revelator, why would I do that?" Alex nearly shouted.

"Maybe to cover up something illegal you've done?"

"Something like swipe official files?" Alex shot back. She closed her eyes and took a deep breath, trying to calm down. Her heart pounded, and bands of panic wrapped around her chest. "Revelator," she said again, her voice finally under control. "I need to...I need to think about this." When Liam didn't answer, Alex looked up at him, eyes burning. "By myself."

Liam nodded and pushed back from the table, his mouth tight. He left without another word.

In hindsight, it was brave of Liam to leave the stolen file with her. She could have done anything: destroyed it, called her alleged bosses in Enforcement and told them someone was digging in their files, turned Liam over to Exordia's authorities for unlawful use of CityGrid access... Maybe he was stupid instead of brave. After several minutes of staring blindly out the rain-stained windows, Alex recognized the gesture for what it was.

Trust.

She sighed. She'd asked Liam for help, and he'd gone so far as to hack Enforcement files to do so. *He's looking out for me.* The thought thawed her icy anger.

She reopened the file and read the report, comparing it with what she'd been told. She could find no gaps. The only thing wrong was the file itself—or what was missing from it.

It would have been easy for someone to slip the file onto the CityGrid to correlate any low-access identity search she could conduct. Only Liam, from inside the filing offices of the Council itself, would have been able to discover that her life was a sham, created by someone for—what? Why had Pallagen gone to so much trouble to hide her identity from her?

Claire was right. I can't just ignore this. She shut down her mobile and stared out the window. *Whatever Pallagen wanted to keep from me, I need to know.*

She rested her forehead against the cool glass and closed her eyes. She traced every nightmare or flash of memory she'd had since she woke up, but nothing happened. There was no revelation of memory. No gateway of information. Just the emptiness at the back of her mind.

Alex wrapped her arms around herself. She sniffed and squeezed her eyes shut. She didn't know what to do or who to trust. She had no one to cry out to for help. Taking a deep breath, she looked at her pale reflection in the window.

"I'm sorry," she whispered to the likeness in the glass. "I'm sorry I don't know who you are, but I promise I'll do my best to find out."

She switched her mobile on and deleted the file.

She remembered what Claire had told her weeks ago at the rehab center. *You get to decide who you are now.* Was she someone who hid from her nightmares, afraid of what Pallagen could do to her? Or was she someone who faced them and demanded to be told the truth?

Whatever decision she made, she needed someone with her. She might not trust anyone but herself, but her instinct said Liam could be trusted—her *heart* said Liam could be trusted. For now, that had to be enough.

Alex looked at the half-eaten dinner and realized she'd sent Liam home hungry. She sighed, walked over to the control panel, and hit the intercom button to speak with him. She hoped he'd answer.

"Yeah?" His voice sounded cautious over the comm.

Alex let out the breath she didn't realize she had been holding. "Can you come back over?" she said. "Claire said something, and...if you're going to help me figure this out, you need to hear it."

Chapter Twenty-Five

Brant wove the gravcar in and out of traffic with reckless abandon.

"Your driving is absolutely atrocious," Lena said through clenched teeth.

"You have to let loose sometime," Brant said, directing a crazed grin at her.

"Track!" Lena screeched. "Watch the track!"

Brant jerked the gravcar back into their lane.

Lena closed her eyes and caught her breath. "You know, if we get stopped for reckless endangerment, we're going to get arrested, and I don't think I need to remind you why that would be a terrible idea."

Brant shrugged. "We're in Fifth City. No one gets stopped here."

"Still." Lena relaxed a little as Brant slowed the gravcar. "So, why are we visiting a safe house again? It's completely against procedure."

Brant gave her an odd look. "What 'procedure'? There are only three of us."

Lena sighed. For all his military training, Brant had a loose interpretation of the word "structure." Lena, in the deep end of a mess she'd helped to make, clung rigidly to every rule and guideline she could set.

To protect people, she told herself.

So you have someone to blame when something goes wrong, her conscience shot back.

She scowled, both at Brant's words and her silent commentary. "Keep explaining, and keep your eyes on the phaeting road."

"A few of the people were acting oddly."

Lena frowned. "We just pulled them out of a lab focusing on human experimentation. They're not going to function normally."

"No, that's not it." Brant shook his head, frustrated. "Just wait. You'll see."

The safe house was in the basement of a restaurant. Fifth City was home to high-end eating and entertainment—much like Second City, but all legal. Holodrama theatres and virtual reality experiences were spread throughout the sector and interwoven with restaurants known more for their aesthetic than their food. Fortunately, the owners of their safe house restaurant were as fragile as the delicacies they served, and were easily strong-armed into believing they were housing members of a dangerous smuggling cartel. They left Lena and her team alone as long as they didn't disrupt the operation of the restaurant.

As a rule, once they had secured and stocked the safe houses, they didn't return to them. Victims were provided with the address of a safe house and allowed to make their way there if they were able, or transported and dropped off if they were not. Dani electronically delivered a new identity for each person, and after a few weeks, the victims were told they were free to go. It was a system meant to keep Pallagen's victims safe and the team as anonymous as possible, but it also kept them from getting personally involved with anyone they rescued.

Getting attached was the biggest challenge they'd faced since hitting Pallagen's live testing labs. Most of the people who disappeared were fractious teenagers, street kids, or other unattached, hostile people. However, there had been some children and teenagers with families still searching, as well as adults that had been snatched from jobs or loved ones. Telling them they couldn't go back to their former lives was almost as distressing to Lena as it was to the victims. It was even more difficult to step back and let them go their own way without any more help than a clean identity and a few credits to their name.

There was no closure to the process, and closure was one thing Lena craved. *Someday,* she promised every victim. *Someday, Pallagen will pay for what they did to you. I'll see to it, if it takes me the rest of my life.*

Winding through the dinner traffic in Fifth City, it was starting to feel like it *would* take Lena the rest of her life.

She braced her hand against a control panel as Brant zipped into an alleyway at the back of the restaurant. "What makes them so different?" she asked again. "Did Pallagen try something new?"

"Yeah." Brant landed the gravcar and opened the hatch. "Just talk to them."

Lena frowned and limped down the hatchway, then ducked into the back entrance of the restaurant. There was no railing on the steep steps into the basement, and she let Brant hold her elbow on the way down to keep from falling.

Dani sat on top of the table in the middle of the basement, legs folded under her. There was a toddler in her lap and another standing on the table, leaning over her shoulder. They were obviously siblings, and they were listening with rapt attention to whatever Dani was explaining about the tablet she held.

There were two other people in the room, a man and a woman, both unhealthily thin, their faces washed completely of color, dark circles under their eyes. They were wrapped in castoff sweaters and stood several feet apart, uneasily observing the children and each other. Despite the wispy hair and hollow eyes of both the adults and children, Lena could clearly see the resemblance in the color of their eyes, the shapes of their faces, and their snub noses. "Okay. So, they took a family this time. I still don't understand why we have to have a meeting about it."

Dani scowled at Lena and hopped off the table, carefully peeling the children off her as she did. She put them on the floor, but instead of seeking their parents, they clung to Dani's pant legs.

"They don't know each other," Dani said quietly.

Lena's eyes narrowed. "What do you mean?"

The woman on the other side of the room stepped

forward. Her arms were folded tightly across her stomach, and her eyes were red. "I can see that they're mine," she said, her voice hoarse. "Miss Fowlkes showed us a picture of me with them. They look like me and *him*," her breath hitched as she pointed to the man, "but...I don't remember them."

Revelator. Lena swallowed. She knew Pallagen was capable of worse things than tampering with someone's mind—Dani was living proof of that—but the thought that they were willing to pull a family apart like this left Lena nauseous.

"Why would they do that?" Dani demanded, her green eyes flashing in anger. "Why would they wipe the memories of an entire family? Did they see something they shouldn't have?"

Lena took a deep breath. "If they had, Pallagen would have..." She trailed off, eyeing the children. *Would have killed them*, she thought. "I don't know, Dani," she finished helplessly.

The small family stood awkwardly as a silent conversation passed between the three rebels.

"Okay," Lena said finally. "We need to know more about this. Dani—"

"Already on it."

"Good. Brant, these people are going to need deep cover. If they're part of a new project, Pallagen will want them back. Badly."

Brant shoved his hands in his pockets. "Beyond giving them new identities..."

"Can you place them with separate families? Ones that we can keep track of?"

Brant was silent for a few seconds. "Maybe," he said slowly. His forehead wrinkled, and he rubbed the back of his neck. "I'd have to contact some old Enforcement friends."

Lena hesitated. She knew Brant hated using contacts from his previous life. He avoided Enforcement or anything having to do with them like the plague. But right now, he was the only one that could offer an escape for this family. She would make up for putting him in this position later.

"I'm sorry, Brant. But if we keep them together—"

"Yeah, I know." Brant sighed and ran a hand through his light hair. It stuck up wildly in every direction. He looked more frazzled than Lena had seen since she hired him. Dani, too, wore a haunted look. Revelator, a new Pallagen mind-based experiment was the last thing they needed.

"Can we reverse it?" Dani asked softly.

Lena grimaced. Of course she'd ask that. It was disturbing for Lena to see the effects of Pallagen's latest research, but she couldn't imagine how hard it must be for the technopath to get another look at Pallagen's mind-scrambling. After everything Pallagen had done to Dani, she deserved to be able to leave it behind, to recover mentally, not just physically. But here she was, dragging Dani into the middle of another Pallagen scheme.

Sometimes, Lena really hated herself.

"We won't know until we find more information," Lena said, keeping her voice low. She met the eyes of Brant and Dani in turn. "We'll go from there. Brant, find a way to keep track of where we send them, in case we find out we can reverse it."

It was a dangerous concession. But, Revelator, they needed a win.

"It's not a mind wipe program," Dani said as soon as Lena stepped into the apartment.

"What?"

"Project Slate." Dani held up her tablet, information scrolling across the screen. "It's not a mind wipe."

Lena pushed her hair out of her face. "Then why couldn't they remember anything?"

Dani shook her head. "That's not what I mean," she said, frustration tingeing her voice. "They did take away their memories. But that wasn't Project Slate's endgame."

"It did seem like an odd tactic." Lena hadn't been able to figure out how a group of amnesiacs could be construed as the kind of "dangerous" Pallagen was known to produce. "So what was Pallagen hoping to do?"

"They were going to program them—imprint them with different memories or commands."

Lena's brow furrowed. "But who would use that kind of programming?"

"Enforcement," Dani answered immediately. "They already use Pallagen's Hazing process. They could use Project Slate for undercover work."

Lena folded her arms. "So, they arrest some gang member..."

"Wipe his mind, imprint commands, allow him to be rescued..."

"And let him do their dirty work without the risk of sending in an officer." Lena closed her eyes and ran one hand over her face. "Great."

Dani fiddled nervously with the tablet. "Lena, we need to

tell someone about this."

"Who?" Lena's voice was strained. She pulled out a chair and sat. "I tried that once. No one listened."

"You didn't know everything then!" Dani's hands were clenched, her leather gloves squeaking against sweaty fingers. "Lena, Project Slate is too dangerous. We can't keep this secret—"

"No." Lena cut her off with an abrupt gesture. "Look, I know you want to open-source our knowledge, and you're right, people need to know what Pallagen is up to, but—"

"It's not just about what Pallagen can do with Enforcement!" Dani stepped closer. She was paler than usual, the outline of her goggles imprinted on her forehead. "Project Slate could be used to program anyone, not just criminals. Pallagen could reprogram anyone in Exordia that doesn't conform to their demands!"

"I agree with Dani," Brant said from behind Lena. She turned around to face him, her eyebrows raised in disbelief. His face was missing its usual smirk. "We can keep rescuing Pallagen's victims, but I'm not sure that's the best way to fight anymore, not with Project Slate as a threat."

"You were the one who wanted to start rescuing people in the first place," Lena scoffed. "What's changed?"

"I'm not saying we stop." Brant's eyes blazed with determination. "But we're getting nowhere, Lena. We're not winning. We're barely staying ahead of Pallagen. If we want to take them down, we need to let people know what they're up to. We can't do this alone anymore."

Dani met Brant's eyes and nodded her agreement.

"Besides," she added, "the people of Exordia have the right to know. Pallagen and Enforcement keep all information locked down so tightly that people don't question it anymore. Project Slate would let them make sure no one *ever* found out what they were doing. Why else are we here, if not to show people the truth?"

Lena took a deep breath. It was no small thing, Brant and Dani agreeing. They were looking at her now, waiting for her to come to a resolution. Lena knew whatever decision she made, they would listen. She had their trust, if not their agreement. She knew she needed to trust them just as much. However invincible she wanted to seem to Pallagen, her team deserved absolute honesty from her, even if it meant not having the answers.

"I don't know," she finally admitted. "I don't know the right decision. I know it seems simple to you, but Exordia is fragile. We've all seen it. How many people are already victims of Project Slate? Who has Pallagen programmed and put into power? What will it do to the rest of the colony?" She paused, letting her words sink in. "If we blow the whistle on a secret like this...I don't know, guys."

Brant nodded, recognizing her concession, but Dani's face fell.

Lena reached out and touched her arm. "We need to determine if we can reverse Project Slate. We need to know if there's a way to find others who have gone through the programming process. There are three of us, Dani, and right now, we have a family depending on us to put them back together." She paused, waiting until Dani met her eyes. "After that, I promise, we'll revisit this. You're right—the people of

Exordia have a right to know. But for now, we need to deal with what's in front of us."

Dani met Lena's eyes and fiddled with the edge of her glove. "Yeah, okay. I guess that is a lot for three people to handle."

"It will take time, but we'll figure something out." Lena tapped the edge of the tablet Dani held. "And the first step is finding the next lab."

"I already picked one," Dani said, flipping the tablet around and pulling up a set of building schematics. "It's in Third City."

Brant leaned over her shoulder to get a better look. "Hang on, isn't that an AI coding lab?"

Dani held out the tablet to Lena, her eyes wide and pleading. "You should probably have someone inside who knows what they're doing."

Lena stifled a laugh. "That's a good idea," she said, pretending she didn't see the eagerness in Dani's eyes.

"Like she needs any more computer boyfriends," Brant scoffed.

"At least I *have* friends," Dani shot back. Brant put a hand over his heart and leaned back, a mock-devastated look on his face.

Lena rolled her eyes. "Fine. Let's make a plan and suit up. You picked this lab, you're helping us raid it."

Dani grinned. Lena let the brightness of her smile wash away some of her guilt.

Revelator, she thought. *Let this be the right decision.*

Chapter Twenty-Six

Alex decided that she loved to run.

As with every other discovery about herself, it happened on accident. She left her apartment to buy more peaches when one of Exordia's fall rainstorms swept in—harsh, short, and drenching. Not wanting to wait in the small, crowded grocery full of people she didn't know, she turned up the collar of her heavy jacket and dashed back to her apartment through the rain. Her knee complained, but the ache was more a sign of overuse than injury now. She trudged into her apartment, breathless and soaked to the skin, but smiling.

She called Claire.

"Running," she said, as soon as the psychiatrist answered her mobile. "I was definitely a runner."

There was a short silence, then Claire chuckled. "*Not mad at me anymore?*"

Alex let her grin seep into her voice. "Oh, I'm still mad. Just not at you."

"*Ah.*" There was a shuffling noise over the mobile. "*Are you busy? The rain will be gone in a couple of hours. I can come over then."*

"Sure." Alex trapped her mobile between her chin and shoulder and shrugged out of her jacket. "Don't wear heels. I need to talk to you about something important."

"Right." There was a short pause. *"Two hours, then."*

Alex threw her mobile onto the couch and draped her wet jacket over the back of a chair. She changed into dry clothing, but she still felt chilled and damp, so she made coffee and curled up on her couch. She glanced out the window at the rain. She was restless, nervous about talking to Claire, and wired from her run.

"When in doubt, call Liam," she muttered, and picked up her mobile.

Liam answered almost immediately. *"Yeah?"* He sounded distracted. In the background she heard the sound of metal on glass.

"You have two whole hours to convince me not to talk to Claire about my suspicious past."

There was a sharp *clang* as Liam dropped something close to his mobile, and Alex winced at the noise.

"Are you all right? More importantly, is *dinner* all right?"

"That's hilarious. Hold on."

Alex waited, fingers tapping against her mug, as Liam finished...whatever it was he was doing. There was a bit more clanging, then the kitchen noises faded into the background.

"Okay, sorry. You're going to ask Dr. Tverdik about this? Are you sure that's wise?"

"I don't have a lot of options," Alex said dryly. "We've plumbed the depths of your knowledge."

"*Good point.*" Alex heard a soft shuffling, as if Liam had settled onto his own couch. She tipped her head back and imagined him stretched out on the couch, one arm hanging over the back, eyes crinkled and thoughtful as he considered Alex's words.

"She has resources we don't have," Alex went on. "Access to parts of the CityGrid you don't have clearance for. And she did get me out of Sixth City Rehab."

"*True.*"

"So, really, if I want to know anything about who I was before Pallagen got their hands on me, Claire is the only person to ask."

"*So you're calling me to argue about this, because…?*"

Alex took a gulp of coffee and wrinkled her forehead. "*I…*" *I didn't think about it. I just wanted to talk to someone, and you're all I have.* Alex shook her head. She couldn't tell Liam that. "You're as much a part of this as me, now. You broke the law for me. You should know I'm talking to Claire about it."

There was a short silence, as if Liam was reading into Alex's words. "*Well, thanks for the heads up,*" he said. "*And I do think it's a good idea to talk to Dr. Tverdik. Just…*" Alex heard Liam take a short breath. "*I know she knows about me, but try not to mention that I was the one who pulled the accident report, okay?*"

Alex scrunched her eyebrows together. She didn't think Claire would disagree with Liam's actions. After all, Claire had pulled strings to get her released against Pallagen's wishes. But Liam had risked his job for her. She owed him his suspicions.

"I won't say anything."

"*Thanks.*" The relief in Liam's voice was apparent. "*Look, I need to check on the sauce again. You still coming over for dinner, or is Dr. Tverdik staying?*"

"No, I'll be over," Alex answered.

"*Great. See you then.*"

Liam hung up as abruptly as Claire had. Alex glanced at the time on her mobile. She'd managed to kill a whole five minutes with that conversation.

She let her head flop back onto the couch and groaned.

She met Claire at the door, jacket already on. "Thanks for seeing me."

Claire smiled. "Of course. I told you before, I'm here to help."

"You're fine with walking, right?" Alex gestured behind her to the windows. "The rain quit."

Claire nodded and stepped out the door, but Alex caught her elbow and gently pulled her inside.

"What—"

Alex held up a hand and pulled her mobile out of her back pocket, setting it on the table. Eyebrows raised, Claire slowly pulled her mobile out of the inside of her jacket and laid it next to Alex's.

Alex motioned Claire out the door and followed, keying it shut behind her. They took the elevator down, and Alex led Claire out the back door, skipping the busy lobby.

"There's a park not too far away," Alex said as they

stepped outside. "Liam showed it to me."

She scuffed her boots through the gravel, not sure where to start. *I'm sorry I didn't believe you? Thanks for telling me the truth once I asked? Thanks for getting me out of a place that did something to my memory and changed my name?*

Alex took a deep breath of the cool, rain-washed air. "I looked up the original accident report on the CityGrid."

Claire's breath hissed sharply through her teeth. "That's highly illegal."

"So is lying to a patient." Alex stopped and faced Claire. "My name isn't Alex Kleric."

Claire stared at her for a moment before nodding. Her eyes glinted. "Was that an apology?"

"Yes." Alex grinned. *That was easy.* "And a thank you. You were right. I should've listened to you. Pallagen was lying to me."

Claire grimaced at the words and glanced around, but the path was empty of anyone but the two of them. "Be that as it may, try keeping it a little quieter, Alex."

"Why do you think I left my mobile in the apartment?"

"Unexpected wisdom. Good thinking." Claire slid her hands into her jacket pockets, frowning worriedly. "Do you have any idea why?"

"No." Alex started walking again. "But I'm going to find out. I was hoping you could help me."

"I thought you were okay living the life Pallagen created for you," Claire said, voice dry.

Alex grimaced. She might have been, until Liam showed her how shallow her created life truly was. She kept her promise to Liam, though, and gave Claire another truth instead.

"I'm having nightmares." Her shoulders hunched. "They've been getting worse."

Claire turned to look at Alex, concern wrinkling her brow. "Do you want to talk about them?"

Alex shuddered. "No." She glanced sideways at Claire. "They don't make sense."

"That's the nature of nightmares," she said gently. "Perhaps talking about them would help."

Alex swallowed hard, pushing back the fear she felt at the thought of reliving her headache-inducing memories. "I don't want to talk about the nightmares unless it's the only way to figure out what happened to me. If Pallagen wanted to erase me that badly, then I need to know why."

"Yes, you do." Claire's voice was heavy. "Of course I'll help you. Anything you need."

"Thank you." Alex stopped walking and met Claire's eyes. "I don't know how much of a risk you took to get me away from Pallagen, but—"

Claire held up a hand. "It was the least I could do." She squeezed Alex's arm. "I'm sorry, Alex. I don't know who you are, but I'm sure you didn't ask for this to happen."

Alex smiled crookedly. "You never know."

Alex sat up in bed gasping for air, her body covered in sweat. She pressed her hands against her eyes, but the images of her nightmare still flitted at the edges of her mind. *White walls, gray uniforms, blood in her eyes, on her hands.* Her head throbbed in time with her pounding heart, and she moaned. *Revelator, make it stop!*

She fumbled blindly for her mobile and pulled up her contacts—all three of them—with shaking fingers.

Claire answered after the second ring. "*Alex! Is something wrong?*"

Alex swallowed hard and pushed her hand against her heaving chest.

"*Alex?*"

"I'm okay," she said. Her throat hurt, and her voice sounded like she'd swallowed gravel. "I had a nightmare. I'm sorry. I shouldn't have called so late."

"*No, it's fine, Alex. Don't worry about it. What do you need?*"

"Can you look up a name for me?" She felt like she was drowning. She closed her eyes and pushed her fingertips against her eyelids.

There was a pause before Claire answered. "*A name? Did you remember something?*"

"I didn't remember it, exactly," Alex said. It was only a little lie. She hadn't remembered. She'd woken up screaming it.

"*Okay, I'm ready. Tell me.*"

"Dani Fowlkes."

Alex pulled on her softest sweater and splashed cold water in her face. She made coffee, but didn't drink it. She sat at the table, staring into the mug, watching the steam rise. Her stomach still roiled, and she wasn't sure she'd keep anything down.

The kitchen chair became uncomfortable after a while. Her head ached and her foot fell asleep, but Alex didn't want to move to the couch. She was too afraid she'd fall asleep and dream again. She waited out the early morning, elbows propped on the table with her head cradled in her hands.

The lights of the city blinked out one by one as the sun rose. Alex stared out at the skyline, watching the sun slowly tint the sky a fiery shade of orange.

A flutter of memory made her wince, and she closed her eyes against the sunrise.

The door chimed. This early in the morning, it could only be Claire. "Open," she commanded, grimacing at the hoarseness in her voice. She took a gulp of stone-cold coffee.

Claire strode over to the table, her expression stony, and Alex's greeting died on her lips. "You've been lying to me," she said, voice hard and quiet.

Alex blinked. "Um, no, I—"

Claire slapped a tablet down onto the table. "Tell me what you know about Project Slate."

"What?" Alex reached for the tablet, but Claire slapped her hand away. "Hey!"

"Tell me!"

"I don't know anything!" Alex pushed her chair back from the table and stood up. She didn't need this, not after last night. Her fists clenched. "I have no idea what you're talking about!"

Claire was glaring at her. She was angry, Alex realized. Actually, truly angry. Her face was flushed and drawn, her eyes bloodshot. *She's been crying*, Alex thought.

"Claire, what's wrong?" she asked quietly.

Claire's face relaxed somewhat. "I found Dani Fowlkes."

"Wait, I thought we were talking about Project something."

"We are," Claire said. "I found Dani Fowlkes."

Alex shrugged. "Okay…"

"She's dead."

Alex's breath caught, and her head throbbed again.

"She was a technopath. A good one. Pallagen created her."

"They *what*?"

"She fell in with a couple of social reformers. Rebels, really. They attacked a Pallagen facility, and she was killed." Claire paused and met Alex's eyes. "*Orbits ago*, Alex."

Alex swallowed, and her stomach twisted again. *Then how do I know her name?* "No, that can't be right. That doesn't…" She blinked, trailing off. "Why did they attack Pallagen?"

"Like I said, Pallagen created her. Apparently they didn't ask for her permission before experimenting on her. My guess is the attack was some sort of revenge."

"I…didn't know Pallagen did that." Alex's mouth was dry. She thought about the months she'd spent in the Pallagen rehab center, unconscious. Helpless. She rubbed her forehead. *Too much happening, and not enough coffee.* "Okay, so, this project you mentioned…?"

Claire looked at her for a few minutes. Her face was lined with worry, her tasteful makeup absent and her hair pulled back instead of pinned up in a bun. That scared Alex almost as much as her nightmare. She'd never seen Claire this shaken.

Claire pulled a chair out and sat down, pushing the tablet across the table. "Project Slate was another Pallagen project.

I started looking into it after I saw your brain scans. The details are on the tablet, but...Project Slate was a memory wipe program."

Alex sat down, hard. *Revelator.*

"So there wasn't an accident," she said, her voice dull. She felt like she couldn't breathe.

"No, there wasn't." Claire reached for the tablet and pulled up a file. "As far as I can tell, you were one of Project Slate's first...participants." Claire's mouth twisted into a scowl as she spoke. "It took some digging and I called in some favors, but I'm sorry, Alex. Whoever you were before isn't in the system."

"What do you mean?"

"They erased you. Completely. I'll try to find what I can, but don't get your hopes up." Claire hesitated. "Look, I know this is a lot to process—"

"No, you don't," Alex snapped. "You have *no idea.*"

Claire's mouth shut. She dropped the tablet on the table and drew her hands back. "Look...everything's on the tablet. I've been awake since you called me. I'm going to crash on your couch, okay?"

"Fine," Alex said. She still hadn't touched the tablet.

"Alex..." Claire stood. Her hand fluttered toward Alex's shoulder, but she pulled it back before touching her. "I'm so sorry."

Alex didn't respond, so Claire walked away.

Alex picked up the tablet and stared at the reflection looking out at her from the screen, hollow-eyed and pale.

Flat. Shallow. Two-dimensional.

She let the tablet clatter to the table and buried her face in her hands. Was that all she was now? The shadow of someone Pallagen had wiped away?

And what had she done to deserve it?

Chapter Twenty-Seven

Lena propped her hip against the countertop and folded her arms. She shut her eyes as she waited for her coffee to brew. Dani's nightmares had been especially bad, and the few hours of sleep Lena had gotten weren't going to be enough to get her through their next raid. She was going to need more than one mug of coffee if she wanted to make it back in one piece.

Brant was already awake and eating at the table, swiping at a tablet with one hand, his fork in the other. Lena watched him as her coffee finished, and chuckled as she picked up her steaming mug.

"What?" Brant asked, looking up from the tablet.

Lena shook her head and sat down across from him. "Us," she said, gesturing toward the untinted windows that let in the red light of sunset. "Our life. Exordia is going to bed, and we're just waking up."

Brant smiled and went back to his meal—toast and eggs, Lena noticed. Apparently Brant didn't care what time of day it was. The first meal of the day had to be breakfast food.

"Second City is awake, too," he pointed out, his mouth full of toast.

"True." Lena sipped her coffee, enjoying the bitter taste on the back of her tongue. Her body had adjusted to the backward schedule of waking up at night and sleeping during the day, but it still took her a while to feel alert in the evenings. She nodded toward the tablet. "Anything happen we should know about?"

"Not really. Nothing out of the ordinary, anyway. A couple of murders in Fourth City. A break-in in Seventh. The usual list of crimes happening in Second." He shut the tablet off. "No missing persons or anything like that. Looks like we're good to go for tonight."

Lena nodded. Halfway through her cup of coffee, she sighed. "I guess we should get Dani up."

Brant suddenly stood up and swiped her mug from her hands. "I'll get the dishes if you wake the technopath," he said, smiling insincerely.

Lena scowled at him as she walked to the bedroom, feeling like a condemned woman. Lena woke up slowly, her mind foggy and sluggish. Dani woke up prickly on good evenings and angry on bad ones. If the nightmares were any indication, this was not going to be a good evening.

Settling on the floor next to Dani's mattress, Lena poked her shoulder tentatively. The technopath didn't like to be touched. Even awake, she would flinch away from contact. Brant had gotten a black eye the first time he tried to nudge her awake, and after that, he gave up. Lena had learned from his mistakes and resorted to cautious taps and bribery.

Dani rolled over and blinked groggily. Lena couldn't help but smile at the way Dani's bright red hair stuck up, frizzled, in all directions. Maybe this would be an easy wake-up. "Come on. Food to eat. Crimes to commit. People to rescue."

Dani muttered something under her breath and rolled back over. Lena sighed. Not so easy. She didn't waste any more words, just grabbed Dani's goggles from the floor beside her pillow and walked back into the kitchen.

"Hey!"

Lena set the goggles on the table next to the plate of toast Brant had left. Dani wandered in a few seconds later, scowling deeply at the world in general and Lena in particular. Lena ignored the glare and took a plate from Brant, who had, in fact, been sending the dishes through the sanitizer.

"Briefing," she said, nudging him away from the counter with her shoulder.

Brant grabbed his tablet and began jabbing the screen. "This lab will be harder to get into. They're guarding more than just Pallagen tech. It's beneath a data center that holds part of the CityGrid infrastructure. There will be more surveillance, heavier armor, and more rifles. They'll be ready for us."

Lena smirked. "Will they be ready for Dani?"

"No." Brant grinned and patted Dani's shoulder as he walked past. "She's our ace in the hole."

Lena frowned. "Our what?"

"Old Earth phrase," Dani said, pulling on her goggles and leaving half the toast on her plate. "A hidden advantage. Secret weapon."

Lena made a mental note to force lunch on her later. "I

understand how Dani knows all of this random Old Earth information, but how do you know this stuff?"

"Enforcement officers travel a lot, talk to other people—"

"Have way too much time on their hands to read outdated history files," Dani interrupted sarcastically. Her fingers danced restlessly on the table, interfacing with a part of the CityGrid no one but her would ever see. "The lab will have extra manpower, but no extra digital security. If you two take care of the guards, I'll take care of everything else."

"When haven't we?" Brant spread his arms wide. Lena reached out and poked him in the ribs, right where a guard had kicked him two days ago. He doubled over with a groan.

"Fairly recently," Dani said pointedly.

Lena looked outside. The sky was almost completely dark now, light pollution hiding all but the brightest of stars. Luna One was out of phase, and Lena felt her internal clock start counting down the hours of natural darkness they had before Luna Two rose. She wrinkled her nose, hoping her ever-present sense of urgency would go away once they defeated Pallagen and returned to normal sleep schedules.

"Okay, let's gear up."

Her team needed no more instruction. Brant pulled on his vest gingerly, careful of his bruised ribs. Lena pulled on her own vest and checked her stunner. Dani disappeared to braid her hair. Lena pushed her own hair out of her face and sighed.

"Something wrong?" Brant asked as he handed her an earpiece.

"No," Lena said, fitting it into her ear. She tapped her fingers against it to activate it and heard Dani swearing under her breath at her hair. "It's just, this is routine now. We get up, we raid Pallagen, we come back and sleep it off."

"So?"

"So this wasn't the plan." Lena gestured at the apartment. "This was supposed to be a quick job, not a long game. Now, for every live lab we clean out, two more show up. I never meant to keep you or Dani here so long."

Brant held out Lena's stunner but didn't let go when she wrapped her fingers around the grip. "I don't mind staying here," he said, meeting her eyes. "I don't have anywhere else to be."

Neither did Dani. Neither did Lena, not anymore.

Brant let go of Lena's stunner and picked up his own, checking it over. "And it feels good to help. I don't remember what I did while I was with Enforcement, but it probably wasn't respectable. I like using the skills they gave me to help others."

Dani walked in, still pinning stray hairs out of her face. "I'm ready. Let's go save people."

Brant tipped his head at Lena and smiled before he followed the technopath out of the apartment.

Lena spun on one heel, dodging a stunner blast. She braced against the wall at her back and aimed a kick at the guard's knee, knocking him off balance. She raised her stunner and shot him in the face before he could recover. He fell to the ground next to two other guards. Lena turned to see Brant knock the legs out from beneath the last guard. Panting, she braced her hands on her knees to catch her breath.

She was glad Brant had continued to drill her in martial arts. His skill alone wouldn't have been enough to keep them alive during this mission. His arm had been burned by a rifle blast, and he kept it tucked close to his chest as he confiscated the security team's weapons, either melting them with the rifle or stuffing them into his belt.

"Eventually this isn't going to work," Brant said, his voice thin with pain.

"Eventually," Lena agreed. "Until then..." She straightened and rubbed her cheek. Her fingers came away bloody. She grimaced and wiped them on her jacket. "Dani, are we clear?"

"Clear," Dani said. *"All guards are down. The only cells in this lab are behind you."*

Lena turned around. There were three doors, and only two had small observation windows. She tapped on the first cell door. "We're going to open the door. We're here to help."

Dani remotely unlocked the door, and it slid open. Lena jumped back. The prisoner inside was standing near the door, close enough to touch. Lena's hand went to her stunner.

"I didn't mean to startle you," the man said.

Lena swallowed. "You didn't. But I'm used to finding people huddled in a corner."

The man smiled, and his broad shoulders shook in a silent chuckle. The shapeless white shirt and pants he wore were comically small on him, the cuff of the pants falling well above his ankles. His dark hair was plastered against his sweaty forehead, but he didn't look as drugged or malnourished as the people they usually pulled out of

Pallagen labs. Lena had to tilt her head back to look him in the eye—eyes that were set in weathered, wrinkled skin exposed to weather that didn't exist inside the city.

"Revelator," Lena breathed. "Who are you?"

"He's one of the Dallusin," Brant said. He stood next to Lena, staring at the man with a frown.

"The who?" Lena watched as Brant and the man locked eyes. "Who are the Dallusin?"

"There are no records of any group in Exordia claiming such an identity," Dani said.

"They're not from Exordia," Brant said through clenched teeth. "They live outside the city."

Lena flinched. "The desert outcasts."

The man chuckled. "Only the people within your city consider us outcasts," he said. "Most of us left this colony on purpose many orbits ago." He stepped forward and held out a hand. "My name is Tavi."

For a split second, Lena didn't know what to do. She felt Brant standing stiffly beside her, watching Tavi carefully. But Tavi, whatever his credentials were, was an enemy of Pallagen, locked inside one of their cells, and Lena was here to help. She shook his hand.

"I'm Lena Ward," she said. "This is my partner, Brant. We need to talk, I think, but first we need to finish our mission here and leave."

"I'll get the other one," Brant said. He looked uncomfortable, but he wasn't glaring at Lena. As long as they talked later, things would be fine.

Tavi was another problem altogether. She held up her

med scanner to check his vitals, and they came back clean. "We can't take him to a safe house."

"*We have a couple that are empty now.*"

"No." Lena shook her head. "He doesn't have an identity to replicate. We can't turn him loose. Pallagen would find him again."

"I don't need help," Tavi argued mildly.

Lena scowled at him. "Obviously you do. We just pulled you out of a Pallagen cell. Besides, we need to know what you know. You're the first person we've met from outside the colony." She looked directly into one of the cameras, knowing Dani was watching. "He goes back with us. Figure out a route to Second City that won't get us caught."

"*On it.*"

Brant appeared from the other cell, his arm wrapped around the waist of the only other prisoner, a woman. "That's a terrible idea."

"Do you have a better one?" Lena snapped. She took a deep breath. "I'm sorry. But he has to come back with us."

Brant nodded reluctantly and helped the woman around the sprawled guards. Lena motioned Tavi out before her.

"You seem very efficient," Tavi said, eyeing the bodies.

"We've had a lot of practice."

"So this is what you do? Break people out of places?"

"Explanations later," Lena said. "For now, we have to disappear."

Tavi didn't ask any more questions. They rendezvoused with Dani outside the factory. Dani tossed her coat over the woman's white gown, but none of them were tall enough to have clothing that remotely matched Tavi's size. Brant sighed and handed over his jacket. The sleeves were far too short, but at least some of the white was covered up.

When they parted ways, Lena took Tavi with her. They found a gravbus, one of the late-night private lines that didn't require a chip to ride. Once in Second City, Lena breathed easier. Even barefoot, Tavi didn't stand out in the eclectic crowd.

Brant and Dani were already in the apartment when they arrived. The weapons Brant had confiscated were hidden away, but his blaster was still strapped to his thigh. Clearly Brant wasn't ready to trust Tavi.

"Make yourself at home," Lena said, gesturing toward the table. "Dani has some work to do, and you probably need something in your system other than whatever drug Pallagen was giving you. Then we're going to talk." She took some prepackaged sandwiches out of the fridge and grabbed the small stack of clean plates next to the sanitizer. She pulled packages of dried fruit out of a cabinet, and dumped everything in the middle of the table so everyone could grab what they wanted.

Tavi didn't hesitate to help himself to the food. Lena wasn't surprised. Pallagen had probably fed him just enough to keep him alive. She put a sandwich next to Dani, who kept pushing her goggles up to look at Tavi. Lena took the opportunity to nudge Dani's sandwich closer. It wasn't often something human distracted Dani enough to keep her off the CityGrid.

Lena started in on her own sandwich but paused mid-bite when Tavi bowed his head over his meal. She stared for a second and glanced over at Brant, who shrugged. She flushed when Tavi looked up and caught her staring. "Sorry."

"No need." Tavi picked up his sandwich. "Is that the first time you've seen someone pray? You invoked the name of the Revelator."

"I don't pray." Lena shrugged. "But you're welcome to."

Tavi smiled in a way that made Lena think he hadn't been asking for permission.

"So," she said. "The Dallusin."

"Yes." Tavi took a bite of sandwich. "How much do you know about Exordia's history?" he asked, his cheeks filled with food.

Lena shrugged. "What everybody else does, I guess. We lost contact with Old Earth. Created laws. Somehow, you people got yourselves exiled."

"We were thrown out of the city because of what we believed," Tavi said. He tipped his head. "Many of us left of our own accord, but the first Dallusin were exiled because they believed that what the Revelator mandated superseded Council law."

Lena shifted. "Yeah, that would get you thrown out. You're lucky they didn't execute you."

Tavi laughed. "Lucky, yes. Or the Revelator was watching over us. Either way, we've been living outside Exordia for almost two hundred orbits."

"How did Pallagen capture you?" Brant asked. "I don't remember much about Enforcement, but I know we didn't take prisoners."

"No, you do not." There was a brief flash of anger in Tavi's eyes. Lena was glad to see an emotion other than impassivity from him. His calm was unnerving. "I wanted to see what Exordia was like. See if there were any other followers of the Revelator here. I'm not the only one in the city, you know."

Dani brought him a glass of water, and he smiled at her and took a drink. Lena frowned. The technopath was hanging on Tavi's every word, and Lena wasn't sure she liked it.

"What were you really doing? You don't go to the trouble to sneak into a place like Exordia just to see the sights." Lena folded her arms. "Was the Council right? Are you a threat to us?"

Tavi raised an eyebrow. "I would think you would want to ally with anyone the Council considered a threat."

"We're trying to save Exordia from Pallagen, not start a revolution." Lena's voice was hard. The city was a mess, but it was hers, and she wasn't going to help some desert outcast harm it.

"We don't want anything to do with your city." Tavi waved a hand dismissively. "I just wanted to talk to a few people inside. That's all."

Lena tapped her fingers against the table, watching Tavi's face as he warred with telling her the truth and protecting his mission. Lena understood his hesitation, but Tavi was in her city, in her crummy apartment. She could wait him out.

Tavi sighed. "One of our water purifiers has been damaged. I snuck into the city to…acquire what we need to repair it."

That hadn't been what she expected. Lena sat back in her chair and crossed her arms, trying to shake her lingering suspicion. *Give him a break. Not everyone is sneaking around*

Exordia for nefarious reasons.

Brant frowned. "Where are you getting the water?"

Lena scowled at him. A wealth of questions to ask, and that was the one he chose?

Tavi put his sandwich back on his plate and rearranged the dehydrated apple slices. He tapped the sandwich with one finger. "Exordia." He pointed to the apple slices on the edge of the plate. "My people live here. Beyond that—" he gestured to the cluttered table, "—lies a vast ocean. Too salty to drink, and almost too salty for anything to live in. We've been able to purify enough water to keep ourselves and a few crops alive. With one of the purifiers down, though, it won't be long before more than one Dallusin will be trying to sneak into Exordia. And not just for spare parts."

Dani leaned forward, eyes wide and eager. "I didn't know we had an ocean."

Tavi smiled and raised an eyebrow. "I'm sure there's a lot about your world you don't know," he said patiently.

Dani spluttered at the condescending words and looked over at Brant. He nodded. He believed Tavi's story.

So did she. Lena sighed. If Tavi's story was a lie, it was an impractical one. Lena figured any trap Pallagen tried to lay for them would masquerade as a citizen asking for help, not an outsider in trouble. Besides, Tavi was too sincere to be lying. If nothing else, they owed him the second chance they gave to all of Pallagen's victims. "Well, your Revelator is looking out for you. You managed to find the only three people in Exordia who both believe you and can do something to about it."

Tavi's eyes lit with cautious hope. "You would take the

word of a complete stranger? Put yourselves in danger for the sake of people you've never met?"

Lena pushed back from the table. "That's why we pulled you out in the first place. And besides, I'm not so morally burdened that I can't help the enemy of my enemy." She patted Dani's shoulder. "It will take us a few days, but we can help you. We have the best technopath in the Cities. She'll erase all the information Pallagen was storing about you, and Brant and I will work on stealing what you need. Until then, it would be best if you stayed in the apartment." Lena let her sternness show. A common enemy notwithstanding, she wasn't going to allow someone to jeopardize the safety of her team.

Tavi nodded. He looked a little shell-shocked. "Thank you for your help and hospitality. May the Revelator bless you."

"Um...thanks." Lena shifted uncomfortably. There was something about the way Tavi said "Revelator" that made her think the name mattered to him. Shaking her head, she pushed the thought aside and started making another sandwich. She had enough to worry about without considering an old religion for which people had once left the safety of the colony.

Though, as she worked, she couldn't help but think of all the times she'd called on the Revelator.

Had he been listening after all?

Chapter Twenty-Eight

Alex dumped her cold coffee down the sink and made a fresh cup. She moved quietly around the kitchen, trying not to wake Claire, who was curled up asleep on one end of the couch. Alex drank the entire mug and made another before she felt ready to face the tablet Claire had brought.

Alex scoured every line in the file, but there was almost no information about Dani Fowlkes. The lack of data made sense. Pallagen didn't want her to know about Dani, so they'd erased Dani's records just as they had erased hers.

There was, however, a great deal of information about Project Slate. The file contained no names, but it detailed the process of chemically and psychologically conditioning a person's mind to forget their previous life and implanting new memories. There appeared to be only a few "successful" patients. Alex assumed she was one of them.

She put the tablet on the table, her stomach and mind churning.

There was a shuffling sound behind her as Claire walked up to the table. She gently rested a hand on Alex's shoulder.

"Are you all right?"

"I'm programmed?" Alex's voice caught.

"No." Claire's hand tightened. She reached for a chair, pulling it closer to Alex as she sat. "You've been wiped. Programming would have been the next step. Sixth City Rehab is owned by Pallagen, but it's staffed by civilian doctors and nurses. They signed your release papers on my recommendation before Pallagen could begin the next phase."

Thank the Revelator. She may be a blank slate, but at least she wasn't someone else. "I owe you for that."

Claire frowned and drew her hand back, folding her arms. "Hardly." There was disgust in her voice. "I couldn't fix what happened to you, but I could keep it from progressing any further. It was the right thing to do. Nothing more."

Alex blinked at Claire's anger. "It wasn't your fault," she said gently, meeting Claire's eyes. She was incredibly grateful for Claire's intervention.

Claire's face softened. "I know."

Alex looked down at the tablet. "I'm not getting any of it back, am I?"

"Your memories?"

Alex nodded.

Claire leaned forward and laid a hand over Alex's. Her fingers were warm and soft, and her eyes were sad. Alex knew the answer before Claire spoke, but she wanted to hear it from her. "I don't think so. Small snatches, maybe, like your nightmares. But consciously? I doubt it."

Alex pulled her hand away and blinked back the tears stinging her eyes. "They...they *erased* me, Claire, and I don't even know why."

"I don't know why you were so carefully mind wiped, but I have a theory." Claire reached for the tablet and tapped another file. "I think you knew something important, perhaps something dangerous you weren't supposed to know. Other test subjects had memories implanted over existing ones, but with you they were very intentional about removing everything. Whatever you knew, someone was very afraid of it."

Alex breathed deeply, forcing herself to calm down. "Okay." Her voice broke, and she cleared her throat. "Can you find out more from the same place you found this?"

Claire hesitated. "It's not that simple, Alex. I think you might've lost more than a few orbits. Possibly quite a bit more than that."

That was a disturbing thought. "How long do you think?"

"I don't know. I'll have to look up your medical records." Claire glanced at the screen of her mobile. "Look, Alex, I have another appointment…"

Startled, Alex looked at the time readout on the tablet. It was after noon. "Sorry."

"No," Claire said, pushing hair out of her face. "This is important. I'll come by later, okay? We can talk more then."

Alex nodded. "Sure."

Alex walked Claire to the door. She keyed the lock, suddenly feeling vulnerable in a building full of people she knew nothing about. What if Pallagen was already looking for her? She needed to ask Liam if anyone else had moved into the building around the same time she had.

She rubbed a hand across her face and groaned. She was

supposed to shop with Liam again tonight. She owed him an explanation.

How dangerous had she been for Pallagen to erase her? Whatever they had done had worked. She was exhausted, but too afraid of her nightmares to sleep again.

She didn't want them to win, but she felt like they already had.

Chapter Twenty-Nine

There was literally no space for Tavi in the apartment.

He was sitting on one end of the sagging couch, a blanket wrapped around his shoulders. Lena assumed he'd slept there, since the floor was bare and Brant's mattress was pushed to the side to create a path from the living area to the kitchen.

He'd already eaten, too, apparently. Lena sighed and pushed aside the extra mug and plate on the counter. Even that much clutter was noticeable. She hoped they could help Tavi and send him on his way soon. She was used to sharing space with Brant and Dani, but Tavi's presence was irritating her. She ran the mug through the sanitizer and dumped instant coffee in it.

"Is that for me?"

Lena flinched and stepped backward into Brant, who was standing behind her. Unbalanced, he flailed for something to hold on to. Lena caught his hand and held him steady until he was firm on his feet again. His face was pale, and there were dark shadows beneath his eyes. It looked like he hadn't combed his blond mop of hair in a week.

"You look awful." She shoved the mug of coffee into Brant's hands. "Here. You clearly need this more than I do."

Brant didn't say anything until he'd downed half the mug's contents—in two gulps, Lena noticed with horrified interest. "Yeah. Didn't sleep well."

Perplexed, Lena glanced back into the living area. Dani had appeared, wide awake for once, and was peppering Tavi with questions as she perched on the couch next to him. Lena looked back at Brant curiously. "What, does he snore or something?"

Brant shrugged and finished the coffee.

Tavi reached out and touched Dani's elbow. The technopath cringed—as she did when anyone touched her—and Brant took a step forward, mug abandoned and fists clenched.

Ah.

"Stand down, Brant," Lena murmured.

The ex-soldier glared at her, but relaxed.

"Are you keeping an eye on him? Is that why you didn't sleep?"

"No," Brant lied, avoiding Lena's gaze.

Lena smiled fondly. Thank the Revelator for reliable, over-protective ex-soldiers. She reached out and squeezed his shoulder. "You're amazing. Please tell me you used all of that not-sleeping time to figure out where we can find parts for Tavi's purifier."

At the mention of his name, Tavi glanced their way. Brant straightened and reached for a tablet on the countertop. "We could break into the hydroponics in Third City, but that would be difficult. The one thing Enforcement guards more closely than Pallagen is the gardens."

"Hmm." Lena crossed her arms. "I'm not sure I like the idea of meddling with our food supply."

"Another good point. I found a lab that stores various liquids for Pallagen—everything from blood samples to drugs. They'll have what we need, and we can kill two birds with one stone."

Lena nodded and took the tablet from Brant.

Dani crowded into the kitchen, staring at the tablet over Lena's shoulder. Lena flicked through the schematics for a few seconds before handing it to the technopath. "Any reason why we can't hit it tonight?"

Brant shrugged. Dani, engrossed in the tablet, didn't answer.

"All right then. Brant, help Dani suit up. Pallagen rents the space—they don't own the building—so there'll be private security all over the place."

"I don't want a blaster." Dani frowned, still staring at the screen.

Brant snorted. "Sorry, freak show, you get one."

Dani turned pleading eyes in Lena's direction, but Lena shook her head. Brant was in charge of keeping them alive, and she wasn't going to argue with his methods.

"Can I help in any way?" Tavi asked.

"Stay here. Don't touch anything. Don't try to answer the door. It won't open for you." She grimaced at the harshness in her voice. "We'll be back soon. There's plenty of food here, and Dani can give you access to one of the tablets."

Tavi smiled. "At least allow me to send you with a blessing." He bowed slightly, his hands folded behind his back. "May the Revelator go with you."

Lena hesitated. Was there a proper response? She nodded slowly. "Thank you."

What could it hurt? They needed all the help they could get.

Although Lena often let Dani help her and Brant pull people out of labs, she hadn't let the technopath directly assist with a break-in. There was too much Pallagen could do to Dani if they recaptured her. With a facility this size, though, Lena needed her third teammate.

They hid behind a low hedge that ran the length of the electrified fence surrounding the lab. Even on the ground, Dani was still the eyes of the team. Lena imagined the technopath's gaze flicking from side to side as she watched information scrolling across the inside of the dark goggles.

"You were right about the private security," Dani said, pausing to do a head count. "Six on the ground floor, one in the control room, and four walking the perimeter."

Brant whistled, low and quiet. "Well, this should be fun." He glanced from Lena to Dani, who had turned away and was staring into the distance. He nodded in Dani's direction. "Maybe we should—"

Lena cut him off with a shake of her head. "No. Dani stays with us."

The technopath pushed her goggles up to her forehead and looked back at her teammates. "I'll be okay."

"Of course you will. You're with us," Brant said, rolling his eyes. His words belied his anxiety, and he shot Lena a worried glance. He still didn't like the plan.

Lena understood his concern but was grateful he didn't argue. If he had, she would have reconsidered her plan, and they didn't have time for that.

"Okay, let's go," Lena said, standing up. "Dani, cut the power to the fence and keep the guards on duty from seeing us. We'll leave the perimeter guards alone for now and deal with everyone inside. Keep them from contacting anyone outside the building."

Dani pulled her goggles back down and nodded. "Got it."

"All right then. Brant, take point."

The ex-soldier slipped into the night. He disappeared silently despite his limp.

"Wait," Lena said, as Dani moved to follow. "Cut power to the fence."

Dani closed her eyes. She tapped her earpiece. "Done."

"Okay, give me a second," Brant said. They heard the buzzing of his laser-edged knife as it cut through the thick wire. *"We're in."*

Lena tugged Dani's sleeve, and they pushed through the thin hedge. Brant knelt next to a gap in the tall fence, holding one edge back from the opening. His face was shadowed in the dim moonlight, and he motioned for them to hurry.

"Guard on the other side of the building for the next twelve seconds," Dani said, adjusting her goggles.

"We'd better hurry." Brant pushed the technopath through the opening. He followed, keeping one hand on her back as they bolted through the darkness to the maintenance entrance at the back of the building. Lena ducked through the fence and dashed after them.

"Cameras off," Dani whispered. "Communication with outside guards disabled."

Lena pulled a hacked card out of her pants pocket and slid it through the door's keypad. It opened, and she ushered her team inside.

"Nicely done," she said, giving Dani a pat on the arm. "Stay behind us. We'll take care of the guards."

"I'm not a child," Dani grumbled, but she stayed a few paces behind Lena.

"You are, technically, a minor," Brant said, rifle up.

"You think they'll slap 'endangering a minor' onto your list of crimes when they arrest you?"

Lena chuckled. "Sorry," she said when Brant glared at her. "Dani, where are the guards?"

"Two straight ahead. Keep walking, we'll run right into them."

"Great," Lena muttered. "Where is the control room?"

"Go straight, left when I say, then it's the first right."

"Got it." Lena squinted up at the automatic lights switching on as they advanced down the hall. It meant an attentive guard would be alerted to their presence, but the lights would also turn on for anyone coming their direction. They'd have a little bit of warning before running into the guards.

Far ahead of them, another light flickered, the silhouettes of the approaching guards barely visible. Lena's grip on her stunner tightened.

"Can they see us yet?" she asked quietly.

"No comm traffic," Dani whispered, fingers tapping nervously against her tablet's casing. She edged closer to

Lena. "They're not sounding any kind of alarm. They must be expecting to meet some of the other guards."

Lena glanced at Brant and he nodded, dropping behind Dani to watch their backs.

"Dani, let me know if they notice us," Lena ordered.

The guards didn't see them until they were within range of Lena's stunner. She shocked them, then jogged forward.

"No armor." She pulled the stunners from their holsters and searched them for access cards. The hacked card from Dani would work, but it would be better for them if it looked like guards were opening doors. She handed one to Brant and kept the other. "Who's in the control room?"

"Two now," Dani said. "No armor. Same as these guys."

Brant led the way. They took the next left, the first right, and found the control room door. Brant slid his card through the keypad, and the door opened. The guards were stunned, and the team was hidden in the control room in a matter of seconds.

Dani pushed her goggles up. "Two of the remaining guards are armored." She activated the surveillance screens and pointed at one. "The last one isn't, but he looks tough enough to take a few shots before going down."

"Okay. This is where we leave you, Dani." The technopath opened her mouth to argue, but Lena raised a hand. "No. When we've taken care of the other three, you can check out the lab while we look for parts."

Dani scowled in protest, but plopped into a chair in front of the screens.

"Keep telling us where the guards are," Lena said, handing Dani her access card and reaching up to activate her earpiece. She slipped out the door behind Brant.

"Muscles is near the front of the building. Wait for him to come to you. The armored guards are in the main lab."

"Great," Brant muttered. He hefted his rifle. "Hopefully they—"

"Lena," Dani interrupted, *"I think they know we're here."*

"What? How?"

"They're heading your direction," the technopath said, the fear evident in her voice. *"Lena, be careful—"*

The guards barreled around the corner and Lena shot their helmets. It wouldn't do more than short-circuit their visuals, but it bought them some time. "Where to now, Dani?"

"Blue door in the lab behind you," Dani said.

Brant followed her, keeping an eye on the guards as they wrestled with their helmets. Just as the first guard pulled his off and aimed his rifle in their direction, the blue door slid open, and Brant pushed Lena inside.

The door took the impact of the blast, and Lena squinted at the keypad. "You're locking it, right?"

"Sure," Dani said, her voice steadier now. *"They'll be able to melt through the lock with their rifles though. They've both got their helmets off now."*

Lena sighed and turned away from the door. *So much for a smooth mission.* "Where do we find the parts Tavi needs?"

Behind them, the guards were pounding on the door. Brant and Lena ignored them.

"Storage closet." Brant pointed.

Lena pulled the door open and began rummaging through drawers, comparing parts and tools to the

schematics Tavi had given them. It only took a few minutes
to find the components. Lena stepped out of the closet
and nodded at Brant, who had been standing guard at the
entrance. They moved on to the lab.

It was all chrome and white tile, and the sterile smell of
chemicals stung Lena's nose. There was a long worktable
cluttered with beakers and med scanners. A cold storage chamber
with glass doors lined one wall. Brant stepped up to inspect it.

"Lena," he said softly. "Look."

Lena examined the vials on the shelves. Most of them
were blood samples, but one section was dedicated to
experimental drugs. Lena swallowed and stepped back to
the worktable, activating one of the data screens. "Let's
download and wipe what we can and get out."

"Do you think this is a testing site?" Brant glanced at the
vials uneasily.

"Hurry up, guys, the guards are almost through."

"No." Lena scrolled through files. "I think this is just
research."

"Good," Brant said, giving one last hard look at the
storage chamber before turning to help Lena. "Hey, I—"

"They're through!"

Lena winced and touched her ear gingerly. She looked at
Brant.

"We really need two of these," he said tersely, hefting
his rifle.

"It would help," she agreed, switching her stunner to
maximum voltage. She hoped it would do some damage
against the armor the guards wore.

"I gave Dani the old gun," Brant said apologetically. "Thought she'd handle it better. Sorry."

Lena had no time to answer as the guards charged around the corner.

The first guard slammed into Brant, rendering his rifle useless in close combat. Brant grunted at the impact and slid backward.

The second guard aimed a rifle at Lena. She ducked. The blast melted part of the lab table behind her. Lena's heart pounded. *Revelator, that was close.* She ran toward her attacker as his rifle recharged.

She was half the size of the guard, but her boot was armored. She aimed a kick at the guard's knee. It threw him off balance long enough for her to get her fingers underneath the edge of the armor at his neck. She yanked it to the side and jammed her stunner into the small gap she'd created. She held the trigger down, sending a full voltage stun inside his armor. The guard dropped and Lena fell, tangled with him. She pushed his limp legs away with one hand and shoved her stunner back into its holster with the other. Scrambling to her feet, she picked up his rifle. It was heavy, but she'd fired Brant's before. She focused on her partner's struggle with the second guard, waiting for an opportunity to help him.

Brant was holding his own. He'd discarded the rifle, kicking it out of reach. Lena knew he had another blaster and at least one laser knife hidden somewhere, but he wasn't trying to pull either of them out. Maybe he knew something about the armor that Lena didn't. She raised the rifle and aimed it at the guard, getting ready to fire. Her finger tightened on the trigger, but she tumbled forward as something hit her from behind.

It was the guard she had fought, recovered from the shock. She swung the rifle around and shot him in the chest. The armor melted, and the guard screamed. He fell to the ground, clutching a nasty, circular burn in the middle of his chest. He curled around the wound and stayed down, heaving for breath with sobbing gasps.

Lena spun around and saw the other guard shove Brant into the glass doors of the cold storage chamber. She shot him in the back before he could make another move on her partner.

Breathing hard, Lena kept the rifle aimed at the guard's back for a moment before slinging the rifle over her shoulder and walking over to Brant.

"I can see why you like this thing," she said, giddy with adrenaline. She held out a hand to help Brant up, but the ex-soldier shook his head quickly.

"What?" Lena asked, suddenly wary. "What's wrong?"

"*What's going on?*" Dani sounded worried again, but Lena ignored her, eyes on Brant's white face.

"Don't touch me," he said, voice raspy. "Don't *touch* me."

Lena stepped back as Brant got an elbow beneath him and pushed himself to a sitting position. There was shattered glass and liquid around him. Lena's breath caught.

He'd landed on the shelf of drugs and poison.

Brant held up his hand. The sterile white light of the lab glinted off the glass that peppered his skin. There were a few small cuts and one large gash across his palm. "I don't feel so great," he said, finally meeting Lena's eyes, a terrible knowledge on his face.

Lena swallowed.

"What? Lena, tell me what phaeting happened to Brant!"

"I need your help. We need to get Brant out of here." He opened his mouth to protest, but Lena shook her head. "No. We're getting out now. Then we'll figure out what to do."

She stepped carefully over to the shattered shelf. Only one tray had been knocked over. Fear knotted her stomach as she read the names on the labels—not just drugs, but vaccines, diseases, poisons. Lena looked frantically around the lab, searching for the blood scanner she knew had to be somewhere.

"Over on the desk next to the door," Brant said quietly. He looked a little less frantic now. Lena grabbed the scanner off the desk and held it over Brant's outstretched hand. The results flashed across the screen almost immediately.

Revelator. The poison of a desert snake. Lena rubbed her forehead and looked back at Brant.

"What?" Brant smirked but there was fear in his voice. "That bad?"

"Hold still," Lena said. She grabbed a bottle of liquid antiseptic from a supply drawer. "This will sting." She upended the entire bottle over Brant's hand.

He cursed furiously, his uninjured hand clenching and unclenching, but he kept the gash exposed to the liquid. His face was tight with pain.

"We need to wrap it." She and Brant jumped as Dani rushed into the room, shoes pounding on tile. "Find some gauze and tape," she ordered the technopath.

Dani didn't move for a second, her frightened eyes resting on Brant.

"Dani!"

The teenager flinched.

Lena took a slow breath and gentled her tone. "Find some gauze, okay? And then we can leave."

Dani quickly located the first aid kit. Lena took it and pushed Dani farther away from the mess before carefully crouching amidst the shattered glass. She gently wrapped Brant's hand. By the time she was done he was sweating, and Lena was holding on to the shoulder of his vest to keep him from falling over.

"Okay," Lena said, "let's get out of here."

She heaved Brant up to a standing position. He stumbled, and Dani reached out to steady him. He slung his uninjured arm over her shoulders and smirked. "See what fun you've been missing out on?"

His voice was hoarse, but it carried none of the pain and weight Lena had heard earlier. She wanted to be angry at him for wasting his energy, hiding his pain from Dani. By the rapid onset of symptoms, he had to know how badly off he was.

Dani calmed a little at his words, and some color came back to her cheeks. She glanced sideways at him. "Whatever. I'll stick to the roof next time."

They shuffled around the fallen guards and through the narrow entrance of the lab.

"Sorry you didn't have time to make any more AI friends," Brant said, his voice slurring.

Dani rolled her eyes. "I'm fine with the friends I have."

Lena's arm tightened around Brant's waist. She'd never heard Dani admit to liking Brant aloud like that. Her chest ached, filling with fear.

Now if only she could keep those friends alive...

The trip back to the apartment was hell.

The lab they'd hit had been close to Second City, thank the Revelator. They'd taken a gravbus to their destination, and now they walked—staggered—home. Brant had to stop to throw up twice, and by the time they reached the apartment, Dani and Lena were supporting all of his weight.

They dropped him onto his mattress. Brant moaned and rolled over, curling up around his stomach.

Tavi scooted forward on the couch. "Can I help?"

"No." Lena's voice was hard. Tavi stayed back.

Dani stood next to the mattress, her fists clenched, scowling at Brant. Every breath he drew was an obvious struggle. It hurt to watch, and Lena looked away. Her hands were shaking and clammy with cold sweat. She wanted to scream that this wasn't fair, that she'd been careful, that Brant shouldn't be dying because of her mistakes.

He wouldn't have been in that lab if it wasn't for her. This was her fault. She'd failed him.

Lena closed her eyes and took a deep breath. She couldn't fall apart now. Later, maybe, after fate decided whether Brant Hale lived or died.

When Dani wasn't looking at her like she held the secrets of the universe.

Lena knelt next to Brant. "Dani, where's your scanner?"

"Bedroom."

"Go get it," Lena said. "And a bottle of water, the antiseptic, and that electrolyte stuff."

The technopath fled like a frightened rabbit. Lena grabbed the front of Brant's vest and hauled him into a sitting position.

"Stop," he said, his eyes glassy. He weakly batted at Lena's fingers. "Don't wanna move."

"You'll be a lot more comfortable with this vest off," Lena said patiently, undoing the straps that held his vest in place. She fumbled, trying to pull the vest off one-handed. "If I let go, can you stay up?"

Brant blinked a couple of times before answering. "Maybe." His words slurred. "Might...throw up on you."

Lena wrinkled her nose. "Please don't."

She finally untangled the vest from Brant's arms and tossed it aside. She started pulling off the belt and knives strapped to his waist. "Okay. You can lay down now."

Brant collapsed sideways onto the mattress. He tried to roll over but Lena put a hand on his shoulder, keeping him on his side.

"If you throw up again, I don't want you on your back."

"Mm." Brant closed his eyes, and Lena moved to take off his boots.

"You don't have to do that."

"Yes, I do," Lena said softly. "You're uncomfortable enough as it is."

A few heartbeats of silence passed, broken only by the sound of Brant gulping air and trying not to vomit. Lena pulled off his boots and sat next to his head.

"It's bad, isn't it," he said, his eyes half open. He was watching her carefully, as if she were a med scanner with his prognosis written on her face.

"Yeah. It's a desert poison."

Brant swallowed hard. "Revelator."

Lena wasn't sure if it was a prayer or a curse.

Dani slipped into the room, her hands full of supplies.

Lena stood, taking the water from her. "Re-bandage his hand. I'll get him to drink."

"Won't keep it down," Brant said as Lena forced him upright again.

"Don't care." Lena put the bottle to his lips. "If you keep throwing up, the dehydration will kill you faster than the poison."

Lena glanced at Dani. The technopath blanched as she unwrapped Brant's swollen hand. Lena's heart twisted, seeing Dani's realization of Brant's condition. She was willing to bet the technopath had never lost anyone close to her. Probably because she'd never allowed anyone to get close. What a phaeting terrible time for Dani to realize she cared about Brant.

"Can you help?" Dani asked suddenly, looking up at Tavi. "It's a desert poison. Do you know a cure?"

"I'm sorry, I don't." The Dallusin shook his head. "I can do nothing more than pray for your friend."

Lena suppressed a snort. Prayer wouldn't do much.

Brant threw up again.

Lena swallowed the bile that rose in her own throat, trying to hide her fear. Her arm tightened around Brant's shoulders.

Perhaps asking the Revelator for help wasn't a bad idea.

Chapter Thirty

The apartment was stifling after Claire left. It was too quiet and still, too unchanged. The tablet, now shut down and passcode locked, was the only sign of the terrible secrets they had discussed. Alex's world had shifted. Again. She didn't belong in this apartment, with this name, living this life.

Either that, or she'd drunk too much coffee.

I need to get out. It was early afternoon, and the sun was shining. A walk in the fresh air would help her clear her mind and decide what to do next. She scooped up her jacket and stepped into the hallway.

She stopped in front of Liam's door and hesitated. Should she tell him? *He started this. You might as well tell him he was right.* She knocked on his door, but there was no answer. He was either out or ignoring her. Alex sighed. *He has a life*, she reminded herself. Maybe it wasn't a good idea to discuss her newfound knowledge before she had more information. Until she knew what was going on, the fewer people who knew what Pallagen had done to her, the better. She stuffed her hands in her pockets and headed for the elevator.

She started out walking, but the sunlight was deceiving. It was cooler than she'd thought, and she shivered beneath her jacket. She broke into a jog, then started running, taking the same circuit she'd walked with Claire the other day. She went a little farther, a little faster, trying to focus on her pumping blood and racing heart instead of her brain, which was whirling with thoughts of her lost identity. Fowlkes' name stuck in her mind. Why had that been the one thing that jogged her memory?

Alex arrived back at her apartment building, panting and sweaty. She took a few moments to rest and catch her breath in the dead grass behind the building before tackling the stairs to her floor. The plastic of the building was warm against her back, and her pounding heart had drowned some of her worry. She was considering taking the elevator instead of the stairs when she heard Liam's voice in a nearby alley. Alex smiled and pushed herself to her feet.

Angry voices joined Liam's, and Alex paused, suddenly wary.

"I told you, I don't know!" Liam said angrily.

"Look, we know you and the girl are together—"

"We're not," Liam snarled. "I haven't seen her in days. Go ask your spies at Enforcement if they know anything about her."

Alex's mouth went dry, and her fists clenched. In the alleyway, she heard the *crunch* of dropped parcels, and someone gasped.

Alex stepped around the corner.

Three men had Liam backed against a wall. His chin was raised and his fists were clenched at his side. Vegetables and bread lay scattered on the ground. Two men wore the gray and orange of Pallagen's security, and one wore a sharp, black business jacket. Alex cleared her throat loudly, and they turned to look at her.

Her heart pounded as she stepped forward. "You wanted to talk to me?"

The man in the business jacket smiled and stepped toward her, his hand held out. "Ah, Miss Kleric—"

Alex didn't let him say any more. She drew back her fist and punched him in the jaw.

He stumbled back, clearly not expecting such a volatile reaction. Alex flexed her fingers with a sense of awe and fear. Where had that come from? The voice in the back of her head, the one she'd been trying to ignore, was screaming *Danger!* at the sight of the gray and orange uniforms.

The other two men pointed blasters at her. Alex smiled and waited for the suit to regain the ability to speak.

He cowered behind his companions and their weapons, rubbing his jaw. "We just want to speak with you." His words sounded mushy, and there was blood trickling from the corner of his mouth.

"No," Alex said. "You're too late. I know what Pallagen did to me, and I'm not speaking to you." She edged closer as she spoke, eyes on the blasters. Liam had circled around behind the leader—intending to do what, Alex wasn't sure.

The leader stopped rubbing his jaw and wiped the blood from his mouth. He tugged on the edge of his cuffs, straightened his jacket, and forced a crooked smile. "I'm not sure what you've been told, but Pallagen is assisting with your recovery. We are trying to help."

"By what? Erasing my memory?" Alex was within arm's

reach of one of the blasters. "Sorry. I've had enough of that kind of help."

"I see." The suit dropped his friendly façade. "Well, I suppose we can—"

Alex had heard enough. She grabbed the wrist of the man closest to her and jerked him off balance. She wrapped her fingers around his weapon, aimed it toward his partner, and squeezed the trigger.

The man went down.

The first guard pulled away from her and jabbed a fist toward her head. She ducked, but not fast enough. The punch caught her on the side of the head, and her ears rang. She heard a cry of anger and saw Liam launch himself toward the leader, who was trying to unholster his stunner.

Something snapped inside her, and she saw red.

Alex seized the man's wrist again. She twisted it and felt something pop. The man screamed and dropped the blaster. She kneed him in the gut and he fell to the ground. Alex snatched the blaster and pointed it at his face. He was kneeling now, panting, fingers wrapped around his wrist.

Alex glanced behind her, looking for the guard she'd shot. He lay on the ground, unmoving. Alex hadn't aimed well but she knew he was dead. The suit was unconscious, his nose and cheeks bleeding. Liam stood nearby, his fists clenched, breathing heavily.

Alex turned her gaze to the remaining guard at her feet. Her hands trembled, and she tightened her fingers around the blaster. Revelator. Where had she learned to do that? Adrenaline pumped through her veins, and she found her voice. "I want you to tell Pallagen they're done with me. Whatever they want, they can't have it."

The man laughed. "They won't stop coming. Do you know who you are? They're going to—"

Alex shot him. Liam gasped, but she waved a hand dismissively. "I switched it to stun. He'll be fine." She looked back down at the guard. "Except for the wrist."

Her chest ached like it had when she first woke up, and she closed her eyes, concentrating on taking slow, deep breaths. She wavered, knees shaky. There was a touch at her elbow. She recoiled and opened her eyes, but it was only Liam, steadying her.

"We should call Enforcement," he said.

"No." Alex shook her head. "We really shouldn't."

Liam's grip on her elbow tightened. "Then what do we do?"

"I need another blaster," Alex said. "And a new apartment."

"No, I meant about the bodies."

"Leave them." Alex knelt beside the dead guard and took his blaster. Her fingers ached as they curled around the weapon. "Pallagen will retrieve them. They'll keep Enforcement out of it. They won't want to be seen as incompetent."

Liam stepped back from the leader and stuffed his hands in his pockets, as if afraid Alex would ask him to pick up the third stunner. "He was right, you know. Pallagen will come for you."

"I know." Alex met Liam's eyes. "Look, about the other night…"

"I didn't *want* to be right," Liam interrupted. "But from what you just said, I was more right than I knew."

"Yeah." Alex sighed. "Let's get upstairs, make a plan, and

eat something. I haven't eaten since dinner yesterday, and I'm not running from Pallagen on an empty stomach."

"No wonder you're so thin," Liam grumbled, salvaging what groceries he could from the pile on the ground.

They rode the elevator in silence. When they arrived at Liam's apartment, he disappeared into his bedroom. Alex pulled an ice pack from the freezer and wrapped it around her knuckles, hissing at the sting of cold on split skin.

"I'm sorry," Alex called. "I guess I've dragged you into this mess."

"I'm not too worried."

"Oh, really?" Alex threw the ice pack into the sink. "Why phaeting not?"

Liam entered the room with a backpack slung over one shoulder. It was too full for him to have packed it in the few seconds he was in his bedroom. Alex raised a suspicious eyebrow as Liam set the pack on the counter and vehemently unzipped it.

"How soon can you leave?" Liam asked, throwing dehydrated food into his pack.

Alex grabbed Liam's hands, full of packaged protein bars, stilling his frenzied movement. "What are you doing? What's wrong with you?"

"Alex, you just killed a man!"

"Enforcement will leave us alone," Alex said, gut-sure, and not knowing why. "They won't get involved with Pallagen's cleanup. We have a little time before Pallagen regroups and sends someone else after us."

"I'm not so sure of that." Liam pulled away and ran

a hand through his hair before meeting Alex's gaze. "It's possible those men weren't here for you."

Alex crossed her arms, waiting for Liam to explain. He squirmed uncomfortably under her stare before clearing his throat. "Pallagen tried to recruit me, orbits ago. I was only ten."

Alex frowned. "What did they want with a child?"

Liam scratched the back of his neck. "I'm not normal. I...I remember things."

Alex tilted her head. "So?"

"No, I mean, I remember *everything*. I'm a hyperthymesiac."

Alex's eyebrows shot up. "You're a *what*?"

Liam tapped his forehead. "I don't forget anything. I remember what I ate for breakfast two weeks ago. How much I paid for groceries this day last orbit. How it felt the first time I fell and scraped my hands. Whatever happens to me stays forever."

"That..." Alex trailed off. "I don't know if that sounds appealing or terrifying."

"It's both." Liam shrugged. "Pallagen thought my brain would be useful. My parents said no."

Alex's mouth tightened. "Okay. So you, what? Changed your name? Faked your death at ten?"

Liam gave a short laugh. "No. Pallagen left us alone. As long as I keep a low profile, they don't bother me. That's why I took the filing job. I can redirect any mentions of me."

"Clever," Alex said, nodding her head. "But the men in the alley asked about me specifically. From the sound of it, they knew who I was before...everything."

"Yeah." Liam hefted the backpack. "So, I think we should go talk to my brother."

"You have a brother?"

"Keagan. Haven't I mentioned him?"

"I don't know, you tell me, hyper-boy."

"Very funny," Liam grumbled. "Well, he...um, he watches Pallagen. Makes sure they don't get to me."

Alex blinked. "Not only do you have a sibling you've never told me about, but he also spies on Pallagen?"

"Yeah, well, it never came up." Liam looked wistfully around his apartment. "He told me this wouldn't last. He's usually right about stuff like that."

Alex ran a hand through her hair, pushing it out of her face. The adrenaline of the fight was gone, leaving her jittery and her thoughts scattered. The idea that she had to leave behind the one home she remembered was frightening, but she couldn't think of another option. Pallagen would come for her, sooner rather than later. "All right. Give me a few minutes to pack. I own less stuff than you do."

It didn't take long to gather her things. She had no memories to attach sentimental value to any of her belongings, so it was easy to grab the backpack from her closet and choose a few pieces of clothing and necessities to take with her. One of the stunners went into the backpack, and she tucked the other into her belt. Alex didn't think Liam would take one.

She took one last look around her kitchen. When it came down to it, Alex didn't mind leaving. The apartment had never felt like home. There were dirty dishes in the sink, a loaf of bread on the counter, a couple pieces of fruit, a half-empty coffee mug. The few data discs she owned were stacked haphazardly on a shelf, but other than that, there was nothing to show that she'd lived here. No strewn clothes. No pictures, no personal items. She realized the only part of the apartment that looked lived in was the kitchen, where she and Liam spent most of their time.

On a whim, she grabbed the tiny aloe plant from the counter and tucked it carefully into the top of her backpack. She walked out the door, keying it locked behind her. It felt like the most final thing she'd ever done.

Liam was staring blankly at his apartment door, shoulders slumped.

Alex reached out and squeezed his arm. "Maybe we can come back," she offered. The words sounded thin, even to her. "Maybe this will blow over."

Liam smiled bitterly. "Right." He laid a hand on his door. "I liked it here. It's just a place, though." He looked sideways at Alex, his face softening. "I'm glad I didn't have to disappear without you."

Alex smiled as they headed toward the elevator. "Yeah, I wouldn't have been too happy running off alone either. I probably would've starved to death."

Liam laughed. "I don't know about that. You're getting better at cooking."

"Ha." Alex scoffed. "I'm just glad I know how to reheat food. Speaking of which, we never did eat."

"True." Liam brought his backpack around, pulled out a protein bar, and handed it to her.

"I'm shocked," Alex said, tearing open the wrapper. "I didn't know you knew pre-packaged food existed."

Liam chuckled as they stepped off the elevator. "Don't

worry. I know how to make those from scratch too."

He pushed open the door to the outside, and paused for a moment. He closed his eyes and breathed in deeply. Alex got the impression that he was breathing in the city itself.

"Okay," he said, "here we go."

Chapter Thirty-One

The team held council around Brant's mattress. He had kept some water and electrolytes down, but his muscles still twitched uncontrollably.

"What if we took him to a hospital in Second City?" Dani asked. "Told them he was screwing around with drugs, got a hold of something..."

Lena pinched the bridge of her nose. "Desert poison isn't something you simply stumble upon. They'd either turn us in or hold Brant until we told them where we got it." She sighed. "I could ask my parents for help," she said slowly. "They're on the Council."

Brant snorted. "They wouldn't help you." Even with his hoarse voice, the disdain was obvious.

"They might," Lena said defensively. "If I could get them to listen for five minutes, they'd probably help us. It's not like we fought about anything important. I just...dropped off the radar."

"They still won't help you." Brant gasped, clutching his stomach. "Look, girls, why don't you just—"

"No," Lena said firmly. "We're not leaving you."

"You could." Brant gulped. "Lena, I—"

Lena helped him sit up to throw up again. When she laid him back down, there was blood on his teeth and in the shallow bowl.

"We don't have time to argue about this," Lena whispered to herself.

Dani took a deep breath. "I know a guy."

"Wait, wait," Brant said, his face gray. "You know a *human* guy?"

Dani shot him a look that would kill him faster than the poison. She turned back to Lena. "He can get us the antidote."

Lena looked from Brant to Dani. She was nearly as pale as Brant, her freckles stark against her skin. They didn't really have a choice.

"I can go alone," Dani offered.

"That's not an option." Lena pointed at Tavi. "If he dies while we're gone..." She trailed off, dread tightening her throat as she thought about Brant dying alone.

Tavi bowed his head. "Don't worry. I won't let him."

Lena knelt next to Brant and opened her mouth to say something—she didn't know what. Finally she shook her head and squeezed his hand tightly. She leaned down and whispered, "Don't go anywhere, okay?"

Brant closed his eyes. "I'll do my best."

Dani didn't say anything, but her fingers were clenched around her ever-present tablet so tightly the casing creaked. She peeled them off long enough to pull Brant's headset out of her pocket and tuck it gently into his ear.

Lena pushed herself to her feet and pulled Dani toward the door. "Lead the way."

Fourth City was just as criminal a sector as Second City, but it was less alive. The apartment buildings were falling apart, the cement walls chipped and the glass windows broken and covered with plastic. There was more of the planet's gray-blue sand than there was pavement, and the weeds that sprouted were scraggly and brown. The few people they passed either hurried by with their chins tucked into jackets or huddled in the shadows, staring out with unfriendly gazes. Dani didn't seem to notice the cold stares they received as they hurried through the maze of broken pavement, but to Lena it felt like having a target taped to her back.

Dani led the way to a slightly sturdier-looking building with a group of muscled teenagers scattered in front. One of them stood as Dani walked up.

"Fowlkes." He sounded surprised. "I didn't think you were coming back."

"Didn't plan on it," Dani said. She shoved her hands in her pockets. Her voice sounded relaxed, but Lena read the tension in the technopath's shoulders. "I need to talk to Kebrice."

The teenager frowned. He looked to be about Dani's age, and Lena wondered if this was someone Dani had known growing up. "You know Kebrice doesn't like strangers," he said, glancing pointedly at Lena.

Lena stiffened. She knew how out of place they must look. Dani with her bright red hair braided out of her face, looking more confident and dangerous than anyone lurking the shadows. Lena, in her tall boots and tailored jacket, chip scar on her hand, clearly high-class.

"I can wait outside." Lena's gut wrenched at the thought. She most assuredly did not want to wait by herself, but if it would get Brant the antidote he needed, she would cope.

"No." Dani lifted her chin. "Lena's not a stranger. She's with me. And Kebrice owes me a favor."

The teenager raised an eyebrow and stepped aside, waving them in. He eyed Lena suspiciously as she passed, probably wondering what business she had with Dani, much less Kebrice.

Lena quietly followed Dani into the apartment building. It was dim inside, the only light coming from windows high on the walls.

"I recognize that name, by the way," Lena whispered, looking at a long flight of rickety steps. "How many of those stairs do we have to climb?"

Dani tested the shaky-looking staircase with one foot. "All of them. Kebrice lives on the top floor." She grabbed the rail and started climbing. "And of course you recognize the name. He's run the black market for the past few orbits. I'm surprised we haven't run into him yet."

"I see," Lena panted, trying to keep up with Dani's steps. For someone who spent most of her time hunched over a tablet, the technopath moved remarkably fast. "I'm more concerned with why he owes you a favor."

"He's my cousin," Dani said simply.

Lena stopped mid-step.

Dani didn't notice until she was a few steps ahead. She turned and looked behind her. "Are you coming or not?" she asked irritably.

Lena shook her head. "Yeah, I'm coming," she said, taking a deep breath and beginning the climb again. "That's information you could've led with."

"You'd never have believed me."

Lena thought about Dani's knowledge of Exordia's underground and the cold pragmatism she sometimes showed. "No, I think I might have." A few steps later, she felt as if she'd caught her breath enough to speak again.

"If he's your cousin, I'm surprised he didn't cause more trouble when Pallagen took you."

Dani glanced over her shoulder. "We're not that close. If I hadn't saved his life when we were kids, we wouldn't have been allowed through the front door."

Great. This plan was going to end badly.

They reached the top of the building—eight stories up— and stopped before a black, metal door. It looked armored, and it was the least shabby thing Lena had seen since entering Fourth City. Dani stood in front of the door, hands shoved into her pockets.

"Do we knock?" Lena asked, eyeing the door warily.

"No," Dani said calmly. "We wait."

Lena was starting to feel nervous when the door finally opened. A man wearing a dark suit held the door open for them. The bulge of a blaster beneath his shoulder didn't inspire confidence in their welcome. Dani wasn't moving, so Lena stepped through the door.

Inside, the apartment was spacious and well-lit, a direct contrast to the shabby building it was housed in. It was thickly carpeted, and it looked like several walls had been knocked down to allow the room to sprawl across a few different apartments. There were a few pieces of comfortable-looking furniture scattered throughout the space in white and slate-blue tones. The entire outside wall was made of glass and looked toward the Sixth City skyline.

There were two men standing in front of the windows. A young man in a business suit with his hands tucked behind his back looked to be private security, judging by the scowl on his face. The other wore trousers and was relaxed, smiling with the confidence of someone in complete control of his surroundings. If Lena had any doubts about his relationship to Dani, his bright red hair would have erased them. He turned toward Dani and smiled genuinely enough, despite what she had said about there being nothing between them.

"Dani!" he said, spreading his arms out. "Welcome back!"

Dani shoved her hands further into her pockets. "Whatever." She looked around the apartment appraisingly. "Where's Gray?"

"Near the food, as always." Kebrice nodded in the direction of the kitchen.

Without further comment or introducing her teammate, Dani made a beeline for the kitchen.

Lena stood silently in the middle of the room, staring after the technopath in disbelief. "Well, all right then," she said, stepping forward. She had been in weirder—and more dangerous—situations. "I'm Lena Ward."

"Are you now?" Kebrice carefully looked her up and down,

then met her eyes. His gaze was challenging, assessing. "I'd heard Dani teamed up with you, but I didn't believe it."

Lena blinked, unsure if she should take the blunt observation as an insult or not. Apparently red hair wasn't the only trait Dani and Kebrice shared. Lena smirked.

"What?" Kebrice asked, his eyes narrowing.

"You really are her cousin, aren't you?"

There was a short pause, then Kebrice laughed. "Our family can be very... straightforward." He relaxed, and Lena found herself relaxing too.

"Very." Lena looked over to where Dani had disappeared. "Who's Gray?"

"My cat," Kebrice said, waving Lena toward a comfortable-looking couch and settling himself into a high-backed armchair. Lena sat and tried hard not to compare it to the lumpy piece of furniture in their apartment. "But I'm guessing she didn't drag you here because she missed Gray."

Lena thought of Brant and instantly sobered. "One of our associates was poisoned on a mission. Dani told me you could get us the antidote."

Kebrice glanced at the young man in the suit before responding. "Of course, we can help you obtain whatever you need," he said. "But why should we?"

"Dani said you owed her a favor."

"Two favors, actually." Dani walked into the living area, a gray, purring cat curled in her arms.

Kebrice leaned back in his chair and crossed his legs, folding his hands over his knees. "So I do. And you're willing to trade both your favors for this?"

Dani frowned. Lena remembered that Kebrice, all resemblance to Dani aside, ran one of the most lucrative and ruthless black markets in Exordia.

"I am," Dani said. "Help me with this, and you're clear of me for good."

The corner of Kebrice's mouth twitched upward at Dani's statement. Lena didn't think he'd been trying to get clear of his cousin at all. Get rid of the favors, perhaps, but he didn't seem unhappy to see her.

"You're welcome in my home anytime, Dani," he said patronizingly.

Dani bristled at his tone, but Lena was used to being condescended to—sometimes even by Dani. "Please. We don't have much time. If you have other terms, tell us so we can come to an agreement."

Kebrice cocked an eyebrow at her, but Lena squarely met his gaze. *I'm dangerous too,* she tried to project. *I face Pallagen on their own ground. What scary things have* you *done lately?*

"Only one other term," Kebrice said, his eyes never leaving Lena's face. "I require that you win."

For a moment, his cheerful mask cracked. Lena saw a flash of anger cross his face, and she knew he was more concerned for the technopath than Dani thought. Dani had cut herself off from her family and friends, and Lena supposed this was the only way Kebrice felt he could protect his cousin.

"Accepted." She shook the hand Kebrice held out.

He nodded to his assistant, who silently held out a hand. Dani passed the assistant the med scanner with Brant's blood sample and followed him to the opposite side of the room, presumably to get the antidote. She was still carrying Gray. She hadn't stopped running her long fingers through his hair. Lena wondered idly if it would be practical to get a cat for the technopath.

"I'm glad she has you," Kebrice said quietly, breaking into Lena's thoughts. "Dani may not care about family, but I do."

Lena snorted. "I dragged her into this. I'm not sure I'm the best thing that could've happened to her."

Kebrice smiled. "Dani never has taken anything sitting down. She would've gone after Pallagen on her own, eventually. With your help, she might live through it."

Lena's chin came up, and her shoulders straightened. "She will if I have anything to say about it."

Dani walked back in and reluctantly set the cat on the back of the couch. She scowled at Kebrice. "Thanks," she said grudgingly, holding up a small vial.

Lena frowned. "Will that be enough?"

"It better be." Dani glared at the silent assistant.

Kebrice laughed. "It was good to see you too, Dani. Please, don't be a stranger."

Dani sniffed. "See you around, Kebrice." She turned and walked out the door.

Lena winced. "Thank you," she said apologetically. She held out her hand again, and Kebrice shook it.

"I didn't say this," he said, "but if you need anything else, I really do owe Dani a few favors."

Lena forced a smile. Just what she needed: the help of Exordia's most wanted criminal, next to herself. "Don't worry.

I'll try not to cash in on them."

She followed Dani out the door and down the long flight of stairs. The technopath was walking fast, the vial clutched tightly in her hand. They were almost back to where they'd stashed the gravcar when they heard the whine of an energy rifle charging.

"Please remain where you are," a projected voice said. "Do not resist, and you will not be harmed."

Dani and Lena took one glance at the Enforcement patrol vehicle cruising through the air behind them and bolted.

They didn't separate. They probably should have in order to shake their pursuers, but Dani knew her way around Fourth City and Lena didn't. Dani dove into a narrow alleyway and started running. Lena followed. They wove through a maze of alleys, deeper and deeper into Fourth City, but always away from Kebrice's headquarters. The last thing they needed was the wrath of a crime lord.

Lena was out of breath, her chest aching, and she could still hear the sounds of pursuit behind them. The cruiser was slowed by the narrow streets, but it wouldn't be long before Enforcement found them.

They slid into an alley between two tall apartment buildings. "What happened?" Lena demanded of no one in particular.

"Someone turned us in," Dani said bleakly. "There's a pretty sizable reward on our heads."

Lena closed her eyes and shook her head, trying to think through the adrenaline. "Well, we're not getting out of Fourth City. They'll have it blockaded."

"Yeah." Dani looked around thoughtfully, trying to choose

which alleyway to take next.

They would find no help here. Lena felt the first edges of panic grip her. "Look, one of us has to get back to Brant." She thought of the ex-soldier dying alone with Tavi, wondering what happened to the team he'd sworn to protect. "I'll lead Enforcement in a different direction. Maybe you can get back to your cousin. Maybe once they've caught me they'll stop looking for you, and he'll help you get back to Second City—"

"No!" Dani interrupted harshly. "That's a terrible plan!"

"It's the only plan!" Lena drew herself up. "Anyway, I'm in charge!"

"I'm not leaving you!" Dani shouted.

"You have to!"

"Or," a third voice said, "you could come with me."

Lena and Dani jumped and turned. One of the side doors in the apartment building was held open by a young woman.

It was Arya.

"Follow me," the girl ordered.

Lena's first instinct was to ignore Arya. With Enforcement chasing her, the last thing she wanted to do was drag someone she'd rescued back into Pallagen's sights. But the sound of patrol gravcars behind them convinced Lena otherwise, and she allowed herself to be pulled through the dark doorway. Arya led them down a long hallway, their heavy breathing echoing off the close walls.

Lena slowly caught her breath. "Arya," she called quietly. "Arya, listen, I appreciate this, but we can't let you put yourself in danger—"

The girl turned, her dark eyes flashing in the glow of the overhead lights. "You're not 'letting' me do anything," she said. There was a challenge in her voice. "You're not in charge of me."

Lena didn't have a good answer, and Dani was glaring at her, so she shut up and followed.

Arya led them up two levels, down dimly-lit hallways, and back down another level. The windowless corridors were cluttered with trash and debris, and paint peeled off the cement walls. Lena was thoroughly confused. She hoped Enforcement, wherever they were, were just as lost as she was.

Finally, Arya let them through a door and into an apartment. The room was small and dingy. Clothes were strewn across the back of the stained couch, data discs lay stacked in a haphazard pile on a low table, and takeout containers were scattered across every surface.

"Make yourselves at home," Arya said, motioning around the tiny room. "Just...clear a spot wherever you want to sit." She closed and bolted the door.

Dani was already poking through the apartment, but Lena turned to face their host.

The last time she'd seen Arya, she was skeletal and sickly. Now, her cheeks were plump, and there was a defiant light in her eyes. Lena's heart sank. She'd tried to get Arya away from Pallagen so the girl could start over, not so she could fight back.

"Arya," she tried again. "We can't hide here."

Arya held up a hand. "I know what you're going to say: that I don't owe you, that you don't want anyone else involved. But you don't get to decide anymore." She crossed her arms. "You started something, Lena Ward, and you need help finishing it."

Lena saw her own stubbornness reflected in Arya's face, and sighed. "All right. But Enforcement will probably search this building."

Arya nose wrinkled as she smiled. "They're welcome to try." She turned and followed Dani into the kitchen.

Lena sighed and rubbed the back of her neck, frustration evident in the motion. Frustrated with herself, with being stuck here while Brant was dying. That Brant had been hurt on her watch, that she'd put him in danger in the first place. Her stomach roiled. *It's my fault*, she thought again, pressing clenched fists to her eyes.

Arya tapped her on the elbow, and Lena jumped. The girl held out a plastic mug of steaming tea.

"Thanks," Lena said softly, taking it.

Arya perched on the back of the couch, pushing aside a pile of sweaters. "What brings you to Fourth City? This is the last place I'd expect to see someone like you. Too many people out for quick money, not enough people looking out for each other."

Lena raised an eyebrow. "And yet, you live here." She settled gingerly on the edge of the couch, her hands clutching the mug. "I'm sorry."

Arya folded up her knees beneath her chin. "Sorry for what?"

"For this." Lena gestured at the apartment. "I tried to give you a second chance, but it doesn't look like it's turning out well."

Arya shrugged. "It's better than other places I've been."

Lena grimaced as an image of the empty lab they'd found Arya in passed through her memory.

"Very true." She took a sip of the tea. It was strong and sweet. It wasn't coffee, but it warmed her insides and helped her relax a little.

"So, Lena Ward. Pallagen isn't in Fourth City, so what are you doing here?"

Lena hesitated, not sure how much to reveal. "I...have a man down."

"Ah. Kebrice." Arya nodded. "He's all right, as long as you don't cross him."

"Yeah." Lena ran a hand through her hair, impatient to be on her way. "When do you think Enforcement will quit searching?"

"Not until they've covered every part of the City," Arya said. She stared at the cup in Lena's hand until Lena took another sip. It was good tea—the kind from Seventh City. Lena felt unexpectedly homesick. "It'll take them most of the night to search every building, but you should be able to slip out after that."

Lena's eyes narrowed. "In the meantime, how do we keep them from finding us?"

The stunner was still in her waistband, and though there were fewer AIs to work with in Fourth City, she was sure Dani could manipulate them. If all else failed, she and Dani could fight their way out. It would draw a lot of attention, though, and a few Enforcement officers would probably be killed. They might stay ahead of Enforcement long enough to get back to Brant, but then they'd be running for their lives. Lena didn't like their odds of being able to stay under Pallagen's radar after that.

Arya grinned. "Have you ever heard of the Old Earth shell game?"

Chapter Thirty-Two

The safe house wasn't far from Alex and Liam's apartment building. It made sense. If Keagan used it to keep an eye on his brother, he'd need to be close by.

It was a home, not an apartment—one of the old, square-shaped, plastic-sided homes Old Earth colonists had erected when they first built Exordia. The fresh paint and desert plants along the walkway gave the house a well-kept façade, but inside it was dark, the air musty and stale.

Liam headed straight for the kitchen, turning on every light he passed.

"There's one bedroom," he called back. "I'll take the couch."

Alex surveyed the room with a critical eye. "I know you're trying to be a gentleman, but I think I should be the first person someone meets when they walk through the door."

Liam poked his head back into the room. "Huh. You're probably right." He looked at Alex carefully. "You should change before Keagan gets here."

Alex cocked her head, unsure of what he was talking about. Liam gestured toward her arm. Alex looked down and realized her sleeve was stiff with blood. She stared at it, her stomach churning.

"Yeah," she said quietly. "I probably should."

Liam opened and closed his mouth before he figured out what to say. "I'm sorry you had to do that."

Alex was silent for a moment. Was she upset at her actions? It was the first thing she had done since waking up in rehab that felt natural to her. She had been protecting herself as well as defending her friend.

"I'm not sorry," she said, rubbing the dried blood with her fingers. Her eyes lingered briefly on her sleeve before meeting Liam's again, afraid of what she would read in his face. What would he think of someone whose natural instinct was violence?

Liam looked serious but not upset. He crossed his arms and gazed at Alex, as if he could read her mind. "I don't know who you were before, but you can't have been that bad."

"How do you know?" Alex's hands clenched into fists. "You have no idea who I was. I could've been a serial killer for all we know. I..." Alex looked down at her hands, her shoulders sagging under the weight of the unknown. "I don't know what I've done. I don't know what I can do."

Liam stepped forward and wrapped his fingers around Alex's hands, keeping them from fretting at the bloodstain. "Pallagen can only do so much, Alex. The human personality is extremely complex. No one could completely erase it. Besides," he shrugged, "what does it matter who you were?"

Alex tipped her head back to meet Liam's gaze. His eyes were full of compassion.

"You get to decide who you are now." Liam squeezed her hand. "Pallagen has no control over that."

Alex was silent. She desperately wanted to believe Liam, to believe that what Pallagen had done didn't matter. She wanted to see herself as an innocent victim, someone worthy of Liam's acceptance. But she'd killed that Pallagen guard on reflex, without thinking. Like she was used to it.

Whoever she was, her slate was anything but clean.

"I have blood on my hands, Liam," she whispered.

"Maybe," he said, "but whose? You stepped up to defend me without hesitation. Wherever your instincts came from, they don't make you a bad person."

Liam walked back into the kitchen and left Alex to think by herself.

Liam managed to coerce Alex into helping with the food. As always.

"I'm miserable at this," she said, standing in front of the stove with sauce all over her shirt and a pan lid in her hand.

"No, you're not." He shoved a spoonful of Alex's sauce into his mouth and tried valiantly not to grimace. "You're just...it's just...you're not miserable at it."

Suddenly, the ridiculousness of the situation struck her. Running from Pallagen. Cooking dinner. Standing in a safe house, covered in sauce. Alex couldn't help it. She began to laugh uncontrollably. She put the lid down and leaned forward, hands resting on the countertop, eyes tearing up and her shoulders shaking.

Liam gave her a funny look, and Alex took a deep breath. "Okay," she said, wiping her damp eyes, "I'm going to scrape dinner off my shirt. You should probably make something else to eat."

Liam looked so relieved that Alex almost started laughing again. "Yeah, I should." He grinned. "This is the first time I'm dragging you home to meet my family, and we want to make a good impression."

Alex smacked him with a towel. "Whatever," she said, leaving the kitchen. "Just hurry. I'm starving!"

She rummaged through her backpack and pulled out another shirt. She hesitated befre grabbing the blaster as well, tucking it in the back of her waistband. She tossed her sauce-covered shirt in the bathroom sink and turned the water on. Glancing up, she studied her reflection. She was pale, and her long, frizzy hair hung loose around her face. Despite her laughter, there were deep lines of tension around her mouth, and she tried to force some of the worry out of her face. She trusted Liam enough to show him how unsettled she was, but she'd never met his brother.

She was wringing water out of the shirt when she heard the door opening. Of course, someone *would* show up while her hands were soaked. She left the shirt in the sink and rubbed her right hand on her pants before reaching for her blaster.

"Keagan!" she heard Liam say, and she relaxed. "Look, I know you said never to bring anyone here, but she saved my life—and I'm aware she's not really my type, but you never did approve of my type, so if you could please not fight with her at first sight that would be great."

Alex rolled her eyes and grinned. She'd better get out there and rescue Liam before he tripped over his own excuses.

Still smiling, she walked into the room and raised a damp hand in greeting. "Hi, you must be—"

There was a blaster in her face. Alex froze.

"...Keagan."

Chapter Thirty-Three

Lena and Dani spent the rest of the night playing musical apartments.

A few minutes after Arya had brought Lena tea, someone knocked on the door and, without waiting for an answer, opened it and poked his head in. His eyes widened at the sight of Lena's stunner pointed at his face, but he leaned farther into the room and shouted Arya's name.

"Enforcement is here," Arya said, a hand on Dani's elbow. "Time to go."

"Go where?" Lena demanded, eyeing the newcomer. He looked even younger than Arya.

"Look, Lena, it's nice that you don't want to endanger other people, but now is not the time to fuss about that. This is Gunn. He'll take you to your next stop."

Lena hesitated, but Dani reached out and touched her arm reassuringly. "I grew up in this City. I'll know if they're up to something."

Lena followed Dani and Gunn out of the apartment. After giving them a jaunty wave and grin, Arya closed the door.

"Will she be all right?" Lena asked, looking behind her at the closed door.

"Oh sure," Gunn waved a hand dismissively. He looked like he belonged in Second City rather than Fourth with his black clothing and neon sweat band. "Enforcement is only interested in you two. Once they know you're not with Arya, they'll leave her alone."

Gunn led them out of the dim, winding hallways and into the maze of alleys. They crossed a few intersections, but no one stopped or even seemed to notice them. Gunn knocked on a beat-up door, and it opened, swinging inward. Evidently, the building wasn't controlled by an AI. Lena glanced at Dani, but she didn't seem bothered. *She's used to this*, Lena thought. She was the one out of place.

The girl behind the door couldn't have been more than thirteen orbits. Her features resembled those of their guide, and Lena guessed they were siblings. "Enforcement already searched this building," she said. She was staring wide-eyed at Lena.

Lena shifted, uncomfortable with the girl's obvious hero-worship. "They'll come back when they don't find us anywhere else."

"We're not the only ones Arya has recruited to help." Gunn whispered, motioning them through the door. "Hurry up. I don't know everyone in this building. For all I know, the person who turned you in could be here."

As if startled by the thought, Dani hurried after Gunn. As much as Lena dreaded being caught by Pallagen, she knew the technopath's fear had to be worse.

They entered another tiny apartment, this one cleaner and showing obvious signs of a responsible adult in residence. Lena shuddered at the thought of explaining who she was and why she was here to a parent, but they proved to be absent for the time being.

"It'll be a while before you have to move again," Gunn said. "Find a seat. Maisy is cooking dinner." He looked at his sister and grinned. "Or, y'know, unboxing it."

Maisy stuck out her tongue.

"I'm not really hungry, but thank you," Lena said. Her stomach was twisted in too many knots to consider food. She immediately regretted her words when Maisy's face fell.

"Well, I'm starving!" Dani said, perking up more than she had since Brant was hurt. "Can I help you with the food?"

Maisy grinned and disappeared into the kitchen, her brown ponytail flipping side-to-side behind her. Dani shot Lena a dirty look before following her.

Lena sighed and looked at Gunn apologetically. "I'm sorry. I didn't mean to offend your sister. It's been a long night."

Gunn nodded, accepting the excuse. "When Arya comm-ed me for help, she told me you were here to see Kebrice. Whatever you needed from him, it must be bad to risk coming into Fourth City."

"It is. How will we know when to move again?"

Gunn shrugged and plopped down onto the couch. "There are people watching the Enforcement officers. They'll let us know when it's safe to leave."

Lena raised an eyebrow, not sure if she was reassured or impressed. "Arya has quite the organization, apparently."

Gunn grinned. "She showed up here a few cycles ago. None of us liked her. She acted too good for us, she had a chip scar, and she...I don't know, she looked *hunted*." Gunn looked toward the kitchen at his sister. "But Maisy liked her, and after a while, everybody else started to. Everyone in Fourth City has a past they'd rather not talk about. When she told us about Pallagen, and how she escaped..."

Lena frowned as Gunn's voice trailed off. Were all of the victims they saved so easy to spot? She started to respond when Maisy and Dani walked into the room carrying reheated food in plastic takeout boxes.

Dani shoved a box into her hands, but Lena just stared at it. After a moment, she placed the food on the floor and leaned back on the couch, covering her eyes with one hand. She tried not to think about Brant, about the time they were wasting waiting for Enforcement to stop their search.

Several minutes later, she felt Dani settle on the couch next to her. Lena looked up. Maisy and Gunn had disappeared into the kitchen. Lena hoped she hadn't hurt Maisy's feelings by refusing to eat, but she'd have offended the girl even more if she'd thrown up afterward.

"I'm going to call Brant," Dani muttered. "I don't want him trying to crawl off and find us."

"Tavi won't let him." Lena rubbed her forehead. "But you're right. We should let them know what happened."

There was silence for a few seconds, broken by Maisy and Gunn's voices arguing good-naturedly from the kitchen.

"This bothers you, doesn't it?" Dani asked. "What Maisy and Gunn and Arya are doing."

Lena didn't answer right away. *This is what I wanted... isn't it? I wanted people to pay attention and react to what*

Pallagen was doing. I wanted them to stand up for themselves and those around them. I didn't want people to die. Dani was silent as Lena tried to give voice to her thoughts.

"I wanted...I don't know, a lawsuit, maybe," she said at last. "I wanted to shut Pallagen down. I didn't mean to start a revolution."

Dani snorted disdainfully. "Pallagen controls half the city. How exactly did you plan on stopping them *without* a revolution?" Lena didn't answer. "Besides," Dani went on, pulling out her earpiece, "I'd hardly call a gang of kids in Fourth City a 'revolution.'" She fiddled with her tablet, pulling up the line to contact Brant.

Lena shifted on the couch. A bunch of Fourth City kids might not seem like a threat, but neither did three people in an old apartment. Just because they weren't supposed to be able to make a difference didn't mean they wouldn't succeed.

Brant didn't answer any of Dani's attempts to call him. After a few tries, she threw her tablet on the couch, anger and worry warring on her freckled face.

Lena tapped her fingers on the arm of the couch, and she kept glancing toward the door, frustration rising within her. She stumbled through a few awkward attempts at conversation with Maisy and Gunn, but the siblings sensed the growing nervousness in their guests and left them alone.

A few hours later, they were shuffled to another apartment, this one owned by a gray-haired couple that tried to feed them watery Fourth City tea and stale cookies. Before the water boiled, they were escorted to their last apartment, inhabited by an iron-faced woman with sandy hair and light eyes.

"You'll leave from here," she said, her voice carrying the barest trace of an accent. "Enforcement lifted the blockade when they pulled out of Fourth City. Still, you'll have to be careful."

Lena nodded slowly. "I..." She paused, not sure where to begin. If Enforcement ever found out what these people had done, they—and all of Fourth City—would suffer for it. "Thank you," she said, meeting the woman's eyes.

The iron-faced woman stared back at her. "You are not the first people Pallagen has victimized," she said softly.

The way she spoke led Lena to believe that Arya wasn't the only person in Fourth City hiding from their past with Pallagen.

"No," Lena said, lifting her chin. "But I hope we're the last."

The woman nodded. "Revelator go with you," she said as she opened her door.

Lena gave her an odd look as they left. Two people who followed the Revelator in the past few days. That felt more than coincidental. She shook her head and concentrated on slinking back home like the criminals they were.

Once they were out of Fourth City, they caught a gravtrain. Dani interfaced with the cameras to make sure no one spotted them, but it was the middle of the day, and the gravtrain was too crowded for them to draw any attention. Once they made it to Second City, Lena resisted the urge to run back to their apartment, choosing instead to lead Dani through the most deserted parts of the sector.

Tavi was waiting for them just inside the apartment door. His face was tense, but he nodded at the question in Lena's eyes.

Brant was barely breathing. His face was waxy and there was blood on his lips, but he was still alive. Dani's hands

shook as she handled the vial of antivenin, so Lena took it
from her, slipped it into an injector, and measured out the
dose. She jabbed the needle into Brant's thigh, regretting the
small sting that would add to his pain.

There was nothing left to do but wait. Tavi wandered into
the kitchen, and Lena was grateful for the illusion of privacy.

Dani curled up by Brant's head, two fingers on the pulse
point in his neck, holding the med scanner with her other hand.
Lena slumped against the wall, her head tilted back and eyes
closed, listening to the uneasy sound of Brant's raspy breathing.

"Do you pray?" Dani asked suddenly, not looking up from
the scanner.

Lena shifted. "To who?"

"I don't know. Anyone." Dani shrugged. "The Revelator,
maybe."

Lena leaned forward in surprise. "Do you?"

Dani met Lena's gaze, her eyes serious. "When Pallagen
captured me, it took me a long time to pray. At first it wasn't
so bad. They were feeding me, and I had a warm place to
sleep. But when they discovered I was compatible with their
technopath project..." Dani swallowed and looked down at the
scanner. "I prayed a lot after that."

"To the Revelator?"

"Yeah." Dani fussed with the blanket covering Brant. "I
prayed that he would get me out."

"Did he?"

"I don't know." Dani scooted closer to Lena and hugged
her knees to her chest. "They still made me a technopath,
but something went wrong. They didn't lock me down like

they should have, and I was able to escape."

Lena nodded slowly. This was the first time Dani had opened up about what happened to her, and she resisted the urge to ask Dani how she had escaped or what exactly Pallagen had done.

"Aren't you angry, though? That the Revelator, if he was listening to you, still let you be turned into a technopath?"

"If I wasn't a technopath," Dani said softly, "I wouldn't have you two."

Lena couldn't find the words to respond, so she simply nodded and edged closer to Dani. Hesitantly, she put an arm around her. Dani leaned in and rested her head on Lena's shoulder.

"I'm sorry that happened to you," Lena said. "But I'm not sorry you're here."

Neither of them moved until Brant's breathing eased and he slipped into sleep instead of unconsciousness.

Chapter Thirty-Four

"Keagan!" Liam yelled, reaching for the blaster in his brother's hand. Keagan shook him off and pushed him back.

"Who is she?" Keagan's voice was deep, cold, and calculating.

Alex lowered her hand to her side, fingers instinctively clenching into a fist. She forced her voice to remain steady. "I'm Alex Kleric. I lived next door to Liam."

"Seriously, Keagan, I've been talking about her for *weeks*."

Keagan's eyes hadn't left Alex since she walked into the kitchen. It was difficult for her not to react. The same instinct that had screamed *danger!* when she saw the Pallagen guards was blaring a warning in her mind, but she didn't think fighting Liam's brother in his own kitchen would help ease the situation.

"That's not Alex Kleric!" Keagan's voice left no room for argument.

Surprised, Liam and Alex glanced at each other. Liam shifted uncomfortably from one foot to the other. "About that..."

The tension in the room broke. Keagan's eyes grew wider,

and indignation chased some of the cold anger from his face. "Wait, you know who she is?"

"Yes. No! Alex, help me out here."

A little hard with a blaster in my face, she wanted to say, but she took a deep breath. "Neither of us knows," she said slowly. She forced her fingers to unclench. "I woke up in a hospital a few cycles ago with no memory of who I was or what had happened to me. Alex Kleric was the identity assigned to me."

The blaster wasn't moving, but Keagan's eyes grew thoughtful. He shook his head. "I don't believe you."

Alex shrugged. She felt her stunner pressing hard against her spine. "Irrelevant. If you point that blaster at me much longer, you won't be conscious enough to worry about who I am."

Revelator. Where had *that* come from?

Keagan's shoulders stiffened at her words, and his grip on the blaster tightened.

"Wait!" Liam grabbed Keagan's sleeve. "Please, can we just, I don't know, sit on the couch and talk for a while? Also, the barely-passable sauce Alex made is burning."

"Hey," Alex said, playing along with his attempt at normalcy. "It's better than it was last time."

"True." Liam jostled his brother's arm again. "Last time it was *horrific.*"

Keagan's arm tensed against Liam's hand. Alex slid one foot back half an inch, ready to move if he so much as twitched a finger. Keagan caught the gesture, but instead of reacting he nodded once and lowered his blaster.

Alex let out a long breath and held out a hand. "Shall we try again?" she said. "I'm Alex Kleric, Liam's next-door neighbor."

Keagan took her hand and shook it slowly. "I'm Keagan, and I'd like to know how you—"

"It's *ruined!*" Liam wailed. Startled, Alex and Keagan turned toward the kitchen, where Liam held up a scorched pan. "I'll have to start over."

He looked so heartbroken that Alex started laughing again. *Revelator,* she thought. *What would I do without him?* The thought warmed her and made her remember Liam's words from earlier.

"Wait," she said between giggles. "You've been talking about me for *weeks*?"

Liam fussed over the food on the stove while Alex fidgeted in her seat at the table, trying to ignore Keagan's stare.

Keagan's eyes locked on her bruised knuckles. "I'm assuming you ran into trouble, since you're here in the first place."

"My fault." Alex grimaced. "Pallagen was looking for me."

Keagan glared at her. "Pallagen was looking for you, and you led them to my brother?"

"No." Alex lifted her chin defensively. Keagan looked like he wanted to pull his blaster out again.

"I found her file," Liam interrupted, shoving a plate of food at each of them. Neither of them started eating. "At least, I found Officer Alex Kleric's file. It was a fake."

Keagan blinked. "So why do you keep using the name?"

"I don't have another one," Alex answered. "Like I said— woke up in a hospital with no memories, and they told me my name was Alex."

Keagan frowned. "Which hospital?"

"The rehab center in Sixth City."

Keagan's shoulders slumped. "Oh."

Alex frowned. "What?"

"It's a Pallagen facility," Liam explained.

"I knew that. So...?" Alex prompted.

"You don't know anything about yourself?" Keagan asked. There was a look on his face Alex couldn't quite interpret. Wariness. Fear. Despair, perhaps.

"I'm sorry, I don't."

Keagan swallowed. "I think I might be able to help with that."

Alex laughed, short and sharp. "You had a blaster to my head ten minutes ago. Why should I believe anything you tell me?"

"I thought you were...I don't know. A spy. A clone. An AI. Something Pallagen made."

Ice curled up Alex's spine. Her hands started shaking, and Liam reached out and covered them with his own.

"Why?" she demanded. "Do you know who I am?"

"Yes," Keagan said slowly, "I think I do. And...I'm sorry."

Chapter Thirty-Five

It took a single call to one of Brant's Enforcement contacts to secure Tavi's departure from Exordia.

"Thank you for your help," Lena said to Tavi as he stood by the door, ready to leave. She looked at Brant, still pale, but sitting upright at the table arguing with Dani.

Tavi smiled. "I'm not sure I did much."

Lena shook her head. "You were the only one that prayed. I'm not sure if it helped, but thank you."

"It was the least I could do." Tavi held out a hand. "I'm sure you never need help, Lena Ward, but if you do, I would be honored to help in any way I can."

Lena smiled and shook his hand. "You remember how to get to the rendezvous?"

Tavi smirked. "I snuck in, remember?"

"You got caught," Lena reminded him.

"True." Tavi said as he moved into the hallway. "Don't worry. The Revelator will protect me." He waved farewell as Lena closed the door.

Lena stared at the door for a moment, then shook her

head. "He was a little weird, but he might've been on to something." She turned and met Brant's shadowed eyes. "We got very lucky this time."

"You want to test our luck again?" Dani asked, holding up her tablet. "I found where Pallagen is storing information about the Dallusin."

Lena stepped over to the table and snatched the tablet out of her hands. "What?"

"Tavi told me what to look for." Dani leaned forward. "If we can release that information, we can prove that Pallagen and Enforcement are fighting Exordians."

"The Dallusin aren't Exordian, Dani-girl," Brant said.

"No. But they're not monsters, either. I'm not even sure they're a threat. Tavi certainly didn't seem to be."

Lena put the tablet down. "We could do two things at once," she said thoughtfully. "Blow Pallagen's cover by releasing what we already know about them as well as any information we find in that lab. That would expose Enforcement too."

No one said anything.

"It's worth a try," Brant said after a long pause.

"Taking out Pallagen *and* Enforcement?" Dani shook her head. "That seems too good to be true."

"It does. But can we live with ourselves if we don't try?" No one needed to answer. "We hit this info bank next. We can decide what information to release after we have it."

"I think Brant should've gotten stuck on the roof this time. I'm dying up here."

Lena rolled her eyes. It was amazing how Dani managed to convey petulance over a comm link.

"I'm no good on the roof, Dani-girl," Brant answered.

"Yeah, but you're recovering!"

"Children, please," Lena said soothingly. She stopped at a crosswalk with a small knot of pedestrians waiting to cross the busy Seventh City street. "Dani, what do you see?"

"The top floor is clear," Dani said. *"But there's something weird going on here, Lena."*

"Of course it's weird. It's Pallagen."

"No." Dani's frustration carried clearly over the comm. *"The building seems…off somehow."*

"Okay," Lena said. "We'll take it slowly. Brant, start on the first floor and work your way up." She had more instructions to give, but at the moment she was simply standing in the sunshine, talking on her mobile like everyone else. If she voiced specifics about the job, she would draw attention to herself.

Lena stepped closer to the crosswalk, tapping her boot impatiently and looking up at the building her team was in. Her palms were damp with sweat, and she readjusted her grip on her mobile. She didn't like the idea of raiding a Pallagen facility in the middle of the day, but this was an info bank with only a few employees on record. Lena wanted to make sure a lab tech was present to help them search for what they needed, so a daytime raid was necessary. "I'll meet you inside."

"Found the stairwell," Brant said. *"There's a key pad outside the door. Enforcement-level security clearance code.*

I'll meet you on the third floor."

Lena crossed the street. "All right, Dani, let him in."

Dani was silent as she worked. Lena walked into the building through the front door. She smiled and nodded at the receptionist, pointing toward the elevator and holding up her hacked access card. The receptionist waved her past. Once Lena was out of her sight, she slipped into the stairwell to avoid guards or former coworkers.

"Found the entrance to the lab," Brant said. *"Hurry up."*

"You know, for a soldier, you don't show much respect."

"Mind-wiped," Brant sing-songed.

"Maybe they wiped too much," Dani retorted.

Brant sputtered. Lena smiled as she exited the stairwell on the third floor. Halfway down the hall, Brant stood next to a propped-open door.

"Huh," Lena said as she joined him. "Dani's right. This does feel weird."

Pallagen was a master at hiding in plain sight, putting their faith in their secrecy and digital security. But if this was where Pallagen was keeping sensitive files, there should have been a manned security checkpoint inside the door.

"Want to leave?"

It wasn't too late to back out, but Lena didn't want to lose the chance to gain a real advantage over Pallagen. "No. But be careful."

Brant nodded, and Dani said nothing, which was as good as agreement. The technopath never hesitated to let it be known when she disagreed with something.

The long hallway beyond the door was eerily silent. Brant

held his blaster in both hands, keeping it pointed in front of them. Lena shed her coat, revealing the protective vest beneath it. She drew her blaster and set it on stun.

Brant paused before another door and gave her a questioning glance. She nodded, and Brant swiped his own hacked card through the access panel, opening the door.

The room was empty but for the long tables filled with computers. Lena frowned. At this time of day, there should have been *someone* in the lab. "Dani, how do we look?"

"*Good so far.*" There was something off about Dani's voice. "*Lena, I—*" Dani's voice cut off with a sharp hiss of pain.

Brant stiffened. "Something's wrong."

"Go get her." She stepped away from the door, gesturing toward the computers. "I'll find the files."

Brant shouldered his rifle and ran down the hallway.

"Talk to me," Lena murmured. She stepped to a screen and began flicking through files, looking for anything she could find about the Dallusin.

"*Halfway there, boss,*" Brant reported, panting as he hurried up the long staircase to the roof.

"*It's my mind,*" Dani said, her voice strained. "*Lena, it's like something's attacking it—*"

Lena stopped short. "*What*?"

Another strangled gasp came over the line. "*I think they know we're here. You and Brant need to leave.*"

"*Not without you, Dani-girl,*" Brant growled.

Lena set her jaw and shut down the screen. Brant was right. They needed to get to Dani, but, Revelator, she didn't want to lose both of them at once. Her gut knotted as she ran toward the stairway, boots pounding in time with her pulse.

"Hurry up! I'll meet you halfway down."

"*No!*" Dani gasped, the anger and pain clear in her voice.

Brant didn't argue with her. "*Watch your back, boss.*"

"Keep breathing, Dani," she said as she heard the technopath start to hyperventilate. She pushed open the stairwell door. "Just keep breathing."

"*Can't,*" Dani said. "*Hurts too much. Can't think.*"

Lena felt the icy fingertips of panic grip her chest. She'd been prepared for guards. Weapons. She hadn't been prepared to hear her friend being ripped apart from the inside.

Focus! She shook herself. *React later. Dani needs you right now.* "Talk to me, Dani. Tell me what you're feeling."

Dani groaned. "*It's like...I can't think. Like someone flipped a switch...cut off the signal.*"

Lena stopped, one hand on the railing. "So they're not attacking you. They're blinding you."

Dani didn't answer, but her heaving breaths continued to filter over the comm. Lena imagined her huddled on the roof, knees drawn up to her face, hands clenching her hair. She heard the pounding of Brant's boots on the stairs.

Lena closed her eyes, and for a split second, the word *trap* flitted through her mind.

Then the world exploded into flame.

Lena felt cold tile against her skin and smelled the sharp, acrid scent of a chemical explosion long before she managed to open her eyes. When she did, all she saw was white. She blinked a few times, trying to make the hazy, wavering shapes come into focus. She fought nausea as she turned her head to gain her bearings. Her forehead throbbed and blood dripped into her eyes, but Lena managed to push herself to her knees.

Brant knelt a few feet away, hands cuffed behind his back. He was staring at her with a distant, glazed look. Lena closed her eyes. One of her knees wouldn't hold her weight, and there was a sharp ache in her ribs. She pressed a hand to her chest and tried to breathe through the pain.

"They're awake," someone said.

Lena didn't open her eyes. She knew they would be surrounded by more soldiers than she could ever hope to fight.

Dani's not here.

The haze of unconsciousness fled and adrenaline flooded her veins, banishing the pain enough for her to think clearly. She looked up and watched as a sea of orange and gray uniforms parted to allow a white-suited man to pass. His indifferent eyes stared down at her.

Lena wanted to stand up, to face him as an equal rather than a failure kneeling on the cold tile in defeat. But her knee throbbed. It would send her back to the floor if she tried to stand. She settled for glaring.

"Lena Ward," the man said, hands stuffed in his pockets. "I've wanted to meet you for a long time."

"Where's the rest of my team?"

"Dani Fowlkes is dead," the man said.

The words hit her like the blast from a rifle. Reeling, Lena looked at Brant. He'd been on the roof by the time the building exploded. He would know what had happened to the technopath. He was staring vacantly at her, and he shook his head sorrowfully.

"I lost her." His voice was hoarse and broken. "I lost her, Lena. I couldn't get to her in time."

Lena swayed. *This isn't happening. Revelator. Not Dani.* Her eyes pleaded with Brant to tell her that this was all a nightmare, but Brant was silent, no protesting or angry words. She wanted to hide, wanted to lay down and sleep, and wake up to find it was some horrible hallucination, but the blood on her face and leg convinced her that she was living her deepest fear.

"You won't get away with this," she said. Her mind raced, trying to form a plan, trying to find a way out. "You didn't just make a few people disappear. You blew up a building. People are going to notice that. They'll notice *you*."

"True." The man snapped his fingers, and one of the security guards pushed a chair over to him. He sat in it and leaned toward her. His face was smooth and composed, his hair slicked back. He was the exact opposite of Lena, kneeling bloodied and broken on the floor. "But I have a convenient criminal, currently missing in action, to blame this on."

Of course they were blaming it on her. She shouldn't have expected anything else. And Exordia would believe Pallagen. They would have to. Pallagen wouldn't give them any other choice.

She'd failed. Herself, her team, and her city.

"What are you going to do with us?" Brant asked.

"I don't intend to do anything with you."

Brant snorted.

The man smiled and leaned back in his chair, waving a hand dismissively. "Not now, anyway. I'm sure the lab will find some use for you eventually."

Lena smirked. "What, no public execution?"

The man gave her a flat look. "I have no interest in creating martyrs. There will be no execution. You can't kill heroes, after all. You have to destroy them." He folded his arms. "But before I resort to anything drastic, I want you to understand that Pallagen is not the evil you think it is."

Lena blinked. She thought of Dani, her eyes hollow in her blank face. Brant, the memories of his family and work gone. The Pallagen-employed doctor who'd lost his daughter to the people he worked for. She remembered her young, ambitious self, wearing an orange Pallagen patch above her heart. What could possibly justify anything Pallagen had done? Anger and disbelief burned in her gut. "You've killed people."

"So have you."

"We drew lines! We didn't *use* people. We helped them!" Lena shouted. Her chest hurt and her hands ached for the grip of her stunner, or Brant's rifle, anything that would make this man stop talking. "Whoever you are fighting—I don't care who it is—that doesn't make what you're doing right!"

"No," the man said, "it does not."

Lena panted for air and shook her head. "Then you need to stop."

"You misunderstand. Pallagen exists for Exordia—to protect it, not harm it. We fought the Dallusin centuries ago when their beliefs threatened to destabilize society. Now, we fight people like you." He leaned forward again. "You've worked so hard to destroy us. Do you know why we exist in the first place?"

Lena shook her head, trying to keep the blood from dripping

into her eyes. "Now is hardly the time for a history lesson—"

"Exordia is a fragile colony, Miss Ward. We've been independent from Old Earth for so long that people don't remember how precarious our lives are on this desert world. We're one disaster—natural or created—away from extinction. Order within the colony must be maintained so that we can survive instead of becoming another one of history's great tragedies." He stood and paced in front of Lena, hands folded precisely behind his back. "It's taken you a little more than an orbit to destabilize the peace that has taken Pallagen years to achieve. What if we allowed everyone in the Cities such liberty?"

Lena felt the thrill of victory at his words. *Not so untouchable, are you?* She straightened a little. *We made a difference.* The thought gave her courage to speak again. "I don't see how creating someone like—like Dani—" Her voice broke, and she swallowed the ache that rose at the mention of her. "You hurt the people you were trying to protect. What in the Revelator's name justifies that?"

"Ah, the technopath." The man stopped pacing and faced Lena. "She was the reason you were able to succeed for so long. She truly was powerful. Able to interface with almost every system in Exordia and access information about any citizen at any time. At least, until we were able to counter her interference." He met Lena's eyes. "Dani Fowlkes was never meant to be a weapon, Miss Ward. You turned her into one. To us, she was a safeguard."

Lena swallowed back bile. "Against what?"

"Against you. Against the rest of Exordia." He unfolded

his hands long enough to gesture toward Lena and Brant. "Like I said, our existence is fragile. To be able to survive, Exordia needs stability. It can't afford revolutionaries like you. The technopath was supposed to help us keep order by doing the same thing for us that she did for you: controlling Exordia's infrastructure. With access to cameras, databases, communications...no one would be able to hide their secrets from her. People like you would be stopped before they ever had the chance to begin."

Lena's hands clenched into fists and she swayed, dizzy. Because of her injuries, or because of the man's words, she wasn't sure.

"You live on the fringes of something you can't understand." His voice was soft, like a patient teacher to a difficult student. "You see only what you choose to see. But in the eyes of society, in the eyes of history, Pallagen is the hero, not you." He gestured at the white walls around them. "We keep Exordia safe because we're willing to choose small casualties over greater ones. Would you risk throwing our world into chaos for the sake of a few unnoticed people?"

"Yes," Brant snarled, but Lena was silent.

The man ignored Brant. "You're so focused on your personal vendettas that you never saw the bigger picture." He looked at Lena as if she were the only person in the room. He wasn't angry or threatened, Lena realized. He looked tired.

"I don't know what you want from me," she said finally. "If you're expecting me to change my mind, I can't. I won't."

"I know," he said sadly. His eyes shifted to look behind Lena.

She surged to her feet, but her knee collapsed and two guards caught her arms. Lena fought wildly, muscles straining against the grip of the guards. Her chest burned with pain, and her heart tightened in anger and grief, fear and loss. But she was injured and outnumbered, and someone bared her neck and slid a needle under her skin.

Lena shut her eyes, and darkness closed around her.

Chapter Thirty-Six

Keagan led Alex and Liam to the bedroom. The single bed took up most of the space, but Keagan wordlessly motioned them to step away from it, crowding them into a corner. He hooked his fingers under the plastic mattress platform and lifted it in one smooth motion. He didn't even have to strain, Alex noticed. He was a taller, more muscled version of his brother. Alex wondered what he did in his spare time, when he wasn't looking after Liam.

She bet it wasn't cooking.

Keagan held up the mattress with one hand and stuck his head and shoulders into the hollow frame. Alex heard the faint beeping of a keypad code, and she leaned closer, trying to see what was hidden beneath the mattress. She caught a glimpse of a tiny metal box with a couple of stunners before Keagan stood and let the mattress drop.

"Here." Keagan held out his hand, gesturing for Alex to come closer.

Alex stepped forward to see what he was holding. It was a data chip, like the one Claire had given her. "What's on it?"

"It's an ID file. Yours, I think."

Alex looked up at Keagan in shock. "What?" She glanced at Liam. He looked as surprised as she did. "I thought there wasn't anything about me on the CityGrid."

Liam spread his hands defensively. "There's not!"

"This didn't come from the CityGrid." Keagan closed his fingers around the chip and took a deep breath. He met Liam's eyes for a moment, then turned his gaze to Alex. "I don't know how much Liam told you about me—"

"I didn't know you existed until today," Alex interrupted drily, crossing her arms. "All he said was that you keep an eye on Pallagen and make sure they stay away from him."

Keagan seemed more confident knowing that his brother had not given him away. He straightened his shoulders and nodded gratefully at Liam. "Well, Liam's not the only person who can dig up suspicious files. I've...*found* a few things while watching Pallagen."

Realization dawned on Liam's face, and he stifled a gasp. "You mean you broke into a databank a couple orbits ago." Liam rubbed a hand over his face. "Revelator, that was you?"

Keagan's nose wrinkled. "I thought you would've figured that out by now."

"No, obviously I hadn't! What were you *thinking*?"

"So, you broke into a databank," Alex interrupted impatiently. "And found..." She pointed at Keagan's hand "...that?"

"The information on it belongs to you, I think." Keagan opened his hand and held out the chip again. "I had no idea what to do with it. I didn't think there was anything I *could* do with it. It's just an ID file. But now that you're here, maybe it can do some good after all."

Alex eyed it warily but did not take it from him. "I'm not sure I want to know."

Liam rolled his eyes. "Right. Because having no memories has made your life comfortable."

Comfortable, no. Familiar, yes. She'd just started to get used to the idea that Pallagen had erased her memories, her past. Now she had the chance to find out what exactly Pallagen had done to her, and why.

Answers to her nightmares. Her reflexes. The empty feeling in her chest.

She took the chip.

"You shouldn't read it alone," Keagan warned.

Alex met his dark eyes for a moment, then looked over at his brother. "Liam's here. He can help."

"I'd be happy to—"

"No. This is..." Keagan shook his head and ran a hand through his short hair. "This is something you need to do carefully, Alex. You don't know what Pallagen did to you. You don't how you'll react to what's on the chip."

Alex blinked slowly. "What, you think I can't take it?"

"Don't start again," Liam said warningly, putting a hand on Alex's arm. "Call Claire. She'll know what to do if anything happens to you."

Alex's mouth tightened at the thought of needing supervision.

"Not that it would!" Liam held up his hands in protest. "You're pretty tough. But it doesn't hurt to have a backup plan."

Keagan's eyes narrowed. "Who's Claire?"

"My psychiatrist." Alex said, looking from Keagan to Liam.

"I'm not sure it's a good idea to get her involved. She's helped me, but that was before I killed someone who worked for Pallagen. I don't want to drag her into something like this."

"Your psychiatrist is Claire Tverdik?" Keagan's eyebrows rose. "You should definitely get her involved."

Alex gaped. "You know Claire?"

"I know of her." Keagan shifted uncomfortably. "She has a...reputation in certain circles."

Alex closed her eyes and sighed. "Revelator. My entire life is one big conspiracy theory."

Liam wrapped a hand around Alex's, the one holding the chip. "Do you want to wait? Sleep on it, maybe, and figure this out tomorrow?"

Alex laughed hollowly. "Right. As if I could sleep after this." She shook her head. "I'll call Claire. I doubt we have time to waste. Pallagen is probably still looking for me."

"Fair enough." Keagan tapped his brother on the shoulder. "I'd rather not be around when Claire's here."

"Why, because of her 'reputation?'" Alex asked dryly.

"No, because of *his* reputation," Liam stage-whispered.

Alex grinned. It was a poor attempt at humor, but she appreciated the effort.

"Go," she said to Keagan. "Take Liam with you. Tell him what you know about me. I'm not sure I want two people hovering over me at the same time." And if she was going to have a meltdown, it might as well be in front of someone who'd already seen her at her worst.

"I do not hover!" Liam protested.

"You hover." Keagan grabbed his brother's arm and met

Alex's eyes. "I'm sorry," he said again.

Alex shrugged. "It's not your fault."

Keagan opened his mouth to say something, but stopped and shook his head. "Let us know when you're..." He gestured vaguely. "When you're ready to talk." He tugged on his brother's arm, but Liam pulled away.

"I wouldn't hover," he said seriously.

Alex smiled at him. "Of course not." She squeezed his hand. "I'll be fine."

Liam nodded and followed his brother out of the safe house.

Once she was alone, Alex wandered into the living area and dropped onto the couch. She turned the chip over in her fingers, then sighed and rested her forehead in one hand. A few days ago, her biggest concern had been going outside by herself. Now she was on the run from Pallagen. Her life had been a blank slate, but now she held the key to her secrets.

She hoped the tradeoff was worth it.

She pulled out her mobile and tapped the screen. "Call Claire Tverdik."

Claire arrived at the safe house less than a half hour after Alex called her.

Alex answered the door as soon as it chimed. "Wow," she said. "That was fast." She eyed the psychiatrist critically. Claire had on pants instead of her usual skirt suit, and her hair was still pulled back in a ponytail. She looked exhausted.

"I went to your apartment. Pallagen was all over it." Claire pushed past Alex and into the living room. "What happened?"

Alex glowered at the accusation in Claire's voice and closed the door. She turned to face her and said coldly, "Pallagen showed up to take me. I didn't let them."

Claire stared at her. "All right then," she said gently, "tell me what happened."

Alex led Claire through the living room and into the kitchen. She sat at the table next to a plate of food Liam had left, now cold.

Claire rummaged through cabinets until she found a tall glass. She filled it with water and shoved it at Alex. "Drink," she ordered. "Then tell me what has you so rattled. Besides being on the run."

Alex drained the glass. She hadn't realized she was so thirsty. "Someone I know gave me this." She held up the data chip. She'd decided to leave Keagan out of the conversation until she knew what was in the file. "He said it contained information about who I used to be. I didn't want to read it alone."

"Alex, you know that could be anything—"

"I know," Alex interrupted. "But I need to see. I've had a few flashbacks, and some of what he's said makes me think that he might be right."

"I wish you'd told me about those," Claire said, frowning. "I could have helped."

"I couldn't tell you. Some of the things I've seen... Claire, I need to know." Her fingers were clenched tightly around the chip, knuckles white. Claire pried her fingers away from it.

"All right," Claire said softly. "I'll help you. Do you want to open it?"

Alex shook her head.

"Okay." Claire loaded the file onto her mobile and glanced at the first picture before she showed it to Alex. It was a wanted ad. The words *Reward for Information on Whereabouts* scrolled beneath the photo. It was her face in the picture. Her hair was short, and her face was younger and rounder, but it was the smirking mouth and laughing eyes that made Alex take a sharp breath.

That Alex had personality. That Alex knew who she was, what she was doing, and why she was there.

Claire cursed under her breath, and Alex looked up.

"Look at the date," Claire said, her voice tight.

Alex squinted at the tiny numbers at the top of the ad. "227 AE. That's…" She blinked rapidly, trying to push back the panic rising in her chest. "That's…what, sixty orbits ago?" *Revelator.*

Claire was watching her. "We can stop, if you need to."

Alex took a deep breath and shook her head. She'd come this far. She wasn't about to stop now. "No. Keep going."

Claire swiped over to the next image. It was an identification file, one with a small print of the first picture in the corner. Claire held out her mobile, hands trembling. "Alex, look."

Alex took it and read the name at the top.

No.

She read it again.

No, no.

"Alex, breathe."

The words on the screen blurred, but she forced herself to read them again.

"Alex!" Claire's hands were on her arms, shaking her. Alex stood unmoving, staring blankly, unable to process the flashes of memory flowing through her mind. "Alex!" Claire shouted as she slapped her across the face. At the shock, Alex took a deep breath.

Chemicals, water, smoke, blood—

"How long does the process take?"

"Physically, we'll have to wait until she's recovered from her injuries. However, mental conditioning can begin immediately."

"Good. Put her under."

"Alex, listen to me. I know it's hard, but you need to focus, all right? Focus on my voice. Alex, can—"

"—you hear me?"

"Loud and clear, boss."

The blood soaking her knees and dripping in her eyes was slick on her fingers—no, not blood but tears streaming down her cheeks.

"I lost her. I couldn't get to her in time."

Claire slapped her again. "*Lena!* Look at me!"

Alex opened her eyes.

Part Three

Chapter Thirty-Seven

Alex couldn't stop shaking.

There was no sudden flood of memories. No huge revelation. Pallagen had been too thorough, taken too much away for that. But she kept getting flashes, little pieces of memories, just like in her nightmares. She tried to pin down snippets of conversations and voices in her mind, but they always disappeared.

Sixty orbits. Her mind flashed the date from the ad over and over. *You lost sixty orbits.* She couldn't even remember enough to know who else she'd lost to time.

Claire shook her shoulder, and Alex jolted out of her reverie. Claire took a seat on the couch, extending a glass of water toward her.

Alex accepted it and took a sip. She frowned at the glass, more recent memories surfacing easily. "How many of these have I had?"

"Six." Claire leaned forward and put a hand on Alex's knee. "Alex, I have to leave."

Alex's hand tightened around the glass, panic clawing at

her. "No, please don't—"

"I won't leave you alone," Claire said reassuringly. "Where's Liam?"

Alex closed her eyes. *Revelator*. What was she going to tell Liam? She thought her life would be simpler once she knew who she was, but she felt hollow, left with the devastation of losing two people whose faces she couldn't remember.

"Alex." Claire prodded her gently again. "Where's your mobile?"

"Kitchen counter." Her voice scraped over her raw throat, and she took another sip of water.

Claire disappeared, and Alex heard a hushed conversation. She caught her name—both her names—several times, but she was too tired to follow the words. Eventually the psychiatrist came back into the living area.

"Liam's on his way. Will you be all right if he stays with you?"

Alex wasn't sure how to answer. She didn't want to be alone, but it wasn't Claire's or even Liam's presence that she missed. She pushed her hair out of her face, and—

"If you grow your hair out, I'll teach you to braid it."

"Sure, and give Pallagen security something to grab on to—"

Alex gasped at the hot spike of pain that accompanied the memory.

Claire's hands gripped Alex's shoulders. "Alex, take a deep breath. Good. Now look at me."

Alex met Claire's eyes.

"Good," the psychiatrist said again. "Listen, I don't want to leave you like this, but I need to take care of a few things. I can't just disappear like you did. Too many people would notice."

Alex gave a half-hearted laugh and pulled back from Claire. "Keagan did say you had a reputation."

Claire's eyes narrowed. "What? Who's Keagan?"

Alex sank further into the couch. *Whoops.* "He gave me the file. He recognized your name."

Claire's face relaxed, and she shrugged. "He may have," she admitted. "I already told you, I got you away from Pallagen, but it wasn't the first time I've done something like that. I'd prefer it to not be the last, which is why I need to leave." She leaned forward and wrapped her hands around Alex's. "I want to keep helping you. We will talk about this later, when I have more time, and when you aren't..." She trailed off.

"When I'm not falling apart." Alex closed her eyes and took a deep breath. She pulled her hands away and crossed her arms. "I'll be fine. Go."

Claire opened her mouth to say something, but Liam unlocked the door and walked in. She sighed and squeezed Alex's shoulder. "It'll be okay, Alex. You'll be all right."

Tears stung Alex's eyes.

The psychiatrist gave Liam a meaningful glance as she left the house. Alex closed her eyes again, trying to regain her composure. When she opened them, Liam was crouched next to the couch, hand outstretched as if unsure whether or not to touch her.

She took his hand and squeezed it.

"What do you need?" Liam asked quietly, pulling Alex into the first real hug she'd had since she woke up. She buried her face in his shoulder and breathed deeply. Liam smelled like cool, rain-washed air, like the curry he loved to cook. He smelled like home.

She wondered what her old home had smelled like.

Alex leaned into Liam and cried herself to sleep.

It was a real sleep with no dreams. No nightmares or flashes of memory. She dimly remembered Liam finding a blanket and making room for himself on the couch. She remembered burrowing into his chest, trying to chase away the cold emptiness inside her.

When she woke up, the room was dim and quiet, the blanket tucked carefully around her. Liam wasn't on the couch, but she could hear him stirring in the kitchen.

She sat up and rubbed her face. The crushing despair of yesterday was gone. She felt more centered, more present. She sighed and pushed back her hair. *Enough moping*, she told herself. *You wanted to know who you were. Now you know. Time to get up and deal with it.*

Besides, there were no more tears left in her.

Alex stiffly wandered into the bathroom and splashed cold water on her face. She meandered back to the kitchen, the blanket still wrapped around her shoulders.

"Hungry?" Liam asked. The look on his face said it wasn't a question.

Alex shrugged. She didn't want to eat, but her stomach growled. She dropped into a chair, and Liam plopped a bowl of hot cereal in front of her. There was fruit in it and some sort of spice spread over the top. Alex poked it with a spoon before taking a bite. And then another. Her stomach warmed. Trust Liam to find the perfect comfort food, even on a day like this.

Liam looked at her appraisingly. Waiting, as always, for the verdict.

"It's good," Alex said through a full mouth.

Liam smiled, but it lacked his usual cheerfulness. He didn't say anything, just drank his tea and let Alex make her way through the meal. She wished he'd chatter like he always did, telling her how he'd perfected each flavor or where he'd found the recipe.

"I guess this is kind of weird," Alex said, pushing the empty bowl away. She'd gained knowledge, if not memory, but Liam had to be wondering if she was the same person he'd met a few cycles ago.

He shrugged. "Probably not any weirder than it is for you."

Alex laughed humorlessly. "Let's just leave it at weird for both of us." She folded her hands on the table. "Is there anything you want to ask me? I can't promise answers, but I can try."

"Are you..." He gestured at her head. "Are you *all right*? Keagan told me what was on the chip, but he didn't give me any details. He just said Pallagen had—" He broke off and swallowed hard. "That they'd wiped your memory."

Alex blinked a few times, the image of white walls and the smell of chemicals overwhelming her. But that, at least, was old news—older, anyway. She picked up the spoon from her bowl and twisted it between her fingers. "Claire said it was a pretty complete memory wipe," she said, her voice low, eyes fixed on the spoon in her hand. "I'm all right physically, but I'll never regain more than bits and pieces of what Pallagen took from me. Maybe a little more, now that I know how to fit some of the pieces together." She met Liam's eyes. "I didn't wake up a different person."

"Oh, good," Liam said, the relief obvious in his voice. He winced. "I mean—"

"I know what you meant." Alex smiled, but it quickly faded. "I'm not having much luck putting pieces together. I can remember how I felt, but I can't remember what happened."

"Maybe you just need more information." Liam folded his arms on the table. "Lena Ward was pretty well documented, if you had the right file."

"And your brother had the right file." Alex sighed. "About that. Why did your brother have that file? I mean, I understand having a safe house to get away from Pallagen, but Keagan recognized me as soon as he saw me. How?"

Liam shifted uncomfortably in his chair. Alex tapped the spoon against the tabletop, waiting.

The door chimed.

"I'll get it!" Liam said, hopping up a little too eagerly.

Alex rolled her eyes and carried her bowl to the sanitizer. So much for a straight answer.

Keagan walked in with Liam hovering behind him.

"Lena," he said slowly, his hands shoved in his pockets.

Alex's headache spiked, and her breath caught at the pain her real name had caused. "Not really." Her voice shook, and she cleared her throat. "Not anymore, at least. Alex is fine for now."

Keagan looked wary.

"You're not going to try and shoot her again, right?" Liam said, eyeing his brother suspiciously.

"I might. Slate was a project to program over memory, not just wipe it. She could be dangerous."

Liam bristled, but Alex sighed and sat back down. "Pallagen didn't finish whatever it was they were trying to do. Claire got me out in time."

Keagan stared at her for a few seconds, then nodded slowly. Not quite ready to trust her, Alex thought, but willing to give her a chance. He sat across the table from her. Liam thrust a bowl of hot cereal and a cup of coffee at him.

"So." Alex gestured around the house. "Whose safe house is this? Yours or Liam's?"

The brothers exchanged a glance. "Liam's," Keagan said after a pause. His eyes narrowed and focused on Alex's face. "I set it up for him, but I use it sometimes too."

"For what?" Alex leaned forward. "And how did you recognize me?"

Keagan stared at Alex for several seconds, his eyes searching hers. She held her breath. She knew he didn't trust her, yet, but she needed to know.

Keagan finally put down his spoon and pushed the bowl away. "You know how much time you lost, right?"

Panic flickered at the edges of Alex's mind, but she pushed it away. "Sixty orbits."

"Just about." Keagan folded his hands on the table. "Pallagen blamed an apartment explosion on you—the last raid your team made. Most people knew it wasn't the truth, but Exordia is so used to Pallagen covering things up, they didn't push it."

Alex's mouth was dry. She got up and refilled her glass with water.

"But you and your team rescued dozens of people," Keagan went on behind her. "They couldn't really go public with that knowledge, not without ending up...you know..."

Alex turned around and leaned against the counter, one hand wrapped around her ribs, the other holding the glass. "I know." She took a gulp of water.

Keagan cleared his throat. "But those people told their families that you saved them. They couldn't fight back the same way you did, but they refused to let Pallagen get away with saying and doing whatever they wanted. Maybe they were afraid, maybe they didn't have anyone who was crazy enough to think they could win...I don't know. But the one thing they could do was tell their families the truth."

"And you're part of that." Alex said, sitting down at the table. "You're, what, part of some kind of underground movement?"

Keagan grimaced. "Not really. We're not organized, or anything."

"I feed him information," Liam broke in.

"Liam." Keagan scowled at his brother.

"She deserves to know." Liam crossed his arms and looked at Alex. "Whenever I come across a suspicious incident report, I send a copy to Keagan. He figures out if it was something Pallagen covered up."

"It usually is," Keagan said, picking up his coffee mug and taking a long drink. "I find out what really happened, if I can, and release it to news sources anonymously. No major network picks up the stories, but at least some people are hearing the truth."

"Eventually someone will listen." Liam pulled two mugs out of a cupboard and dumped instant coffee into them. "The evidence will pile up. You can't ignore something like Pallagen forever."

"Although Exordia seems to be giving it their best shot." Alex rested her head against the back of the chair and closed her eyes. She couldn't blame them. With a headache pounding behind her eyes and her memories irrevocably gone, ignorance sounded appealing.

She smelled coffee and opened her eyes. Liam held a mug out to her.

"Thanks." She smiled up at him and took a sip of the hot liquid.

"They may listen eventually, but they'll have to listen to someone else," Keagan said. "Liam can't go back to his job now that Pallagen knows he's with you."

Alex winced. "Sorry about that."

Keagan leaned forward, elbows on the table. "I know how you could make up for it."

There was an edge to Keagan's voice, an eagerness that made Alex nervous. She shifted in her chair restlessly.

"What would you say to finishing what you started so many orbits ago?"

Alex's heart sank and she felt like panicking at the thought of fighting back again, fighting for something she couldn't remember. Standing up to Pallagen hadn't done her any good so far. "It hurts to even hear my real name, Keagan." Her shoulders slumped. "I couldn't win against Pallagen before they wiped my memory, how could I possibly—"

The thought set her heart pounding, and a cold sweat covered her hands. She was going to panic again—

A heavy hand rested on her shoulder. *Liam.* She leaned into it and took a deep, calming breath.

Keagan's eyes were soft with compassion. Alex wondered if it was meant for her, or for the person Lena had been. "I realize fighting Pallagen is probably the last thing you want to do right now. But if you can tell us what you remember, or help us plan ..." Keagan paused, as if trying to decide what to say next. "I have a mission you might be interested in."

Alex wanted to say no, wanted to refuse as her pulse quickened and white flickered at the edges of her vision, but there was too much of Lena still in her. She pushed herself up in the chair. "What mission?"

Keagan rubbed the back of his neck. "I was chasing down one of Liam's leads when I found a file. I wasn't sure what it meant at the time, so I didn't do anything with it, though I wish now I'd investigated sooner..."

Alex tapped the tabletop impatiently.

Keagan straightened in his chair and met Alex's eyes. "I know the location where Brant Hale is being held in stasis."

Chapter Thirty-Eight

Alex had another panic attack when Keagan brought up the file with Brant's picture. Afterward, calm but shaking and enveloped in a blanket, Alex asked if they could wait for Claire before looking further. Liam wrapped her in a hug and told her that was fine.

Alex was pretty sure Liam had been waiting for the chance to pounce with hugs. After their first hug, Liam had taken every opportunity to wrap his arms around her.

She wasn't going to complain.

The three of them ended up in the living room, Alex curled up in the corner of the couch and Keagan and Liam sitting on the edge of the cushions with a pile of tablets in front of them. Keagan had quite a bit of useful information on Pallagen. As long as she read the files that had no connection to her old team, Alex was able to comb through it safely.

The door chimed.

"I'll get it." Liam pushed up off the couch, but Keagan pulled him back down.

"We don't know who it is," Keagan said warily. "*I'll* get it."

Tension settled on the room, but it was Claire's voice that responded when Keagan opened the door, and Alex relaxed back onto the couch.

"Hey," Claire greeted them hesitantly as Keagan led her in. She eyed the mess of tablets and empty dishes on the table, and held up a plastic takeout box. "I brought dinner."

Alex smiled and stood up to take the box. "Thanks for coming."

"Of course." Claire squeezed Alex's fingers as she handed her the food. She nodded at Keagan, still standing next to her, and held out a hand. "I know Liam, but I don't believe we've met."

"This is Keagan, Liam's brother," Alex said as they shook hands. "Keagan, Dr. Claire Tverdik."

"I've heard of you," Keagan said. Alex thought he sounded a little awed.

"Ah, right." Claire smiled, but it was more polite than warm. "My 'reputation.'"

"There are worse reputations to have than fighting Pallagen." Liam said from the couch, eyes focused on a tablet.

"True." Claire's smile softened, and her shoulders lost some of their tension. She looked down at the tablets and cocked an eyebrow. "Is that what you're doing?"

"Sort of." Keagan shoved his hands in his pockets.

Frowning, Claire edged closer to Alex and put a hand on her arm. "I'm not sure you're up for this. Are you feeling all right?"

"Fine," Alex said. "I've only had two panic attacks."

Claire turned and scowled at Liam. "I thought I told you to take care of her, not cause her more stress."

Before Liam could respond to the accusation, Alex jumped to his defense. "I'm fine, Claire. I promise. I ate and everything."

Claire dropped her hand. She didn't look convinced, but she didn't continue asking questions. "I suppose humor is a good sign." Her mouth twisted wryly. "Even if it was in poor taste."

"Sorry." Alex dropped onto the couch next to Liam and patted the cushions. "Have a seat."

Claire settled in and picked up a tablet. "I meant what I said, Alex. You shouldn't be pushing yourself like this." She frowned as she looked at the contents on her tablet screen. "Are these the schematics for Sixth City Rehab?"

"Brant Hale is being held in stasis there," Keagan said. "We're going to get him out."

Silence descended on the safe house. Alex's mind flashed back to a tiny apartment and the long silences that had stretched between her team. Comfortable, companionable silences, not the unpleasant one she suffered through now.

"All of Pallagen is looking for you." Claire's voice was flat, and she dropped the tablet onto the low table by the couch. "The last thing you should do is walk back into their arms."

Alex's jaw clenched. "What am I supposed to do, Claire? Leave him there?"

"He's not your responsibility."

The room faded as another memory washed over her. *I'm not your hitman,* she heard, in a voice she couldn't place. *No,* she remembered saying. *You're here to keep Dani and me alive.*

Someone gently tapped her face. Liam. Alex blinked quickly, then closed her eyes. Her cheeks were wet with tears, and her breathing was short and rapid.

"Calm down, Alex," Claire said soothingly. "I'm sorry. Take a breath."

Liam's hand was on her shoulder now, warm and comforting. Alex reached up and squeezed it before speaking.

"I remembered Dani Fowlkes," she said, her voice hushed, almost whispering. "Before anything else, I remembered her. I remember what it felt like when someone I was supposed to protect died because of me." She swallowed hard and opened her eyes. She looked up and met Liam's eyes, then Keagan's and Claire's in turn. "I don't remember much about Brant Hale," she went on, only half-lying. Like Dani's name, it felt like it fit into one of the empty spaces in her mind. "But I won't let someone else die on my watch."

Claire sat back and studied Alex carefully for a moment. "All right," she said softly. "If you think you can handle it."

"I can handle it." She *needed* to handle it.

Liam wrapped his arm around her shoulders. "We'll be there with you. We won't let anything happen to you."

There was an undercurrent of protectiveness to his voice, and Alex scooted a little closer to him.

Keagan sighed and picked up another tablet. "We don't have a way in yet. We need to figure that out before we worry about anything else."

"Tabba," Alex and Claire said together.

"She would help us, I'm sure." The psychiatrist crossed her arms. "I can get in and out of Sixth City Rehab easily. Two of us should be able to get him out."

"Maybe," Keagan said. "Though I'd rather not rely on the help of someone who doesn't know what's happening."

Alex took a deep breath. "I'm a former patient. I could get into Sixth City Rehab."

Liam's arm tightened around her shoulders. "No! They'll be looking for you!"

"No, they won't," Claire said slowly. Her eyes were on Alex's face, judging if Alex was prepared for this. "Sixth City Rehab is staffed by civilians. Pallagen hasn't contacted Enforcement or anyone else about Alex. No one outside of Pallagen is looking for her."

Liam's jaw set. "Then I'm going with you."

"No," Keagan said, his voice hard and unyielding. "I can't tell Alex what to do, but I can tell you. You're not getting anywhere near a Pallagen facility."

Liam opened his mouth to argue, but Alex held up a hand. "I'll be fine." She slid out from under his arm and stood, running her fingers through her hair.

"I don't like this," Liam grumbled.

Neither did Alex. The thought of walking back into Sixth City Rehab, knowing what Pallagen had done to her, made her want to throw up. But Brant was there, and though she didn't remember him, she knew he had walked into worse situations for her sake.

She met Liam's eyes. "Don't worry." She forced every shred of confidence she had into her smile. "This won't be the first time I walk into a Pallagen facility right under their noses."

But, Revelator, I hope it's the last.

Chapter Thirty-Nine

By the time they finished making their plans, Claire's takeout was cold. She had skipped dinner, unlike everyone else, so Liam led her into the kitchen to reheat it.

Keagan waited until they left the room to take a seat on the couch next to Alex. "There's something else you should know."

Alex sighed. Of course there was. Part of her—the part, she suspected, that was Lena—appreciated Keagan's direct manner. The rest of her still felt incredibly fragile.

"Do you remember any of your missions?"

"Only parts of them. No details." Alex twisted her fingers in the neatly folded blanket, resisting the urge to disappear beneath it again.

Keagan cleared his throat and flicked his eyes in her direction, no doubt nervous he'd bring on another panic attack. Alex felt too tired for that, but she let Keagan fumble his way through his story.

"Your last mission, do you remember what you were after?"

"I don't," she admitted, shaking her head. "When

I tell you I don't remember much, I'm not lying. I have impressions, emotions. I have a few flashes here and there, but nothing solid."

Keagan sighed and ran a hand through his hair. "You raided a databank, which was unusual for your team."

Alex winced as her headache spiked, and she glared at Keagan. "So?"

"So, you must have been after something specific."

"We could do two things at once." Alex's voice echoed in her head. *"It's worth a try,"* someone else said. Alex pressed her fingers against her temples, trying to will away the rest of the memory before it caused her more pain, but the memory kept coming, bringing with it the answer to Keagan's question.

"Alex?" Keagan rested a hand on her shoulder, concern lacing his voice.

"It was a file," she said, gritting her teeth and lifting her head to meet Keagan's gaze. "We were after a file." Keagan's face lit with hope, but she continued. "I don't remember what was in it. Maybe it wasn't that important."

"Maybe what you were after is still there," Keagan shot back.

Alex shook her head wearily. "That building blew up sixty orbits ago, Keagan. Whatever was there—"

"—was transferred to the data bank beneath Sixth City Rehab."

Alex froze.

Keagan took a deep breath and leaned closer. "Whatever you were after must have been important. You raided that building in the middle of the day. The CityGrid shows a large data transfer from that building just hours before...you know."

Alex swallowed. They'd been so close.

"I tracked each transfer. The data hopped around to a few different locations before being transferred to Sixth City Rehab. We can get whatever file you were after. You can still win, Alex."

Alex closed her eyes.

"Listen." Keagan plunged ahead, his voice carrying an edge of desperation. "We have to go after Brant Hale anyway. Why don't we access the database while we're in Sixth City Rehab and take the file? If it was information that would take down Pallagen, we can put it on the CityGrid."

Alex shook her head. "I can't imagine you would be able to access a file like that. Whatever was in it, they'll be keeping it somewhere protected, or—"

"I don't think so. Exordia is different now, Alex. Pallagen has been safe for the last sixty orbits. They're complacent. Why would they need to be cautious? Lena Ward, their biggest threat, was gone. *You* were gone."

"I keep telling you, I don't remember." She spread her hands in frustration. "I don't know how to put together a plan like that anymore. Even if I did, we don't have a technopath who can get us in and out of the rehab center without anyone noticing." Her voice caught at the mention of Dani, but she kept talking. "I don't remember how to steal a file like that, much less get it onto the CityGrid."

"It wouldn't be much different than what Liam and I were doing before." Keagan leaned closer, looking intently at Alex. "We can do this."

Alex felt the weight of eyes other than Keagan's, and she

looked away from him. Claire was watching her, a plate of food in her hands, as was Liam, leaning against the wall between the kitchen and living area. They were waiting for her decision, Alex realized. They were letting her take the lead as she had so many times in an unremembered past.

"It's not my choice to make," Alex said softly. "Exordia isn't my city anymore. I don't have the right to drag any of you into an old war."

"It's not an old war, Alex. Pallagen is still doing the same thing they did orbits ago. There's just no one brave enough to stand between them and the city."

Revelator. Keagan sounded just like Lena's voice inside her mind. Alex's head pounded.

"Besides, do we look dragged in?" Claire stepped into the living area. "Maybe this is a second chance at victory."

"You know what happened last time, right?" Her words were hoarse, scraped out of a throat filled with gravel. The grief she'd managed to push down welled up again, drowning her.

"Then let Dani's sacrifice mean something. Don't let Pallagen win because you're afraid of losing. They've taken everything from you, Alex. What else can they do?"

Alex blinked back tears and tightened her fists until her fingernails cut into her palms. She met Liam's eyes. "I put people I cared about in danger, and Pallagen took them from me. I won't do that again."

She caught the pointed glance between Claire and Keagan. "We won't force you to do anything," Keagan said slowly. "But with or without your help, we will try to get that file."

Alex was suddenly angry. Didn't they realize how hard

this was for her? She rounded on Keagan, her face flushed and fists clenched, and he flinched backward.

"You knew about that last mission. You even knew about the data transfer. Why haven't you done anything about it before now?"

Keagan's face softened. "You have no idea, do you?"

Alex shook her head defiantly.

"Come with me," he said. "There's something you need to see."

Alex pulled her jacket closed. "Should we be out here?" she hissed, close enough to Keagan to bump elbows.

"We're fine. I know the streetcam's blind spots." He glanced at her. "Besides, they're looking for you, not me. Keep your head down, and no one will notice you."

Alex ducked her head and fought the urge to pull the hat Liam had given her farther over her face. But the wind was biting, and everyone they passed was too busy tucking their chins into their coats or scarves to notice her.

"You can stop staring at the pavement now," Keagan said when they turned a corner. "The streetcams don't work here."

The wind was suddenly gone, cut off by the long wall in front of them. Alex raised her chin from her collar and stared, perplexed by what she saw.

It was the side of an old building. The plastic was scorched and warped, and the roof was gone. Only the one wall remained. It was one of many damaged, disintegrating buildings they had passed on their way through Seventh City, but this one was covered in writing.

Alex stepped closer to the wall. Something brushed at the back of her memory, making her knee and chest ache, but she pushed it aside. She stopped several inches away and stretched out a hand, brushing her fingers lightly over a name scrawled in red.

"What is this?" she whispered.

"These are the names of every person you and your team saved," Keagan said. She turned to look at him. He had his hands shoved in his pockets, and he spoke quietly, eyes focused on the wall. "After you were killed—after Exordia thought you were—someone came and left their name here. Do you recognize the building?"

Alex turned back to the wall and fought against the emptiness still clawing at the back of her mind. Nothing. She shook her head.

"It's the building Pallagen blew up to trap you. Before they could raze it, someone graffitied their name on it. By the next morning, there were more than a dozen names."

Alex swallowed. "There is no way we saved this many people."

"No. But the ones you did save brought their children here, and they've brought their children. Pallagen has tried painting over the names, but someone always destroys the streetcams and repairs the damage. Once, a few orbits after you died, Pallagen took the whole wall down. Someone rebuilt it. There was a huge news story, conspiracy theories...Pallagen left it alone after that. Probably figured it did them more harm than good to draw attention to it." Keagan turned to look at

Alex, his eyes burning with passion. "This is what Lena Ward was to Exordia. She may have failed in the end, but she made a difference in the lives of a hundred people, who went on to help another hundred."

The wall blurred as Alex blinked back tears.

"So, yes, I knew about your last mission. I didn't do anything about it because the whole reason I started spying on Pallagen was to keep Liam safe. I wasn't willing to risk him, not for any reason. But it's too late for that. We're already in danger, so why not make it worthwhile?"

Alex turned her back to the wall to meet Keagan's gaze, tears spilling down her cheeks. "I'm not Lena Ward."

"Yes, you are," Keagan said firmly, eyes boring into hers. "You're Lena Ward, back from the dead, and right now I feel pretty phaeting invincible."

Alex closed her eyes. She'd made this choice over sixty orbits ago, when she decided—in arrogance and anger— that she was going to destroy Pallagen. She'd made this choice when she gave up stopping them to help those they victimized.

"Sometimes part of being unbreakable is believing that yourself, y'know?" Dani's voice echoed in her memory.

Oh, Dani, she thought. *I'm so sorry.*

She took a deep breath, pulled on every part of her that felt like Lena, and looked at Keagan again. "All right," she said. "I'm in. For this *one last* mission."

"That's all we need," Keagan promised.

Chapter Forty

Alex walked through the front door of Sixth City Rehab and smiled at the receptionist. She waved her old patient identification badge, and the receptionist motioned her on. Claire had told her entering the building wouldn't be difficult, but Alex breathed easier after she was past the desk.

She switched her patient badge for a stolen visitor pass and wandered through the maze of patient wards and visiting areas. She got lost in the white tiled hallways and nearly panicked, but she turned another corner and found a nurse's break room. She leaned against the wall and took a deep breath, listening for the sound of Tabba's voice. She heard it, thanking the Revelator that she could remember that much correctly. She glanced at the room designation on the wall and tapped the numbers into her mobile to let Claire know where she was. A few moments later, the psychiatrist slipped around the corner next to her.

For a few minutes there was only the muted silence of the hallway. A nurse walked by with a patient in leg braces, and she nodded at Claire. Alex's visitor pass didn't draw any attention, and Claire was well-known in the rehab facility.

Alex's heart slowed down and she closed her eyes, trying to push away the memories of past missions that flickered in her mind. Her head ached a little less with each recollection, but the pain was still distracting.

But here, in a place so much like the Pallagen facilities she had raided with Dani and Brant, it was hard to keep the memories at bay. She remembered assuming a mask of calm when all she felt like doing was chewing on her fingernails. She remembered how it felt to have constant knowledge of where Dani and Brant were. Whether Dani was on the roof above them or skulking in the dark with them, Lena had never been out of reach of either teammate. She suddenly remembered Brant and his rifle, stalking the halls, watching for any danger. Alex opened her eyes, and her jaw tightened against a sharp flare of pain. She rubbed her temple. Claire touched her elbow, concerned, but Alex shook her head. Now was not the time. Her calm was fragile enough.

Before Claire had a chance to ask anything, Tabba walked out of the break room. Alex quickly grabbed the nurse's arm and pulled her around the corner, out of sight. Tabba elbowed Alex in the gut and stomped on her foot, causing Alex to stumble back gasping for air.

Claire grabbed one of Tabba's wrists before she could do more damage. "It's me, Tabba. Calm down."

"Well," the nurse said breathlessly, voice quiet to match Claire's. "It was hardly you two I expected to see sneaking around." She pulled her wrist free and pushed her hair behind her ears, studying Alex. "You've healed nicely in the last few cycles." Her words were light, but there was a note of worry in her voice as her eyes darted back and forth between Claire and Alex.

"You two can catch up later. Right now, we need you to get us into the patient data room," Claire went on in her best unreasonable-patient voice. Alex recognized it. She had been on the receiving end of it more than once.

Tabba's eyes widened in astonishment. "Oh, really? Patient data?" She shook her head. "I don't know what's gotten into you, Dr. Tverdik, but you know very well I can't just let people in there."

Claire glanced uncertainly at Alex.

"I might be able to hack the keypad," Alex said slowly. "It would take time though. More time than we have."

Tabba frowned at her. "Did you gain a bunch of criminal memory back or something?"

Alex grinned. "Or something."

"We don't have time for this," Claire said. "I can't explain right now, Tabba, but we need to access a file there. *Alex* needs the file. It's vital to her...recovery."

Tabba crossed her arms, giving both of them a hard stare.

"She's a terrible liar," Alex said quietly, "but I do need your help. I can tell you later, but we don't have time right now."

Tabba's lips thinned as she stared at Alex. Alex tried not to look nervous, tried not to think about every precious second wasted while Tabba made her decision. Finally, Tabba sighed. "Okay, but I get a full explanation as soon as this is over. Hold on." She stepped into the hallway. Claire made a motion to stop her, but Alex held up a hand. Her gut told her Tabba was fine.

Sure enough, the nurse waved them out a few seconds later. She faced Claire. "You look like you belong. Just loosen up a little. No one's going to think it's strange that you're here." Claire's shoulders relaxed as she tried to assume her professional demeanor.

"As for you," Tabba said, eyeing Alex up and down, "try to look a little less like you're going to murder someone with your bare hands."

Alex huffed indignantly.

They walked down the hallway, Alex a step or two behind Claire and Tabba. They passed a few patients and nurses who ignored them. One doctor nodded and smiled at Claire, but no one tried to stop or speak to them. Tabba led them down the fire escape stairwell. There was a door at the bottom with a keypad beside it.

"I can get you through this door," Tabba said. "Confidential files are kept here. I'm not sure what else."

"We know what we're looking for," Claire said.

"There will probably be a guard."

"I can take care of the guard." Alex put her hands on her hips, her thumb brushing the stunner tucked in the small of her back under her jacket.

Tabba gave her a sideways glance. "You know what," she said, punching in her code and pushing open the door, "I think I'll come along to keep an eye on you two."

There was no guard or receptionist in the outer office, and it took them a minute to find a second door at the back of the room, hidden behind rows of servers. Tabba tried her code, but it wouldn't open.

"Hold on." Alex pulled off the keypad cover and stared intently at the wiring underneath. She closed her eyes, trying to draw on the second-nature knowledge that had already saved her life. It made her head hurt. She opened her eyes and scowled at the panel. "This was always Dani's job."

"You can do it," Claire encouraged.

Alex took a deep breath. Without thinking too hard, she crossed a couple of wires, reconnected the panel, and punched in a random set of numbers. The door slid open.

"Wow," Tabba said. "And who's Dani?"

Alex didn't answer. She was balancing precariously between remembering enough to get through this job and not giving herself a migraine. Talking about Dani would make it worse.

She stepped into the dark room. There would be a guard here, she felt. This was where Lena would have let Brant go first, let him take his rifle and clear the room.

Now, that was her job.

"Be quiet," she whispered. "Stay here. Don't let the door close behind you."

Claire and Tabba obeyed, but Tabba looked worried. Alex stepped farther into the darkness.

She could hear the humming of machines, taste the metal and chemicals on her tongue. It was the smell, though—the same smell that haunted her dreams—that caught her off guard. For a moment the room was overlaid with a white one, and she saw herself kneeling on tile. She paused for a moment, closing her eyes to push back the feelings of helplessness and grief that welled up within her.

When Alex opened her eyes, she felt the air around her

shift and she ducked. Something whistled through the air above her head. She heard someone—Tabba, probably—gasp.

Alex smiled in the dark.

This, she knew how to do.

She couldn't see much, but she let muscle memory take over. She feinted right and reached one hand out to grab the blaster coming around to point at her forehead. She wrenched the arm backward and heard a dull *pop* as the joint was forced out of place. She used the sudden cry of pain to judge where the guard's face was, and slammed her elbow into his nose, still holding the wrist of the hand with the blaster. She felt the guard stumble, and she yanked on the dislocated arm. The blaster clattered to the floor, and the guard dropped to his knees. Alex caught him in the chin with her knee as he went down. He dropped like a stone.

Breathing hard, she turned to look back at the door. Claire was holding Tabba's elbow—to keep her from running to help, or *for* help, Alex didn't know.

She straightened. "Claire, watch the door and keep it open. Tabba, can you find the lights?"

The nurse fumbled along the wall for a moment, and with the flip of a switch, the room was flooded with sterile white light. Alex blinked rapidly to allow her eyes to adjust and stepped away from the body at her feet. Blood pooled beneath the guard's face. He'd be lucky if he ate solid food in the next few weeks, or regained full use of his arm.

Tabba's face was pale as she stepped carefully around the guard, avoiding Alex's eyes. Alex wanted to apologize for frightening her, but she doubted anything she said would help.

She turned away from the guard and scanned the room. There were a few metal desks with tablets and clear computer screens. Those she knew how to operate without dredging up any painful memories. Alex pulled up the interface on one of the computers and found full CityGrid access. Tabba's access code allowed them to do a name search only, but when Alex typed in *Brant Hale* it gave her a number-letter combination.

"Room number?" Alex asked, turning to Tabba.

The nurse's eyes were wide with confusion. "Probably not. A file maybe." Tabba frowned and scrutinized the screen. "Brant Hale is *dead*."

"He's not dead," Alex said. That explanation would take far too long, and she silently vowed to make it up to Tabba later. "We need to find where they're keeping him," Alex explained patiently, forcing a mask of calm over her mounting frustration. She was doing the job of three people, and working without a team who knew her next move by heart felt like writing with the wrong hand. She rubbed her forehead. "Look, Tabba, we don't have time for this. Do you have any idea what the numbers mean?"

Tabba studied the combination on the screen. She inhaled sharply. "Morgue. It's the same format of the ID numbers on the morgue drawers."

Alex glanced toward the back of the room at the wall of people-sized drawers there. "Okay then," she said, memorizing the numbers. She strode to the end of the room, scooping up the guard's blaster on the way. She heard Tabba following a few steps behind.

Instead of access codes on the panel next to the drawer

matching Brant's ID number, there was medical data being displayed. Tabba looked closely. "This isn't a mortuary chamber. It's a stasis drawer," she said, realization dawning on her face.

"Can you pull him out safely?" Claire asked from the doorway behind them, voice tense.

Alex felt the pressure mounting. If they didn't rescue Brant now, they might never get another chance.

"Yes," Tabba said, already pushing buttons. "It's required training for all medical personnel working here. Volatile or critical patients often arrive at the center in stasis." She glanced sideways at Alex. "You were one of those patients."

Alex nodded impatiently, watching Tabba initiate the process to bring Brant out of stasis. There were some alarming noises of water draining and a strong smell of chemicals, then with a click and a hiss the drawer slowly slid open.

In shock, Alex realized she recognized the face in front of her. The pictures had jogged only a faint recollection, but now, with Brant lying in front of her, his clothes soaked and hands folded over his chest, Alex realized she *knew* him. She didn't know she was reaching for him until Tabba grabbed her wrist.

"Wait," she said. "Give him a minute."

"We don't have a minute." Claire impatiently looked through the door with a sharp, fretful movement. "We need to get him—and us—out *now*."

Tabba's mouth tightened into a thin line, and she nodded.

Alex and Tabba pulled Brant's arms over their shoulders and dragged him off the table. Alex staggered under the limp weight, but Brant was nothing but skin and bones beneath the damp hospital shift he wore.

Tabba pulled a small monitoring tablet from her pocket with her free hand and began scanning his vitals. "You know the way out, right?" she asked Alex without taking her eyes off the tablet. "He's going to need a place to rest as soon as possible."

"We have a place." Alex handed Brant off to Claire. She carefully closed the stasis drawer and jogged back to the desk. She pulled out the data stick Keagan had given her and placed it next to one of the screens. She brushed her ear, activating her comm for the first time. "Can you download what you need from here?"

"*That's perfect, Alex. Just give me a minute. I'm going to download anything that's not current patient records. Then we're done.*" Keagan sounded tense, but that was to be expected. Alex was the only part of this hastily-constructed plan that had any idea what she was doing, and even then, it was spotty memories. She grimaced. That wasn't an encouraging thought.

The screen on the desk registered the passing of seconds, but to Alex it felt like long minutes. She tapped her foot impatiently.

"*Okay, we're done,*" Keagan said at last. "*I have everything, Alex. You can leave.*"

Pocketing the data stick, Alex turned out the lights and locked the door behind her, leaving the guard to explain his incompetence to his superiors. She wished she could erase the security footage and personal access codes, but there was no time for her to figure out how to do it.

Besides, maybe it was better if Pallagen knew who had

been here. Alex paused long enough to locate the camera in the room. She looked directly into it and, bringing every memory of Dani to the front of her mind, smiled. Not a nice smile, not even a victorious one.

A smile that told Pallagen they had won one war, but they were about to lose the second.

Chapter Forty-One

Keagan was waiting in the alley outside the rehab center, just as planned. Alex kept watch at the entrance to the alley as Claire and Tabba loaded Brant into the gravcar. Claire climbed into the transport after Brant, but Tabba hesitated.

"We used my access code to get through that door," she said, looking at Alex. "Dr. Tverdik stayed off-camera, but they'll definitely see me." Her voice carried the weight of knowledge that a line had been crossed, and there was no going back.

"I'm sorry, Tabba," Alex said quietly. Though, if she were being honest, she wasn't really sorry. Seeing Brant's face had rekindled a sort of desperate devotion to her team, as well as a desire to keep them safe. If it had meant changing the lives of a hundred people like Tabba, she still would have gone after her partner. "You're part of this now. You can come with us, if you'd like."

Tabba laughed scornfully. "Right. Great idea." She peered into the transport. "I suppose I can't leave that man—whoever he is—in your incapable hands, can I?"

"I'm a medical professional too, you know," came Claire's

voice, faintly offended.

Keagan turned around in his seat. "We need to leave, Alex."

Alex nodded and pushed a reluctant Tabba into the transport before climbing in. Keagan took off.

"How long do we have before they figure out he's gone?" Keagan asked, merging onto the main gravtrack.

"When do the guards change shift?" Alex asked Tabba.

"Not for another couple of hours."

Good. They had some breathing room. "At least a few hours, then. We didn't set off any alarms because we used Tabba's access codes."

Keagan glanced back, an incredulous look on his face. "Revelator, Alex. Just how long does it take you to corrupt everyone you come in contact with?"

Alex grinned crookedly, though the smile didn't quite reach her eyes. Tabba had helped her so much in those first few days after waking up, and now she'd ruined the nurse's life. Alex glanced at Tabba. *I'll make it up to her. Somehow.*

"She's always been that way," said a hoarse but familiar voice. Everyone looked at Brant, startled. Tabba continued to monitor him. His color looked better, but he shivered and his eyes were glazed. "What happened? No, don't answer," he said, his words slurring. "We'll just blame it on Dani."

"Hardly anything is ever Dani's fault." Alex said the words without thinking and winced when her head throbbed. She hesitated, one hand hovering near Brant. *Revelator. What do I say to him?* She rested her hand on his shoulder and squeezed it. "Just...go back to sleep for now."

"Mmm. Whatever." He closed his eyes and shifted as if

trying to get comfortable. They blinked open again when Tabba put two fingers on his neck, checking his pulse. "Hey," he said, a smile barely forming. "You're cute."

Alex rolled her eyes as Tabba sputtered an incoherent response. "Sleep, Brant." She patted his hand, then wrapped her fingers around his wrist. "Seriously, go to sleep."

But he had already fallen asleep, or passed out again. Tabba didn't look worried though, just shell-shocked.

Her eyes rose to meet Claire's. "What's going on here?"

"We'll explain later." Claire clutched the back of the seat in front of her as Keagan careened around a corner. She shot a cross look toward the driver's seat. "Maybe we'll let Keagan do it."

"Oh no," Keagan said. "You took over my safe house without warning. One of you guys gets to do the explaining."

Claire made a face, but Alex stopped paying attention to anything but the steady thrum of Brant's pulse beneath her fingers.

Claire and Tabba helped Brant into the safe house while Keagan parked the gravcar on a different street. Alex hovered behind her partner and friends, one hand on her stunner, until they were safely behind the locked door.

Liam wrapped her in a hug as soon as she had keyed the lock. She leaned into him, burying her face in his chest.

"Are you okay?"

Pressed up against him, Alex felt more than heard the words. "I'm fine," she said shakily.

"Sure you are." Liam's voice carried plenty of disbelief.

He gently pushed her away and examined her face. "I made coffee," he offered.

"Perfect." She forced a smile. "But I need to check on Brant—"

"Tabba's with him," Claire said, stepping into the living area. "Look, Alex, I know you want to speak to him, but he needs to hear about what happened from someone other than you."

Alex bristled and clenched her fists, but Liam squeezed her shoulders gently. "Let her explain," he said softly.

"It's for your sake as well as his," Claire went on. Her eyes were steady, never leaving Alex's. "We don't know what Pallagen has done to him, and clearly it hurts you to remember anything. You've both been through a great deal of trauma. Let him hear an explanation from someone who won't have a panic attack halfway through the story."

Alex's shoulders slumped. That was a fair point. "I still want to talk to him."

"You will." Claire turned to step back into the bedroom. "Give me a few minutes. I'll let you know when he's ready."

She disappeared into the bedroom, and Tabba walked out a few seconds later, closing the door behind her.

"I forgot how bossy Dr. Tverdik could be," she grumbled, hands on her hips. She met Alex's eyes. "Now. Will someone *please* explain what's going on?"

The front door opened, and Liam's face brightened. "Oh, Keagan would *love* to explain." Without giving his brother time to protest, he grabbed Alex's hand and pulled her into the kitchen.

Liam handed her a mug of coffee and hovered close to her as she drank it. Claire was still in the bedroom by the time the coffee was gone, so Alex walked into the living area. Keagan was sitting on the edge of the couch next to Tabba, talking softly to her.

Alex stewed silently and paced back and forth outside the bedroom door. Liam followed her into the living area but didn't push her to talk, choosing instead to plop into a chair with a tablet.

Alex's stomach twisted. What would she say to Brant? Even half-conscious in the back of a darkened gravcar, Brant had recognized her. Had Pallagen left his mind alone? What would he think of her now, with her brain washed out with chemicals?

And what would he say when he remembered Dani was dead?

She stood in front of the door with her arms crossed, waiting. Staring at the door as if her glare could burn holes in it. Keagan walked over and put a hand on her shoulder.

"I can't do this," she said quietly. "He's waking up sixty orbits in the future, we lost our fight against Pallagen, and I got Dani killed." She closed her eyes. "I failed him. He'll never forgive me."

"He'll understand." Keagan turned to face her. "He's your brother."

Alex looked at him in surprise. "No, he's not. We aren't even from the same part of the city."

Keagan shook his head. "There doesn't need to be blood between you for him to be your brother. The guilt you're feeling right now, the way you looked at him when he woke up—he's a brother to you. You walked back into a Pallagen facility to rescue him, after all they did to mind-wipe you." He glanced behind him at Liam, who was pretending to concentrate on the tablet. "I'm sure Brant feels the same way, or he wouldn't have followed you in the first place. He'll forgive you."

Alex stared at Keagan, hearing the truth in his voice. She remembered that she wasn't the only person trying to protect people from Pallagen. "What would Pallagen have done to Liam?"

Keagan didn't respond right away. Claire's voice, low and calm, filtered through the door. Brant's retort was muffled but sharp. Alex knew it wouldn't take him long to ignore Claire and walk out the door to find out the truth for himself.

"Liam's not...he doesn't think the same way others do," Keagan said haltingly. "I don't know how much he told you..."

Alex smiled. "He told me about his memory. He remembers everything." And she couldn't remember anything. Her mouth twisted at the irony.

Keagan nodded. "Pallagen would have used him like they used you." He looked her in the eyes. "The way his mind makes connections, stores information...they were going to use him as a computer with the advantage of human instinct. There would have been nothing left of my brother if they got their hands on him."

Alex tried to imagine soft-hearted Liam as hurt and confused as she had been. She shuddered.

"Don't hurt him." Keagan stepped closer, his shoulders tense and jaw tight. "Don't do that to him."

Alex was startled by the fire in his eyes, but she nodded. "I understand."

Keagan turned abruptly and walked back to the living room, but Alex felt the tension between them ebbing away in the wake of finding common ground.

Tired of waiting, Alex raised a hand to knock on the bedroom door, but Claire opened it before she got the chance. The psychiatrist let it slide shut behind her.

"Is he all right?" Alex asked impatiently.

Claire shrugged. "I didn't tell him much. I don't think he would have believed me anyway." She glanced sideways at Alex. "He's demanding to speak to you."

Alex closed her eyes.

"He survived stasis well enough," Claire went on. "Nothing seems to be wrong with his memories."

"So he wasn't mind-wiped like I was."

Claire sighed in confirmation.

"Why me and not him?" Alex whispered. "If I'm so dangerous to Pallagen, why wake me up? Why keep me alive in the first place?"

"Keagan showed you what you meant—what you still mean—to Exordia. Removing your past was probably Pallagen's version of defeating you. Take away everything that made you Lena Ward, proving that no matter who you were or how much you fought, they are still in control."

Alex stared at the door. "They're not though. Not anymore."

"No," Claire agreed. "They're not."

Alex rubbed her forehead.

"Do you want me to go with you?" Claire asked softly,

putting a hand on Alex's shoulder.

Alex shook her head. "I'll be okay. I just need to figure out how to explain what's happened." And find a way to apologize. Hopefully Keagan's words were true, and Brant would listen to her.

"You could start by opening the door."

Alex made a face at Claire, but the psychiatrist smiled and pushed her toward the bedroom.

Alex's heart pounded. Her breath came short and sharp. *You can look Brant in the eyes,* she told herself. *You faced down Pallagen. You walked back into the Rehab Center, even after they beat you. Even if he doesn't understand, he can't take that away from you.*

She keyed open the door.

Chapter Forty-Two

Brant sat on the bed, scowling at his bootlaces. His fingers shook as he tried to knot the cords. He looked up sharply when the door slid open.

"Lena." There was something in his voice that made Alex want to cry. "Revelator, Lena."

His face was white, and his hands trembled. But with dry clothes and mussed hair, he looked more like the Brant she had begun to remember.

Suddenly Alex knew she couldn't explain things in the house, in hearing range of everyone else. Brant was looking at her as if she held all the answers, but she didn't want to admit to him that she couldn't even remember the question.

"Let's walk," she said. She may not remember who Brant was, but she didn't have to look to know he was following her.

They couldn't walk around the city like Alex wanted to, so she chose to go to the tiny fenced-in garden at the back of the safe house. They settled cross-legged in the dead grass. Brant shivered, and Alex wished she'd grabbed a blanket from the couch. Instead, she scooted closer until their

EXORDIA

shoulders and knees were touching. They sat in silence, their memories decades apart.

"How long has it been?" Brant asked.

Alex closed her eyes. "Sixty orbits."

She felt Brant shudder. Alex remembered her own shock when she thought she'd only lost two, and wondered if a gap of more than half a century would be too overwhelming to process.

"They called you Alex," he said. "What is that, a new cover?"

Alex sighed. Of course he'd caught that. "Do you remember Project Slate?"

Brant froze. He looked at her with wide eyes. "I knew something was off—is that what happened to you? How did you reverse it?"

"I haven't," Alex admitted, unable to look Brant in the eye.

Brant laughed bleakly. "Do you remember who I am?"

"Of course I do," Alex said sharply. She bit her lip. She couldn't lie to him. "I don't remember you completely, but I get flashes here and there. I know you sit really still like that when you're trying to solve a problem, but I can't remember how I met you."

Brant didn't say anything for a while. He stared up at the gravtrain that rushed through the gray sky above them. Alex frowned. They couldn't stay out here much longer. Someone would notice the two figures matching the descriptions that must be out for their arrest by now. The safe house was their last refuge in the city.

"What about Dani?" Brant asked, his voice barely above a whisper.

"No." Alex swallowed. "It's just us."

"It wasn't your fault." His words were hoarse and distant.

Alex looked at him. His head was turned away from her. Her throat tightened, and her eyes burned with unshed tears. "I forgot you. I forgot *her*." She wrapped her arms around her middle and squeezed her eyes shut. "Everything was my fault."

She felt Brant shift, his shoulder brushing hers. She angrily wiped the tears away from her cheeks and opened her eyes. Brant, of all people, didn't deserve to bear the weight of her guilt.

But Brant's eyes glinted with understanding. His smile was small, the corners of his mouth barely creasing, but it was genuine. "Same old Lena. Had your brain wiped by Pallagen, and you're still taking responsibility for everything that happens." He wrapped his arms around her like she was a fragile, prickly plant. Alex wasn't sure he'd ever hugged her before, but she leaned into it, accepting his forgiveness.

"I don't blame you, Lena." Brant's arms tightened around her. "Dani wouldn't have, either."

Alex shook her head but didn't argue. After a few moments, she took a shaky breath and pushed away. Brant met her eyes. There was a weight to his gaze that Alex hadn't seen from anyone else. Brant knew her. He'd worked with her for so long. He knew her reactions, her moods, how to read her thoughts. She wondered if there was enough of Lena left in her for Brant to recognize.

His eyes were bright with tears, but he smiled. "We got sent to the future. That's the weirdest thing that's ever happened to us. Which is saying a lot."

Alex laughed wistfully. "I wouldn't know." Brant's grin faltered. "Sorry. The amnesia jokes are kind of a thing now, so, if you're planning to stick around..."

"I guess I'll have to get used to them," Brant finished. He straightened and gestured toward the house. "So, I'm assuming there's some kind of plan?"

"Sort of. Keagan and Claire are working on it."

"Who are they anyway? Your new team?"

"Sort of," Alex said again.

"You're full of answers," Brant grumbled.

Alex smirked, one of Brant's old excuses flickering across her memory. "Mind-wiped." She shrugged, hands up.

Brant chuckled. He pushed himself to his feet and held out a hand to Alex. "How about we get inside and show these rookies how it's done?"

Alex grinned and took his hand.

Liam stress-cooked a massive breakfast for everyone. They started out gathered around the table, Tabba peppering Brant with questions, Claire and Keagan conspiring over a tablet, Liam bouncing between the table and the stove. When the food was gone, they drifted away one by one, leaving Alex and Brant alone at the table. Alex knew they were trying to give the two of them some space, but she wished Liam would have stayed. Looking at Brant didn't make her head hurt, but the flashes of memory came more often when she was around him. It left her aching for something to anchor herself to, and Liam had always helped her feel centered.

Alex absently tapped the tabletop with her fingertips. The silence felt familiar, and as long as she didn't let her mind wander to the past, it felt comfortable. Brant didn't let it last, though.

"So," he started. His hands were wrapped around a mug of steaming coffee. "The name thing."

Alex grimaced.

"No one calls you Lena but me," he said. "And you do that weird scrunchy thing with your eyebrows whenever I say it."

"It hurts when I hear my old name," Alex admitted. She tapped her temple lightly. "I don't know exactly what Pallagen did, but whenever I remember something from my past..." She shrugged. "It's getting a little better, but Claire said it probably won't go away completely."

"So it's permanent." Gloom colored his voice, and his fingers tapped restlessly against his mug. "Pallagen really did erase you."

Alex's vision whited out. *You can't kill heroes*, someone said, *you have to destroy them.*

"Lena?"

Her pulse pounded against her skull. She blinked a few times and took a gulp of coffee. "I'm fine," she said hoarsely.

Brant had abandoned his mug and was leaning forward as if he'd been about to jump out of his chair. He relaxed and shifted back in his seat. "Does that happen often?"

Alex looked down into her coffee and didn't answer. Revelator, this was hard. She'd thought getting Brant back would be a good thing for her, but he fit into her old life, not her new one. Liam and Claire, even Keagan, were used to her damage. Brant still saw her as indestructible.

"Look." Brant's voice cracked, and he swallowed before continuing. "I'm not trying to make this harder for you. I know it must have been horrible, being alone, not knowing who you were. But I just woke up today. You've been awake for a few cycles, but I don't know where I am or what I'm doing, and every time I look at you, it's like a stranger is looking back at me."

Alex couldn't answer. She longed to reassure him, to ease the panic in his voice. She wanted to give him the answers he needed, to be the person he'd followed into hell, but she didn't know where to start.

After a long, awkward silence, she whispered, "I didn't get over Dani." This was the last connection they had, and her gut told her to use it.

Brant looked up.

"I didn't get over her," she repeated, meeting Brant's eyes. "I kept dreaming about the apartment explosion. I saw the blood on my hands and knees, and I dreamed about Dani hurting, and not being able to get to her."

Brant's face softened. "It wasn't your fault—"

"It doesn't matter whose fault it was," Alex said, slamming her mug on the table. Brant shut his mouth, and Alex sighed in resignation. "That's all I dreamed about for weeks. I woke up screaming her name, and I knew, whoever she was, I needed to find her." She dropped her eyes, unable to meet Brant's gaze any longer.

Brant didn't say anything for a long time.

"I'm sorry it was me," he said finally. "I'm sorry you found me instead of her."

Alex looked up sharply. "Don't say that," she said, putting as much snap as possible into her voice. "I miss her. Revelator, she was the best one of us, wasn't she? I'm just glad to have either of you back."

Brant seemed to be measuring her words. "That sounds like something Lena would have said. I guess she's still in there somewhere."

"Somewhere," Alex agreed wryly. They sat for a little while, not speaking.

"We'll figure it out, Brant," Alex said eventually. "I know I'm not the Lena you're used to, but I promise, we'll figure this out."

Brant smirked, but there was an edge of bitterness to his voice. "Don't make promises you can't keep, Len-*Alex*." He pushed away from the table and, grabbing his mug, walked back into the living area.

Alex slumped in her seat. She tried not to think about what Dani would have said. Despite the ache in her head, her mind conjured up the technopath's face. Dani would have known how to hack the CityGrid and make the stolen file publicly accessible. She probably would have been able to make it play it across every screen in Exordia, without any risk to the team.

Any good we did was because of you, Dani, she thought. *Without you, we never would have made a difference.*

Alex wondered if she could make a difference now.

She wondered if she even wanted to try.

The safe house felt decidedly overcrowded with five people sleeping in it. Tabba claimed the bedroom on grounds of having her life destroyed, and couched in those terms, no one could deny her the privilege of the only bed in the house. Brant stretched out on the couch, and Keagan disappeared to stalk the streets. Liam fell asleep slouched at the table, and Alex dozed off and on in a comfortable chair in the living area.

She finally got tired of tossing and turning and stood in the entrance to the living area listening to Brant's steady breathing.

Abruptly, she remembered nights—days—like this. Dani poking at electronics at unreasonable hours, and Alex—Lena—trying to sleep through the noise. She hadn't remembered how loudly Brant snored.

She jumped when Liam wrapped his arms around her from behind. In one hand he held a glass of water, and he opened the other to reveal two painkiller tablets. "I know Claire said these won't do much good, but you've got a permanent crease in your forehead now."

Alex took the water and painkillers and untangled herself from Liam's arms. She downed the tablets in one gulp. "Thanks," she said, handing back the glass and smiling at him. "You've been really great about this. I don't know how most people react to someone who's been mind-wiped, but I'm pretty sure they're not as understanding as you have been."

Liam grinned and shrugged. "We're a matched set now." His smile turned mischievous. "I've got everything in my brain, and you've got nothing."

Alex rolled her eyes and jabbed him in the ribs with an elbow. Liam grabbed her arm and pulled her into his embrace again, resting his chin on top of her head.

"I wouldn't say 'nothing.'" She tipped her head back. "I

saved you from those Pallagen guards."

"And then dragged me into this mess," Liam joked.

Alex's face fell. She knew Liam was kidding. She could feel the chuckle rumbling through his chest, but his words still stung. "I'm sorry."

"You're fine," Liam said easily. "We'll figure it out. Besides, we won't be running from Pallagen for long, now that you're back."

"About that." Alex took a deep breath. "I'm not going to fight Pallagen."

Liam stiffened. "We can't stay in the safe house forever," he said, his voice wary.

Alex sighed. "I wish we could." She felt Liam take a breath to argue, but she didn't give him the chance. "I don't have a plan, all right? I don't know what to do next, but I want to stay as far as phaeting possible from Pallagen." She turned to look at Liam's face, not sure what she would see. Anger, maybe. Fear. Liam had been hiding from Pallagen for orbits, and Alex had brought him to their attention.

Story of her life.

Liam looked confused. "You're Lena Ward," he said. "Can't you just—"

"I'm *not* Lena Ward!" she shouted. Brant's snoring stopped, and Alex pulled away from Liam. "I'm not that person anymore. I don't have the knowledge or the skill she had." She looked over at Brant, who was now awake and watching her. "I can't fight Pallagen again. I tried, and look where it got me. This is bigger than we can handle."

"Your team is larger now," Liam said.

Alex laughed bitterly. "My team?" she scoffed. "Before, I had an ex-soldier and a scarily-capable technopath. Now, I have a walking memory, a nurse, a psychiatrist, and an information broker." Alex shook her head. "We're not a team, Liam. We can't stop Pallagen like this."

Liam looked as if he'd been slapped. He nodded slowly and walked away.

Immediately, Alex wanted to follow him. She wanted to apologize for snapping and hurting him.

But she knew she was right.

Alex closed her eyes and hung her head. "Go ahead, say it. That was a little harsh."

She heard Brant shift on the couch. "Okay," he said slowly. "It was a little harsh."

She looked up at him. He patted the cushion next to him, and she sank into it, burying her face in her hands.

"I don't want to do this again," she whispered. "I won't—I *can't* lose any of you the way I lost Dani."

Brant's hand settled on her shoulder, comfortable and heavy. "Then don't. The city doesn't own you, Lena-Alex." Alex flinched as Brant stumbled over her name, but he scooted closer. "You've done enough. Let it go."

Alex sighed and looked at her partner. "I can't let it go," she said hollowly. "Liam is right. Someone has to do something. But I don't want to be that someone."

Brant didn't say anything.

"Okay," Alex said, leaning closer. "There's that 'thinking silence' again."

"Exordia doesn't own you," Brant said slowly. "And you

could just walk away..."

"But...?"

Brant met her eyes. "That file you swiped off Pallagen's databank won't be enough to take them down."

Alex frowned. "You don't know that—"

"Oh, come on, Alex," Brant scoffed. "We raided half their labs and couldn't make a difference. Keagan and Claire might catch some attention with the information, but not enough to be considered a real threat."

Alex spread her hands. "Breaking into their labs doesn't work. Telling Exordia the truth doesn't work. So, we just *lose*?"

"No." Brant ran a hand through his hair and pushed himself up off the couch. He paced unevenly back and forth. Alex's headache flared at the memories of Brant caught up in a thought or plan, pacing despite the pain of his old injury.

"Your mother was on the Council," Brant finally said, stopping in front of her.

Alex tried to remember her parents, but no flickering memories presented themselves. She shrugged apologetically. "Okay."

"You didn't talk about your family much, but you once told me that the Council could be bought off by anyone with power. That's why Pallagen got away with so much." He tipped his head. "And, in hindsight, probably why you didn't get along with your parents."

Alex rolled her eyes. "Great. We're up against Pallagen, Enforcement, and the phaeting Council."

"But the Council is still an elected body," Brant said patiently. "Pallagen may be paying them off, but it won't do them much good if they all get voted out of office by angry citizens from every city."

The first glimmer of a plan began forming in Alex's mind. "If the people of Exordia put enough pressure on the Council, they would have to act against Pallagen." She leaned back on the couch and crossed her arms, her forehead furrowing. "That seems too easy. Why didn't we do this orbits ago?"

Brant dropped back onto the couch, stretching out his leg. "We weren't big enough then. We were just vigilantes, and Pallagen's crimes were just rumors. Some people might have listened to us, but the Council could always discredit us as criminals. Now, you're a legend. We pulled people out of those labs—people who told stories about what we did. The city remembers you, Alex."

"Only some people." Alex closed her eyes and rubbed her forehead. "Not enough to make a difference. It's been sixty orbits, Brant, and no one's done anything. They're too scared."

"Of course they are. They watched the one person who stood up to Pallagen lose."

Alex flinched at his words and opened her eyes. "Did you and Keagan talk? He said the same thing." She sighed. "It doesn't matter, Brant. We lost. Exordia won't listen to me."

Brant leaned forward, his eyes burning with conviction. "You're Lena Ward, back from the dead. They'll listen."

Alex's heart pounded. She was exhausted. The expectations of her friends weighed heavily upon her. Too heavily. "I can't stay here. I can't keep fighting them, Brant. I know you want me to be that person, but I can't."

"Then don't be." Brant's voice was quieter now,

pleading instead of insisting. "You couldn't win as Lena, so do something Lena would never have done: appeal to the people of Exordia. Leave it in their hands."

Alex didn't answer. She didn't want to admit he was right, but in spite of herself, her mind began rushing ahead, making a plan. "*If* they would listen, I could tell Exordia what happened to me. I could tell them what we did."

"Between your testimony and that file, people will be furious, and—"

"—the Council would have to investigate Pallagen or be voted out of office." Alex took a deep breath. "It could work. But, Brant, no part of Exordia would be safe for us anymore. Pallagen would turn the entire colony upside down to find us. We won't be able to hide from them—not even in the worst parts of Second City."

"Then we leave."

Alex looked up. "Leave Exordia?"

Brant shrugged. "We could. Do you remember the time I got poisoned?"

Alex scowled, caught off guard by the change in subject. "You're making that up."

"I most certainly am not." Brant rubbed the back of his neck. "We rescued this one guy right before the explosion. Revelator, you really don't remember this, do you? There was a Dallusin in the lab we hit, and we got him out of Exordia. If we left the city, he would help us."

Alex took a deep breath, and for the first time since Keagan had handed her the data chip, she felt hope flare in her chest. "That was a long time ago," she said, cautiously optimistic. "He might not be alive now."

"If he is, he would remember you." Brant shook his head, staring into the distance. "No one could forget that phaeting mission."

Except Alex, apparently. "Well, it's a start. I suppose the next step would be convincing everyone to leave?"

She looked at Brant for reassurance, and he smiled wistfully. Alex thought about how difficult it must be for him to wake up in a world where his entire team, as he knew them, was dead. "Yeah. That'd be where Lena would start."

Alex stood. "Would Lena succeed?" she asked.

Brant shrugged. "I don't know. But I'm pretty sure Alex will."

Alex gave Brant a half smile before walking toward the kitchen, hoping that Liam would be there. At the very least there would be coffee.

She felt Brant's eyes on her, but now it felt like he was watching her back, not her ghost.

Chapter Forty-Three

Alex decided to lead with an apology. "I'm sorry I dragged you into this."

Liam slouched at the table tracing invisible shapes on the tabletop. "I'm not." He sighed and leaned back. "I'm sorry too. I know you're not Lena Ward, and I don't want you to be."

Alex slid into the chair next to him and put her hand over his. "I thought I was doing the right thing, fighting Pallagen. But it didn't end well. I don't want to risk losing anyone else."

Liam met her eyes. "Really?" His face was incredulous as he grasped her fingers.

Alex frowned. "Of course I don't want to lose you. I thought that—"

"No, I mean—maybe it didn't end well for you, but think about the rest of Exordia. You pulled nearly a hundred people out of Pallagen's testing labs. You showed people they could stand up to Pallagen. That's why I'm here instead of locked in a Pallagen cell. My parents said no to them because of what you did. My name should be up on that wall somewhere."

"I'm glad what I did kept you safe." Alex's hand tightened

around Liam's. "And I don't want to let them get away with what they did. But I won't let history repeat itself. I lost someone I cared about. I can't do that again."

Liam leaned closer. "If you leave, I'm going with you."

Alex smiled, but inside she felt like crying. "I wouldn't leave without you." Liam put an arm around her, and she leaned against his shoulder. "What about your brother?"

"He'll probably come too. He can be a little protective."

"No, really," Alex said dryly.

"What about Claire? Or Tabba?"

Alex sighed. "I think they should leave as well. I doubt Claire will, though."

"You'd be right about that."

Alex and Liam jumped and turned to see Claire standing in the kitchen door, her face set.

"It's a good plan," she said, pulling out a chair and sitting across from Alex. "But you're right. I won't leave."

"Claire, if they find out what you did for me, what you did for Brant—"

Claire shook her head. "They won't. I'm used to staying under their radar." She looked between Alex and Liam. "Liam's right. You pulled a lot of people out of Pallagen's grasp, and their families still remember. My father was one of them." She smiled. "I owe it to him to stay."

Alex's forehead creased in confusion. "With that history, how can you work for Pallagen?"

"I work for *Exordia*. Which, admittedly, is not much different." Claire folded her hands on the tabletop. "I got involved so I could help. I grew up with the stories of what you did for him and so many others. By staying, I can honor that legacy and do my part to help the colony."

Just like Keagan, Alex thought. Like Liam's parents. Revelator, how many people were scattered across Exordia, living their own quiet rebellion?

"You can't fight Pallagen any longer," Claire said quietly, her gaze sympathetic and steady. She reached into her jacket pocket and pulled out a data stick. "Take Brant's advice, Alex. You've done enough."

Alex reached out and took the data stick. Her breath caught as she turned it over in her fingers. "Keagan found what we needed?"

"Everything's there," Claire said with a satisfied smile. "Why the Dallusin were first exiled. How many lies Pallagen told about the Dallusin to convince Exordia their research was necessary. How many people were hurt by Pallagen's experiments. It's all there." Claire took the data stick from Alex and held it up. "This will be the end of Pallagen—maybe not right away, but it will dig their grave. Not all of Exordia is spineless. Once the truth is out, they'll take action. Pallagen won't get away with turning people into weapons anymore." Claire tucked the data stick into her jacket pocket and met Alex's eyes. "Let me finish this, Alex. Let me do that for you."

Alex closed her eyes, fighting the tears that threatened to spill out. The image of a dingy apartment flashed through her mind. *You started something, Lena Ward,* someone said, *and you need help finishing it.*

"Okay," she said, her voice hoarse. She opened her eyes and smiled at Claire. "You win. But let me do something for you first." Her shoulders straightened, and she felt the weight of her past fall away. She took a deep breath and let it out slowly. "Get the others. I have one last plan, and I'll need their help."

Claire gaped as Alex told everyone her plan.

"You can't be serious," she said. "The physical ramifications alone—you can't even say your name without getting a headache—"

"I can handle it." Alex looked at the faces of everyone gathered in the living area. Keagan leaned forward in a chair, elbows on his knees, and Brant slumped on the couch with his legs stretched out, Tabba next to him. Claire stood by the couch with one hand on Tabba's shoulder. Alex could feel Liam standing reassuringly behind her, his arm brushing her shoulder. Alex turned her gaze back to the psychiatrist. "Liam and Brant were right. That data stick may not hold all of Pallagen's secrets, but I can make sure you take them down. I've been given a second chance to beat Pallagen, and I'm not going to waste it."

Claire didn't say anything, but Alex saw her expression change as the idea took root in her mind. Her face lit with cautious hope.

"What happens after?" Tabba asked, crossing her arms. "You go public with something like that, and, Council influence or not, Pallagen will kill you."

"We can't stay, obviously. Brant knows someone who will shelter us if we can get out of Exordia."

Tabba looked away from her, mouth tight and eyes hard.

Alex fought the urge to sigh. Instead, she met Keagan's eyes. "You're our best bet at escaping the city. Can you get us out?"

Keagan nodded slowly. "It would involve calling in several favors."

"Favors you won't need anymore," Brant said, nudging Keagan's ankle with his outstretched boot. He smirked when Keagan glared at him.

Tabba shifted uncomfortably on the couch. "I don't understand. What's outside the city?"

"Outcasts," Brant said, his voice deep and ominous. "Desert dwellers. Radicals."

Alex rolled her eyes.

"The Dallusin are a peaceful people, by all accounts." Claire looked disapprovingly at Brant.

"We rescued a Dallusin named Tavi," Brant said in his normal voice. "He was all right. Got a little weird about the Revelator, but I think he might've been on to something." He frowned and his eyes lost focus. Alex made a mental note to ask him for the full story later.

"If we can get to the Dallusin camp and find Tavi, he'll shelter us," Alex continued. "Brant said he promised to help us if we ever needed it."

Silence descended on the room. Alex looked at Tabba. She was pale, and panic flooded her features. The nurse had been nothing but kind to her, and now she was running for her life.

"I'm sorry," she said, meeting Tabba's eyes, "but I don't have another plan. If we stay here, we'll never stop running. I don't have a technopath that can erase us from the system. We might be able to run from Pallagen for a while, but eventually they will catch us."

Tabba looked away, and Alex's stomach twisted with guilt. She'd taken away any choice Tabba had when she went after Brant.

She still wasn't sorry.

"When will you leave?" Claire asked.

Alex looked at Keagan. He shrugged. "I can talk to some people, maybe get us out within the next few hours."

Alex nodded. "The sooner the better."

Tabba rose from the couch. "I need to..." She gestured vaguely. "Get some air."

Claire squeezed Alex's shoulder. "I'll talk to her." She followed Tabba outside.

Keagan stepped forward. "Do we know where to go once we're out of Exordia?"

Alex looked questioningly at Brant, and he nodded. "Tavi told me some stuff when I was..." He trailed off and looked at Alex uncomfortably, then cleared his throat. "Yeah, I can tell you where to go."

They definitely needed to talk about that mission.

"Great." Keagan didn't sound confident, but he turned to face Alex. "You're right, it's the only plan. And it's a *good* one. It's not your fault it's come to this."

She still felt responsible, though. What would life have been like for everyone if she hadn't challenged Pallagen?

She knew the answer to that.

Claire would never have been born. Liam would be trapped in a Pallagen laboratory, his mind picked apart. Brant would be dead in a street fight. Dani would still be alive, and

Tabba would still have a job. Alex squeezed her eyes shut.

She felt Brant's hand on her arm. "Maybe Tavi was right about the Revelator."

Alex opened her eyes and looked at Brant. "What do you mean?"

"You're alive, I'm alive…"

"That's just luck. Or coincidence."

"Maybe not," Brant said, shoving his hands into his pockets.

An image of Brant with blood around his mouth flashed into her mind. She winced and massaged her forehead. "You were dying, weren't you? Something happened, and you almost died."

Brant shifted his weight. "Yeah. Tavi was with me." He bowed his head. "You and Dani went after the antidote, and he prayed the whole time. It was…" He paused, tipping his head back. "It wasn't weird. I think it helped." He glanced sideways at Alex. "I'm not sure I would've made it if he hadn't been there."

Alex nodded slowly. "Maybe you should ask the Revelator if he'll help us get out of Exordia. And find the Dallusin."

They were going to need all the help they could get.

The burned-out apartment building covered in names was a reminder of what Alex had lost. A reminder of all the people she'd forgotten.

She'd never considered what it would mean to Brant.

He stood where Alex had when Keagan first brought her here, silhouetted in dim moonlight, silent and shivering— from the cool night, or from memories, Alex didn't know. For him, this building had blown up only a few days ago.

She stepped closer, her fingers brushing his elbow. "Are you all right?" she murmured.

Brant shook his head. He reached out to trace the scrawled letters of one signature, and Alex wondered how many faces or stories he could put to each name.

"We only have a few minutes," Keagan said from behind them, his voice heavy with disapproval. "We shouldn't be out in the open for long."

Liam scuffed his shoes in the gravel impatiently. "Where else are we supposed to do this?"

"Nowhere." Keagan sighed. "Just…we're leaving the city in less than an hour. Let's not get spotted before then."

Alex nodded and tugged nervously at her jacket, straightening her collar. She braced herself for the impending migraine. "Ready."

Brant turned away from the wall and stuffed his hands into his pockets, putting most of his weight on his good leg. He stood behind Alex, to her left. He had refused her request to say something on the holovid, but he stayed close to her, lending credibility to their story with his presence.

Liam stood a few steps away, holding Claire's mobile in front of him. Alex met his gaze for a moment, reading the encouragement in his eyes, then looked straight into the tiny camera and lifted her chin.

Liam nodded as he began recording.

Alex remembered the old picture in her file and tried to pull off the same smile, the same tilt of the head, the same confident posture. She tried to put the same fire in her eyes.

She took a deep breath and squared her shoulders.

"My name is Lena Ward." Her voice was calm and measured, the same voice, she hoped, Lena would have used. She felt Brant straighten behind her, so she must have succeeded.

"You have heard many stories about me and my team," she went on, gaining confidence. "Allow me to tell you the truth about what I have done to Pallagen, and what they have done to me."

She told her story. Talked about Brant's determination to fight, how Pallagen had tried to take everything from him, and how he still resisted them. She talked about what Pallagen had done to Dani. She told them about Project Slate, and how Pallagen had used it to erase her. She didn't cover for the gaps in her memory, letting Exordia see the full extent of the damage Pallagen had done. She kept her voice calm, even though it caught when she spoke of their final mission, and how it ended.

"I did all I could for Exordia." Her palms were damp with sweat, and she fought the urge to cross her arms protectively over her aching chest. "I almost died for this city. But this isn't my fight any longer. It's yours." She held up the data stick with Pallagen's files. "By the time this is released, I'll be gone, but everything you—the people of Exordia—need to take Pallagen down will be on the CityGrid. Use it. Go to the Council. You've forgotten you have a voice. Speak up about the crimes Pallagen has inflicted on the innocent. For two centuries, Pallagen has controlled this colony through fear. They assumed there wouldn't be enough people with the courage to stand up to them."

She let a smile spread across her face, the same sharp-edged smile she'd given Pallagen's security cameras in the basement of Sixth City Rehab.

"It's time for you to prove them wrong."

Chapter Forty-Four

Alex expected their escape from Exordia to be flashy. Exciting and heart-pounding, complete with hair-breadth escapes from Pallagen security or Enforcement officers.

Instead, they split up at dusk. Keagan took the gravcar with Brant and Tabba to the outskirts of Second City. Liam and Alex pulled on jackets, scarves, and caps to hide their faces. They walked to the worst part of Fourth City and caught the cheapest gravtrain. They exited at a station close to Second City, using the alleys to circumvent the main roads until they rendezvoused with the others.

Keagan led them to the border of Exordia. On the edge of the city were nothing but huge warehouses and deserted first-colony homes. There was no wall. The city simply ended where the terraforming had stopped. Coarse grass met slate-blue desert, a few sage-gray spires poking up bravely through the sand. Besides Enforcement posts, there was no need for any other security—or so Exordia thought. Why would anyone want to leave when the only thing the desert could offer was a colony of half-forgotten outcasts?

Alex was sure Pallagen would have guessed their plan and coordinated with Enforcement to keep them in, but they had no trouble leaving the city. Maybe they thought she would try to live up to her past and cause a rebellion. Maybe they were confident in their ability to use the infrastructure of Exordia to catch them.

Or maybe the Revelator was looking out for them.

Either way, Alex left Exordia more quietly than she had ever lived in it. Keagan dropped a substantial amount of coin into the hands of an Enforcement soldier, and Brant led them out of the city.

After a few hours of walking, Tabba began complaining about blisters on her feet. Alex didn't want to admit it, but she was footsore, too. It was hard to walk in sand after walking on nothing but gravel or plastic or carefully manicured yards.

Brant was limping ahead of everyone. He wasn't complaining, but his face was tight and pale. Alex stepped up and pulled his arm over her shoulder.

"I can help," Keagan offered, but Alex shook her head. She wanted to do this.

"You know where we're going, right?" she asked Brant quietly. "You're not just winging this?"

Brant huffed. "How would you know if I was?" He struggled through the sand for a few more steps. "Tavi said to walk south, and we'd hit the settlement in a few hours." He glanced at Alex. "But I don't know if that's changed in sixty orbits."

Alex nodded. If it had, there wasn't anything they could do about it. They hadn't had time to search out any new information on the Dallusin, if there was any to be found.

They'd have to trust in Tavi's Revelator to lead them in the right direction.

The desert was silent except for the soft whisper of footsteps through sand. They could still see the glow of Exordia's lights against the night sky, but all the noise of the city had long since disappeared. No one talked much as they walked. They would point something out or ask to stop to shake the sand out of their shoes or comment on how far they'd walked. Alex felt the weight of what they were leaving behind, in search of a place none of them were sure of. She didn't feel much like talking, and she suspected everyone else felt the same.

Luna One set, and Luna Two began its slow descent. Alex's shoulders ached, and she reluctantly let Keagan help Brant. She slogged through the sand beside Liam, hands tucked in her jacket pockets. Their height difference made it too hard to hold hands while they walked, but he stayed close enough that their arms brushed.

Tabba was stiff-shouldered and tense, much quieter than everyone else. She did, however, keep reminding everyone to drink. They had to ration their water carefully in case it took more than a few hours to reach the Dallusin.

As the sun rose, they hit rockier ground. They stopped to rest on an outcropping of dark stone. Alex dropped her pack onto the ground and leaned against a boulder, facing the sun. Liam settled on one side of her and Brant on the other, stretching his leg out. He hadn't complained once, but Alex could tell he was in pain. The longer they rested, the more he relaxed.

"The planet's so big," Alex whispered, gesturing to the desert around them. "There's a whole world out here that no one in Exordia has ever seen."

Liam's nose wrinkled. "I'm not sure the desert is much to look at."

"They say that all of Old Earth was explored," Brant said. He tipped his head back against the rock. "People lived all across the planet. Outside of cities, even in desert places like this." He shuddered. "So many people on one planet."

"I like the quiet." Alex leaned against Liam. "It's just ... strange. All those people in Exordia. Pallagen. Enforcement. It seems like that's all that exists when you're living there, but out here..." She sighed. "It seems so insignificant."

Liam chuckled. "You're not used to your own smallness, are you?"

"Maybe not." Alex frowned. "I don't understand, though. If I'm so small, out here in an empty world, why am I awake?"

Liam shifted. "You wish you had never woken up?"

"That's not what I mean." Alex pushed away from Liam "I mean, why wake me up now? Why give me a second chance?" She shook her head. "If someone has a plan, why wake me up just to run away?"

"Maybe it's time to let someone else take responsibility for a while." Liam folded his arms. "Maybe you waking up isn't about Exordia. Maybe it's about you getting a second chance to live instead of fight."

Alex didn't answer. She'd felt uncomfortable when Claire told her that her memories had been purposefully removed, uneasy with the idea that she was important enough to erase. She felt the same way now. Who would care about the good she'd done, in spite of failing?

SARAH E OTT 383

Maybe Tavi would know.

Keagan stood. "We should keep walking," he said, helping Tabba to her feet. "We don't want to get caught out here all day if we can help it."

They were footsore and weary, but they kept walking. The sun had hit its zenith when a settlement loomed into view. Alex saw tiny figures hurrying between tents. As they got closer, people gathered at the edge of the settlement. There were no hostile movements. No one brandished weapons or challenged them until they reached the edge of the small crowd.

One of the men stepped forward. "Welcome, travelers," he said, bowing. "It has been many orbits since we have sheltered anyone from Exordia. How may the Dallusin serve you?"

Alex stepped forward. "I'm—" She hesitated, feeling Liam's eyes on her back and Brant's steady presence at her side. "My name is Alex Kleric. My friend once helped a man from your settlement—Tavi. He offered us help if we ever needed it."

The crowd murmured and slowly shifted as someone from the back moved forward. His face was wrinkled, his shoulders bent with age, and he walked slowly, leaning heavily on a cane. Alex didn't recognize the old man's face, but Brant stepped forward and smiled.

"We're not thrilled to have to call in the favor," he said. "But we could use a place to stay that's not in Exordia."

The man—Tavi, Alex realized—formally bowed. "Welcome to my home." He smiled and stepped closer, holding out a hand to Alex. "I think you will find it more spacious than the fine couch you once offered me."

Brant laughed. Alex felt the hole in her mind again, the knowledge that she was missing something she should remember. But Tavi didn't say anything about the name she had given, or how she and Brant hadn't aged. He simply waved an arm in front of him, parting the crowd so Alex and the others could walk through.

Tabba stayed close to Keagan, and Brant accepted the help of a curious boy who helped him limp into the camp. Liam reached for Alex's hand and wrapped his fingers around hers.

"So is it Alex or Lena, for good?" he whispered.

Alex closed her eyes. If this was her second chance, she wasn't going to waste it trying to recapture something she would never become. "Lena Ward died the night Pallagen captured her." Alex looked behind her, imagining the distant skyline of Exordia. She tried to imagine what would happen when Claire leaked the files and the holovid: the media coverage, Pallagen scrambling to cover their losses, the aloof betrayal of Enforcement, the Council's put-upon outrage. She shook her head, suddenly glad she wouldn't have to deal with the chaos. She smiled up at Liam. "I'm ready to just be Alex."

Liam waited with her as the crowd slowly trickled away, talking eagerly with Brant, Tabba, and Keagan.

"Do you know what 'Exordia' means?" he said suddenly.

Alex shook her head, still staring into the distance.

"It's an Old Earth word. It means 'the beginning of anything.'"

The beginning of anything. Alex smiled. She tightened her hold on Liam's hand and turned her back on the city.

Acknowledgements

Aaron: social media ghostwriter, haranguer, late-night plot twist provider, helpful book buyer, purveyor of creative and entrepreneurial wisdom.

Susie: who put up with deadlines and distractedness, weathered my existential crises, read and responded to a whole novel's worth of texts, and believed in me more than I ever have.

The Parents: who taught me to read and write, who taught me that you are what you read, who handed me Ivanhoe *and* Lord of the Rings *and* Star Trek *and* Star Wars.

The Editors and The Press: who believed in this story, and who made this book better.

Everyone who stopped me to ask "How's the book going?" and who reminded me it was cool to write a book.

Here's where you can find Sarah E. Ott online:

Website: www.saraheott.com
Twitter: @Ott2Write
Instagram: sarahlizzieo

Thank you for reading *Exordia*! If you're inspired, please leave a review on Amazon.com! I'd love to hear your thoughts and feedback. Also, get connected with Uncommon Universes Press for more great reads!

About the Author

Sarah Ott was born and raised in rural Kansas. She's spent her life telling stories of all types. She majored in English, taught students, mentored kids, wrote curriculum, and discovered that she loves conveying truths best through science fiction and fantasy. She now resides in Omaha, Nebraska, with her husband and two cats, where she writes in both creative and professional fields.

PRICELESS

AN IRONFIRE LEGACY NOVELLA

Nula Thredsing might finally have it all. If she survives to enjoy it. Fortunately, she has a dragon on her side...

JUNE 2018